Daughters of a Nation

A Black Suffragette Historical Romance Anthology

Kianna Alexander
Alyssa Cole
Lena Hart
Piper Huguley

Contents

In The Morning Sun

Lena Hart

With the election of 1868 underway, Madeline Asher's mission is clear: educate and enlist the freedmen of Nebraska to vote. After losing the man she loved to war—and a small piece of herself along the way—Madeline leaves her life in Philadelphia behind, determined to reclaim her life's purpose by making a difference in others.

With America's Southern Rebellion at an end, so are the efforts of Union veteran James Blakemore. Tired of the injustices still plaguing the young country, he sets his sights toward his Canadian roots—until fate guides him back to the love he thought he'd lost.

Vowing never to leave her side again, James joins Madeline in her cause to help the freedmen of Dunesville, despite rising threats and violence. But with Nebraska's enforcement of anti-miscegenation laws, Madeline will be forced to choose between a life with her new husband or the chance to shape a greater nation.

For the mothers and daughters, fathers and sons, who fought for our right to vote—and who continue to fight for our unalienable rights to life, liberty, love and happiness.

"So close is the bond between man and woman that you cannot raise one without lifting the other."

Frances Ellen Watkins Harper

PROLOGUE

June 1866
Chicago, IL

"I can't go through with this. I won't."

"Madeline, you can't just...run off. Where do you plan to go? What about Mr. Mercer? And Mrs. Dobson?"

Madeline Asher stared at her travel companion, the uneasiness in Gracie Shaw's incredulous tone almost making her reconsider.

Almost.

"I'll figure something out," Madeline said. "But I can't marry that man. Not when my heart still belongs to my Jimmy."

Sympathy flashed across Gracie's pretty brown face, though her obvious concern did nothing to ease the panic churning in Madeline's stomach. She just wanted Gracie to return to the hospital where their chaperone Mrs. Dobson lay indisposed with an extreme case of cholera.

"Madeline, I can only imagine your pain, but you're going to have to let it go. Jimmy is gone, but I'm sure he would want you to find someone else to love again. To be happy with."

Maybe so, but Madeline wasn't ready to let go yet. She certainly wouldn't find love in Montana, where they had been headed before Mrs. Dobson had fallen ill.

Madeline didn't know what had possessed her to agree to the arranged marriage clear across the country, with a man nearly twenty years her senior. Their stop in Chicago, however, had given her a clarity she had been missing since her sister shipped her off to New York to work for Mrs. Dobson as an assistant in her school.

Madeline wasn't going to find her purpose in this life by marrying a man she didn't know. She certainly didn't have room in her heart for a man who hadn't bothered to send her one personal correspondence. How could she love another? Her core was already filled with loving memories of the man who had gone off to fight for a cause greater than themselves.

"That is why I have to go," Madeline said more to herself than Gracie. "I know I won't be happy marrying some stranger and I can't give myself to a man I don't love."

Frustration was plain in the heavy breath Gracie blew out. It took a bit more convincing on Madeline's part to remove the doubt and concern from Gracie's dark eyes. But after a few desperate pleas and a promise to write Mrs. Dobson and her would-be husband as soon as she arrived back to New York, Madeline managed to convince Gracie to let her be.

Except, Madeline wasn't going back to New York, but that was a small detail she didn't plan to share with her travel companion.

Before Madeline turned to the waiting train, she surprised Gracie with a quick hug. They hadn't been close, but Gracie had always been kind to her during her brief stay in their small New York community.

"Thank you, Gracie. I pray you find your happiness out there."

Clutching her satchel close to her chest, Madeline eventually made her way into the train, leaving an anxious-looking Gracie on the train platform. Madeline settled down on a bench in the last car of the train and watched as the green fields rolled past her.

Though she was eager to return home to Pennsylvania, Madeline didn't have a clear idea of what her next move would be once she got there. With slavery finally at an end, the next course for change was obtaining equal rights for women—and remaining idle had never been in Madeline's character.

She would just have to convince her sister Elaine that her future didn't have to be reduced to just becoming some man's wife, as Madeline's idol, Frances Harper, had written about. Then again, that sentiment may not go over too well, seeing as her older sister had settled into a life of domesticity and appeared content with that.

There was only one man Madeline had ever considered becoming a wife to and he was dead. Grief curdled in her belly at the thought of Jimmy. No matter how much time had passed, she couldn't seem to accept it.

Madeline pulled out the last letter he had sent her, along with a *carte de visite* of him wearing his new officer's uniform. She had kept both close to her heart, had studied his handsome face in the miniature portrait, and had reread his letter until she had it committed to memory.

She stared down at the small card photograph now. His expression was serious but there was a fire in his eyes that embodied the kind of man he was—compassionate, honest, and incredibly braze. He had been the kind of man to stand up and die for what he believed and she knew that side of him well. There was no doubt in her mind that he had died courageously on some ravaged battlefield.

Madeline's eyes welled with tears and she blinked them away. She unfolded the brief letter, the bold strokes of his handwriting offering her an odd, yet pleasant sense of comfort. As she had done so many times, she read over his final words to her—words that read like poetry but always left her aching for a future that would never exist...

"My dearest Maddie, I never cease thinking about you. With each day that comes, I see your face in the morning sun, and it fills me with renewed life and hope that we will soon be together again. When that day comes, we will take that journey to Horseshoe Falls, and I promise you, my love, I will never leave your side again."

Madeline carefully refolded the letter. It was dated two years ago, on September twenty-fourth, yet it had been on a particularly frigid November when the letter had arrived to her. Three months later, she had received notice of his death. That journey to those majestic Canadian falls he had told her so much about would never come.

For the first time in months, she let the tears fall. They offered her a small comfort, allowing her to release the anguish of her overwhelming loss. She knew she would have to eventually let him go. But not tonight... Tonight, she would hold onto the memory of his love and light just a little while longer.

Madeline eventually fell into a fitful sleep, her satchel clutched tightly to her chest. It was dusk when the train finally pulled into the Philadelphia train station. She hopped out of the train, along with the other passengers and surveyed her surroundings. The enormity of what she'd done—and the position she'd put herself in—suddenly hit her when she found herself alone and without any money to get her to her sister's home.

Well, there's no turning back now.

Resigned to that unavoidable fact, Madeline started the long walk to Elaine's. There was a bit of activity buzzing around the streets, which made the journey less intimidating. It had been a while since she'd made the trip to her sister's place, a trip she certainly had never made by foot. And if

Madeline had gotten her way, she wouldn't be headed there now. But their father's death last year had only motivated her sister to "unburden" herself by selling their family home and sending Madeline off to New York.

Ten minutes into her journey, Madeline realized nothing looked familiar. She continued on, hoping she would recognize something soon, but the longer she walked, the more isolated and deserted the streets became. Somewhere back, she had taken a wrong turn and a slow hum of panic began to buzz inside her.

She immediately squashed the feeling. Nothing good would come from falling into hysteria.

Right before she reached another crossroad, Madeline turned and began to retrace her steps. She came upon two men in uniform, their dark, navy-blue Union coats recognizable from where she stood. The taller of the two had his back to her, but the tapered ends of his dark-brown hair peeking from beneath his wool cap held a familiarity that made her heart stop.

It couldn't be...

Without thinking, Madeline rushed toward the man and grabbed his arm. "Jimmy!"

The man turned, astonishment in his brown eyes.

Not green eyes.

Her small bubble of hope burst as swiftly as it had inflated.

"I'm sorry," Madeline stammered to the stranger, her face heating up with embarrassment. "I thought you were...never mind."

She started to back away, too humiliated to continue her explanation. But before she could dash off, the man grabbed her arm.

"Are you lost, miss?"

Madeline glanced from him to his friend, the two assessing her with an intense curiosity that she hoped was on account of her being a colored woman dressed in fancy skirts and boots—all provided by her wealthy would-be husband in Montana—and not because she was a woman traveling alone.

Madeline pulled her arm out of the man's grip and fixed her gaze on him. At least he had manners enough to release her without challenge.

"I seem to be a bit turned around. I'm looking for Franklin Road."

The taller man whistled. "You took a wrong turn, darling. Franklin's back that way."

Madeline followed the direction where he pointed, relieved that it wasn't as far off as she'd believed.

"My friend and I were actually headed that way. We'd be happy to escort you there."

From the sharp look his friend shot him, he didn't appear pleased by the sudden offer.

"That's all right," Madeline murmured. "No need to trouble yourselves."

"It would be no trouble at all, miss…"

"Madeline."

The man's smile widened. "Pretty name. My name's Ryan. And this here's Paul. A fine woman like yourself shouldn't be out here alone. May I?"

Madeline glanced down at his outstretched hand, then back up at his gentle smile. With a brief moment of hesitation, she handed him her travel bag. He started down the path toward Franklin, and Madeline fell into step beside him. His friend followed behind them, a frown still marring his round face.

"So where are you traveling from, Miss Madeline?"

"I'm on my way to visit with my sister," she said instead, not wanting to think about the future she had deserted. She indulged in the man's small talk during their short walk, listening as he whimsically spoke of home. They may have walked a block and a half before she realized they were headed in the wrong direction.

"Sir, I think we may have missed our turn."

Suddenly, Ryan stopped and released a loud sigh. "Now that I think about it, Paul and I may be just as lost ourselves."

Madeline tilted her head in confusion. Then realization struck her as he threw her travel bag to his friend. He caught it with one fluid motion, his frown intensifying.

Her heart sank. She was being robbed, and there was nothing she could do to stop them.

"See if she has anything nice in there, Paul."

His friend stared down at the bag, dumbfounded. "What the hell for?"

"Something tells me this fancy Negro has enough to spare." Ryan grabbed her arm and jerked her close. "Don't you, darling?"

Madeline stood there, frozen. All she could do was shake her head numbly, while her insides shook with panic.

"She doesn't have anything in here, Ryan." His friend threw down her bag as if the strap seared his palm. "Now, let's get the hell out of here."

"She has something." Anger and frustration darkened his features and he released her long enough to retrieve the bag.

Her instincts took over. Gathering her skirts, Madeline turn and fled.

Her booted heel snapped against the cobbled road with a fierceness that matched her racing heart. She darted down the dark road, praying the panic coursing through her wouldn't let her legs buckle beneath her.

But with all her determination, she didn't get far.

Strong, rough hands grabbed her by the waist and lifted her high.

"Oh no, you don't, missy. My friend and I fought hard for you people. We deserve to get something for it."

Madeline wanted to scream but the large lump in her throat kept all sounds lodged there. Using what strength she had, she kicked and clawed at her captor, but her struggles were in vain. With surprising ease, the man managed to pin her arms at her sides then lifted her high against his chest.

"Paul! Grab her legs."

Madeline kicked out but strong hands wrapped around her ankles and held them firm. In that moment, she found the unspeakable strength and drive to belt out a scream. The shrill sound barely pierced through the quiet night air before Ryan had his hand clamped over her mouth and nose.

"Goddamn you! *Shut up.*"

His tight grip over her face was suffocating her and she barely held on to consciousness as they carried her further into the night shadows. Through the dull thudding in her ears, Madeline could hear the earnestness in Paul's voice.

"Ryan, let's just leave her here. She doesn't have anything."

"Yeah, she does. Now shut up, and put her down here."

It wasn't until she felt the hard, flat surface against her back that Madeline realized they had dragged her into a dark, abandoned building. From the short ends of the table, she realized they held her down on a desk. The windows were boarded and the stench of old wood and dust were distinct.

Ryan grabbed her wrists and jerked them above her head. "Come here and tie her hands."

Paul released her ankles but instead of following his friend's directive, he began to slowly back away from her. Ryan glanced over at his friend then cursed.

"What the hell are you waiting for?"

Paul shook his head. "I don't want any part of this."

With another curse, Ryan bound her hands with something rough and heavy. The gravity of her situation came crashing down on her and Madeline thought she would suffocate from it.

"Help me, please!"

Those were the last words she spoke before he stuffed a coarse rag between her teeth. She tried to scream but it only brought the rough cloth deeper into her mouth.

Guilt and uncertainty clouded Paul's pale face, before he turned and fled, taking with him any shred of mercy she had silently hoped for.

"Goddamn yellow-belly." Ryan jerked up her skirts and stared down at her. "Guess that means more for me."

A heavy cloak of shame came over her and Madeline shut her eyes from the humiliation. Ignoring the blunt fingers that dug into her thighs, she stole away inside herself.

She conjured up memories of a crooked smile, dancing green eyes, and a handsome face that took her into a ravine full of happy memories—to a place as deep as Horseshoe Falls, where she could remember and preserve a part of herself.

And no one, not even the monster grunting above her, could touch.

CHAPTER 1

August 1868
Southwestern Nebraska

Two years later…

"You're a dangerous woman, Miss Madeline Asher."

Madeline sheathed the small knife into the holder strapped around her wrist. "Better to be a dangerous one then a dead one," she muttered, tugging down the long sleeve of her dress to conceal it.

"What do you plan to do with that gun?"

Madeline ignored her friend and fellow missionary, Sherry Thomas, and proceeded to slip the small Derringer into the holster strapped around her boot ankle.

Teresa Miller snickered. "Someone forgot to tell her the war's over."

Madeline snapped her gaze over at the other woman. "If you think that, then you're a fool. We're not safe as colored people and we're especially not safe as colored women. Until that day comes, the war will never be over."

Teresa rolled her big, chocolate-brown eyes—an action that left Madeline irritated on enough occasions to make her want to smack the other woman just to see how far back her eyes could roll.

"Don't start up again, Militant Madeline, or I'll have Oliver make you ride outside the stagecoach the rest of the way to Dunesville."

Madeline let her lips stretch into a smile that held no humor or warmth. Their travel from Philadelphia had been long and she about had it with the infuriating woman.

"That's fine by me, Teresa. Your brother keeps better company and it'll save me from having to suffer through your endless chatter."

Teresa sucked in a sharp breath of outrage and as usual, Sherry jumped in to intervene.

"Now, now ladies. It's been a long ride to Nebraska. We're almost to Dunesville and you two need to muster up some of that Philly charm and start getting along. At least through the end of our contracts. Those poor folks out there don't need to suffer through six months of your bickering. Remember, what we're here to do is bigger than your petty squabbles."

Sherry was right.

Madeline couldn't let her irritation with sassy-mouth Teresa Miller turn her into a petty child. She had volunteered to join the missionary so that she could help educate the freedmen of one of the largest Negro communities in Nebraska, not argue sense into Teresa. Now that the old territory had been admitted into the Union as the thirty-seventh state, it was critical that every able-bodied man cast their vote for this election— including the Negro men. And if that meant linking arms with all her sisters to make that happen, Madeline would set aside her differences long enough to do so.

But before Madeline could apologize, Teresa slapped on her travel bonnet.

"Oh, quit your meddling, Saint Sherry." With those crisp words, Teresa stormed out of the room they had all shared for the night.

Madeline turned to Sherry. "I swear that woman exists just to annoy me. I don't know how you put up with her."

"I've known her longer than you."

"Then you really are a saint."

Sherry giggled. "She's really not all that bad."

That remained to be seen. Madeline had only met Sherry last year, after joining the American Missionary Association in Philadelphia, but they had become fast friends—something that almost never happened for Madeline. But where Sherry was pleasant, genuine, and passionate about their cause, Teresa was uppity, arrogant, and praise-seeking.

And what are you?

Wasn't she also here for her own self-serving reasons?

Madeline pushed the uncomfortable thought aside and pinned up the soft coils of her hair atop her head. She took one last look in the mirror, pleased with the way the simple blue gown concealed everything she wanted it to hide, including the remaining bits of fear and anxiety that had travelled with her from Philadelphia.

Her decision to come to Dunesville to teach had not been an impulsive one. The association had been transparent about the dangers the previous instructors had faced by those who had seen their presence as an insult to their bigoted beliefs that Negroes ought to remain uneducated, uninformed, and disinterested in their country's government. She had read about the savagery that had befallen men of color in certain parts of the country who presented any interest in exercising their right to vote, but that had not deterred Madeline from signing on to help with the effort.

As much as she longed for the day when women would be granted those same rights, she couldn't continue to sit idly by, listening to those injustices. It was that same anger and disgust that had led her here, farther west then she had ever been, and she could only hope she could do her part for the freedmen of Dunesville. Maybe then she would find the inner peace that had eluded her for the past two years.

With a wary sigh, Madeline grabbed her small travel bag and started toward the door. "I'll meet you downstairs, Sherry. I need to stop by the postal office before we start off again."

"You're not having breakfast?"

"I'm not particularly hungry this morning." And her nerves were strung too tight for her to try and force down any food. "I won't be long."

Madeline slipped out of the room, her mind already on her next and final task before she, Sherry, and Teresa were dropped off in Dunesville.

Clutching her valise in one hand and the long letter she had written to her sister in another, she made her way down the busy streets and toward the small postal office. It had taken her about three drafts before she had been satisfied with the final letter.

Her final goodbye letter.

Madeline couldn't anticipate how her sister would take the correspondence but if she had to guess, she would assume shock first followed by immense anger. The last thing Madeline wanted to do was anger her only living relative, but the past two years in Philadelphia under her sister's charge had been unbearable. She could no longer stand to be in a city that reminded her so much of what she had lost—nor could she take any more of Elaine's pitying looks. The kind that suggested Madeline would never amount to more than being an unclean and unhappy spinster.

But she was much more than that.

Now that she was of age to access the small inheritance her father had set aside for her, Madeline planned to start a new life for herself elsewhere. Someplace she could be an asset and truly make a difference—and Dunesville made a great starting place.

Madeline crossed the street and walked down a row of shops. Right before she entered the small postal office, a distinctly tall profile caught her attention. The man stepped out of the bank, his features hidden behind the brim of his hat but there was something oddly familiar about his wide shoulders and smooth, easy stride. He started across the street, his long-legged stride taking him further away from her, yet leaving behind a sense of recognition she couldn't shake.

For a moment, Madeline was held captivated as she was jerked five years into the past…

"I don't want you to go, Jimmy."

His expression softened. "I have to join, Maddie. The victory at Gettysburg was only the beginning. If we want an end to come to this rebellion, the Union needs more men to fight."

"But what of those who have been selected for conscription? The government will have the number of men they need to enlist."

"You've read of what's happening in New York. Those riots are a big setback to our cause and drafting men to fight can't be the only solution. I, for one, will not just sit and wait to be called to fight."

Madeline grabbed his hand and held it tight. "But you can do so much more for our cause here than in any battlefield. You don't need to risk your life!"

"I have a chance to do more than write recruitment bills and articles. Let me help the Union secure victory against the southern rebels and then you'll see. Soon, everything we've fought hard for will finally be realized."

She swallowed hard, her next words barely a whisper. "And what if you die?"

He brought her hand to his lips then gifted her with his signature smile. "You worry for naught, love. This war is close to coming to an end and you forget. I'm too stubborn to die."

And yet, he had.

When will you stop being so foolish, Maddie? You need to let him go.

The quiet reprimand pulled her out of her stupor and she quickly shook the memory away. Her silly heart and imaginative eyes needed to stop creating visions of him where there were none and accept the fact that her Jimmy was dead. Gone. And after everything she had been through, she should have learned by now that pining for the dead was a waste of time.

Turning on her heels, Madeline pushed open the post office door and stepped inside.

⁂

James Blakemore stepped out of the bank, fifty dollars richer. It wasn't much but what little he had managed to save from his paltry pension was now rolled up in his boot—and was just enough to see him back home.

He crossed the busy street of the bustling Nebraska city, eager to get started on his long journey east, then north, and finally home. To Canada.

His steps faltered, however, when a strange, warm tingle suddenly moved over him. It was the kind of sensation that came from the penetrating gaze of another. He knew how it felt to have eyes glued on him, and he tended to ignore it.

But this time, it was different.

Turning back, James quickly scanned the crowd for the gawker. There was no one. He caught the glimpse of wide blue skirts disappearing through the doors of the post office. For a moment, the soft sway of the woman's hips brought back a familiarity that made his chest squeeze. James was tempted to go after the lady, but luckily he came to his senses.

It's not her, you blind fool.

With a small shake of his head, James continued down the street. That was the problem of having only one working eye—it kept him from seeing straight. He needed to stop deluding himself. It wasn't her. It couldn't be. His love was far away from here, far away from *him*.

The last he had heard, the woman who should have been his wife had gone to marry some well-to-do miner in Montana. At first, the news had crushed him, but then James had come to accept it. He wasn't the same man he had been when he'd left Philadelphia in hopes of putting an end to one of the greatest atrocities against humanity. He had fought for the Union and emancipation had been declared, but he was now damaged goods.

What did he have to offer a fine woman like Madeline Asher?

"Colonel!"

James turned to find one of the young residents of the new Veteran's House rushing toward him. At the earnestness in the young man's stiff gait, James tensed.

"Philip, what's the matter?"

James waited as the young private stopped to catch his breath. Philip Cooper was a resilient kid, having lost his ability to ever walk straight again during his short stint in the war. But that hadn't stopped him from running the distance he had and James couldn't help but admire that.

"It's Major Anderson, Colonel. He's left the home, but no one's willing to go out and look for him."

James cursed. "Does he have a weapon?"

Philip nodded. "Someone said he stole a chef's knife from the kitchen."

James cursed again. He couldn't blame the other men or paid caregivers for keeping their distance. Major William Anderson could be extremely dangerous. With a knife, he was deadly.

"Do you know which direction he went?"

Philip pointed to the south of them. "I believe he went down to the river. He was shouting something about going to save you."

James pressed his lips in a tight line. When Will began rehashing his time in the prison camp, he was the most unpredictable.

"Thanks, Philip. You did good." He cuffed the young man on the shoulder. "Now head back to the house and make sure no one else runs off."

"Yes, sir!"

Though the other men in the home weren't as mentally fragile as his friend Will Anderson, it would give the young man something to do while James went to fetch his friend. Turning toward the direction Philip had pointed, James ran down toward the river.

It had taken him quite a bit of convincing before the home would admit his friend. They had thought Will better suited for one of the veteran hospitals back east, but James knew those places were nothing more than dressed up asylums and the conditions would only do more harm than good.

James wouldn't discard his friend in such a place, as many families had done to those who had returned home after the war. Will had no close ties to his family, or anyone willing to take him in, yet a life in an asylum wasn't a fate James could leave his friend to. Not after everything they had been through together. He would see to it that Will lived out the rest of his days in comfort.

As he neared the riverbank, James kept himself vigilant. He couldn't be sure what he would encounter when he got there, but he was careful not to make himself a target.

It didn't take long for James to spot his friend standing in the shallow edge of the river. Will had stripped out of his clothes and was slicing through the water with the long kitchen blade, muttering threats and curses to himself. James jerked off his boots, his hat following next, before he made his way toward his friend.

"Major Anderson! Throw down your weapon. *That's an order.*"

It was a senseless order, since Will appeared more interested in carving answers from the water than following his command. But the goal was to either get Will to drop the blade or distract him enough so James could disarm him of it.

"Those bastards got Jim," Will muttered. "I've got to find him, and then make those bastards pay for what they did."

"No, you don't, Will." James stepped into the water but stopped when Will raised the knife toward him. "It's me, brother. Jim. Your old friend. No one's got me."

Will paused, assessing him with a shrewdness that hadn't been in his bright blue eyes in a while. Then he shook his head wildly.

"No, you're not!" Will began pounding the side of his head. "Jim's dead. *I saw him die.*"

James glanced at the knife in his friend's hand, coming dangerously close to his temple, and his gut twisted. Will could hurt himself— intentionally or not—and with the distance between them, James feared he would be too late to do a damn thing about it.

"Will, look at me. Do I look dead to you? I got this funny looking eye patch but as you can see plain, I'm very much alive."

Will stared at him, recognition flashing across his flushed face. He lowered the knife and took a tentative step toward him.

"Jim?"

James nodded, keeping his eye on the blade. He held out his hand, urging his friend to hand it to him.

"Yes, brother. It's me. Now why don't you give me that blade and we'll get you back in your uniform."

These days, their uniform consisted of a pair of trousers, one shirt, and a jacket. With the constant fight with the government for adequate pension pay, they were lucky to have those simple provisions.

Will stared down at James' outstretched hand, but instead of taking it, he brought the knife down and slashed it across his palm.

"Liar!"

James jerked back from the intense pain, biting back a vicious curse. Will raised the knife again but this time, James wasn't caught off guard. Grabbing his friend's wrist, he twisted it then slammed his fist against his jaw. Will collapsed with a low grunt. Before he could fall into the river, James caught him and hoisted him over his shoulder.

He carried his unconscious friend to a grassy patch of land and placed him down before he too collapsed beside him. James stared up at the clear sky, waiting for the rapid thudding in his heart to slow. He hated to admit defeat but this struggle between what he wanted for Will versus what was best for him was proving to be a difficult one.

And it was a decision James was starting to realize he wasn't the right person to make.

Will wasn't getting any better and it was time he considered other arrangements for his friend. Before Will seriously hurt himself— or someone else.

As much as he hated it, James knew what he had to do.

Taking in a deep breath, he shut his eyes against the early morning sun, letting the warm rays wash over him. Deep, dark-brown eyes and a pretty smile filled his mind and he smiled back at her. His Maddie.

But the sweet smile he had held constant in his memory turned solemn as he recalled their last night together…

"Maddie, what are you doing here?" James pulled her into his small apartment.

"You're leaving tomorrow, and I know I can't change your mind, so…" She inhaled a shaky breath, her hands clasped before her. "I want to spend tonight with you."

There was an earnestness in her tone that made his heart ache and James reached for her. "Come here, Ladybug." He took her hand in his, and his fingers brushed against something stiff. "What's this?"

Her shy smile only added to his curiosity.

"I had this made for you."

James carefully took the small card from her outstretched hand and turned it over. Staring back at him was her dark, knowing gaze on her smooth, beautiful features. His heart warmed at the sight.

"I have nothing to leave you, love."

She walked up to him and folded her arms around him. "That's all right. Just write to me. Every chance you get."

And he had.

As often as he could, he had sent her countless letters, along with a *carte de visite* when a photographer had been spotted on their camp. Unfortunately, however, her photo and the letters she had written him were now all lost to him, destroyed during the ambush on his regiment.

But James could never forget the love that had shone in his Maddie's eyes that night.

She was the sunlight of his days, the delight of his dreams— and the anchor that had kept his mind from snapping the same way his friend's had.

CHAPTER 2

"This will be your lodging, Miss Madeline."

She turned away from the tall, well-dressed community leader who would be their host and attendant while she, Sherry, and Teresa were in Dunesville. She surveyed the small, single room cabin and tried not to grimace.

It's only temporary, Madeline reminded herself. She had seen happier living quarters but this one would have to do. And the benefit was that she wouldn't have to share the space.

"Unfortunately, there was some flooding here recently, so it may not be pretty but it's sturdy," Eldridge Duncan said. "Reinforcements were added around the foundation of each place so no need to worry. Only a tornado could knock this place down."

Madeline shared in his short chuckle, though she nervously glanced around the small cabin again. Since tornadoes were frequent in these parts of the country, it made that possibility an uncomfortable, and frightening, probability.

But Madeline set that worry aside for now. Tomorrow would mark her first day as a teacher and she needed to concentrate on her students, their education, and getting through the next couple of months before the election.

"Thank you, Mr. Duncan. This will do just fine."

Eldridge nodded, a relieved smile breaking across his dark, handsome face.

"We passed by a school on our way here. Is that the one I'll be having my classes in?"

"Indeed, it is," he confirmed. "We were lucky to receive funding to rebuild a new school and church after they were…"

"Burned?" His lips tightened and she gave a small smile of reassurance.

"We know all about the vandals that came here and destroyed what you all worked so hard to build, but it hasn't stopped us from coming here and helping."

Another wave of relief flashed across his face. "I'm glad to hear that, Miss Madeline. It was hard finding educated individuals like yourselves to return to Dunesville after that. This community is important to me and my family and we're trying to keep it as safe for our people as we can."

The love and loyalty for what was a thriving community glowed on the man's face. His enthusiasm for the safe haven his family had developed for so many people only added to Madeline's anger that anyone would try to destroy it.

"Well, you don't have to worry about me abandoning you, Mr. Duncan." She offered him a teasing smile. "It's going to take a tornado to sweep me away from here."

He returned her smile and took her hand. "Please, call me Eldridge."

Madeline tensed and stared down at her hand clasped in his. It had been a while since a man had taken her hand that way—with gentleness and affection. But she didn't want his affection.

She wanted nothing from him.

Madeline jerked her hand out of his grasp and his eyes widened in surprise. It was immediately replaced with embarrassment and a sudden awkwardness settled between them.

Regret at her impulsive reaction brought an apology rolling off the tip of her tongue but Madeline swallowed it. What was she to say? That the new Madeline preferred not to be touched, that as much as she liked and respected what he was doing for his community, she didn't want anything other than friendship from him?

The old Madeline wouldn't allow her to be so ill-mannered, so she asked the one thing that mattered.

"What time should I report to the school tomorrow?"

"I believe my mother, Mrs. Ophelia, will discuss that with you all tonight after supper," he said, clasping his hand behind his back. "But everyone is excited for the school term to start again. The children, especially."

"Children?" Madeline frowned. "I specifically requested to teach the adults."

At Eldridge's curious expression, she dropped her gaze down to the button on his coat. Being allowed to teach only the adults had been a big part of her decision to join the mission. Though she may not have been formally trained to teach anyone, she wasn't prepared to deal with children.

"I…I had plans in my curriculum to teach government and politics," Madeline added. "That's where my expertise lay."

"To be frank, I don't really know the details of the teaching assignments, but I don't see why that should present a problem. There will be a noon and evening class schedule for the men to accommodate those who have to work through their noon meal, so you'll have your choice of one."

Madeline released a sigh of relief. Noon or night, it didn't particularly matter to her, so long as it didn't include being near the little ones. Though she knew her preference bordered on ludicrous, she couldn't change how she felt. There were times just the sight of a young child would send her into a panic, or fill her with immense grief. The only way for her to control her reaction was to keep her distance.

After giving her a few more instructions on her accommodations in her temporary residence, Eldridge finally took his leave.

Finally alone in the cabin, Madeline sat down on the edge of the bed, surprised by its comfort, and took in her surroundings once more. She hadn't imagined her first step toward a new life would come to this— sitting alone in a dim, one-room cabin—but distance from her sister and her past made it worth it.

There was just one person in her past she couldn't seem to let go.

Lifting her travel bag onto the bed, Madeline took out the stack of letters from her suitcase. All of them were from her Jimmy, and every last letter was sacred to her.

Tugging at the thin ribbon around the bundle, she pulled out the top envelop and laid the stack beside her on the bed. It was the first of many letters he had written her and the one she turned to whenever she needed his words to lighten her spirits.

She took out the letter dated five years ago on November fourth, three months after his enlistment and began reading.

My dearest Maddie, I have wanted to write you much sooner as I've missed you more than you can imagine. Though I do not regret my decision to join the Infantry, as I have met with the most honorable and courageous of men, I do regret that we did not wed before my departure. Our last night together is all I can think on. It has firmly bound me to you, as it has bound you to me. You are all that is good and pure of heart, and it is your smile and your passion that sustains me in a place where defeat and despair is rooted in so many. I know in my heart we fight for a great cause, and that this war will soon be over, but I can barely wait for the day when I can truly make you mine. Keep me in your thoughts, my love. I remain always and very truly yours.

Madeline shut her eyes against the sting of tears that burned behind her lids. She knew it was pointless holding on to such mementos, but James Blakemore was the one thing she couldn't seem to leave behind.

Stuffing the letter back into the envelop, Madeline got up from the bed and began settling herself into her new, temporary home.

ↄↄ ↄↄ ↄↄ

The first day of class was a massive disappointment.

Madeline sat in the empty classroom, her hands locked together and resting on the desk. She waited over twenty minutes before she accepted the fact that no one was going to show. With a small sigh, she rose to her feet and began to gather her things.

"I was afraid of this, though I had hoped at least a handful would show."

Madeline looked up from her packing to find Mrs. Ophelia Duncan walking into the classroom, her lips pinched with disappointment. Aside from the grays in her neatly-pinned hair, Madeline would never have guessed the head mistress of the school to be in her late fifties. It certainly wasn't evident on her smooth brown face or in her patient brown eyes.

"Perhaps they weren't sure of the time," Madeline offered in response to the empty classroom. She hated to think anyone would pass up the opportunity for a free education.

"I doubt that. We've announced these classes for the past few weeks now, even during the Sunday service. Notices have also been posted around the community." Ophelia sighed.

Madeline could feel the weariness of that small action from where she stood. Last night, she and her missionary mates had shared dinner with Ophelia and from that short time, Madeline had gotten to learn just how much love the Duncan family had for their community.

"Noon may then be a difficult time for them to step away from their work or chores. Perhaps the evening class will be different."

"You're right. Maybe the turn out would be better then. Would it be asking too much if you could lead the evening class? At least until we can figure out a schedule that works for everyone."

"No, it wouldn't be any trouble at all."

That evening, Madeline returned to the school and was relieved to find a few men sitting behind the old desks, waiting for her. It was only a handful—some ranging from young men about her age to a few who could have been old enough to be her father, had he made it to sixty.

She smiled a greeting toward the men only to be met with grim, tired expressions.

"Good evening, class. My name's Madeline Asher and I'm here to teach you reading, writing, and government for the next six months."

Madeline didn't know where her sudden nervousness had come from, but suddenly her hands were clammy and her throat begged for water. She had never taught a group of people before, and the sudden realization that she had absolutely no idea of what she was doing nearly overwhelmed her.

However, the longer she stared out at their expectant faces, the more she realized she needed to get over her nerves and see to her duties. These men had the chance to shape the future of this nation. The laws weren't going to change in the next three months to give the women the right to vote, and with the presidential election barreling down on them, she needed to do the next best thing—equip the freedmen of Dunesville with the knowledge they'd need to cast an informed vote this coming November.

"Miss Madeline? Are you all right?"

Madeline pulled herself out of her daze and offered her class a quick smile. "Yes, thank you. Why don't we go around and introduce ourselves?"

One by one, each man said his name, and told whether he was new to the community. It appeared many of the more enthusiastic men were, in fact, newcomers to Dunesville.

"By show of hands, how many of you know the alphabet?" Madeline asked.

One hand came up.

Madeline bit the inside of her lip. Well, at least now she knew where to start. She took a few minutes to explain what the alphabet was and why it was important to learn. Some of the men listened to her intently and with genuine interest. A few others, however, were not as invested. She tried to ignore that unfortunate fact, yet the more cynical their expressions turned, the more she began to lose her confidence—and her resolve.

So she decided to tackle the most stubborn bull of the group head on.

"Mr. Barnes, what would you like to learn to write first?"

Surprise flashed in the older man's dark eyes before it was replaced with sharp skepticism. "Miss Madeline, I appreciate all that you're trying to do here, but truthfully, I see no point to it. These white folks don't give a lick about our vote. They gon' put whoever the hell they want in that big ole' house and there ain't nothing we can do about that."

Madeline glanced around the room as some of the men murmured in agreement. She could understand their frustration, especially with news of the Black Codes taking root and spreading across the South. Those unsanctioned laws made it difficult for Negro men and women to function as equal citizens of the country.

But Madeline couldn't let the attitude of one influence the others. Not when there was so much at stake.

"Mr. Barnes, we can only make a difference if we take a stand and let our voices be heard. I'm trying to give you the tools you need to march to that voting poll and cast your ballot for the candidate you believe has an interest in your rights as an American citizen."

Mr. Barnes scoffed and settled back in his seat, his thick arms folded across his wide chest. "Darling, I'm too old and too tired to believe in those fairytales you spinning. You can stop with all that voting mess. I'm not about to get lynched for putting down a name on a piece of paper for some white man who's feeding us nothing but lies."

He received more murmurs and nods of approval and Madeline's heart sank. They were losing faith in the system and her class without really giving it a chance.

"Think about this, Mr. Barnes. If the election weren't so important, there wouldn't be people out there right now trying to keep you out of it. As a newly freed man in this nation, you can't let your fear or frustration keep you from practicing your constitutional right. At the very least, don't let what all those brave soldiers fought for become a lost cause."

"If you ask me, it's already a lost cause. They killed the only white man in power who seemed to be on our side. They already got us back in chains. And it's a real shame, because this time, a lot of us just can't see it."

At Mr. Barnes words, many of the other men grew vocal in their agreement. But it was the indifferent callousness of what he said that struck her—and made her see red.

It's already a lost cause?

How could he say that? With all that she had lost—all that she and so many others had given up—she couldn't accept that it had all been for nothing.

With short, careful steps, Madeline went to stand in front of the desk Mr. Barnes sat behind. She dragged the desk back and slid it off to the side.

"If that's how you feel, Mr. Barnes, then you are free to leave my classroom." Madeline turned to the other men in the room. "All of you are. I won't waste my time with a bunch who cares nothing about their future, much less the future of their children. I particularly won't waste my time with an ignorant, selfish bunch that can't appreciate the opportunity they've been given."

A few hung their heads low, but Mr. Barnes continued to glare defiantly back at her. She knew there were still some who followed his belief and total disregard for the American democratic system. Though she could understand their apprehension, their fear, she couldn't tolerate their disregard of those who had fought and died for them to have this moment.

"You have a chance here, gentlemen, to honor your country and those who gave their lives so you could have this right. You also have an opportunity to honor your mothers, sisters, and daughters and be their champions for change. Those women look to you to be their voice in a country that says they can't have one, simply because they are women—a decree passed on by men brought into this world by women. *That,* gentlemen, is the true shame."

The silence in the room was louder than a cannon blast—and just as unnerving.

Madeline's heart thudded in her chest as she continued to glare down at a quiet Mr. Barnes. She felt the eyes of the other men on her but kept her gaze on the one stubborn bull who had started her on her tirade.

"So, Mr. Barnes, are you going to leave here and give those who mean to terrorize and oppress us exactly what they want? Or will you remain here with me and let me help you serve and honor what this country stands for?"

The older man slowly rose to his feet and Madeline took a step back, a sinking sense of failure crawling up her spine. But to her surprise, Mr. Barnes grabbed the desk she had set aside and slid it back to its original place. He fell into his seat.

"My name."

Madeline cocked her head to the side. "Excuse me?"

"You asked what I wanted to learn to write first." Mr. Barnes cleared his throat. "I want to write my name."

CHAPTER 3

"That looks pretty bad, Jim. You sure you want to ride out tonight?"

James glanced down at his bandaged hand and shrugged. Considering the various injuries he had endured since his enlistment, a knife to the hand amounted to nothing more than an inconvenience.

"I still got one good eye and one good hand. I'll live."

Clayton Palmer snorted. "You always managed to see the bright side of things."

James placed his signature on the last of the government documents and handed them to his attorney and fellow Union vet.

"Well, I believe happier things come when we keep our eyes locked toward the sun." That way, his shadows would always stay behind him. "Besides, I'm already a day behind on my journey. The sooner I'm on my way, the better."

Clay sighed. "I wish you would reconsider. There's still so much work to be done."

"I've done all that I can do, Clay. I've signed more petitions then I can remember and sat in more assembly meetings than I can stomach. Perhaps when the bureaucrats in Washington are ready to enforce half of the promises they've made to their countrymen, to the men who fought for them, then perhaps I'll consider continuing the good fight. Until then...my work here's done."

The solemn, half-hearted smile on Clay's face was all the acknowledgement James needed. They both knew he had a point. They may not agree on the level of change that needed to take place, but they both agreed that it wasn't happening soon enough.

"In the short time I've known you, Jim, I always pegged you as a man with strong beliefs, but I've always wanted to know why..."

"Why, what?"

"Why fight? Why risk your life for a country you had no stake in? You clearly don't plan to stay, so why?"

The corner of James's lips lifted into a half smile. He was not offended by the question because he had asked himself that very thing when times had been beyond bleak, and when those times had appeared damn-near hopeless. There were countless reasons, little of which having to do with him being in love with a colored woman and a lot to do with the fact that America was part of his roots.

"I may not be American born but my great-grandmother was part African and part Iroquois," James confessed. "Her tribe fought with the Americans during the revolution. I like to think I'm finishing that fight for *all* Americans to be free."

In many ways, his ancestry made him as American as any man here, and a land that embodied the spirit of freedom and new life shouldn't continue to stain its legacy with the enslavement of people.

If the knowledge that he was the descendent of a colored woman surprised Clay, his friend didn't show it. His fair skin, dark-brown wavy hair, and light green eyes hid that part of his heritage, allowing him to move about this country as freely as any full-blooded white man. But in the eight years James had lived in this country, he knew that the knowledge of his full ancestry would put an end to those privileges he was granted.

"Well, we're going to miss you around here," Clay said, apparently choosing to ignore that bit of damning information. "Fighting the good fight."

"It certainly was a fight well fought," James muttered.

And if he were honest with himself, James was going to miss it here, too. More specifically, he was going to miss the friends he had made, the places he'd been, and the ones he had yet to see. He had always had a strange pull to this country. Maybe it was the tales his father had told him of the first James Blakemore. Their family's original patriarch had fought fearlessly for the British during the birth of this young nation—until he had met the woman that he would choose to give it all up for, just so they could be together.

That had once been a dream of his as well—to return to his home in Canada with the woman he loved. But fate had seen to it that his Maddie found love and happiness with another. As much as James resented the thought of her with another man, he couldn't begrudge her the one thing he had always wanted for her.

Happiness.

James rose to his feet, ignoring the unrelenting tightness that always seem to invade his chest whenever he thought of their broken future. As much as he would miss this great land, there was nothing left for him here.

"Well, I better be off. It's high-time my family saw my charming face again, not to mention the new nieces and nephews I have yet to meet. You know where to contact me, if you need me."

Clay stuffed the documents giving him power-of-attorney over James' U.S. assets into a file before he too got to his feet. "Everything I need is all in there. And not to worry about Anderson. Until I hear back from his kin, I'll be sure he gets his pension, and whatever else he needs at the home."

James nodded. Guilt over leaving Will behind, before he had a chance to get in touch with his half-sister, almost made him second guess his decision to leave. His friend was sick, the kind of sick no doctor could fix. James could only hope that Will's sister did right by him and used his pension to see to his comfort.

"Write to me if you run into any issues."

Clay took his hand and gave it a firm shake. "Of course. Safe travels, Jim."

With a quick tip of his hat, James left Clay's law office and headed toward the post office. He had one last errand to run before he started on his long journey home.

He entered the small office and went straight to the front counter. It was hard to miss the gaping stare of the young clerk. James ignored him. There were times he managed to forget about the patch covering his right eye, forget the scars that traced a jagged path down the side of his face.

Today, however, wasn't one of those times.

"I need these three letters postmarked today." James handed the older clerk behind the desk the envelopes, trying his damnedest to ignore the fascinated gaze of the young man off to the side. He hated being gawked at. Oftentimes, people stared long enough to satisfy their curiosity, but they eventually had the damn decency to look away.

"Where is this one going?" The old man's eye-glasses sat perched on the bridge of his nose as he squinted down at one of the letters in his hand.

"Canada," James replied.

The old man grunted, then made a notation on the envelope. Without looking up, the clerk slid a short form across the counter toward him. "I'm gonna need some more information from you, sir. Derrick, that mail ain't gonna sort itself."

James glanced over at Derrick as he took the form. The young man remained standing there, a stack of mail clutched in his hands and his wide-eyed gaze held transfixed on his eye patch.

With a sigh of exasperation, James shifted until he was standing directly in front of the young mail clerk. Leaning against the counter, James got as close as he could and flipped open his eye patch.

"Here's a closer look."

The blood drained from Derrick's face and to his surprise, the boy collapsed were he stood. James released the eye patch and it fell back into place. Leaning over the counter, he peered down at the unconscious boy, mail littered all over him.

"Well, hell."

The old man sucked at his teeth and shook his head. "He's always had a weak stomach. Didn't figure him a fainter too."

"Your son?"

"Nope. My late sister's boy, so I guess I got to claim him." The man moved to grab the boy's feet. "Help me with him, would ya?"

James came around the counter and grabbed Derrick's shoulders. Together, they moved the boy's motionless body to a nearby seat. The man stood back with a grunt then turned and studied him closely.

"I'm guessing you lost that eye in the war?"

James gave a curt nod. Though he hadn't lost it fighting in battle, the result had been just the same. He wondered just how good a look the man had gotten at the damaged, hollowed socket. The older clerk hadn't flinched when he'd exposed the scarred remains of his right eye socket. James could only assume he hadn't gotten that good a look because he knew just how grotesque the sight was. There were days where he avoided his own reflection.

"Lost a brother in that damn war." The clerk shook his head with pity. "I reckon, though, he'd rather be dead then a—"

"Cripple?" James finished for him.

The man's face flushed with embarrassment. James ignored the man's obvious discomfort. That was the problem with some westerners, he had come to realize. They always had an opinion and never knew when to keep it to themselves.

"I knew a few men like that, too vain to live a life with a mutilated face," James said evenly. "But if you ask me, nothing beats death. Not even vanity."

Derrick began to stir in his seat. "Uncle Aaron…?"

The old clerk went to tend to his nephew, clearly grateful for the distraction.

James started back around the other side of the counter when he realized he was crushing a letter beneath his boot. He snatched it up and started to toss it back on the counter when the handwriting caught his attention. It was the way the letters scrolled neat and elegantly across the front of the envelope that drew him.

He clutched the envelope in his hands as he carefully read the name of the sender. Then he re-read it again, not wanting to put his trust in fate again—or allow himself to believe in miracles.

Yet the name on the envelope didn't disappear...

Madeline Asher.

He knew that handwriting well. With every letter that had made its way to him during the darkest moments of his hell, he had studied her writing, memorized her words. This was her name, her handwriting, and—he brought the letter to his nose—her scent.

James whipped around to the clerk and his nephew. The look on their faces made him question his own sanity. Maybe the sweet, delicate smell he remembered was all in his head, but he didn't care. He knew with every fiber in his being that this was her.

And he needed to find her.

"The woman who brought this in, when was she here?"

The two men stared blankly at him. James cursed.

"*When*, damn it?"

Aaron snapped out of his stupor. "I don't rightly know. We had a lot of traffic yesterday and today..."

"This patron would have been hard to miss. She's about yay high." James levelled his hand up to the center of his chest. "She has big, chestnut brown eyes and smooth, amber-brown skin. The color of sweet butterscotch." James shut his eye briefly, wanting to imprint the memory of her in his mind. "She has the sweetest smile and the softest laugh..."

"I'm starting to realize, Mr. James Blakemore that you have this perverse need to tease me."

"I can't seem to help myself, Miss Asher. It must be the fire in your eyes that I find irresistible."

She laughed again and shook her head. "You are as peculiar as you are vexing."

He smiled down at her, enchanted by the sweet sound of her laugh. "I assure you, I'm as ordinary as they come. But a passionate lady deserves an impassioned suitor."

"Am I to presume that suitor to be you?"

"Well, love, you have managed all three of the impossible."

Her eyes widened at the endearment, but she didn't shy away. "And what is that?"

Further emboldened, James took her hand and kissed her wrist. "You have aroused my mind, inflamed my senses, and corrupted my thoughts."

He opened his eye again, having lost himself in that short glimpse into the past—to his initial courtship of the most captivating and easily goaded woman he had ever met. James caught the shared look between the two clerks and a bit of warmth crawled up his cheeks.

But he refused to lose his resolve.

"I need to find her. Now, do you know where she is?"

"No," Aaron said. "I don't remember a woman by that...colorful description coming in here."

"You have her letter right here," James snapped. "She came in here sometime today. Now think!" He turned to the younger clerk. "What day were those letters you were sorting postmarked?"

Derrick's already pale face lost what little remaining color it had. "Th-th-they were collected yesterday."

"So you saw her?"

The young man's eyes darted from him to his uncle. "Maybe...I-I don't remember. I think so."

James sighed and bit back a curse. He was getting nowhere but needed a starting place if he was going to find her in this busy town.

"Do you remember a colored woman stopping in here? Perhaps one you'd never seen before?" The boy opened his mouth, indecision plain on his face. "Think long and hard before you answer, Derrick."

Something in his tone must have convinced him, because the boy shut his eyes and James watched as the pupils moved rapidly behind his eyelids. Then suddenly, they sprang open.

"I remember!"

James' gut clenched in anticipation.

"She came in very early. I believe you were in the back, Uncle Aaron."

"Do you know where she's staying?"

"No, sir. But I heard of some colored missionaries staying at Patty's Saloon. She could have been traveling with them."

"Traveling?"

"Y-yes. She asked about renting a box for her letters. Asked about our schedule, too, so she knew what times to travel into town."

"Did she say when she would be back?"

The young man shook his head vehemently.

James took a step forward. He was so close! "Are you certain?"

"He said he doesn't know," Aaron interjected. "Now, I think it's about time you finish your business here, mister, and be on your way."

James snapped his gaze over to the older man.

Maddie is my business.

But he kept the sharp retort behind his teeth. At least now, he had a starting place.

And by the following night, he finally had a destination.

Dunesville.

CHAPTER 4

"I heard you gave your class a proper and thorough set down last night, Maddie."

Madeline swung her gaze over at Sherry, embarrassment warming her cheeks as she thought about her rant to a room full of grown men.

"I wouldn't call it a set down..." Madeline began.

"Then what would you call it?"

More like a meltdown.

When she'd had a moment to calm down, Madeline realized how improper her behavior had been. Though the men had stayed until the end, including Mr. Barnes, and had showed a little more interest in her teaching, Madeline wouldn't be surprised if none of them showed today. Why would they?

Upon further reflection, she had a chance to think about the men's arguments. As colored men, they faced constant humiliation and degradation from the hands of their counterparts. The last thing they wanted was an "uppity" colored woman talking down to them. It certainly was the last thing they needed.

"Well, whatever you call it," Sherry said, "it seemed to work. It's all anyone can talk about today."

"Wonderful," Madeline muttered. "I'm glad I'm the source of everyone's afternoon gossip."

Sherry laughed. "And this morning. I had breakfast with the Duncans and even they were talking about it."

Madeline groaned. She typically chose to skip her morning meal, and was glad for it. Now she would have to find time to explain her behavior to Ophelia.

"Well, enjoy this now," Madeline said. "Because it'll be the last. I plan to apologize to the men tonight for my behavior. At least to whoever decides to show up…"

Sherry shrugged. "From what I hear, there's nothing for you to apologize for, Maddie. The Duncans admired what you did. You're a teacher now, a mentor to your pupils, and sometimes that means ruling with an iron fist."

Madeline frowned. "These are grown men we're talking about, not children. How will I expect to gain their respect if I go around talking down to them and making them feel low?"

Sherry shook her head. "Take it from someone who teaches children, being firm-handed doesn't mean you're talking down to them. You think I go around coddling my kids? No. I praise them often when they have earned it, and reprimand them when they misbehave or challenge my authority. Don't go undoing what you've done, Maddie. You have their attention and respect now. Use that to continue pushing them."

Though Madeline wanted to be as optimistic as Sherry, she couldn't help feeling as if she had already set a negative precedent and she had a lot of work ahead of her if she was going to convince any of them to return to her class.

Later that evening, Madeline realized she had gotten it all wrong. She entered the classroom and her mouth fell open.

The room was packed.

Not only did it include new male faces, there were also some women in attendance. Madeline surveyed the room of black and brown faces—some behind desks, others on the floor—all looking to her with interest and an excitement she hadn't seen before. There were maybe about twenty to twenty-five people in the small classroom and they were all ready to learn.

"If it's okay with you, Miss Madeline, some of us would also like to learn to write our names."

"And maybe read what's in those books you carry around," another called out.

"Yeah, I'd like to learn to read a few pages myself," someone else shouted from the back.

Madeline beamed at all of them, her heart swelling with wonder and another emotion she couldn't name.

"Of course it's all right," she said. "I just hope some of you are comfortable on the ground like that. This class runs for about an hour."

"Yup, Miss Madeline. We're all good down here," someone from the ground called out. "Just as long as the ground is the hardest thing my backside is going to suffer in your class."

Everyone laughed and Madeline couldn't help but join in their amusement.

"I promise you, it is," she assured them. "Now, shall we get started?"

ℰℬ ℰℬ ℰℬ

It was high noon when James rode into Dunesville.

If he had thought finding Madeline in the private community would come easy, he learned swiftly just how private and guarded the people of Dunesville really were.

He'd been there less than an hour, and yet all his questions about Madeline Asher had been met with silence and blank stares.

But James knew she was here. He felt it in his gut. Nothing, not even the residents' wariness of him, would stop him from searching for her.

He made his way to the church, hoping he would find better luck there. The mail clerk had mention something about her being part of a missionary group. If he was lucky, his search would end there.

James drew his horse alongside the large white building and jumped off. He tethered it to a nearby tree, never taking his attention off of the newly but poorly assembled building. After helping construct over a dozen veteran homes these past two years, James could spot poor handiwork and lazy construction from just one glance.

As he neared the church, a loud crash came from inside, followed by a heavy grunt. James rushed inside to find a short, balding man dressed in a long, black robe and starched white neck collar. The man appeared to be about fifty, yet he was attempting to lift a pew that had sunken into the floor boards on his own.

Without a word, James went to the other end of the pew. The reverend glanced up at him, perspiration glistening above his dark brows and brown face, and his eyeglasses were dangerously close to sliding off of his nose.

James grabbed the bottom of the pew. "On three."

He started counting and on three, they managed to lift the heavy bench enough to slide it out of its trench. The reverend straightened and adjusted his robe.

The man gave him a quick once over, his narrowed gaze not hiding his obvious suspicion. A sinking feeling settled in James' gut when he realized his hope for answers would not be found here either.

"You the carpenter from town?"

James nodded stiffly. It wasn't a complete lie since he'd spent the last three months there working on the new veteran home. That had to count.

The reverend's lips pursed with disapproval. "What took you so long, then? Oliver said he sent for you hours ago."

James jerked at the unexpected question. He was just about to tell the man that he was mistaken until he realized his advantage. Though, James didn't like the idea of deceiving a man of God, he had to know if what he felt in his gut was right.

"Sorry about that, Reverend," James began. "I was held up on another job."

The reverend grunted. "You could have sent word. I told them the floors have been groaning for weeks now. Had you been here sooner, I wouldn't be in this predicament."

"Again, my apologies." James held out his hand. "Lieutenant Colonel James Blakemore, at your service, sir."

The reverend shook his hand, and James knew the title had impressed him as he had intended it to. Whatever he needed to do to gain the man's trust...

"Reverend George Lincoln. Named after our two great presidents," the man said proudly. "But everyone calls me Reverend Linc. You a Union soldier, James?"

"Yes, sir. Served in the one-hundred and fifth Infantry regiment." James glanced back down at the collapsed floor. "I didn't have time to get the details from my boss, but I'm guessing you need the floor beds secured?"

"Ha! That's just the beginning."

The reverend proceeded to list all the repairs around the church that needed work. And it was quite a list.

"Do you have all the supplies for these tasks?" James asked.

The reverend shrugged. "I might. Everything during and after the construction was stored in the cellar. You're welcome to take a look to see what else we might need."

James inclined his head. "Lead the way."

Reverend Linc led him outside of the church and around the back. It was then he decided to broach the subject.

"I heard there were some missionaries that arrived here the other day," James began in what he hoped was a casual tone. "Are they all residing here at the church?"

"Oh, no. Those ladies are staying in the red cabins."

James' heart leapt with anticipation. She was here.

"If you ask me," Reverend Linc continued, "they're better off there too. Those small shacks are a far sight better than this building, with its weak walls and floors."

"The church looks new. Why the feeble construction?"

"Why you think? One of those vagabonds in town burnt down our first building. I reckon they figured it'll come down again so why bother building something sturdy?"

James frowned. "Have you taken this up with the sheriff?"

The reverend turned and gave him an incredulous look. "I can't be too certain he wasn't the one who lit the fire." Suddenly, as if realizing he'd said too much, Reverend Linc pursed his lips and continued toward the tall cellar door.

From the wary glance the reverend had shot him right before he had turned away, James could only guess the vandals had been white men. Although he resented the idea of someone of the law neglecting to protect their citizens, James wasn't exactly surprised by it. Before and since the war, he had the misfortune of meeting extremely hateful, bigoted men. As much as James sympathized with the small community's unfortunate situation, he needed to focus on the real reason he was there—before the reverend did like everyone else in the community and completely shut him out.

"So about those cabins, are you sure they're secure? If they're close by, maybe I can drop by and take a look at them."

Reverend Linc unlatched the door and pulled it open with a hard tug. "I believe they're about two, three miles west of here, but it could— Hey! Where you off to?"

James didn't stop in his tracks when he called back. "Sorry, Reverend. I just realized I'm late for an appointment."

About three years too late.

James got to his horse and started off toward the direction the reverend had mentioned. In a mad gallop, he made it to the row of small, red cabins in record time. It was a little after noon yet the area appeared desolate. For a moment, James wondered if the reverend had gotten their location mistaken until he saw a young woman leaving from one of the cabins. He swung his horse in her direction and rushed toward her.

The woman froze, her dark eyes saucers as she clutched an armful of books to her chest. James immediately dismounted and pulled off his hat.

"Sorry, Miss. I don't mean to bother you. I'm looking for Maddie— Madeline Asher. Can you point me to her cabin?"

The woman glanced toward his eyepatch, and then continued staring at him. For a moment, James wondered if she too would ignore him as the others had. He held on to his waning patience.

"Reverend Linc sent me," James lied.

Well, it's not a complete lie.

"The cabin on the end is where Maddie stays," the woman finally said. "But she might still be at the school."

School?

James simply inclined his head. With one final look in his direction, she continued down the path. He led his horse toward the last cabin down the row, his heart thudding in his chest.

Suddenly, he found himself torn between his anticipation to see her and his fear of how she would react when she saw him. As much as he wanted to lay his sights on her, to touch and hold her, there was a part of him that was afraid that she wouldn't be as eager to see him.

Five years was a long time since they'd laid eyes on each other. He wasn't the same man she'd known before the war. He no longer looked the same. With his damaged face, what if she found him repulsive? Frightening?

What if she had moved on from him?

James tethered his horse nearby and walked up to the cabin. Like he had done many times before, especially during the pits of battle, he shoved his fears and uncertainty deep inside himself. Fate—and perhaps even God—had brought him this far.

There was no turning back now.

✿ ✿ ✿

Madeline was pleased with yet another successful day with her students.

The men and women of Dunesville were more eager about their education than she had realized—or had given them credit for. Because the previous evening's class had been overcrowded, she had managed to convince those who could spare the time to attend the mid-day classes, saving the evening ones for those who needed it the most.

Today, she had gotten a decent turnout with a group that was just as eager about the upcoming classes and the thought filled Madeline with a quiet happiness and excitement.

As she made her way back to her cabin, the high afternoon sun beat down on her, adding to her lightheadedness and fatigue from the long walk from the school. She made a mental note to start eating something in the mornings before class, at least until the end of this sweltering summer, or else she wouldn't have the stamina to teach anyone anything.

Madeline continued toward her small cabin, making another mental note to start carrying a hat with her to ward off the harsh sun. By the time she made it through the door of her cabin, she couldn't think of anything more heavenly than the pitcher of cool water inside.

Madeline dropped her bag of books on the ground and rushed to the pantry. She reached for the pitcher and mug until she realized they both weren't where she had left them.

She froze.

The hairs on the back of her neck stood on end, and she could sense with every fiber in her being that she wasn't alone. Panic swelled inside her but she swiftly suppressed it. She wasn't the same helpless Maddie she had been two years ago. She began to slowly slide the knife out of her wrist holster, wishing she had her pistol in the same easy reach.

Once she had the knife from its sheath, Madeline whirled around to face her intruder.

Instead, she came face to face with a ghost.

The bottom dropped from her stomach, along with the knife from her hand. She had dreamed of that moss-green gaze and sensual lips that had stretched into a wicked smile whenever he had fancied a kiss from her.

Madeline shook her head.

No, this can't be him.

The Jimmy she knew was dead and her mind was playing tricks on her. This strange man who bore the ravages of violence on one side of his face was just a larger, coarse, and damaged imitation of the man she had once known. He was here to hurt her and like before, she would be too weak, too stupid, to stop him.

Yet, with just a few simple words—words spoken in the same deep, richly smooth voice she remembered so well—the man managed to strip away the last of her defenses.

"I've missed you, Ladybug."

Madeline gaped at him. Suddenly, something strange moved over her and the blood drained from her head.

To her immense horror, she fainted.

CHAPTER 5

Well, hell.

James barely had time to reach Madeline before she hit the ground. Luckily, he was quick. He lifted her in his arms, and for a moment he stood there, relishing the feel of her in his arms again. It had been too long since he'd been able to hold her, to have her pressed against him like this.

But he'd obviously frightened her to unconsciousness and needed to make sure she was all right. Crossing the short steps to her bed, he placed her down gently. Her smooth, brown cheeks were flushed slightly and he undid a few of the buttons of her high collar.

He went to the water pitcher and dampened a cloth before he rushed back to the bed. James sat down beside her and lightly pressed the cool cloth against her flushed cheeks and down her neck. His gaze moved over her as he took in every nuance of her matured features.

It had been too long since he had been able to lay eyes on her, and yet she was just as beautiful as he remembered, if not more so. And now that he had found her, had seen her, he couldn't wait a moment longer to press his lips against hers and savor her sweet softness.

His gaze drifted down to her full, supple lips. With very little thought, or decency, James leaned down and kissed her. He lingered there for a moment, cherishing the deep pleasure of the stolen kiss and committing the taste of her to memory.

Just as he began to pull away, the hard steel barrel of a gun pressed beneath his chin. James froze. The sharp crack of the gun being cocked disrupted the warm, easy comfort of the small quarters.

"You're right," he said, inching back away from her, his hands raised in surrender. "I shouldn't have done that."

She pushed at his chest, keeping the Derringer leveled at his face. James kept his eye on the gun, vaguely wondering where the hell it had come from and just how well she knew how to handle it.

"Sorry. That was stupid. Now put down the gun, love."

She ignored him, her shrewd gaze held steadily on him. There was a weariness in her eyes that seemed to age her more than her twenty-three years, but beyond that, she looked very much the same.

"Who are you?"

"Maddie, it's me."

He reached for her and she scooted away from him, lowering her arm until the gun was aimed squarely at his heart.

James frown. "I know I've changed, but don't you recognize me? Even a little?"

She slowly shook her head, but her gaze was unwavering. "You can't be him... Jimmy's dead. They told me...they told me he died in battle."

His heart broke at the anguish in her voice.

"I'm very much alive, Ladybug." He offered her a gentle smile. "And I have a waterfall to show you, remember?"

Tears welled in her eyes. She released the hammer and lowered the Derringer. "Jimmy?"

"Yes, love. It's me."

With a loud sob, she tossed the gun aside and threw her arms around him. He tightened his arms around her and held her close, not realizing how much he had missed the way she called his name until that moment. It had been a long time since anyone had called him by that nickname. It brought back memories of her, his family, and his life before the war.

The wetness of her tears slid down his neck and James tightened his arms around her. Her embrace was the loveliest thing he'd experience in a long time. A tight lump formed in his own throat as five years of hell, of not being able to hold her like this, tore through him.

"I thought you were lost to me," he murmured thickly against her hair as her body shook with silent sobs.

The countless days and nights he'd spent wondering if he would ever see her again, wondering if she was happy and safe, came pouring through him and he shut his eye against the sting of emotion that burned in his eye. He hadn't allowed himself to think of what he had given up, of what he had lost, until now.

But now that he had her back, James had no intentions of ever letting her go.

She pushed away from him and stared searchingly at him, her eyes and cheeks dampened with tears.

"What happened to you, Jimmy? Where have you been? Why didn't you come back to me?"

"I wanted to, love." He wiped away the dampness on her cheeks. "Believe me, I wanted to."

She stared at him as if waiting for the explanation he didn't know how to give her. There just were no right words to tell her how broken he had been after his release from the Confederate prison camp, how he had been just a shell of himself after three months in the worst hell he had ever had to endure. It had taken him months to find his center again, his reason for living, and when he had, it had been too late.

She had been gone.

Madeline reached out and brushed her fingers lightly along his eye patch. "What happened?"

James turned away, and she let her hand settle back on her lap. He regretted the embarrassment that now tainted her face but he wasn't ready to expose those dark memories yet. He knew he would have to. It had been a part of his healing, to talk about the atrocities he had witnessed and faced. Yet, he didn't want to revisit those memories now. All he wanted right now was to savor this moment of having her back in his arms and in his life.

James took her hand in his. "I know you have a lot of questions, Ladybug, and that there's a lot for us to discuss, but just know that as soon as I was able, I came back to Pennsylvania only to learn that you had left. I went searching for you all over. Reading, Philadelphia, New York, Chicago. It wasn't until I discovered you had left for Montana to marry a wealthy miner that I stopped looking. I didn't have much to offer you and I didn't want to take you away from what could have been a happy life for you."

"Jimmy, I could never be happy with anyone else." Her hands tightened around his. "I've been miserable without you."

His heart warmed at her words. "I've been miserable as well." He brushed the back of his hand across her cheek. "Now that I've found you, I don't plan to ever let you out of my sight."

James pulled her toward him and sealed that promise with a kiss. For a moment, she was still against him, almost rigid. But he kept his mouth lightly pressed on hers and she slowly began to lean fully into him.

She rested her palm gingerly across his shoulder and he gathered her close, deepening the kiss. He savored the familiar taste of her, her sweet scent and gentle touch. In that moment, he would have given anything to have them naked, her smooth skin pressed against his.

Yet, as much as he wanted to be inside her again, to have her thighs trembling around him as he rode her through the depths of incredible pleasure, he had vowed that the next time they made love, she would be his wife.

James drew back, his breath coming out deep and ragged. He cupped her face, his heart racing with need and swelling with immense love and joy. He couldn't help placing another fast kiss on her lips.

"Tomorrow," he promised. "Tomorrow, we'll have the reverend marry us, and then we'll start out for Canada and…what is it?"

She shook her head. "I can't marry you, Jimmy."

His head jerked back in surprise. "What?"

"I'm sorry, but I can't marry you. Not anymore. Not after…" Her gaze slid away from his. "You'll never know how good it does my heart to know that you're still alive, but things have changed, and I've made a commitment to the people of Dunesville. I can't leave them now."

He frowned. "What sort of commitment?"

"Teaching and recruiting more voters. The men and women here need a basic education and we have only just begun. I can't abandon them now. Not when there is so much at stake."

James could only stare at her. He had expected shock, maybe some uncertainty, but he hadn't expected her to flat-out refuse him. The bond between them was strong and he had hoped she would be eager to continue on with the life they had dreamed for themselves.

"What about *us*, our future? We were supposed to leave for Canada, to build a new life for ourselves there."

She pulled her hands out of his. "That was a long time ago, Jimmy, and dreams do fade. Things are different now. *I am* different. And I don't know if things can be the way they once were between us."

James gritted his teeth as a sinking thought entered his mind. "Is there someone else?" Something in his gut clenched at the thought that she may now be in love with another.

"No, there isn't anyone else, but… You shouldn't have come back for me. You should have just moved on."

"I love you, Maddie. Once I found out you were here, moving on wasn't an option for me."

Tears again welled in her eyes. "But I'm no good for you. Not anymore."

He regarded her closely, and he suddenly saw the somberness in her eyes, a sorrow he had never seen before.

"What happened to you to make you think that?"

Apprehension and shame filled her dark brown eyes, before she tore her gaze away and rested it on her clasped hands. He took her hand in his and laced their fingers together, wanting to wipe away that look from her eyes forever.

"Fate has brought you back to me, Maddie, and I have no intention of ever leaving you again."

ю ю ю

Madeline stared at James, still reeling from the shock of having him sitting right across from her—very much alive.

She also reeled from the fact that he still wanted them to marry. She didn't have the words to tell him why he shouldn't. The shame of what happened to her that long ago night would always stay with her. But it was what she had done after that made it all unbearable. How was she supposed to be his wife with so much disgrace following her?

Madeline pulled her hand from his grasp and stared down at his chest, as if she could find the words she needed to send him far away from her.
"Jimmy, I—"
A sharp rap on the door startled her. It was soon followed by Eldridge's booming voice.
"Miss Madeline? Are you inside?"
His tone indicated something was terribly wrong. She scrambled out of the bed and rushed to the door. She jerked it open and what greeted her left her stunned.
Madeline glanced from Eldridge then to the shotgun in his hand. Standing some distance behind him, were three men she didn't recognize and Sherry, concern and apprehension pulling at her brows.
"Eldridge, what is all this? What's going on?"
But the man didn't answer her. Instead, there was a sudden shift in his expression. Madeline knew then that James had come to stand behind her. Before she could reassure him of James' presence, Eldridge raised his shotgun.
Everything in that instance moved in a blur.
A strong hand snaked around her arm, then jerked her back. Madeline found herself staring at James broad back as he ripped the shotgun from Eldridge's hands and had it pointed at the other man.
Madeline had never seen him move so fast and in that moment, she realized just how much the war had changed him.

"You have some nerve pointing a gun toward a defenseless woman." James kept the gun levelled at Eldridge, his hard tone low and even.

Despite the tense situation, Madeline couldn't help sending James an annoyed glare. She was far from defenseless.

"I would never raise a gun to Miss Madeline," Eldridge said tightly. "I was aiming at you."

"Then give me one good reason why I shouldn't shoot you now."

Madeline gasped at his harsh words. "Jimmy!"

After a few short tense seconds, he lowered the gun but didn't return it to Eldridge.

Madeline rushed between the two men. "Eldridge, this is all a big misunderstanding. Jimmy doesn't mean anyone any harm. He's my…" Madeline stared at him, lost. Five years ago, before he had enlisted in the war, he was supposed to have been her husband. Just yesterday, he had been a nostalgic memory, a ghost.

What is he to me now?

"I'm Maddie's betrothed," James said frankly. "Now would you kindly leave us be?"

He held out the shotgun to a stunned Eldridge, the grim lines around his mouth not hiding his reservations, but he took the weapon from James.

"We were just worried about you, Miss Madeline. A few residents mentioned a white man snooping around here, asking for you. We just wanted to be certain this stranger meant you no harm."

Madeline offered Eldridge a reassuring smile. "You have nothing to worry about, Eldridge. Jimmy's just visiting and will be heading back home shortly."

Behind her, tension radiated from James in waves but Madeline kept her attention on Eldridge, hoping he and the others would not force the matter. Eldridge glanced from her to Jimmy and then back to her. With a small incline of his head, he turned to leave.

"Sorry again for the misunderstanding," she called after him before shutting the door to her small cabin. Madeline leaned against it and turned her attention to James. "You could have apologized to him."

James cocked a brow. "The man threatened to shoot me and *I* should have apologized?"

"You're a stranger here, Jimmy. They haven't had the best experience with outsiders, particularly those who look like you. Of course, you made them nervous."

He stared at her searchingly. "And is that why you want me gone, Ladybug?"

Her heart wrenched at his words. Of course, she didn't. God had granted her a miracle and brought the love of her life back to her. How could she turn him away?

Yet, knowing she wasn't the same woman he fell in love with, how could she let him stay?

Moved by an inexplicable need to touch him, Madeline pushed away from the door and went to him. She wrapped her arms around his neck and his mouth met hers for a searing kiss. She kissed him with all the love and desire she had locked away inside herself for so long. All her grief, all her longing, poured out in their simple embrace and in its place came a slow, delicious warmth that spread throughout her limbs.

They were being given a second chance. She couldn't take that for granted.

His arm tightened around her and he drew her close. "I've missed you so much, Maddie," he murmured against her lips.

Madeline, however, tensed at the unmistakable hardness pressing into her belly. She wanted him like she had never wanted anything—or anyone—in her life, but she didn't think she was ready for that kind of intimacy between them again.

What if you'll never be ready?

As if sensing her sudden worry and doubts, James pulled away from her. There was a love and understanding in his gaze that reminded her why she had fallen in love with him those many years ago.

"I take it that kiss means you don't really want me to go."

It was a statement, not a question, and Madeline couldn't lie to him. She never could. Her gaze fell briefly to his chest and she drew in a weary breath.

"You're right. I don't want you to go."

"But I can't convince you to leave here with me tomorrow, can I?"

She slowly shook her head. She wouldn't walk away from something this important. "I'm sorry. You can't."

James sighed. "Then I guess I need to go apologize to the reverend."

She tilted her head to the side. "Why?"

"I may have misled the poor man into offering me a job. Seeing as I don't plan to leave here without you, I'm going to need that job after all."

"You're staying?"

"You would have to force me out." He cupped her chin. "But just so you know, I'm not giving up on us without a fight."

Madeline's heart fluttered, though she couldn't decide if the tears prickling in her eyes were from joy, or from the possibility that this miracle was all just a dream. Because if life had taught her anything these past two years, it was that there was no such thing as miracles.

❧ ❧ ❧

James watched the mirage of emotion move across Madeline's face.

Now that he had a moment to process everything, he could understand why his sudden presence was still a shock for her. She had been told he was dead and he couldn't imagine what that news had done to her.

He also wasn't oblivious. As much as he wanted her and as much as she wanted him, there was a tension in her that wouldn't be relieved after a few minutes of reuniting. Things wouldn't just immediately return to the way it had been between them. It would take time, and if that meant starting from the beginning, and giving her the space she needed to adjust to the idea of a life together again, he would give that to her.

Slowly, James pulled her into his arms and held her. "We don't have to rush things, love. I know this is all still very new. I've waited this long to have you, I can wait a bit longer."

She wrapped her arms around him and he was delighted by that simple return of affection. They stayed like that for a moment longer before he pressed his lips against her hair then pulled away.

"Where are you going?"

"Back to the church," he reminded her. He reached for his hat and started toward the door. He paused and threw her back a crooked smile. "But don't worry. This won't be the last you see of me."

When James arrived at the church, he was surprised to find the reverend still in the cellar. The man didn't bother to look up from the crates he was searching through when James walked in.

"I trust your appointment went well, James."

"Please call me Jim, Reverend. And yes, everything went as well as I could expect." It hadn't been the reunion he had dreamed of, but it was the best he could hope for. "About the work you need done around the church, I was wondering—"

"Help me carry these out of here, will you?" Reverend Linc interrupted. "I need a closer look through them."

James swallowed the rest of his words and carried three heavy crates into the back office of the church. It was all done under the careful command and direction of the good reverend. If James weren't mistaken, he would have sworn the man was testing him—both his strength and endurance, along with his patience.

But James was used to taking orders, and in this instance, he took Reverend Linc's incessant commands all in stride.

On his final trip to the church with the last of the crates, James dropped it down with a heavy thud.

"Careful, son. We don't want these floors to give in too."

James stamped his foot on the floor board beneath him, to the reverend's horror and dismay.

"I think you're fine here, Reverend. These boards are nice and sturdy."

"Well, I'd like to keep them that way!"

James grinned. "And I can help you do that. I'm ready to get to work today. After I've gotten to assess everything, I can get a better sense of how much work will be involved. Whatever supplies we might need, I can go in to town and get tomorrow."

"Well, don't let me stand in your way, son."

James shifted where he stood, not sure how to broach the subject of compensation with the man. With his work building the veteran homes, much of his payment had come in the form of donations or exchange of other benefits like room and board. But now that he had a future bride to think of, James would need to start making some income. His small veterans' pension wouldn't be enough.

In the end, he came right out with it. "Did Oliver mention anything about the pay for this job?"

"Pay? There is no pay. Isn't this your contribution to the church? You know, charity work."

James stared at him, stunned disbelief pulling at his brow. Charity work?

What the hell had he gotten himself into?

"I think the terms will need to be renegotiated, Reverend," James said. "I think twenty dollars a week is fair, considering my experience and that I'll be working alone."

Reverend Linc pondered his request for a while before he said, "Five dollars a week plus room and board. That's the best I can offer."

James frowned. For the amount of work and repairs the church needed done, he would be a fool to agree to such a low wage. Maybe that was all the church had to offer, but he couldn't be certain. With his skill set, he could go elsewhere and make considerably more. Then again, he would have to leave Maddie to do so.

James sighed. "Why do I have a feeling I'm being took?"

The reverend laughed and patted his shoulder. "Perhaps you'll think twice before lying in the house of the Lord."

James winced, realizing the old man knew about his ruse. "I didn't mean any disrespect, Reverend. I just wanted to find my lady."

Reverend Linc nodded. "I get it, son. And I can see that you're not a bad man, which is why I'm offering you the work. Now, do we have a deal, Jim?"

James had to give it up to the reverend—he had just hustled his hustler. Perhaps he could have pushed for higher pay, but guilt over his earlier deception made him drop the matter.

Wiping the dirt and grime from his hand onto his pant leg, James extended his hand. "Deal."

Chapter 6

"G-O-W-N. Gown."

Madeline beamed. "Very good, Raymond. Now that wasn't so hard was it?"

The young man, one of her quick learners in the evening class, gave her a wide smile. "No, ma'am."

Madeline took her ruler and moved it down to the next word. "Anita, do you want to give this next word a try?"

The woman hesitated, then nodded. "T-O-W-N."

Madeline nodded encouragingly. "Can you read what it says?"

"T...town?"

"Excellent."

Madeline moved her ruler to the next set of words and on it went— brown, crown, drown, frown. She called on many of her quiet students, wanting to encourage them to be active participants in their education. Her evening class students hadn't advanced as much as her noon class, but she had faith they would soon catch up, which was why she continued to push them harder.

Except tonight, her thoughts weren't focused on her lesson as they should have been. They kept wandering to the man who had just rocked her world not too long ago. She hadn't seen James since he'd left her cabin that afternoon, and Madeline wondered when he would come back.

And if he did, would he want to spend the night with her?

Her cheeks warmed at the thought of the last time they had seen each other completely bare...

"You're the loveliest thing I've ever seen."

Madeline stared up at James' flushed face as he gazed down at her nude body. He cupped her breast and her taut nipple pressed against his warm palm. A carnal hunger unfurled inside her as he gave her plump flesh a gentle squeeze before he brushed his thumb across the firm point. She couldn't stop the quivering moan that escaped her parted lips, no more than she could stop her back from arching and seeking more of his delicate torment.

Linking her arms around his neck, Madeline coaxed him down above her. But instead of the heady kiss she was so desperate for, he dipped his head toward her breast and drew her sensitive bud into his mouth. Another soft cry was wrenched from her throat at the molten need burning between her thighs.

Running her fingers through his hair, Madeline tugged lightly at the wavy strands. "Jimmy, please... Stop your teasing and make love to me. Now."

He chuckled low and pressed a light kiss between her breasts. "Not yet, love. I want to savor every minute of tonight..."

Madeline blinked away the memory then realized she had a dozen or so pairs of eyes staring back at her. Her face flooded with heat.

She couldn't believe she would let herself think of that night when his nude body had pressed so intimately against hers—in the middle of her lesson, no less! Trying to ignore the mortification that now made her hand shake, Madeline rested the ruler down on her desk.

"That will be all for tonight, thank you. You all did wonderful."

As they each filed out of the classroom, Madeline busied herself with stuffing her books and papers back into her bag. She also fought her wayward thoughts from returning to places it shouldn't.

"I'm glad my trip wasn't in vain."

Madeline glanced up with a start to find James standing at the door, a teasing smile on his lips. Seeing him even now was jarring. Despite his eye patch and the scar running along the side of his face, he was every bit the man she remembered.

Yet, she couldn't understand of all the places he could be, how was it that he was with her here in Dunesville? This time Madeline fought the urge to run to him and hold him close again.

He came into the room, carrying with him a large crate. "Is there someplace I can put this? It's heavier than it looks."

Madeline shook her head at herself. Sooner or later, she would need to get over her shock.

"You can leave it here." She gestured to the empty space beside the desk. "What is all that?"

"Old school supplies the reverend found in the church cellar. Said it must have been left behind when they had been setting up the school."

"Oh. I'll let Mrs. Ophelia know. She's the headmistress and should probably be the one to look through them."

"Well, I found something I think you might like." James opened the crate and pulled out a short book. There was a mischievous sparkle in his eye when he handed it to her.

Madeline took the book from his grasp and read the title—*Poems on Miscellaneous Subjects* by Frances Ellen Watkins.

Something in Madeline's heart fluttered. "You remember?"

"How could I forget? I think on our first meeting, you practically recited every line of her speech to me on the rights of women."

Madeline couldn't stop the smile that tugged at her own lips. "I didn't know then that you were intentionally provoking me with your infuriating thoughts on women and their appropriate *place* in the household, as you had put it."

He chuckled. "It worked. I got you to talk to me, even if it was in a tone that would have frosted the sun."

Madeline smiled at the memory. She had just turned seventeen that spring, but one would have thought she was approaching thirty with the way she spoke to him with such authority, embodying the words of Mrs. Frances Ellen Watkins Harper as she did so.

Madeline was a huge admirer of the activist and suffragette, and she was excited to have a collection of her poems in her possession. Not only was Mrs. Harper a brilliant writer who spoke out against the sins of slavery and rights of women, she was also the first Negro woman to have her short story published. It had been years since Madeline had read Mrs. Harper's works, but she was already eager to begin incorporating them into her lessons.

"Thank you for this," Madeline murmured. "I think my students will enjoy learning about her and her work."

James inclined his head. "It's probably I who should be thankful. If it weren't for her, you probably wouldn't have anything to lecture me with that night, and thus we might have never met."

"Oh, I'm sure I would have found a way to educate you, Mr. Blakemore," she teased.

But in many ways, he was right. If it hadn't been for that speech Mrs. Harper had given at the Philadelphia abolitionist club, Madeline wouldn't have encountered an overbearing Canadian by the name of James Blakemore the third, who she would later come to fall madly in love with.

James closed the crate and straightened, slowly glancing around the schoolroom. "So this is where it all happens? The education of a freed people?"

Madeline studied him, wondering just how much the war had changed him and his beliefs. The James she knew before—the one that had placed his own freedom and life at risk with his involvement in Philadelphia's vigilance committee, who had helped set up safe homes and hideaways for the underground—had always had a deep commitment to freedom and liberty for all men, well before the war.

But Madeline knew firsthand just how many soldiers had come back embittered—even those who had fought on the right side of the war. Looking at James now, at the evidence of what he had endured, she wondered if it had left him resentful. Like it had so many others.

"Yes, this is the room where change is happening. Thanks to you and those who fought for this moment."

James ran his hand over the wood desk, his gaze remaining fixated on a spot there. "Then I am glad it truly wasn't all in vain."

She took his hand in hers and gave it a squeeze. "No, it wasn't."

Before war had been declared, there had been many who had fought and killed and died for the same cause. It had taken more loss and heartache before an end would come to a vicious enterprise that forced people into bondage and purposefully kept them illiterate.

No, a fight for freedom could never be fought in vain.

Suddenly James laced his fingers through hers, and the action helped pull her out of her thoughts of war and slavery.

"So, Miss Madeline, I would love for you to continue my instruction over an evening meal."

Madeline smiled, remembering how he'd said those very words to her after she had given him a proper scolding for his backward views on women's ability to be productive citizens of the country.

That had been the start of his courtship.

He had been as brave then as he was now because she had made no secret of her initial dislike of him. He had been too arrogant and cocksure for her liking. But, in the end, it had only taken one night in his company to learn that he was also honorable, generous, and very well-grounded.

"I would love to spend the evening with you, Jimmy. But tonight, my friends and I are having supper with Mrs. Ophelia and her family."

His face fell but he offered her a smile. "How about I walk you there then?"

Madeline grabbed her bag and looped her arm around his.

"What are your plans tomorrow morning?" he asked as they left the school.

"We don't have classes tomorrow, so I'll take that time to work on new lessons for next week. Why?"

"I have to ride into town for supplies tomorrow morning. Perhaps you can ride with me?"

Madeline moved closer to his side. Memories of such casual strolls made her forget that there was still three years and lots of questions unanswered between them.

Tonight, however, she would let herself forget.

"I would love to."

℘ ℘ ℘

The sun had barely crested the horizon when James rode up to her cabin.

The soft rays of light that peeked through the morning clouds fell over his profile where he sat high on his single horse wagon. He was exceptionally handsome this morning, with a warm smile ready on his lips.

"Morning, Ladybug. Are you ready?"

Madeline nodded and he jumped down to help her up into the high seat. She didn't mind the dirt or dust that clung to her dress as she settled on the wagon bench beside him.

Their drive into town gave them a chance to talk a bit about his work trade with Reverend Linc and reminisce of their life and time together in Philadelphia before the war. James also talked about the two years he had spent building homes for veterans who hadn't had a place to go after the war.

It appeared he had spent those two years going city to city, building these homes. As much as Madeline admired him for his level of devotion to his fellow soldier, a small, selfish part of her wondered why he hadn't felt just as devoted to coming back to her and building their home together.

"I threw myself into the work when I thought you had married another," he said, as if reading her bitter thoughts. "I figured there was nothing for me to do, other than to help make as many of my comrades as comfortable as I could before I returned to Canada."

Madeline glanced over at him. "You consider all the Union veterans your friends?"

"I do," he said adamantly. "I have fought alongside the most fearless, the most honorable men I know."

She pressed her lips together, wondering if he would feel the same way if he knew that not all of his fellow soldiers held the level of honor as he or his friends. Madeline was not foolish enough to believe that just because one Union soldier had disgraced her, that they were all a bad bunch. She was, after all, in love with the most honorable of them. Yet, she also wasn't naive enough to think that they were all honorable, good men.

Not anymore, anyway.

Madeline steered the conversation back to his work with the associations and groups that were organized to provide assistance to the former Union soldiers.

"In these veteran homes and hospitals, are Negro men accepted?"

His lips tightened and she knew her answer.

"Only in a few," he admitted. "And in those few, there aren't many colored soldiers. However, the Grand Army of the Republic is one of the bigger organizations formed to assist all Union vets, no matter their color."

That piqued her interest. There were a few men in Dunesville and in her class that had served in the war and she had once overheard their conversation of reduced government pensions, among other things. Some had been denied, while other hadn't even received the payments they had been granted.

"Would this organization assist with inquiring about pensions and medical care?" Madeline asked.

James shrugged. "I believe it depends on the individual's situation. I've seen men who've lost their legs get denied pensions or access to proper care. The organization could petition on their behalf but the usual response from the government is housing them in a hospital that's more akin to an asylum. And believe me, that's the wrong kind of help."

Madeline contemplated what he said, feeling the fine threads of despair weave through her at the grim outlook of getting assistance for the men of Dunesville.

"What of those who need basic medical attention or even just medicine? Who or where do they turn to?"

"There are a few hospitals around the country, just not enough in my opinion." He fell silent for a moment before he spoke again. "Then there's the issue of those who become overly dependent of the pain medication and are left worst off than they were before. Not to mention those who have the kind of illness that no medicine or surgery can fix…"

"What happens to those men?"

"They get put in the homes." This time, he slid her a curious glance. "Why do you ask? You know of someone who needs assistance?"

Madeline sighed. "I know several, actually. Some are in my class."

Suddenly, an idea struck her. "Do you think you can come to my class one evening and discuss some of these services available to them? I can announce it in both my sessions that there will be a special meeting just for veterans."

James slowly nodded. "That's a fine idea. Let me know what day you decide and I'll see if the reverend can make an announcement about it during Sunday service."

"Okay, I'll look at the schedule as soon as we return."

"Though, I'll warn you now, I don't know everything," he added. "And because Nebraska was only just admitted into the Union last year, there may not be enough services readily available for the residents of this state. But whatever I can't answer that night, I'll write down and send out an inquiry to a friend who's an active member of GAR."

Madeline beamed at him, a feeling of immense triumph and love coming over her. "That would be such a great help. Thank you."

Suddenly, the wagon went over a large rock and Madeline was jostled in her seat. She found herself leaning against his side, but didn't move away. Instead, she looped her arm around his and moved in closer, careful not to disturb his hold on the horse's rein.

"We work well together, don't we?"

Just like old times.

James leaned down and gave her a quick kiss on the top of her head. "Yes, we do."

As members of the vigilance committee, they had made a great team. Madeline shut her eyes as memories of working side-by-side began to fill her. They had organized meetings, wrote letters to Washington, and exhausted all avenues to raise funds to help individuals and families adjust to a new life of freedom.

They had been like two halves of a whole and it hadn't come as a big surprise when she had realized on one of their most trying and grueling nights that she was devastatingly in love with him. Though her family had tried to warn her against such a union, she couldn't help who she fell in love with. They had been in Philadelphia, after all, and though they had gotten the occasional looks and whispers, she and James had generally been left alone.

The people of Nebraska, however, were not as tolerant.

When they arrived into town, Madeline realized just how far from Philadelphia they really were. She wasn't sure if it was her oversensitivity, but she couldn't remember ever being gawked at this much.

James, on the other hand, didn't let it bother him. At least he gave the impression that it didn't. He strolled through town with her close at his side, as if it were perfectly normal for them to be walking hand in hand. And when they weren't holding hands, he would occasionally have his hand at the small of her back.

Madeline tried to adopt his nonchalant attitude, but it was hard for her to ignore the outraged glares and disgusted sneers. In one particular instance, she tried to move away from him, but his hand only tightened around hers. She realized then that his display of possessiveness was largely a bold response to the townspeople's obvious disapproval.

Madeline sighed. As much as she loved him and wanted to possess the same devil-may-care attitude, a more rational part of her knew they were only inviting trouble.

"Jimmy…" she began in a low voice so only he could hear. "We're not in Philadelphia anymore."

"I know exactly where we are, love."

And his tone said he dared anyone to challenge them.

CHAPTER 7

"I ask no monument, proud and high, to arrest the gaze of the passersby. All that my yearning spirit craves, is bury me not in a land of slaves."

At the last verse of the poem, Madeline closed the book and looked up at her students.

"I like that, Miss Madeline," one of her female students called out. "A Negro woman wrote that?"

Madeline nodded. "Yes, Mrs. Frances Harper was an abolitionist and writer who regularly spoke and wrote against the horrors and degradation of slavery. When she wrote *Bury Me in a Free Land*, however, it was in the hopes that the images she invoked from her words would portray a country that was not holding up its ideals of freedom and liberty for all. Can anyone remind me where this sentiment of justice and liberty for all was first written?"

"In the United States Constitution," one of her male students called out eagerly.

Madeline smiled. It had only been a week now since she had incorporated government and politics into her lessons, but she was glad to see she had some who were just as interested in the subject as she was.

"You're correct, Luis. When the Constitution was drafted after the country won its independence from the British, it was meant to unite the states and citizens under one law."

Madeline spent the next couple of weeks weaving in United States history and government into her students' reading and writing lessons. She enjoyed the change of pace, and it appeared so did her students. Their abilities to apply some of her readings within the context of what was happening in the country now, or what had occurred in the past, never ceased to amaze her.

Such moments even led to passionate discussions about politics or current social issues. She recalled one such discussion that had started in regards to the advancement the country was making in recognizing colored men and women, but had then led to another debate on whether change was happening fast enough.

"I don't agree with the others, Miss Madeline," one of her female students had voiced adamantly. "If Miss Mary Jane Patterson is one of the first Negro women to graduate from Oberlin College, how can we say the country isn't embracing change?"

"That's just one school in Ohio," another of her female students pointed out. "What about the others who won't allow Negroes near the door?"

"Yes, but doesn't it always start with one?" Her usually quiet student Anita joined in. "Miss Patterson being the first only means there's a chance for one of us to be the next."

Madeline nodded in encouragement then added, "You're right. There have been others before Miss Patterson to graduate and go on to be lawyers and professors. In fact, the first colored woman to be hired as a college professor was Sarah Jane Woodson. Can you imagine the doors that has opened for us?"

The usually cynical Mr. Barnes sucked at his teeth. "I don't get this country. One minute, they passing laws to keep us out of their schools, the next they hiring one of ours to teach at their college. This country needs to make up they damn mind. Either they want us here or they don't."

"It doesn't matter what they want," Mr. Gary, another male student about Mr. Barnes age, called out. "We have every right to be here. They gonna just have to get used to seeing my black behind, 'cause I for one ain't going nowhere."

A chorus of laughs went around the room. But as usual, Mr. Barnes didn't miss this opportunity to get in the last word and further ruffle feathers.

"Well, I guess your black behind will learn soon enough just how much rights you got in this country, 'cause I hear Nebraska's about to bring on poll taxes and reading tests for this coming presidential contest."

Mr. Gary waved him away dismissively. "That's just the kind of stories they bring up from the Deep South to keep us from voting."

And with that, another debate was started with some of the students in the class confirming Mr. Barnes claims of such poll taxes and reading tests, while the other half argued that such unlawful restrictions wouldn't find its way into the Nebraska voting polls.

In those instances, Madeline almost never got a word in, or intervened, and that was fine with her. She gave her students the space to debate each other and express their thoughts and opinions, even if it meant going over their class time. But now that they were at the end of their third week since classes had begun, and her students had demonstrated sharp abilities to examine and evaluate, Madeline believed they were ready for the next phase of their lesson.

Independent reading.

"Miss Madeline, can you read us that short story you told us about?" Anita asked eagerly during one of their class sessions. "The one by Mrs. Frances Harper?"

"You mean 'The Two Offers'?" At Anita's excited nod, Madeline sighed. Harper's story of a woman forced to choose between two marriage proposals had been a favorite of Madeline's, not only because it had made history by being the first short story published by a Negro woman, but because it had given Madeline the courage to walk away from her own arranged marriage two years ago.

As it turned out, that had been the best decision she had made for herself. Now, she was free to marry the man she loved. But when she thought of the last few weeks, and the time she and James had gotten to spend together, it was with both exhilaration and agitation. Though she relished the mornings and occasional evenings they spent together, she had to admit there was a restlessness in her she couldn't quite pinpoint. She appreciated his consideration in taking things slow between them, yet part of her yearned for more.

She just didn't know what exactly it was she longed for.

"I'm sorry Anita, but I don't have a copy of that story with me," Madeline said, returning her attention to her class. "But I do have a stack of books that were found in the church with tons of stories you will enjoy."

"What are you going to read to us today, Miss Madeline?"

"Actually, today, you all will select a book to read on your own."

A few murmurs of dismay stirred through the class and Madeline laughed.

"Don't give me those terrified looks. You all are learning at a fast pace and I want to keep challenging you. Besides, the most effective way of learning to write well is by reading often."

"But what if we don't know the words?" one of her shy students, Harriet, surprised Madeline by asking.

"I'll still be here to help you along. All I ask is that you try your best.

Now, I would like each of you to come up one at a time and select a book from the pile."

Madeline waited as each student came up to choose a book on her desk. The last of her students made it back to his seat when Ophelia stepped into her room and waved her over.

"You may start your reading," she said to her class as she started toward the headmistress. There was a graveness in her face that left Madeline tense, but she plastered a smile on her face for her students' benefits.

When Madeline reached Ophelia, the woman motioned her outside.

"I hate to pull you away from your class, Madeline, but there's been an incident."

Dread tightened in her stomach. "What's happened?"

"Sherry and Eldridge...they were attacked and robbed this morning on their way to town."

Madeline's hand flew up over her mouth. "Oh my God. Are they all right?"

"Eldridge wasn't hurt too badly and was able to tell us what happened. But Sherry..." Ophelia's lips tightened in a flat, grim line and Madeline's heart lodged in her throat. "She was badly beaten, she had to be taken to the hospital in town."

Madeline sent up a quick prayer of thanks that her friend was still alive, though her heart ached for Sherry and the pain she must be enduring. Memories of her own attack that long ago night came rushing back to Madeline and she remembered the pain she had been in when she had woken up in a hospital.

"Has the attacker been caught?"

An anger Madeline had never seen before suddenly flashed in the older woman's eyes. "No. We can only pray Sherry makes a fast recovery and justice will be found soon."

"Yes, I'll keep her and Eldridge in my prayers," Madeline murmured, a slow anger sprouting over her feeble wall of composure at the possibility of justice evading her friend's attacker, as it had evaded hers.

"I also wanted to ask one more thing from you, Madeline..."

"Of course. Anything you need, just let me know. I want to help."

A flash of relief filled Ophelia's dark eyes. "Good. I believe between you and Teresa, we can still keep Sherry's classes going."

Madeline tensed. "You mean you want me to teach the children?"

"Yes, although you and Teresa can alternate, of course, so there's no undue pressure."

Madeline shook her head. She wanted to do what she could to help but this… This was asking too much.

"Mrs. Ophelia, I'm sorry, but I don't think I can. I've never taught children before and I… I don't think I would be the right—"

"You don't have anything to worry about, Madeline. You're a bright and capable teacher. If you can handle these adults, you can handle their babies." Ophelia patted her arm reassuringly. "Trust me. They are a lot less scary than you think."

℘ ℘ ℘

Madeline stared down at the children, some were as young as four and as old as six. Their round, innocent faces looked back up at her with eyes like big, chocolate pools of curiosity and wonder.

Between Teresa and Ophelia, Madeline had a drafted lesson planned for the young ones. She had all the supplies and tools she needed, yet she couldn't seem to make herself speak.

Pull yourself together, Madeline Asher.

"Hello, children. My name's Miss Maddie and I'll be your teacher today."

One of the children raised his hand and Madeline pointed to him. "Yes?"

He lowered his hand. "Where's Miss Sherry?"

Madeline ran her palms down her skirt and gave the children a wide smile that strained her lips. "Miss Sherry is taking a break from teaching right now, but she will be back soon. And I know when she gets back, she'll be happy to see you all."

The little boy raised his hand again.

Madeline's forced smile remained. "Yes."

"I heard my daddy say the white man got her. That she's not coming back to Dunesville, like the others."

Madeline opened her mouth and shut it again, not sure exactly what to say, she didn't want to give them false promises and tell them that Sherry would be okay and back to work. She didn't know that—no one did. Everyone in the small community was on edge over what had happened to Sherry and Eldridge, but how could Madeline expose such young children to that ugliness? She didn't think she could take away their bright-eyed innocence by telling them the truth of what kind of world they lived in.

And what kind of world they would grow into.

Before Madeline could find her words, the little boy raised his hand yet again. Madeline's smile slipped and she stifled a groan.

"Yes?"

"Where did the white man take Miss Sherry? I can go find her. My mama said I'm brave just like my daddy. When I get bigger I'm going to be a soldier like him too."

At the young boy's words, warm tenderness spread through Madeline. That had to be the most endearing thing she had ever heard.

"What's your name, sweetie?"

"Ben."

"And how old are you, Ben?"

He held out his hand with all five fingers displayed.

"Can anyone tell me how many fingers Ben's holding up?"

A chorus of fours and fives rang out. A lone one followed. Madeline stifled a laugh.

"It looks like we have a lot of work to do with our numbers. Why don't we all keep Miss Sherry in our prayers tonight, and start practicing our numbers?"

In no time, Madeline found her groove with the children, going through the lesson plan with little disruption. Teaching children was so much different than teaching her adult class. She found their young minds fascinating, like wide, blank canvases demanding to be filled. They asked questions after questions and she was astounded by the energy their little bodies held. Watching them filled her with such wonder—and an incredible longing.

Pushing her wayward emotions aside, Madeline concentrated on her new lot of eager students. Eventually, the end of a long day came and Madeline waited as parents and relatives came to fetch their young ones. The only student left behind was one of the shy girls. She remembered the little girl's name was Rosie, but couldn't remember the girl speaking more than three words all day.

The girl sat on the front steps, her school bag looped around her small shoulders. Her hair was pulled back in a lopsided ponytail with a bright green ribbon tied at the end.

"Rosie, is your mama coming to get you?"

The little girl shook her head. "I don't have a mama. Papa's supposed to come but he's always late."

Madeline settled down on the steps beside her. "Then I'll wait here with you."

Silence settled between them as the girl appeared to count the cracks on the steps beneath them. Rosie seemed content with that distraction, yet Madeline felt she should say something. She had thought she had managed to get beyond her awkwardness where the young children were concerned, but she realized she was better at dealing with them in groups.

She had no idea what to say to a young girl who reminded her so much of herself at that age.

Madeline remembered a time in her life when she had wanted to work with young colored girls. Whether it was mentoring or teaching, she had wanted to be the kind of inspiration Frances Harper and many other colored women had been in her life. She, too, hadn't grown up with a mother—only with an older sister who had been content in living a simple, uneventful life with her husband. Madeline, however, had met and gotten to volunteer with some inspirational women in her earlier life that had molded her into the woman she had grown to be.

Yet, in this moment, she couldn't find anything to say to a young girl like Rosie. Madeline knew better than anyone how important it was for young girls to have people to look up to. Maybe in some distant past, she could have been that woman, but not anymore. Not after what she had done.

Still, Madeline couldn't help but wonder what kind of woman would little Rosie grow to be? What kind of life would she lead?

"Rosie?"

They both glanced up to find a tall, lean man rushing toward them.

"*Papa.*"

Rosie got up and started down the steps before she suddenly stopped and climbed back up them to where Madeline still sat. The young girl threw her little arms around her, and for a moment, Madeline sat there, frozen. She was surprised and confused by the unexpected embrace, but she managed to snap out of it and returned the girl's hug.

Rosie eventually pulled away and flew down the steps to her father. She gave him a big hug as he lifted her into his arms.

"Sorry to keep you waiting, missus," he said, a bit chagrin. "It was my job and—"

"Please don't worry yourself," Madeline interrupted. "Rosie's a sweet girl. It was no trouble at all."

The man nodded then started down the path, away from the school. Rosie turned back to her, waving widely.

"Bye, Miss Maddie!"

Madeline lifted her hand and waved back, a sudden lump forming in her throat. She didn't know if the sudden wave of emotion crashing through her was from the tenderhearted embrace she had done nothing to deserve or from the many hugs she would miss out on.

As Madeline walked back to her cabin, she thought about how different her life would be right now, if she had been strong enough to face her fears.

She stepped into her small cabin and shut the door behind her. It was only then that she allowed herself to give into her tears, crying for the child she would never get to meet—and for the absolution one little girl's hug had offered her.

CHAPTER 8

Thank God for the little children, when our skies are cold and gray. They come as sunshine to our hearts, and charm our cares away.

A hard knock came at her cabin door and Madeline glanced up from the poem she had been reading. She didn't know what she hoped to find in Frances Harper's poem of mothers appreciating and protecting their babes. It did nothing to ease her forlorn mood.

The knock came again and she rested the book down on the bed beside her. Wrapping her shawl around her shoulders, Madeline padded to the door. She knew who stood on the other end. Though she wasn't feeling up for company, she knew James wouldn't leave if she tried to avoid him.

Madeline pulled open the door and the warm smile that was on his lips fell away.

"Maddie, are you ill?"

She shook her head. Though her students in her evening class had asked her the same thing. She had barely been able to concentrate on their lesson, and after a painfully long session, she had dismissed them early, feigning a headache. She believed some rest and time alone would ease the real ache in her heart.

"I'm just tired. I know we were supposed to have supper together this evening, but can we do so another night?"

"Yes, of course," he murmured, regarding her closely. "Have you been crying?"

She glanced away, not wanting to lie to him, but not ready to answer the questions that would surely come if she admitted the truth.

"Maddie?"

"Jimmy, it's late and I would really like to get back to bed."

"Can I least come in for a bit?"

She stepped back and let him in, not wanting to be rude to him, no matter how she felt. Yet, she found herself in a strange mood. Though he had done nothing to invoke these feelings, just the sight of him agitated her.

He came in and looked around. She realized this was the first time he had been back inside her sleeping quarters since that first day he had reappeared in her life. For some reason, the small cabin felt stifling with him there.

"I'm going into town tomorrow," James began. "To talk to the sheriff."

Her brows rose in curiosity. "Why?"

"The reverend thought it would help. I heard about what happened to your friend and it seems there's been quite a few crimes around here that the sheriff has failed to look into. Something has to be done."

Madeline tightened the shawl around her. Mustering up hope that the bigoted sheriff would suddenly care about the citizens of Dunesville, or actually bring the attackers terrorizing them to justice, was not something she was interested in indulging tonight.

Tonight, she was all out of faith and hope to give.

"You believe you can convince him to investigate this latest attack?"

James shrugged. "It can't hurt to ask him about what's being done to find the men behind this. It'll just get worst if these attacks continue to go unchecked. And all I can think about is what if that had been you."

"What if it had been? You wouldn't be able to protect me. Just like you weren't there when—"

Madeline snapped her mouth shut not sure where any of that had come from. She couldn't blame him for what had happened to her. It was no one's fault except the monster who had chosen to violate her and the man who had literally turned his back on her while his friend tied her down. And it was her fault for being so gullible and foolish enough to wait for a man to save her.

Yet, in her raw emotional state, Madeline realized there was a secret part of her that *did* blame James. He should have been there for her; he should have come back to her. Madeline turned away from him.

Where were you when I needed you the most?

He came up behind her. "I would never let anything happen to you, Maddie," he said, his voice rough. "As long as I have breath, I will always protect you."

She shook her head slowly. "You don't have to protect me, Jimmy. I can protect myself. I have been for some time now."

He was silent for a moment before he said tightly, "You say that as if you don't need me."

She turned to face him then. "I don't."

His brows pulled together as surprise and hurt flashed in his eye. In that moment, she wished she could take back what she said. But then maybe this was the moment she needed to finally send him away. He deserved happiness and the kind of future they had both dreamed of...a dream she had given up on a long time ago.

"Maddie, where is all this coming from? We love each other and—"

"I had an abortion."

A painful silence fell between them as he stared at her with what looked like numb shock. She had not planned to be so graceless with her words, but with a secret sin so great, she didn't know how else to say it.

"Was it...was it mine?"

She winced at the low harshness in his voice. She didn't fault him for thinking that. They had made love that very night before he went off to enlist.

"No, it wasn't yours."

His body was still rigid before her. "Whose, then?"

"I don't know."

A look of surprise and disbelief moved across his face. Without warning, he grabbed her arm and jerked her towards him.

"I don't believe you! I know you, Maddie. You wouldn't let any man into your bed unless you wanted him there."

She wrenched her arm from his grip and stepped away. "You're right. I wouldn't, but in this world, it doesn't matter what a woman wants because there will always be some brute who believes just because he can, he can tie a woman down and force himself on her. Again and again."

James' face was pale and stark with emotion.

"That's whose baby I carried inside me for three months, until I could no longer stomach the thought of carrying it a minute longer. I didn't care about anything, not my soul or my faith. I just wouldn't—I *couldn't*—bear the child of a monster!"

A heavy stillness settled in the room. Madeline kept her arms wrapped tightly around herself as her heart raced in her chest. For a moment, she couldn't look at him, regretting her thoughtless outburst. She had said too much. But then again, now he knew her darkest secrets and maybe it was for the best.

"Maddie..."

He reached for her. She jerked back.

"No, I don't want your pity or your sympathy. What's done is done and nothing can change that. And I'm not angry for what I did. I'm angry that I was forced to make such a choice, that my first child wasn't created by my consent or with the man that I loved. I'm angry that I will have to live with what I did for the rest of my life, that no matter what I do, I can never seem to stop thinking about the baby I will never get to meet, and that to me just seems so…*unfair*."

To Madeline's dismay, a sob escaped her and she folded into herself. James reached for her again and she tried to ward him off. But in the end, she couldn't fight him when he pulled her into his arms.

James sat down on the bed, holding her close as she broke down, releasing all of the pain and regret and anger that she hadn't realized were still a part of her. She wept for the time between them that they could never have back, for the dignity that had been stolen from her, and for the child that was forever lost to her.

♡ ♡ ♡

James didn't know how much time had passed, but he continued to hold Madeline close to his side as she slept. Her sobs had been gut-wrenching but he had simply held her as she released the flood of emotions until she had fallen into an exhaustive sleep.

But as night moved into early morning, his tightly-wound emotions hadn't been able to let his mind find any level of rest. The guilt and rage coursing through him was just too great.

He had witnessed the greatest horrors during battle, had experienced even worse during his captivity, but nothing was as crushing as hearing how he had failed her. For everything he had gone after, for everything he had fought hard for, he hadn't fought hard enough for her. As soon as he had been able, he should have gone to her—even if it meant going to the ends of the earth.

Five years of pain and darkness now stretched between them, yet it was the things that had been left unsaid that threatened their future. She had exposed her pain. It was his turn to tell her why he hadn't been ready to return to her after the war.

When you're going through hell, the best thing to do is to keep going.

James remembered the words of the highly religious physician that had done more toward his healing after his release from the prison than any medicine had. By facing the horrors inflicted on him and talking through the trauma, he had been able to make it through the worst of it. He would never forget the moment he had returned to the prison camp to help identify the thousands of bodies left behind. It had been mentally excruciating, but he had reentered his hell and kept going.

Facing his demons so that he could help put those who hadn't been so lucky as to make it out alive had been like a therapy for him. And in many ways, it had helped him find his purpose and sense of self again.

Beside him, Madeline began to stir. When she came fully awake, she tensed against him. James didn't speak, only continued to rub her lower back.

"Jimmy…"

"Yes, love?"

"I'm sorry."

He frowned. "You have nothing to apologize for, Maddie."

"Yes, I do." She propped herself up and stared down at him. The skin beneath her eyes was swollen and a few loose strands had escaped her braid. "I shouldn't have unloaded all that on you. I certainly shouldn't have blamed you for any of it. I was speaking out of anger. I want you to know that I don't blame you for what happened to me."

He sat up in the bed and cupped her chin. "I know that, love. I also know how devastating war can be and how, for some of us, war is never over. I just didn't know the kind of battle you were fighting inside. And I should have."

She shook her head. "You couldn't have known."

Yes, he could. He should have known from the weapons she carried, from the way she kept herself guarded at times, and the way she stiffened ever so slightly at his touch. He had thought it was because she needed time to adjust to him again, and maybe part of that was still true. But she had the signs of someone who had suffered extreme trauma and he should have known. He had witnessed and suffered through some of the same effects.

"I spent three months in a prison camp before the war had finally ended, Maddie," he confessed quietly. "That was the darkest hell I had ever experienced during my time in the war. I watched men starve to death, watched men kill for scraps, and I've had to watch men I had fought side by side with literally lose their mind."

Watching his friend Will descend to madness had been the most difficult. They had become fast friends and had watched over each other during the bloodiest of battles. Yet it had taken just one fight too many during a small riot in the prison camp for James to lose the man he had once trusted his life to.

"Where were you taken?"

"Camp Sumter in Georgia."

She sucked in her breath. "I read stories about that place. I heard many of the men taken there hadn't made it out alive."

"Some did, like myself. But many of us didn't make it out whole."

Her brows pulled together and she reached out and touched the right side of his face. James held his breath but didn't pull away from her.

"Did this happen to you while you were there?"

He nodded. "A small riot had broken out. Over food or shelter, I can't remember. But in the chaos, some of us tried to escape. But we were too weak to get far." He stared off, thinking of that moment when he had dug into his depths, trying to find the energy to keep going. But he couldn't leave Will and when his friend had fallen behind, he had gone back for him. By then, it had been too late. A guard had caught up to them and James had taken a bullet to his face.

Madeline ran her fingers along his eyepatch. "Who did this to you?"

He took her hand in his and held it tight. "A guard fired at us and a bullet went through my eye. I shouldn't be alive but I had God and luck on my side. The next day, the war was declared over and I had a doctor who not only saved my life, but also my sanity by reminding me what I had to live for. It took a full year for me to recover from my injuries. All of them. And I knew I couldn't return to you until I had properly healed."

But, by then, it had been too late. She had been lost to him.

A tear slid down her cheek and James brushed it away.

"Don't cry, love. I didn't tell you this to add to your misery. I just want you to know that we have both done things to survive. In that prison, I was trapped in yet another battlefield, except the men I was fighting were my own. I had to kill or be killed, just to survive. I'm not proud of what I've done, but if it meant saving my life, I would do it again."

Without a word, she threw her arms around him. "How are you here with me?" she murmured, her arms tightening around him. "How are you alive?"

He instantly wrapped his arms around her and held her close. "I'm here because of you. Because I chose to keep facing the sun so I wouldn't lose myself in the shadows."

She drew back from him, her expression solemn yet accepting. "Well, now you know you're not the only one running from shadows."

"As long as we stand together in the light, Maddie, we can truly stop running."

He pulled her down for a kiss that was meant to be short, a resealing of their bond, but it quickly became passionate and in that moment, he wanted more.

He wanted her.

James braced himself on his arms and stared down at her, his heart racing with desire and an even greater emotion. "I love you, Maddie, and I want you badly. All of you." His tone was rough with need. "But I need to know what it is you want."

Her fingers dug into his shoulders. "I want *you*, Jimmy. I do. I just don't know if I could be the kind of wife you need."

He regarded her closely, wondering what was going on behind those luminous dark-brown eyes of hers. "What is it you think I need?"

"You deserve someone you can take to Canada, to meet your family, and start a quiet, comfortable home with. Someone you can start a family with and forget all this...ugliness."

"My life with you was never about moving to Canada and living a fairytale, Maddie. It was about being able to love you the way I want and being able to protect you for the rest of my days." He leaned down and brushed his lips against hers. "I've told you how I felt, but I can't keep trying to convince you, and I certainly don't want us to keep on like this."

Her gaze fell to his chest. "I know. It's not fair to you."

"Then I guess there's only one thing left for me to do..."

CHAPTER 9

"By the powers vested in me by the State of Nebraska and Almighty God, I now pronounce you man and wife."

Man and wife.

Madeline stared at the reverend, stunned that she and James were actually married.

"May your days be good and long upon this earth," Reverend Linc continued. "May your nights be filled with peace and love. May you both—"

"Hurry it along, Reverend," James muttered.

To Madeline's surprise, a giggle burst from her lips. She slapped a hand over her mouth. She couldn't remember the last time she'd giggled but the sound brought out a low chuckle from James.

That won them a sharp glare from the reverend, but he proceeded to close his bible and gave them a curt nod. "You may now kiss your bride."

James turned to her, mirth and warmth dancing in his eye. He swept her into his arms and kissed her deeply. Madeline let herself get lost in his embrace, her arms wrapping tightly around him. Fate had seen to it that he was back in her life, that he still wanted her despite everything they endured, and she didn't plan to ever let him go.

Reverend Linc cleared his throat and Madeline pulled away, heat rising up her cheeks. James's face was also flushed but from his hooded gaze, she knew it wasn't from embarrassment.

"I've waited a long time to do that," James said huskily.

"What do you mean?" Madeline stole a quick glance at the reverend. "We've…kissed before."

His lips curved in a crooked smile. "Not as Mr. and Mrs. James Blakemore, we haven't." He kissed her again, this time light yet lingering.

"Not so fast," Reverend Linc said. "I have to get your signatures on the marriage certificate, then you two can run off to consummate your union."

Their signatures on the certificate made it all too real and for the first time in five years, Madeline's heart filled with giddy happiness. James took her hand and they walked out of the church. It was early in the morning, and for a moment, she wondered if he would indeed take her to her cabin and—

"I have to head into town, love. But when I return..." He brought her hand to his lips. "You'll become my wife in every sense of the word."

Heat and desire flooded her. Her thighs clenched with anticipation just as a wave of disappointment washed over her, but she quelled it. She knew his trip into town was so he could speak to the sheriff about the attack on Sherry and Eldridge and that took precedence right now.

Besides, they had waited this long, she could wait a few hours more.

"Let me come with you," Madeline said. "I'd like to visit Sherry at the hospital, if I can."

☙ ☙ ☙

"What do you mean, you have no suspects?" James glared at the unconcerned sheriff. "Two people were badly beaten. Their possessions along with their damn wagon were stolen. Someone must have seen *something*."

Sheriff Ronald Johnson leaned back in his seat with an indifference in his cold eyes that made James' teeth gnash.

"Look, like I said, we are looking into it. There were no witnesses so our hands are pretty much tied."

James knew he shouldn't be surprised. Most of his time in America had been fighting against and, at times, alongside racist men like Sheriff Johnson. And from what Reverend Linc had told him about the lack of protection for the citizens of Dunesville, it was clear speaking up for them now would just be a waste of his time.

Yet, the alternative would be to ignore it and let the violence and terrorism continue. That, James couldn't do. He had seen the savagery done to Madeline's friend when he had dropped her off at the hospital and that kind of brutal, senseless attack filled James with both quivering rage and panic.

What if that had been Maddie laying in that hospital bed?

James wouldn't let himself think of that. Madeline was safe and he would see to it that she remained so. He had barely wanted to leave her at the hospital alone, though he knew she had wanted him to give her some privacy with her friend.

"One of the victims is still in the hospital. Why don't you go try speaking with her?"

The man shrugged his wide shoulders and James fought to keep hold of his withering patience.

"I don't see no point in it."

"Dunesville falls under your jurisdiction, sheriff," James snapped. "I suggest you get off your ass and do your job."

Sheriff Johnson shot up to his feet and came up to his face. "Or what? It's bad enough I lost my home in Virginia on account of your damn war, I don't need some damn one-eyed Yank telling me how to do my job. You don't like it, you can leave my town. Along with the rest of those niggers."

James saw red as he clenched and unclenched his fist. As badly as he wanted to slug the son-of-a-bitch, he knew it wouldn't be worth getting carted off to jail for.

"In case you forgot, sheriff, you have an obligation to serve the citizens of this town. Like it or not, that includes the Negroes. If that's going to be a problem for you, perhaps then *you* should leave."

The sheriff dropped his bulk into his seat, a smug grin on his face. "Who's going to make me?"

James furrowed his brows and stared down at the man with disgust. He could see he wasn't getting anywhere with the man and it burned at his gut. No matter how many battles were fought, or how many laws passed, there would always be men like Sheriff Johnson who would use power and the illusion of supremacy to validate their existence.

"Those cowards need to be brought to justice. If you can't handle the job, sheriff, I can see to it that someone more qualified be put in your place."

Sheriff Johnson snorted. "Don't waste my time with threats, Yank."

"You misunderstand me, sheriff," James said icily. "That wasn't a threat. That was my promise to you. Now, I suggest you do your damn job and find those bastards who are behind these attacks."

ↄ ↄ ↄ

"I take it your meeting with the sheriff didn't go well?"

James grunted and Madeline took that as a yes.

"I have one more stop I want to make before we head back. Do you mind?"

"Of course not. Where are we going?"

"To see a good friend of mine."

They travelled a short distance before they pulled up to a large, white house with black trimming. The country's flag hung proudly out front. It draped down from the trim and hung above the front door. There was much activity going on outside, but from the men who lounged on the porch, Madeline knew where they were.

"Is this one of the veteran homes you built?"

James nodded, and jumped down from the wagon. He wrapped his hands around her waist and helped her down just as a young man came rushing toward them.

"Colonel, what are you doing back?"

"I never left, Phillip," James said. "I also learned that Anderson's family had not yet come to retrieve him, so I figured I'd drop in and check up on him."

"Major Anderson is doing better today. He's taking his medicine and it keeps him out of trouble."

James pursed his lips, but he nodded. "That's good to hear."

Madeline wondered what ailed his friend and what trouble could he possibly get himself into if he were ill.

"He's in his room, if you want to see for yourself." Phillip grabbed the reins and led their horse and wagon away.

James took her hand and they made their way inside the home. They entered the home and a few people called out greetings to him. It wasn't long before they made their way into a small but sparse room. A tall man sat at the window, and he turned to them as they entered. A brief silence filled the room before a wide grin broke across the man's face.

"Jim, I knew you would come back for me." The man came up to him and the two men embraced.

"I am only here for a short visit, brother," James said. "Just want to make sure they're taking good care of you."

"Are you kidding? This is paradise compared to the hell we went through at Camp Sumter." Suddenly, the man turned to her and his eyes widened in surprise. He swung his gaze back to James. "Is this…?"

"Yup," James said, looping his arm around her and pulling her close. "This is her. My Ladybug. Maddie, this is—"

"Major William Anderson, ma'am. And it's very nice to make your acquaintance. You're as pretty as your picture, if you don't mind me saying."

Madeline blushed and held out her hand. "It's nice to meet you too, Mr. Anderson."

"Please call me Will." He reached out to take her hand then froze.

Will stared intently at her outstretched hand. Madeline realized her dress sleeve had fallen away slightly, exposing a part of her wrist holster. His eyes remained fixated on that area and she began to let her arm drop.

In a blur, Will grabbed her hand and twisted it high. Madeline cried out as his grip tightened painfully around her wrist.

"Will, let her go!" James' harsh command did nothing to penetrate the wild look in his friend's eyes. Instead, he jerked her sleeves back, exposing her wrist holster fully.

"What the hell is this?" he demanded.

"It's nothing," Madeline gasped out. "It's just for my protection." She glanced nervously at James but he kept his sharp gaze directed at his friend, his hand inching towards the gun at his side.

"Will, I am not going to tell you again. Let her go."

His friend ignored him and jerked the small handle from its holster. He pulled out the thin, sharp blade and the sound of James' sharp inhale made Madeline's heart lurch with panic.

"I knew it!" Will snapped. "You came here to kill us. You're nothing but a whore spy!"

Will hauled her forward and her heart sank as he pointed the knife down towards her heart. Before she could react, the crack of the gun blast echoed in the small room. Will's lean body jolted back but he remained standing. His eyes were wide as his stared down at his chest.

Madeline jerked out of his grasp and stared in horror as blood began to spread through his white shirt at the center of his chest, turning the garment crimson.

Shouts and chaos faded into the distance as a blur of activity surrounded Madeline. She remained frozen where she stood, watching until the light dimmed from the man's eyes before he fell to his knees and collapsed on his side.

CHAPTER 10

"Looks like I get the displeasure of dealing with you twice in one day, Yank."

James gritted his teeth at Sheriff Johnson's condescending tone. He had barely recovered from what had just happened. He should have never brought Madeline there. He knew how unstable Will had been, how unpredictable, and yet, James had literally put her in harm's way.

If he were honest with himself, he would admit that he should have taken Will to a hospital for the mentally ill. Will had been a danger to everyone around him, including himself. Yet, instead of acknowledging that, James chose to treat his friend's illness lightly.

And now his friend, his brother-in-arms, was dead.

James briefly shut his eye, said a prayer for Will's soul, then opened his eye only to find a pair of shrewd eyes staring back at him. He needed to deal with the sheriff then he could go and lay his friend to rest.

"It was self-defense."

The sheriff leaned back in his seat and regarded him closely. "So you've said."

"Then why am I still here? Where's Maddie?"

"One of my deputies is talking to the colored woman. We want to be certain we get the full story. Now tell me again, what you two were doing there."

James buried his annoyance and explained in short, concise sentences the entire sequence of events. His stomach tightened as he remembered the sharp blade in Will's hand and how it had been pointed at Madeline. He couldn't remember experiencing such fear. Not in any battle or anytime during the three months he had spent in the Confederate prison.

He also couldn't remember drawing his gun just as fast.

After his recount, the sheriff finally nodded. "That's the same story the colored woman is telling. Since there were no other witnesses, then we will classify this as self-defense."

"Are we free to go then?"

"You are, but the colored woman is being charged with inciting a murder."

It took a moment for the sheriff's words to process. When they did, it was as if the air had been knocked out of him.

"*What?*"

"According to you two, it was her weapon that triggered that poor man's psychotic break, forcing you to come to her defense."

"That's ridiculous." James shot up to his feet and planted his hands on the sheriff's desk. "That's not just any woman. That's my *wife*. Of course, I would come to her defense. Now, I demand you release her at once!"

Sheriff Johnson eyes narrowed. "Your wife?"

"Yes, damn you. And if you keep her a minute longer, I'll see to it that you are stripped of your badge."

The sheriff rose to his feet and he shook his head, a slow grin stretching across his lips. "The only thing I am going to regret is not savoring this moment. Turn around. You're under arrest."

James stared at him, incredulous. "The hell I am."

"Don't make this difficult for yourself, Yank."

"But I broke no laws," James snapped. Taking his friend's life still gutted him but if he had to do it all again, he wouldn't hesitate to protect Maddie.

Hell, if he could do it all again, he would have taken his friend to the veteran's hospital from the start. That was a regret he would have to live with forever.

"I told you. I shot my friend, William Anderson, in self-defense."

The sheriff shook his head again. "I'm not talking about that. You are under arrest for the abomination you just committed. Mixing the races is against the law in this great state of Nebraska and I have a responsibility to bring all criminals to justice, as you so finely put it." He nodded toward his deputy. "Go on. Cuff 'em."

James tensed as the deputy came up behind him. "This is absurd, sheriff, and you know it."

Sherriff Johnson turned back to him and grinned. "How's that for doing my damn job?"

☙ ☙ ☙

The tornado Madeline had feared when she had arrived at Dunesville had finally come and she was wholly unprepared.

Except this storm didn't include wind or lightning, but it shook her world just the same.

She sat on the hard bench of the small jail cell, the stale odor of urine reminding her of the chaos that still surrounded her. She had been charged with two crimes but couldn't decide which of the two were the most ludicrous—the fact that she was being held responsible for her husband's actions or because it was against the state's law to be married to him.

She couldn't fault James for doing what he did. It had quite possibly saved her life. But if she could redo that moment in the veteran home, she would. Watching Will's death had been heartbreaking. Watching the aftermath, the expression on James's face after, had been devastating.

Madeline didn't want to be the cause of anyone's death, though she understood James had done it to protect her. But now he would have to live with that decision and she hadn't even had a chance to speak to him before they'd brought her down to the cells.

Now, she was trapped in the eye of the tornado with no way out.

Madeline clasped her hands together, her fingers grazing the empty wrist holster that was still tied around her wrist. She stared down at the brown leather material that had spurred these horrific turn of events.

Madeline quickly unbuckled the holster and ripped it away from her wrist. She threw it across the dirty cell just as something scurried across her feet. She jerked her legs back and caught only a glimpse of the rat's tail before it disappeared into a crack in the wall.

Dear God, why is this happening?

Her eyes burned as frustration and anger began to settle in her. To be sitting here because her husband had saved her life felt incredibly wrong. To be here because she was married to him was the real injustice.

The jangle of keys slid into the door. She jumped to her feet and rushed towards the bars, hoping the Sherriff had recognized the error of his decision and had come to free her. Her heart sank when she realized a hand-cuffed James was being led inside.

"Jimmy!"

"*Maddie.*"

He pulled away from the guard, but was jerked back and given a swift punch in the gut. James grunted and doubled over. Something in her twisted with outrage.

"Leave him be, damn you!"

The guard snapped his hard gaze toward her. "Mind your tongue, missy." He opened the cell beside hers and shoved James inside. "I better not get any trouble from you two."

Madeline rushed to the other side of her cell. The only things that separated them now were a few iron bars. She took what solace she could from that. She waited until the guard left them alone before she called out to him.

"Are you all right, Jimmy?"

Madeline reached her hand between the opening of two bars. James took her hand, leaned close and just that small contact was enough to give her renewed hope. They would get through this—they had already survived much worst.

He leaned his head against the bars. "I'm so sorry, Ladybug."

She shook her head. "For what? You did nothing wrong. *We* did nothing wrong."

He blew out a weary breath. "I know. But it doesn't change the fact that we are both in here because of what I did." He fell silent for a moment before he said quietly, "I should have never taken you to the veteran home. I should have never put you in danger like that."

Madeline gave his hand a gentle squeeze. "I'm sorry for what happened to your friend, Jimmy, but you saved my life. You took a life for me. Your friend's life. I regret that you had to make that choice, but I don't regret being alive."

James shut his eye. "Will was a good man. You would have liked him, Maddie. But after the war…after we were released from that prison camp, it was like his mind just snapped and there was nothing I could do to fix it."

"It wasn't your responsibility to fix him, Jimmy. Don't put that burden on yourself."

He opened his eye and stared at her. "Yet, I didn't think twice about taking his life, Maddie. I just reacted. I didn't even think about it."

Tears burned in the back of Madeline's eyes. She hated the pain she felt radiating from him, and hated the situation that kept her from being able to hold him.

"You saved my life, Jimmy," she said again. "Had I been faced with the same decision, I wouldn't have done any different. I love you and would do anything in my power to protect you too. I would always choose *you*."

∽ ∽ ∽

"You have two choices, Jim. You can either leave Nebraska or get an annulment."

James narrowed his eyes at Clay. "That's not much of a choice."

"It's not, I know. But they will drop all charges under those conditions. Except, Jim, you will be banned from returning to Dunesville if Madeline decides to stay there."

In the next cell, Madeline visibly tensed. James hated the position they were being forced into. They had barely had a chance to enjoy their marriage, or even spend a proper wedding night together. Hell, the ink on their marriage certificate wasn't even dry yet. Now, he was expected to just walk away from the woman he loved?

James regarded Clay evenly. "I'm not leaving my wife."

"And we can't leave Nebraska," Madeline said. "Dunesville is already down one teacher. I need to stay and help. I have a commitment there I have to fulfill."

James glanced over at her, hating that they were still separated by the damn cell bars, yet grateful that she was close. Clay had made it down to the prison as soon as he had heard of their arrest, but from what it sounded like, the charges were likely to be upheld.

Unless they turned their backs on the people of Dunesville.

James couldn't imagine doing that and he wouldn't expect Madeline to either. It was clear this voting season wouldn't be made easy for the colored men of this town and they could use all the support they could get. But in order for Madeline to see her mission through, they would have to end their marriage.

That, James wouldn't do.

"There has to be another way, Clay. We have to fight this."

"I'm willing to do that, Jim, but you have to know what you're getting yourself into. I'm waiting to hear if a bail has been set. If one has, it could also come with stipulations that could still keep you two separated from each other. And if we do take this to trial, it could take weeks, maybe even months, to fight."

James gritted his teeth in frustration. "Maddie's my wife and I intend to spend my life with her. Why is that anyone's business?"

Clay shrugged. "It isn't, but unfortunately it's the law."

A heavy sense of failure and dread began to settle in James' gut. He looked over at Madeline and recognized the same loss of hope in her eyes.

She had said she would always choose him, but did he want to force her to make that decision?

Her work at the school was important to her, which made it important to him. He didn't want to force her to choose between him and her mission, but neither did he want to be apart from her until that mission was complete.

"I love my wife, Clay," he said, still holding her gaze. "And I want to be with her."

Tears filled Madeline's eyes, but she smiled despite the fact that whatever they decided, heartbreak was inevitable.

"There may be another way," Clay began. "Though, it may be a stretch."

James's brows pulled together and he turned his gaze to his lawyer. "What are you thinking?"

Clay rubbed this chin. "Tell me more about your great-grandmother…"

CHAPTER 11

"Okay, they've agreed on a settlement."

James stared at Clay through the cell bars, suspicious. "Does it include me and Maddie still being together?"

"Yes. You can remain married, and in Dunesville if you'd like. You just have to sign an affidavit acknowledging that you're a colored man."

James head jerked in surprise. "What? That's ludicrous. Surely, you see that."

"I do, but we can spend the next few months fighting this in court or we can get this done and over with. And have you and your wife out of this jail."

James turned to Madeline. If it would free them from this hell and keep them together, he would do it.

"Okay."

Clay blinked in surprise. "Okay?"

"Yes, I'll do it."

"Are you absolutely certain about this?" Clay hesitated before he handed him the document. "You do understand what you're giving up, right?"

"I know," James said. He would be giving up his rights to move freely and without prejudice in a country that placed the value and worthiness of a man based on the color of his skin. "But it doesn't matter what anyone considers me. In the end, I know what I'm gaining."

James signed the papers and by that afternoon, he and Madeline were freed and on their way back to Dunesville.

By late afternoon, they rode into the small community and, to his astonishment, a small crowd had gathered to welcome them back.

He was also surprised by the questions and praise that came from all directions.

"It's nice what you did for Miss Madeline…"

"Is it true, what they say, Mr. Jim? Are you a colored man?"

"I don't think I'd ever see the day a white man claim he's a colored man when he's not…"

James didn't know whether to laugh or groan at the barrage of claims and questions.

"It wasn't a lie," he said instead, as he assisted Madeline down from the wagon. "My great-grandmother was half-African and half-Native American. She was born of the Oneida tribe in the Iroquois nation. Unfortunately, a lot of that culture is foreign to me, since many of the customs were lost or diluted in my family over the years."

"Why didn't you mentioned any of this before?" Reverend Linc asked.

James shrugged. "It's not something I intended to hide from, but it isn't a heritage I intend to exploit either." It was just a part of who he was.

Yet, in exposing that part of himself, he now opened himself to being judged and treated as less than. James hated being gawked at, but instead of curiosity or weariness, the crowd of black and brown faces regarded him with admiration and wonder. In all his twenty-eight years, James had never felt more self-aware of his heritage than he did now.

And he never felt more accepted for it.

He smiled to the small crowd. "Thank you all for the warm welcome, but Maddie and I had a trying few days and would like to get some rest." He took her hand and started toward the direction of the red cabins.

"How does it feel to be a colored man?" someone asked as they moved through the small crowd.

James thought about the past two nights in the uncomfortable cell, the uncertainty that had surrounded their future, and the mental and emotional upheaval they had been put through.

"It's damn exhausting."

A big barrel of a man let out a shout of laughter, and then thumped him on the shoulder as he passed. James couldn't stop the smile that curved his lips.

"You goddamn right it is!"

෬ ෬ ෬

Madeline sat on the edge of her bed, not realizing just how weary she was until they were finally alone. But beyond the fatigue that weighed her down on the mattress was the whirl of emotion that still spiraled wildly inside her.

The uncertainty of the past two days had left her tense and more afraid than she had ever been in her life. She had only just gotten James back, had barely gotten to enjoy the simple pleasure of having him as her husband, and just like that he had almost been taken away from her.

"I know you must be exhausted, love," James said by the door then placed his hat on his head. "I'll let you rest and I'll find something for us to eat."

She shook her head, a slow panic building in her when she realized he intended to leave. But she was unable to find the words to tell him she wasn't ready to let him go. Not yet.

He frowned over at her. "Maddie, you have to eat something."

She swallowed hard as she stared at him, the words she wanted so desperately to say lodged in her throat by a powerful emotion she couldn't place.

He came toward her, his expression softening. "It's all right, Maddie. Once you've had some rest, you'll feel—"

Moving with a speed she didn't know she had, Madeline flew off the bed and threw her arms around him. His strong arms wrapped instinctively around her. She held him tight as if it were the first and last time, because if life had taught her anything, it was that nothing was certain and moments like this were sacred.

"I don't need rest, Jimmy," she murmured against the crook of his neck. "And I don't need food. I need *you*."

Madeline lifted her head and his lips came crashing over hers. They moved in a frenzy, jerking at each other's clothing, their movements awkward as she couldn't seem to tear her lips away from his long enough to get her gown off. Eventually, her dress fell at her feet and she stood before him in her undergarments.

James' gaze ran down the length of her as his fingers flew down the column of buttons on his shirt. At the blatant desire on his face, her nipples hardened and pushed against the thin material of her shift. Eager to see and feel all of him, Madeline began undoing the buckle of his trousers. He jerked the shirt from his wide shoulders, letting it fall from his body, and it was soon followed by his pants.

Madeline glanced down at his torso and froze. The scars that slashed across his skin were jarring. She reached out and lightly traced her fingers against the more pronounced of his battle marks. It ran across his chest and down his side.

James stood motionless under her touch, and Madeline glanced up at him to find him watching her intently. She couldn't read what was in his gaze and that realization served as a painful reminder of all the damage and pain they still kept hidden away from each other.

Suddenly, Madeline wanted no more barriers between them. Reaching down at the hem of her shift, she peeled the garment over her head and stood naked before him. James closed the gap between them and pulled her into his arms. Her breasts pushed against the hard expanse of his chest, sending a surge of desire coursing through her.

He captured her lips in another deep, consuming kiss and Madeline clutched at his shoulder as he moved them down on the bed. He came over her and settled himself between her thighs. His hard shaft pushed between her soft folds and she released a small sigh at the delicious sensation.

"You're truly the loveliest thing I've ever seen," James murmured as he trailed his lips along her neck.

A shiver passed through her and her eyes fluttered open. Madeline stared at him, then reached up to pull away his eye patch. He jerked his head back.

"Don't, Maddie." He was rigid above her. "It's not—"

"Shh, it's okay." She cupped his face and pulled him down for a slow, tender kiss. "I don't want any more barriers between us, Jimmy."

She placed another lingering kiss on his lips, then reached for the patch again. He shut his eye but didn't stop her. She peeled away the black leather covering and stared at his mutilated flesh. Tears sprang unexpectedly in her eyes—not from pity, but from the jolting realization of just how fortunate she was. The man she loved had returned home to her, whole and complete. He may carry the vicious marks of a long, brutal war on his face, but in his core, her Jimmy was still very much the man he had always been—noble, kind, and unbelievably grounded.

Madeline blinked away her tears and pressed her lips just above his brow, and then his cheek. "I love you, Jimmy." She looped her arms around him and lifted her legs high against his hips. "You're by far the loveliest man I know."

He stared down at her and she smiled up at him. There was an emotion in his eye that she was all too familiar with. It was the kind of feeling that was too heavy, too forceful, to express with mere words.

Instead, they let the bonds of the flesh cement their love for each other.

James entered her with a tenderness that made her cry out from the incredible pleasure. He captured her moans and gasps in his mouth as he thrust rhythmically above her. She clung to him as her body clenched fiercely around him. With every deep stroke, he drove away the last of her remaining shadows and replaced them with his warm touch, his heady scent, and his intoxicating taste—until finally, they both came apart in a burst of explosive pleasure.

In the aftermath, she nestled against his side as his hand gently ran down her lower back. They lay silently in each other's arms for a while, but Madeline could sense the thoughts running in his mind.

She brushed her fingers absently along his chest. "What are you thinking about?"

He took her hand and laced their fingers together. "That if I had my way, I would take us far from this intolerant place, to a place where we can just...*be*."

"Like what your great-grandfather did when he whisked your great-grandmother away to Canada?"

"I've told you that story, huh?"

There was feigned bemusement in his voice and Madeline chuckled. "Just a handful of times."

And she didn't mind hearing about it a dozen more times. She could never tire hearing the romantic and daring tale of how a brave Siaragowaeh had saved a wounded English soldier from certain death during America's rebellion against the British and had ultimately fallen in love. Their fascinating story read like something from a dime novel. The risks James' great-grandmother had taken by caring for a fallen soldier proved what kind of courage and selflessness such a woman had possessed. And luckily those same traits had been passed down to her children and her children's children.

Madeline would have never believed such a love capable of surviving back in those early times, but the hard, warm frame she rested against was evidence of how two souls from completely different worlds could defy those odds. Out of nothing more than their love, James' great-grandparents had created a life for themselves and raised a family deep in the moorlands of Canada. Such a life sounded like the kind of peaceful bliss Madeline's old self would have been willing to leave everything behind for.

Her new self, however, understood that she could never be content living a life with her head buried in the sand.

Madeline sighed. "Part of me wants to get away from all this hate and injustice too, Jimmy. But then another part wants me to stay and show those bigots that their plans to intimidate and terrorize us won't work."

He tightened his arm around her. "That's the part I struggle within myself, which means I'll just have to do my damnedest to protect you."

Madeline fell silent. She hadn't been naive to think that emancipation would change things over night, but things were still changing. In the end, she was responsible for the schooling of over two dozen men and women who were a consequence of that change. She didn't have time to waste on anger or resentment.

"Now what is it you're thinking about?"

Madeline lifted her head from James' shoulder and peered down at him. There were no more walls, no more secrets between them, and for the first time in a long time, she truly felt uninhibited…and free.

Cupping his cheek, she leaned down and lightly brushed her lips across his. She drew back as a wicked thought suddenly entered her mind, and her lips curved in a teasing smile.

"I'm thinking we haven't made love nearly enough to satisfy me."

His eye widened with surprise. Then, without warning, he grabbed her and flipped her on her back. He moved over her, his lips inches away from hers.

"I guess I'll have to remedy that."

Wrapping her arms around his neck, Madeline lost herself under the loving caress of her husband's skilled fingers. In his arms, she vowed to herself she would no longer allow fear or regret to keep her from reveling in life's simple pleasures, and would instead live each day alongside him with abandon.

James was her today and her tomorrow—her now and forever. He was her lover, her friend, and the light that made dreams of love and laughter part of her reality.

Epilogue

March 4, 1869
Washington, DC

Six months later…

"The question of suffrage is one which is likely to agitate the public, so long as a portion of the citizens of the nation are excluded from its privileges in any State. It seems to me very desirable that this question should be settled now…"

Madeline stood with the crowd at the U.S. Capitol, watching from a distance as the war hero and now new president of the United States gave his inaugural address. Though she could barely make out President Ulysses S. Grant from where she stood, she was still excited to be among the many who had turned out for his inauguration. This was a momentous occasion and she wanted to bear witness to it, much to her husband's reluctance.

"Come, love," James said close to her ear. "We should start back now before the crowd breaks and the parade starts."

James took her hand and led her through the crowd of huddled bodies, wrapped in heavy coats. Madeline rested her hand over her swollen belly as they made their way to the street.

The weather was bitter and frigid, yet thousands of people, of all colors and races, had turned up on the steps of the capitol to witness the first elected president, since the end of the war, be sworn into office. Grant had won over many of the states and their electoral votes, including Nebraska's, which she believed meant that many in the country were looking to heal and move the country forward.

From President Grant's speech, Madeline was hopeful of better change to come. The recent passing of the fifteenth amendment from the House and Senate had been a move in the right direction. Though women had been omitted from the bill, men of color could no longer be barred from practicing their constitutional right.

James assisted her inside a waiting stagecoach and Madeline settled into the seat. A sudden shift inside her belly made her start and she pressed her hand against her stomach. James climbed in and sat across her. Another kick came and Madeline gasped from the pressure.

James frowned. "What's wrong?"

She smiled over the sharpness in his tone. Taking his hand, she placed it over her round belly.

"Do you feel that?"

His eyes widened as their baby pushed lightly against her belly. It was an extraordinary feeling, carrying a life inside her and feeling it live and grow. With every day that passed, the soft flutters and subtle movements grew stronger and she never ceased to be amazed by it.

"Is that our son in there?"

"It's our daughter," Madeline said, her smile widening. "And she's a little warrior. Just like her father."

James returned her smile then leaned forward and pressed his lips against her belly. "That she is. I can't wait for the day we get to meet her."

"Soon," Madeline murmured, rubbing her belly. She thought of the small life growing inside her and a fierce love moved through her. It was followed by an immense curiosity.

What would their baby be like? What would be her favorite subject in school? Would she be shy or full of energy? How would it feel to hold her...?

She had all these thoughts and couldn't wait to bring their new baby into the world.

"When that day comes, husband, I plan to join the suffrage movement. Our daughter is our future now and this nation can only benefit once it recognizes the value of giving women the simple right to vote."

James straightened and eyed her closely. "You don't have to convince me, love. I'm always on your side."

"I know. I don't mean to lecture you. I'm just tired and frustrated from the lack of progress."

Though the fifteenth amendment had been a positive step forward, the growing rift within the suffrage movement due to women's exclusion in the amendment had created a divisiveness that only helped to further stall their efforts.

"However," James stressed, "I won't allow you to tire or exert yourself while you're carrying our child. First bring our daughter into the world, then we can continue the good fight."

"I wouldn't call writing letters and signing petitions exerting myself. For now, I'll let my pen do most of the work."

"Good. For a moment, I thought you had a notion of following in Mrs. Harper's footsteps in traveling around the country giving lectures."

Madeline laughed. *Maybe one day,* but she didn't voice those words aloud. She didn't want to give her overprotective husband undue worry, and with her current condition, she understood her limitations.

"So we will stay on in Washington?" she asked. "Continue our work here?"

James laced his fingers between hers and kissed the back of her hand. "Yes, love. For now."

Though Madeline would miss the open, rural lands of the west, there was more she could accomplish from the battlegrounds of the nation's capital—or rather from the office of their rented townhome. She wanted to secure a future for her sons and daughters, where they could hold their heads high as Americans. And with the election over, the fight to obtain equal rights for all colored men and women had only just begun.

Madeline gave her husband's hand a gentle squeeze. With a man like James at her side, the hope of such a legacy was just at their fingertips.

THE END

Author's Note

Dear reader:

For those familiar with my story, AMAZING GRACE, in the historical romance anthology *The Brightest Day*, you'll remember Madeline Asher and her lost love. I was excited to tell Madeline and James' love story in *Daughters of a Nation* and give them the happy ending they deserved. If you're interested in reading the "romantic and daring tale" of his great-grandparents, you can find James and Siaragowaeh's love story in A SWEET SURRENDER.

I can't begin to tell you how much I enjoyed writing IN THE MORNING SUN. During my research for the story, I got a chance to uncover so much inspiring history. In *Notable Black American Women* by Jessie Carney Smith, I learned more about women like Frances Ellen Watkins Harper, her writing, and her influences in the women's suffrage movement. In *The Civil War and Reconstruction,* a documentary collection edited by William E. Gienapp, I read personal letters written by soldiers and officers, getting a true account of their feelings and attitudes of the time.

Despite the many issues faced during Reconstruction—issues such as racism, unlawful voter restrictions, the neglect of veterans, and the lack of women rights—there were still the hope of brighter days to come. We may not be where we should be on these issues, but it's my hope that the stories in this anthology can show what it means to our future when we all stand together for equal rights and justice.

Best,

Lena ♥

Additional resources:

• *A Shining Thread of Hope* by Darlene Clark Hine and Kathleen Thompson

• *Black Women of the Old West* by William Loren Katz

• Frances Ellen Watkins Harper poems: http://www.poemhunter.com/frances-ellen-watkins-harper-2/poems

ABOUT THE AUTHOR

Lena Hart is a Florida native currently living in the Harlem edge of New York City. Though she enjoys reading a variety of romance genres, she mainly writes sensual to steamy contemporary, suspense, and historical romances. When Lena is not busy writing, she's reading, researching, or conferring with her muse. To learn more about her upcoming works, join her Reader Group.

THE WASHERWOMEN'S WAR
PIPER HUGULEY

Atlanta, GA – Summer 1881. When Mamie Harper arrives to substitute teach for the Atlanta Baptist Female Seminary, she bears witness to the injustice told by some of the older students who are washerwomen. Mamie's upbringing as the daughter of the most famous Black suffragette in America means that she cannot be silent and resolves to help her students find their voice and openly protest their mistreatment.

When the Black Washerwomen go on strike, summer pastor Gabriel Harmon is brought in to mediate a solution but realizes the feisty leader of the opposition is the young teacher from Milford who previously rejected his attempts to pay court to her. When these two forces collide over explosive events during a hot Atlanta summer, only one will be able to win the battle. However, as they clash, Mamie and Gabriel learn that there is another war, the war for the heart, that's well worth the fight.

For the original Washing Amazons. We stand on their shoulders. Thank you.

ACKNOWLEDGMENTS

To Debra Little, Holly Smith and Kassandra Jolley. Thank you for all of your help.

CHAPTER 1

Milford, Georgia—June 1881

The one thing I swore I would never become is a minister's wife. That's not me. Those women are saints. And sinners. There are some, like Mama Manda, who are nice, kind and gracious. The epitome of womanhood. Others are mean, like snake's venom, ready to spit it out on some poor woman in the name of the Lord.

So when I wanted to kiss a man, I made sure he was not a minister. Why start something you couldn't finish? No purpose in it, as far as I could tell. That meant that during my time at Milford College, it was only the males who were studying to become teachers who had a chance with me. Not the preacher ones. That made the choices less difficult.

There weren't many, mind you. Just some. Enough so a young woman like myself could get a notion of what I wanted for my husband. And now I know.

There wasn't going to be any floundering around for me. Given my lot in life so far, I know I'm not going to be as fortunate as my best girlfriend, March Smithson, oops, March Lewis. She was not searching and this handsome gentleman just dropped in her lap from the heavens. I'm not jealous of her or anything, but March isn't the most enterprising woman. It had to happen for her that way. Which was fine. She's related to most of the eligible men in Milford, since the school started where her family lives. Marrying one of her Baxter cousins would have been just horrible for her. Since I'm not a Baxter by blood, that makes someone like me very desirable, but the feeling was far from mutual.

I love my March and I would have loved to have been her cousin or something, but all of those Baxter men are too holy by half. Sometimes, the itch to preach the gospel is latent in a man. I had to rule them out too. So, there were just a handful I could keep on a string and so I had some fine beaus who were crazy for me, during my time at Milford.

Some of the poor dears thought that meant that I was going to be their wife. No. I'm a woman and it's almost the twentieth century. It's time for me to see what is out in the world.

I was thrilled when Mama Manda, our esteemed presidentress, called me to her oak-paneled office and told me they had an assignment for me to substitute teach. Imagine! I was being called forth to use the skills I had learned in the past year since I had arrived at the college. I would be able to be put to some good use and purpose. Finally. My own mother, my real mother, would have a reason to be proud of her chick.

"Mamie. This is Miss Packard. She will be supervising you in your new assignment. Miss Packard, please meet Miss Mary Frances Harper. We call her Mamie." Mama Manda indicated to me I should shake hands with the older woman of the lighter-hued race. Miss Packard had blue eyes focused in on me. I knew she wanted to see if I presented as teacherly enough.

I tightened my shoulders and stood up straighter. There was no need for shame. I'm rather comely, if I do say so myself. I smoothed down my brown skirt, which Milford made me put on to look more like a teacher. Brown is a boring color to wear, especially if you are brown yourself, but it would do.

"Good day, Miss Harper. Do you mind me asking how old you are?"

"I'll be twenty in a few month's time, Miss Packard."

"Gracious. I had to ask because several of the students will be older than you. Do you find that daunting?"

"Not at all, ma'am. The end of our time in chains has meant that we here in Milford prepare to teach any and all who want to drink from the pool of knowledge." There. That should suit her.

Her eyebrows, which were almost faded to gray and matched her faded hair, rose in amusement. "Really? And what of teaching God's word? Are you ready to do that?"

Mama Manda stepped forward. "Teaching from the Bible wouldn't be a strength of Miss Harper's. She's very quick with mathematics. She would probably best serve in that capacity."

Miss Packard looked a little worried. "I was hoping for someone a little better rounded to suit. Hattie won't be well for a time and I need someone who could teach in more subjects."

"Oh, Miss Harper can help, of course. I was just letting you know what would be best with her."

I spoke up for myself. "I'm well used to the Word of the Bible, Miss Packard. I was raised to know the Lord."

"I imagine so. When I heard you were the daughter of… well, your mother is very well known to Miss Giles and myself. She's quite remarkable."

And there it was. Another time when the greatness of my mother preceded me and I was expected to do the same as she. I smiled. "She is."

"Mamie has her own way of doing things. She's young, but energetic and lively. I'm sure she would suit for a month's assignment."

"Well, the school is growing so much. It's hard to tell who and what we will have coming to us before the term ends."

Mama Manda nodded in her gracious way. "It's wonderful. I'm so glad to hear young women of our race have opportunities to obtain educations. I recall when I lived there, it wasn't easy to educate my daughter in a classroom setting. Between myself and her tutors, it was not easy and that was some ten years ago."

"It's been a blessing for Hattie and I to start this endeavor. It's very humble. Rather mean and lowly, like the place where our Lord was born. But there was greatness for Him and there will be greatness coming for the Atlanta Baptist Female Seminary as well."

"Well, the name is certainly an exalted one," I crowed, and both of them turned to look at me. There it was. I had the habit of saying the most inappropriate things sometimes. Another reason why I would never make the grade as a minister's wife. "I mean the name has everything in it to let you know what it is."

"Part of the job would be to ensure its growth. This is a test term, as it were, but on Sundays, Hattie and I take turns in visiting the congregations of your race to ask if they have any daughters they would wish to learn to read the Bible and to be educated. You will have to help me over these next Sundays while my dear is recovering."

I kept my face smooth. Some of her work sounded like minister's wife activity.

But I'm a teacher.

"Fine. I'm willing to help in any way I'm needed."

"Well, it is an answer to prayer. It would just take too long to get someone from up North to come. And it is just for a month. The Society cannot pay you much. Ten dollars above room and board."

"We know of a place where she can stay in Atlanta." Mama Manda interjected. "Mrs. Turner has long owned a suitable boarding house. She is an old friend and would be just like a mother to her."

Great. Another mother looking out for me. Just what I need.

"Well, that's a relief. I would have been happy to have her stay at the boardinghouse where Hattie and I stay, but…."

Mama Manda nodded. "I understand. Miss Harper is not there to cause trouble. Just to have a place to stay. Then she will make her way back here to Milford to prepare for her next year of study. Correct?"

Her calm, steady gaze held mine and I returned it in equal measure. "Of course." I replied in the same way she spoke to me.

"Wonderful. And we here at Milford College are grateful you are giving one of our students this opportunity, Miss Packard. I trust you'll find Mamie to be extremely helpful in this trying time and I'm hopeful your friend will soon feel better. It's probably the southern air."

"Well, yes. It's been an adjustment, since I'm the one who is usually ill, but I'm sure you are right. The humidity is quite an adjustment."

"Yes. Well, Mamie can pack her grip and return on the train with you."

"That will be best. We do have a church service to attend in the morning."

I watched them both shake hands over my fate. Neither of them shook my hand again, I noted. Mama Manda made a sweeping Queen Victoria gesture of dismissal to me. I knew what to do. I went back to my room in the student house to pack some dresses, since I was told before in school nothing too pretty or gaily striped would do for my teaching duty. My teaching wardrobe was not very expansive. I would have to buy more boring clothes to wear in Atlanta. Three dresses and my pretty pink one would do very nicely, plus some white shirtwaists and a boring black or dark-blue skirt. I still packed my sapphire blue and emerald green striped dress, though. Just in case.

Carrying my grip to the door, I sucked my stomach in, and dragged my footsteps a little. Milford had been a kind of home to me. I would miss it. But given how quickly I had been handed over to the charge of Miss Packard, I wasn't too sure they would miss me in the same way. Oh, well. It was only for a month.

Miss Packard didn't have much to say as we rode the train back to Atlanta. The line of worry etched between her faded gray eyebrows let me know this woman felt the weight of enormous responsibility. I felt some enormous responsibility, too, since I was tasked to lift some of those burdens from this good woman. On behalf of my race, I would do the very best I could. That would be all I could promise.

ℭℴ ℭℴ ℭℴ

Miss Packard looked old to me, but she could move. She just about exploded off of the train once we arrived in Atlanta. It was the early morning and it seemed that things, everything, were already steaming in the June heat.

Now, I have known plenty of cities, but Atlanta was a particularly smelly one. When Miss Packard engaged a hansom cab to come and get us, I remembered all over again the times I had been here with my mother for one of her speeches. Maybe it was the way I had grown quiet, but all of a sudden, I longed for Milford. It was almost as if the woman beside me knew what was in my heart.

"Now, my dear. We cannot let grass grow under our feet. I've been too long in need for someone to help me with this endeavor while my poor Hattie is ill. We're attending a church service where I will make a speech."

Was there any hope of breakfast? I'm not the kind of woman who can do without breakfast. I looked over at Miss Packard and she seemed like the thin type to me. I'm not excessive in size, but I have always enjoyed a good meal.

"Oh, don't worry about food. The church will probably have something for us to eat at some point. They always do. Especially since we will attend the early service at Summerhill Baptist Church."

"I know Summer Hill. My mother would speak at some of those churches. Mayhap, I've been to this one before."

Miss Packard looked over at me. I felt as if I was wilting in the hot June day, but her respect for my experience was real. "You will do nicely. You don't have to give a speech, but if I refer to you, you may have to stand and some of the potential students or parents may want to ask you questions."

"I have no problem with any of that." I folded my hands and matched her gaze.

"Good. It's been providential you were at Milford, and well worth the trip. Then after church, we'll go visit my Hattie for you to meet her and see you settled at your boarding house."

And hopefully there would be something to eat somewhere in there. *Please, Lord.*

The cab let us out at the curb by a handsome red brick church that did, indeed, look familiar to me. A lot of Atlanta skewed to the new, because of how General Sherman and his Union troops dealt this place a severe blow, but I recall this was the place where the church women did, indeed, lay out a healthy reception when my mother spoke here some six or seven years ago on the topic of rights for women. I pressed my corset down in the hopes of food as I followed Miss Packard into the church. So much of it was draped lovingly with touches of red velvet. Such rich fabric served to prove how special this congregation was.

Miss Packard swept up to the first row of the church, nodding to everyone. She was quite comfortable. I had to admit, even in knowing women of her race who dealt with my mother, none seemed so comfortable when dealing with mine in quite the same way. I tried to buck myself up to nod and smile behind her. She seated herself in the second row, and I sat with her, smoothing my hands over my boring navy skirt.

The organ swelled up with an impressive aria and the minister processed in with some other people. I caught sight of his look from the side, thinking him a most impressive and tall man. He turned to me full on and I was struck silent.

The minister of this church was Gabriel Harmon.

I tried to look away, but his intense black gaze landed on me, struck me and fixed me.

Oh, yes, he recognized me.

Recall when I said I didn't want to be a minister's wife? This was a man who had tried, and failed, to reverse the course of my life's direction.

And he had the gall to look more handsome than ever.

CHAPTER 2

I have to explain. I said I didn't want to be a minister's wife and I don't. But part of that was because I was faced with the proposition, and I rejected it.

Soundly.

I got to know Gabriel Harmon last November when the Milford College choir performed in a series of concerts in Southern Georgia, far from Atlanta, late last year. We were on a tour to raise money to help our school to sufficiency and the efforts of our small group went very well.

The fireworks between Mr. Harmon and I happened quickly. He zeroed in on me as the choice of his heart, and I on him. After all, who would not delight in a tall, toasty, traditional man with luscious, full lips topped with a full black mustache and a sonorous speaking voice? He was a wonderful escort.

We were chaperoned the entire time.

Unfortunately.

The first night was a Friday and the church had a lovely spread for us. He asked me if he could bring me punch and I had said yes. He stayed by my side the entire night. If only I had thought to speak with him about his vocation, but his beauty made me quite speechless.

The next day there had been a picnic for the church youth and I played baseball with some of the fellows. March had too. She had brothers, so she knew how.

Some of the others in the choir had been appalled. Gabriel watched and my decorum did not seem to make me unsuitable to him. Some of the fellows in our choir bet against our team, but we won.

We recovered and had a very successful concert in the evening and attended service the next day. The church laid out a wonderful lunch of chicken, potatoes, vegetables, and pie. The works.

After I had eaten a slice of apple pie, I stepped outside for a breath of fresh air and found myself accompanied by Gabriel. "Where do you journey from here, Miss Harper?"

"We will continue our tour into Tennessee for a time and then loop around back to Milford. Some will go home for Christmas. I'll stay on campus."

"It sounds lonely."

I turned around and almost ran smack into the broad wall of his chest. Out of protection to my face—well, curiosity, I raised my hand up and lightly placed it on him. Heat radiated outward from his chest and seemed to seep through my hand and radiated in my fingers like mini-lightning bolts.

I sought to reassure him. "I get along well. I've always been in the care of others, or else I would be on the road with my mother all of the time. The people in Milford are like my family anyway. It will be all right."

It was a practiced speech I used to justify my life and it worked fine. Usually. But this man and his stern, but kindly gaze seemed to see different. "Your mother?"

"The lecturer, poet, abolitionist and woman extraordinaire Frances Ellen Watkins Harper."

He said nothing. Really? Nothing?

"You don't know her?"

"I know of her," he responded quietly and I gained a flutter in my stomach.

"Which is?"

"Her seeking the right for women to vote is not seemly."

"Not seemly?"

"Women need guidance and counsel. They aren't prepared to make that kind of decision without assistance."

I pushed back from his chest. "That's what the lot say about Negro men. Do you agree?"

"No, I don't, but…."

"No, because you are one of them."

"When I become a shepherd of a flock, I must teach everyone in the church the best course of action."

"Dare I hope you meant being a shepherd of sheep?" My hands started to sweat a bit.

I patted his tie. He was very handsome, with long, wavy black hair which certainly betrayed a mixed heritage, as a number of Negroes had, but I wondered what Gabriel's story was about it. I hoped I would have the opportunity to find out, but I said, "When people talk about a shepherd, it's because they take care of sheep or are a minister. You certainly don't look like or smell like a sheep herding person."

"Ahh, you are very smart, Miss Mamie. You are right. I'm in hopes of attaining my church flock very soon."

I stopped patting the solid knot on his tie and stepped back from him. Oh.

That's too bad.

Very bad.

"If you will excuse me, I think I should go inside, lest my friends worry about me."

"What's the matter, Miss Mamie? Did I say something wrong?"

I gulped at a knot developing in my throat. Why? Things were doomed to never turn out my way. I could just give up and tour endlessly like my mother for the rest of my days, trying to get people to see the truth. Women had enough sense to vote and exist without men. That's what should be my life.

So now, looking at him gazing down on me with barely disguised contempt, I had thought teaching in such a place as the Atlanta Female Baptist Seminary for the next four weeks would help me with my goal.

Lord, what do you want me to do? I have told you repeatedly that I am not interested or desirous of a man who is a minister. When will you hear my cry of lamentation?

I lowered my head and prayed, knowing it was a good look in a church service. And because my sore heart was in need of comfort.

Already, I was having a hard time focusing on the text handsome angel Gabriel was preaching because I knew he found me exceedingly cowardly. Well, no one is perfect. I readily admit to being clay in the Master's hands.

Just not clay in Gabriel's well-made, tapered, polished-looking fingers that waved in the air with excitement as he preached on about. Something.

Surely it was sinful to think of what those hands would be like on my person.

I could see that in this congregation of aspiring Negroes in Summer Hill, I was not alone in a very favorable estimation of Mr. Harmon.

I took a deep breath and waved the hand fan I had been given in the increasing mid-morning heat of the late spring day. Summer would happen in another day or two and then the southern heat would really be oppressive. But I knew my sweating had far less to do with the heat of the day, than for Gabriel's regard.

"I want to take a moment, dear friends, for something special." His smooth voice rolled over us and I closed my eyes, attempting to create an island of myself. A place where he could not touch me in any way. "Miss Packard is here and has a word for us."

The space next to me, previously filled with a woman who fairly vibrated with energy, was made vacant as she stood and spoke from the bottom of the stairs, rather than asking Gabriel to yield the pulpit. Very thoughtful. Many congregations were against the thought of women speaking from such a place. She understood.

"We have had some success further into Atlanta, just off of town, with our school. We started out with eleven souls who came, wanting to learn how to read their Bible. We now have grown to fifty-some souls. Our circumstances are meek and low, but we are in a place to help those who thirst for knowledge. So we are blessed."

I opened my closed eyes, not liking the turn of what Miss Packard was saying.

"Please stand, Miss Harper. My dear friend Hattie Giles and I came from the cold north to your warmer climes to start this endeavor on behalf of the Women's Baptist movement. We knew this was a good work to do and we are supporting them in this endeavor. This test term only proves we can do more and better. The tuition for the next few weeks is only five dollars. If you have women or older girls who want to come and seek learning, I'm pleased to announce we have Miss Mary Frances Harper to help us."

I really didn't like the spotlight of attention, but it seemed to land on me always. I stood, turned to the congregation as I swept back my bustle to avoid toppling over and waved with my right hand.

"Miss Harper is an expert in mathematics and we are pleased to have her so my Hattie can continue to heal over these last weeks of the term. Miss Harper has been educated at the esteemed Milford College and is a fine example of what your daughters can become."

All true, very true. I flashed a welcoming smile to the friendly crowd.

"Her pedigree is unblemished, as she is the only child of the esteemed Frances Watkins Harper, who has long fought for the freedom of the enslaved and now fights for women to attain suffrage."

Well, I expected that. People were bound to bring mother into it. I nodded my head.

"Miss Harper would be delighted to have you hear her give a selection in song. She's been a member of the wonderful Milford College choir."

The murmurs grew a bit louder.

The smile disappeared from my face. No one, not even when I was in Milford, mentioned me having to sing.

The summer day reached my throat.

"Does she need some accompaniment?" Gabriel intoned from his high place at the pulpit. "I'm only too happy to help."

"Oh, my, yes. I usually play, but if you would Reverend."

And then Miss Packard returned to her seat and sat down!

Get up!

"I, well," I managed to croak.

"A song, Miss Harper." The good woman—well, not so good—said.

I made my way to the piano on the side where Gabriel had taken off his minister robes, appearing now in a well-fitting, black, broad-cloth Prince Albert suit and sat down at the piano, using those fingers of his to warm the instrument.

"Selection?"

Everyone knows I'm the weak voice in the MCC. I only joined to be with my friend, March. No one would ever think of giving me a song to sing alone. What in the world?

I swallowed that summer down in my throat. "Do you know *Steal Away?*"

"I do."

"Well, then, play that."

I turned to the congregation and flashed them a smile. To make it look as if I were completely comfortable with all of this. Even if I wasn't. "Many of you know it is the project of groups like the Milford College Choir and the Fisk Jubilees to save the music of our beloved loved ones who were in bondage. I am now going to sing *Steal Away.*"

I opened my throat and warbled out that thing as best as I could. When I finished with the singing, the applause was loud and long.

I was not fooled. I had stopped torturing the crowd with my shaky soprano, which was why the applause was so rich and full.

"Well," Gabriel gave me a slight nod of regard and returned to his high-up minister place. "Thank you, ladies. The Atlanta Female Baptist Seminary has much to recommend it. I know several women in the congregation will be at Friendship tomorrow to pursue this desire of being more like the esteemed Miss Harper here. Any man would be honored to have such a jewel grace his life. We should all be so blessed."

Surely, he jested with me.

It appeared I would never know. When the service was over, Miss Packard stood and swept me out of the church.

"I need to go check on Hattie and get you settled with your boarding house. You'll need the time to rest up, as you will need all of your energy to teach school in the morning."

Many sought to shake our hands as we walked to the back of the church. I looked behind me to see where Mr. Harmon was and he was engulfed with matters as befit his status as a minister.

See there? Look at all of the work he had to do. His gaze caught mine once more, and I thought I saw a little smile emerge at one corner of his mouth, lifting up an edge of his mustache.

Then it disappeared. I turned away and followed Miss Packard back to the waiting hansom cab, off to get settled into my new Atlanta surroundings.

I had faced him, months earlier, and I came out fine on the other side of it. So, I guess that's why when I settled into the cab, my knees started shaking. I put my hands on them to be still and obey, but it didn't work very well.

I think my knees didn't like to sing. Who could blame them?

Chapter 3

I wasn't nervous for the next day at all. Miss Packard had kept me so busy all day Sunday, I had no time to really slow down. Fortunately, I was able to get something to eat when we went to visit Miss Giles, her beloved Hattie, who was recuperating from her summer illness. She was younger than the stern Miss Packard and had merry, brown eyes. It was too bad we wouldn't be teaching together. She seemed fun.

Miss Packard and Miss Giles were both amused to see me eat the cold chicken and vegetables with cherry pie they offered, but I was satisfied. I knew I needed to eat well before they took me to the boarding house. Prominent Negro people stayed at Mrs. Turner's in Atlanta.

Mrs. Turner, everyone knew, was not the best cook in the world, so I had my fill when I was able.

She was still a sweet lady and I knew she would be happy to see me and very welcoming when I arrived. That was all that mattered. "Oh, my. You are so grown up, in your first teaching job. How proud your mama would be."

"You believe so?"

"Oh, I know. I have fourteen children myself, you know. Preachers a-plenty, but none of them teachers!"

I suppressed the need to shudder. And they all needed wives, no doubt. Luckily, none of the Turner sons ever looked me up. Her husband was the esteemed former politician Henry McNeal Turner. If I were to ever marry with a Turner son, it would be considered a royal wedding of sorts in the Negro community. But I'm no Princess Louise. It would be a disaster for me.

When I woke the next morning, I took in a three-minute egg cooked in five minutes and a slice of burned toast. I passed on the oatmeal. It was too runny, if there could be such a thing. She handed me a lunch made up of more eggs and bread and I stepped out into the June humidity.

I tried to wear a boring white shirtwaist and blue skirt, but I missed my happy striping. On went the blue and green.

"You look lovely, Mamie. Are you sure you won't be hot?" Mrs. Turner asked.

"I don't think so. I'll be fine, ma'am. Thank you."

A wrinkle appeared on her face, but I don't know why she felt that way.

The school wasn't far from the house, so I walked. This part of Atlanta was also populated with Negroes, but these seemed to be more of the working-class type. As I walked on, I saw the washerwomen heating up their large basins of hot water over fires they had constructed. Some of the basins were made of tin, some were cast iron pots. But they had to be outside. Monday was the first day of the week to do wash and it appeared to be hard, hot, thirsty work.

"Good morning." I said to a young girl with large, liquid eyes as she carried buckets of water to fill one of the large basins. Another boy helped her.

They both looked at me as if I had escaped the mad house. I don't know why. I felt like a happy spirit in my emerald green and sapphire blue stripes with a jabot of lace at the throat. My boots were made of white leather and clicked a tune as I walked along the mud roads.

I piled my black hair high on my head, so it wouldn't come down on my neck and make it hot for the day. I still couldn't help but notice how some of the washing women were helped by young girls, girls who should have been in school. Why did Miss Packard want to recruit students out of the churches? There were young girls right here in the neighborhood who needed an education. I made a mental note to ask her about it.

I arrived at Friendship Baptist Church in about fifteen minutes and a crude sign hewn out of wood strung up on the door directed me to the back of the church and to the place where Atlanta Female Baptist Seminary was. I followed the directions to a flight of stairs. The stairs had been carved into the red earth with some crude planks laid across them. The steps alone caused me to almost lose heart and run back to Milford. For, if the steps looked this way, what would the rest of the school appear as?

I thought of Gabriel in that second and how he might think me being spoiled.

I was, but I wouldn't let him know that.

I descended carefully and opened the door to darkness.

It was a sunny June day outside, but it was hard to tell by the looks of this basement, where hardly any light resided at all.

This was it?

Miss Packard, in her energetic way, came to me. "Welcome, Miss Harper."

She must have noticed the stricken look on my face and patted my arm. "I know. It's very low and mean. As I said. But I was afraid if I told you what it looked like, you wouldn't come. And I was so desperate for help. Fifty all at once is so many to handle alone."

I surveyed the crude wooden benches. The planks on the floor were open in some places and I couldn't swear to it, but I thought I heard some scurrying in a far corner. There was a pot-bellied stove at one end of the room and a slightly raised platform with an obviously used, crooked desk at the other.

I thought of all of the places where I had been to school, Milford as the last one and dear old Henry hall and instead of feeling heart sick, I tensed. Why in the world did people believe this was enough for women of the race?

"Please, don't apologize for it, Miss Packard. I'm the fool, coming here like this. I'm obviously not prepared for the first day."

"Don't apologize for your attire, my dear. It will give the students heart and courage, qualities sorely needed here in our ant-hill."

"Ant-hill?"

"Yes. Several of our detractors call our school the ant-hill school, rather than the illustrious name it possesses."

"Why?"

"Well, not everyone believes it's necessary to educate a colored woman. Surely you know that."

"No, I don't. But since there are detractors— and I can't imagine who they are, Miss Packard—I will work exceedingly hard to help."

Her blue eyes brightened enough for me to see in the dim light of the basement. She led me to the back corner of the room, where there was a tall stool. There were no floor boards underneath my stool. "You may sit yourself here, dear, and lift yourself out of the mud."

"Thank you." I didn't know what else to say. Tufts of dry grass peeked out here and there. It promised to be a long day.

All of a sudden, I heard a clatter down the stairs and some of the students began to arrive. Some of them carried lamps to help light the way in the darkness of the school room, so it was a little better. Well, some.

The increased light brought heat with it, the last thing needed in the June heat.

Sweat trickled down my back and I wanted to rip at my dress in some way to chastise myself for my vanity.

The women who arrived lined themselves up in the cast-off church pews in front of me and precisely at 8:30 a.m. Miss Packard sounded the bell for an opening morning convocation. She opened her Bible and read from Isaiah. "I will I will say to the north, Give up; and to the south, Keep not back: bring my sons from far, and my daughters from the ends of the earth."

Yes, I knew this one well and where Miss Packard was taking it. Just a bit of an admonition to me, I believe. "Remember ye not the former things, neither consider the things of old. Behold, I will do a new thing; now it shall spring forth; shall ye not know it? I will even make a way in the wilderness, *and* rivers in the desert."

"Amen." I said when she finished, showing I could take the Good Word as a lesson, even though I was only nineteen years old.

Miss Packard spoke to my group, who had gathered in the far corner of the room where the scurrying had been. "Miss Harper is here to teach several of you mathematics. She will show you how to account for your works in your businesses. I'm sure you will gain a great example from her instruction."

I noted I was given about fifteen students. The rest were all for Miss Packard, a crowd of some thirty-five. Some had just joined in the new week and Miss Packard was teaching them reading from the Bible. "How has your schooling been?" I spoke to my little troop to try to get a sense of where they all were.

An older student, named Lavinia, raised her hand. "We learned how to read from the word of the Lord. It is marvelous in our eyes."

Some of the students laughed at her, but her words relaxed me. "I'm so glad to hear it. It's a good way to get started. Miss Packard says you have businesses. What do you do?"

"Take in wash." A new voice in the back spoke out, strong and sure. "It's one of the few things we can do."

I turned to the woman who spoke. She looked familiar to me. I saw her on the way to school. She was the young woman with the children in the yard who were lugging buckets of water to her tin vessel. I did not feel it would be appropriate to bring that up, though, so I leaned forward in welcome on my appointed stool. "I would think it would be hard to be here with the washing needed to be done."

"We come as we can."

"What's your name?"

"Deborah. I let my girl and boy watch out for the pots in the morning. I can leave at lunch time and check them before I put the wash in to boil."

"How old are your children?"

"They are nine. Twins. My girl came first."

"Fascinating. But they should be in school."

A fierce look dawned on Deborah's face. "I come to get the schooling and then I can tell it to them. Figure this math you teaching will help me to know more about how some of these misses try to cheat me when I drop off the wash on Fridays."

"Cheat you?"

Lavinia scoffed. "People don't try to be honest with the washerwomen. They always cutting corners, but they want their clothes to be snow-white, like them."

"That isn't fair though. Workers deserve to be paid a fair wage."

Lavinia gave me a close look. "Bless your young heart. We do it because no one else will."

That was clear. I turned back to Deborah. "What about your young ones? Your young girl. Shouldn't she be in school? And for the boy, there is the boy's school, the Atlanta Baptist Seminary."

They looked so frightened at the possibility I shut my mouth, and resolved to take it up with Miss Packard at the end of the day. Instead, I showed them how to take up their slates and divide it into columns to begin to enter in amounts and account for their earnings.

It was good to be involved in some purposeful work. The day flew by. There was a lunch recess, but not all of them returned.

"Why not?" I asked one of the seven students who did come back after the morning session.

"You heard Deborah. Sometimes, they have to see to the washing. Takes a lot of work, so they either come late or they will be back tomorrow."

I taught my students some more about adding up the columns of numbers in the books.

My hem was ringed with red mud at the end of the day, but I was on fire and determined to help more than ever. These women lived such difficult lives. My heart was touched at their desire to learn. What strength and dignity.

I had some questions for Miss Packard as we came up the steps together at the end of the day, and there, in a horse and shay, was the Reverend Gabriel Harmon, looking down at me from on high and smiling.

CHAPTER 4

"How was your first day, Miss Harper?"

"What are you doing here, sir?" I looked far from nice. My happy green and blue stripes were pulled down by the new red mud hem I had acquired. The basement had gotten no cooler during the day. Miss Packard made the decision to dismiss at four so we could come up out of the basement to breathe again before the really hot part of the day took hold.

"I've come to take you home."

Miss Packard smiled. "I do so appreciate it, Reverend. I can get home to check on Hattie much faster and incur no additional expense by taking a cab." She alighted next to him, which left me to scramble up to the back seat of the shay.

"Thank you for the ride." I kept my voice low, and wondered at how his arms bulged from his rolled up sleeves. I determined not to wonder at the way his fingers laced through the leather reins.

"You are very welcome. You neglected to answer my question."

"I'm happy to meet the students and to help them in their learning. I can't help but wonder, though, at some of their circumstances."

"What do you mean, dear?"

"There are older ones who have children. What do the children do while they are in school? Where is the school for them?"

"They are at home, doing some work, or working jobs, from what I understand."

"They are children." My throat thickened. "Why aren't they in the school with them?"

"We tried it at first, dear. But the Mission objected. So, we had to back off of that aim and teach those over fifteen. I think Deborah, who you had this morning, has been instructing her twins at home."

"That doesn't seem to be a great solution. Can't there be a school for the young ones?"

The look Miss Packard and the Reverend exchanged didn't elude me. Oh, how much I had to tell my mother of these injustices. Maybe I should ask her what she thought should happen. "I've been working on some solutions, Miss Harper. Through the church. But there has been some force against it."

"Why?"

"If everyone were in school, there wouldn't be anyone to do the wash. So, someone stays out to work."

"What is this insanity? Everyone needs education."

"But the community of whites here need for the washing to be done at a certain rate of pay. So, this is the way it has worked out."

Something in me wanted to smash things. What kind of world was this where children couldn't go to school, but stayed at home to do wash? Deborah's earnest, brown face rose up before me. I knew she would pass on the rudiments to her children, but there had to be another way.

The shay pulled up in front of Miss Packard's boarding house and she scrambled out. I told her to give Miss Giles my greetings and the horse high stepped over the mud.

"Are you sure you don't want to come up front with me?" Gabriel spoke over his shoulder with too much pleasantness in his voice.

"I'm fine back here, Reverend, thank you."

"You know, I'm the one who could easily be mad at you, Miss Harper."

"For what?"

"I don't know. You ran out on me."

I leaned forward. "Do you want to know why I ran out on you?"

"Please. Edify me."

I shivered at his use of the word. "I don't want to be a minister's wife." There. I said it. Let him think what he wanted of me.

"My. I had only asked you to dinner."

"What is the point of starting something that could only end in heartbreak? Cut the bud off before it has a chance to bloom."

I folded my arms in front of me. Protection.

That wasn't stopping him though. He stopped the horse and turned around to look at me with that gaze of his. "That's not how to live life, Miss Harper. You cannot be afraid to live your life. And I would have you know ministers are men too. Men of God, but men as well."

"That has little to do with me." I pressed in my arms in to calm my heart down.

"I'll show you. Let me take you to dinner."

Oh. This man was trying to get to me through food. He knew me, somehow. He knew I didn't want to go back to Mrs. Turner's and eat her burned something she would have prepared.

Then I thought of something.

"I cannot go to dinner with you, alone. That wouldn't be proper."

"Oh, no. I understand. We're going to have dinner with some parishioners. You'll be properly chaperoned."

Well, then. My shoulders rounded a bit. "Oh. Thank you."

No kisses with this man, then. He might have been a bit of fun, if nothing else. But I am new here, and I should have been happier because he has a care for my person. My hungry person.

"Would you like to refresh yourself at the boarding house before we depart?"

"That's a nice thought, thank you."

The good reverend smiled and turned around to drive with me attached to the back of the shay as if I were a wealthy lady.

❧ ❧ ❧

Mrs. Turner looked hurt I wasn't staying for dinner this night, but when she saw the Reverend out front in his shay, she wished me a good time at dinner. I had no need for her good wishes. It was just dinner.

I put on something more sober and thanked my Lord I had other shoes to wear. My white lace-up boots were coated in thick, red Georgia mud and dust. I put on my fancy, but still dressy, dark blue boots to match my conservative blue skirt and white shirtwaist. It was hot, so I brushed the hair up off of my neck again, but tied on a festive, matching blue bow around my curls.

When I came back out, Gabriel was standing talking to Mrs. Turner and he stopped speaking and regarded me with obvious favor. Mrs. Turner announced, "I made some cornbread, but I know you have some place to be. Have a good time and don't stay out too late. You got school in the morning."

He reached out for my hand and helped me up into the front seat next to him in the shay. I put my hand in his and was surprised at how work-roughened it was. I wonder why. Most preachers I knew, or at least the ones in training, had softer hands. Except for Reverend Smithson, Mama Manda's husband, in Milford. He worked harder than just about anyone I knew. But once I was safely in the seat, I jerked my hand away, lest he get any ideas.

"Where are we going to dinner?"

"With one of my parishioners."

"Won't that be starting something? To have them see you bringing someone to dinner? I've seen it before with pastors who are single who look as if they are courting a woman. It's like vultures."

"Oh, really? How would you know, Miss Harper?"
"I know."

"I'm actually helping you with your recruiting work for the Seminary. These parishioners have young daughters."

I perked up. "Well, lead on, then."

He laughed a little and started the horses. I didn't brace myself for the start and fell into him a little bit.

I righted myself quickly. His body was as hard as the baseboard and Lord knew I didn't need to be thinking that.

"Were you born enslaved?"

Gabriel sobered himself. "I was. Son of the master, as if you couldn't tell."

"Your hair is a dead giveaway. As well as your nose."

He was quiet for a minute, and then he reached up to feel the organ I had just mentioned. "What's wrong with it?"

"It's a little narrow for one of our persuasion. You wouldn't get into the club with that nose."

He laughed and he had a very nice laugh. I knew that already, though. We had done a lot of laughing in November, hadn't we? So why was his laugh something new to me now? "Won't you let me in as an honored guest, Mary?"

He was whispering in my ear now and I tried to shift myself over a bit on the side board, just a little, but not enough to pitch myself over the side. He also had nice pepperminty, kissable breath. I breathed out. "It's not for me to say, Reverend."

"You should just call me Gabriel."

"I cannot. I wasn't brought up that way. Titles must be adhered to. You are Reverend. I am Miss Harper. Maybe if we are friends enough, I can call you Reverend Gabriel. But that's all."

Was he smiling at me? No, he was focused on the road, as he should be. "I see how it is with you. Proper protocol then."

"Yes. Exactly." I folded my hands before me, glad he understood.

୧୨ ୧୨ ୧୨

He pulled up in front of a nice brownstone house in Summer Hill, not too far from his church. Thankfully, he was the soul of propriety in helping me down from the shay. His touch stirred some feeling inside of me, but once I was on steady ground, I took my hand back from his and I smoothed down my skirts, righting myself. I focused instead on the delicious smell wafting from the house tickling my nose. "That smells wonderful, doesn't it, Reverend?"

"The Gregsons always invite me on Mondays when they have roast beef and Yorkshire pudding. But I have to say, that's pretty typical when I get invited to dinner." He opened a little gate in front of the house so I could walk through.

"It is?"

"Why, yes, Miss Harper. Everyone brings out their best when the Reverend comes to dinner. Happens every time. But as you can tell by my shape, I try not to take in too much of it."

Then he walked in front of me so that I could better observe him.

Oh, if this weren't a hot June day. If I had an umbrella, I would have hit him with it. I searched the corners of my brain to prepare a speech to upbraid him with about the evils of vanity. Didn't the Bible say something on it? The fact that I didn't exactly know, further proved my inability to be a minister's wife.

But before I could think of something, the front door opened and an older woman emerged. "Oh, Reverend, I'm so glad you came, and brought Miss Harper with you! We are so honored."

He dipped his head in greeting and touched me on the small of my back to usher me forward. "The pleasure is all mine, ma'am. Thank you. But one word of understanding before we enter your lovely home."

Mrs. Gregson's kind featured arranged themselves in confusion and I studied him as well. What in the world?

I saw some mischief dancing in his warm brown eyes. "Miss Harper is not at all interested in marrying a minister. She is here in her capacity to recruit your daughters to consider attending the illustrious Atlanta Female Baptist Seminary, where she is presently engaged as a teacher."

Mrs. Gregson relaxed herself. "Why yes, of course." She reached over and grasped at my hands. "We certainly welcome you here as a teacher. And as a daughter of such an esteemed poet. My daughters have prepared an evening's entertainment after we eat. I hope you don't mind."

Such entertainment probably entailed some recitation of my mother's poetry, knowledge no well brought up young woman of the race would do without. "Of course, ma'am. I do not know what the good Reverend is talking about."

"Why, Miss Harper. I am only speaking of the conversation we had earlier today. I only wanted the circumstances of your dining here to be clear to any bird's nest we might visit to eat."

Mrs. Gregson let go of my hands and extended her arm in hospitality. "Please enter our home, for whatever reason, and make yourself welcome."

The so-called good Reverend touched the small of my back again, and his touch sent warmth throughout my lower regions. "You don't play fair do you?" I whispered through my tight lips.

"I don't know what you mean." He whispered back.

I sallied forth into the parlor, determined to enjoy the evening in spite of his low tactics.

I knew my own mind and meant to keep to it.

CHAPTER 5

Mrs. Gregson led us to a table laden with the promised roast beef and Yorkshire pudding cooked in the drippings, potatoes, celery and carrots cooked in gravy, salad, and glasses filled with frosty lemonade. A double-crusted pie and a layer cake swirling with white, boiled frosting waited on the side board.

"You certainly set a generous table, ma'am." I sat down in the chair Gabriel held out for me. He went on the other side of the table and sat down, giving me a most unminister-like grin.

"Oh my. We have to take care of Reverend Harmon while he's with us. When I heard he was without a wife, I knew nothing else would do but that we see to him while he's here serving as our summer minister."

"I was not aware of that." I held up my plate for my share, indicating to Mr. Gregson to give me some of everything. Fill my plate up, sir.

"That I have no wife or I'm only a temporary replacement for the esteemed Reverend Jones?"

"Yes, that." I accepted my plate and waited for Gabriel to lower his hooked nose, and say the blessing over the food.

He wasn't long or outrageous with it. He spoke to God with a touching humility and included a nice blessing for the Gregsons and their lovely daughters who were dining with us, Lena, Margaret and another Mary. We were everywhere.

"How did you receive your training, Reverend Harmon?" I asked him as I cut into the fork-tender beef and made a perfect forkful with a little dab of pudding, slice of carrot and one chunk of onion.

"Oh, come, Miss Harper. We cannot have the dinner conversation focused on me. I'm sure these young women would rather hear about your time at Milford College and how you traveled all kinds of places in the past year as a member of the Milford College choir."

"Indeed, not. All of you heard yesterday how I got into the choir on my good graces. No, sir, I would rather you tell how someone like you came to be a minister."

Ha! He would not win all of the points tonight.

"Well, as I told you before we arrived and the Gregsons before, my father was a slave owner who happened to fall in love with one of his enslaved maids, my mother. Because he was single himself, he sought to make provisions for myself and my brothers as much as Georgia law would permit him."

"So you did not grow up in true bondage?"

"Not at all. I was educated in the best possible way from the beginning. He decided the church would be the best place for me to be as a man of color at this time. The first and only place where I would be respected and dignified. And I should use my advantage to help others of my race."

"What a touching love story." Mrs. Gregson put her fork down. I had no such intention.

"It is, ma'am, but I recognize how unusual it is. It's part of my purpose in life to work to a better end for more in our race."

"Well, Reverend Harmon knows of our origins, but coming to Atlanta when the bad times came to an end was something we never regretted. My husband found much success in making bricks here to help rebuild this city after Sherman came though it in '64. So, in the wake of reconstruction, we were able to acquire much and to build a sure foundation for our daughters."

"I see. They are lovely girls. The Seminary has been more in the project of educating older women instead of the younger ones."

"Yes, and all need education, surely." Gabriel interrupted and I was struck to see the look of concern on his face. So we had something in common, then.

"What do you propose to do, sir?" I asked him after swallowing another one of those perfect mouthfuls.

"Well, clearly, Miss Packard and Miss Giles are in need of a better place than the basement of Friendship Baptist Church."

"I would completely agree. Is an invitation to your church forthcoming then?"

Ah. A hit.

"Alas, I've asked. Many of the population Misses Packard and Giles seek to serve live too far from Summer Hill."

"My dear, we are working to help. We have to lift up the women who live on the west side of Atlanta. Education will help. So, it's fortunate people like you were willing to come and help." Mrs. Gregson insisted.

"I did not know what was there, but now I do. It will be hard to leave from what was also intended to be a temporary teaching assignment."

"So, we both lack permanent status then. We have that in common." Gabriel speared a chuck of beef and chewed it with his well-formed and juicy-looking lips.

"There is something about summer and relationships which lack permanence in the cold light of day, I believe."

"We believe differently, Miss Harper. Summer can be the time when the heat sparks the best long-lasting fire."

Mrs. Gregson waved the handkerchief at herself. "More of something, Miss Harper?"

I speared my last potato. Usually, I would have loaded up for more food, but Gabriel's words gave me pause. "No, thank you."

"I'll have more. I have to be ready for any and all battles before me." Gabriel gave the strangest look to the quiet Mr. Gregson, who seemed to be busy wiping at his wiry moustaches with a fine napkin.

Mr. Gregson filled his plate again, while the Gregson daughters drew me off to the parlor in order to show how well and good they knew my mother's fine poetry.

Usually, the depth of my mother's accomplishment went right over my head, but tonight, her words soothed me. The narration of "A Mother's Blessing" which she wrote to celebrate my birth, reminded me I needed to write her to tell her of all that had happened. But I could hardly tell her everything. Something had to remain close to my heart.

ꙮ ꙮ ꙮ

Gabriel's treatment toward me was the main torment of my night and into the next morning when I put on my plainest apparel and walked to the church the next morning. I knew I would pass Deborah's house again, but this time, I wandered down the pathway to the front door of her house. In the front yard, two small children lugged wooden buckets filled with water to a big tin washtub, filling it up as much as they could from a dripping spigot at a stable from next door. "Hello."

The children started at me in my stark apparel. They were no doubt frightened because I looked so stern. But a stern nature was a quality needed for a good teacher and I was bound to do my best. I fished in my pocket for some lemon drops. "Would you like some?"

The boy with short black hair, which furred his head, in too-small clothes reached out for the candy, but the girl, with two stick straight braids ran away to the house, calling for her mother. Deborah emerged at the doorway, clearly harried, but stunned to see me.

"Miss Harper, I'm doing my best to get there."

"It's okay. I remembered I passed here to get to the school and I wanted to stop in and help if I could."

"Help?"

"You seem busy. What do you need to help you get to school?"

"I was trying to make some sandwiches for the children so they could eat later."

"I can help so you can get yourself ready for school. I guess your children are getting your washtubs ready."

An aura of pride dawned on her tired, tan-colored features. "Yes. They is, I mean, are a blessing. My girl is Serena. My boy out there is Pax."

"Fine names. Names of peace."

"Yes, ma'am. They are."

"I offered your girl some lemon drops, but she came in here to you. Pax took them."

Serena ran out and gave me a sidelong glance as she did so. What a beautiful young girl. I felt like a fool wearing my showy dress yesterday.

"She sees more than Pax. Pax is too trusting and I tell him all the time. But I let her know she can trust you."

"I'm glad. I want to help. I will finish their lunches and you can come with me to school." I stood, ready to help her. She pulled a loaf of bread out of a pantry, brought it to the table. Sandwiches. I could do that.

"I'm almost finished mixing up my detergents. Then we can leave."

"You make your own soaps?"

"Yes. A lot of my customers, the white ladies, say it really cleans things up."

"And you are paid how much?"

"Fifty cents for twelve pounds of washing."

I almost choked out the words. Fifty cents? For so much work. And there were a lot of fifty cent piles in this house. "I see."

"I know what you think. It's a whole lot of work for a little bit of money. Sometimes they offer me a job in they houses for some more money. A whole dollar a week. But I have my children. I can't leave them here like their father left us. And I don't want to be in someone's house.

I want my freedom. It would be too much like the bad times."

"I believe what you say. I understand." I finished smearing some kind of weak looking spread on the thick bread slices to form the "sandwiches" for the children. I thought about how I had rejected the food at Mrs. Turner's in favor of richer fare and my heart plummeted. Was teaching enough? Something had to be done to help Deborah and her precious children and washerwomen like her.

Deborah spoke out in her confident voice. "I'm finished. Let me change out of my apron and we can get going."

I was finished too. Serena came to the doorway and peered around at me.

"Would you like a lemon drop?" I offered her once again.

"I don't like candy. I'm okay."

"Of course you are. I just wanted to give a good, responsible girl like you a reward. What a blessing you and your brother are to your mother."

"Thank you."

I could see my words had their intended impact. She reached around to me and snatched the lemon drops from my palm. Her warm, small fingers scraped against my palm as she took them.

Deborah came forward, giving the children directions as she moved on to ensure the pots were ready for boiling more clothes in the hot afternoon sun when she came home for lunch. The children waved as we climbed up the hill to the road which led the Seminary school. The set of Deborah's shoulders squared in determination as she walked away from her children toward the opportunity of education, preparing for the battle of life. Her bravery inspired me to do more. And better.

CHAPTER 6

For much of the day, I couldn't get Deborah and the children from my mind. The more I taught her—the more I noticed her entering her figures on her practice sheets, and the smile, which lit her face up—the more I felt ungrateful. I guess my care showed on my face, because at lunch Miss Packard asked me if I were ill.

"I went to Deborah's house this morning." I explained when most of the students had departed for their midday break. "That may have been a mistake. I shouldn't have invaded her private life."

The sharp look her blue eyes imparted told me she agreed, but she sat in the pew across from me and listened.

"Her home, the children, dressed so raggedy, her spirit."

"Yes, Miss Harper?"

"Are we doing enough in this school? Is this enough to help, to really help?"

"I believe it is. We've given a great deal. Why, Hattie even sold her piano to show the Association we were serious in this quest. Educating women, especially bringing women of your race to the light, is important work. Do you believe otherwise?"

"No, I mean, I do. But the payoff seems so far away. I mean what about now? It's June but how do Deborah and the others keep their children warm at night?"

Miss Packard leaned in and patted my hand. "You cannot let such matters distress you. She is doing what she can to secure a future for her family. Maybe she will meet a nice man, and he will help her in the meantime. For now, we can teach her God's word and hope she stays away from fornication and continues her hard work."

I shrank back. Fornication? Who was even thinking about such things?

But I supposed that was a concern. I never even thought to ask how Deborah had gotten her twins. It never entered my head. My own father died when I was so young, I just didn't think of the twins even needing a father, because I hadn't.

"Reverend Harmon says he will come to pick us up after school again."

"He doesn't have to come every day."

"No, but he does."

"Why?"

"Well, I think he wants to make sure that we get home safely. I have to admit his good actions have helped me to save money and to get home in good time to check and care for Hattie, who improves daily. I have hopes she'll be better next week to come and sit in on your class in the mornings."

The thought of merry Miss Giles sitting in lifted me. A little.

Miss Packard gave me a sidelong glance. "But most of all, I think he admires what you are doing."

I leveled my gaze at her. "I made it plain to him. I have no intentions of marrying a minister."

"Who do you plan to marry, Miss Harper?"

"I don't know. But not someone like him."

I don't know why, but when she turned to unwrap her thick ham sandwich from its paper wrappings, I wanted to clench my fists and pound on the pews in protest.

☙ ☙ ☙

Deborah did not return after the lunch break. When I asked, Lavinia told me, "It's looking like rain."

"Rain is just about the worst thing to happen to laundry. If my girls weren't old enough to do it, I wouldn't be here." Another student informed me.

The thought of Deborah engaged in back-breaking work, trying to best a natural event, distressed me. I kept stammering and finally, I folded the Bible in front of me in frustration.

"What wrong? You doing just fine Miss Harper." Lavinia said.

"Honestly? I don't feel as if I am. Who said it was right and fair for her to be paid only fifty cents per twelve pounds of laundry? That's exploitation!"

"Expa-what?" Lavinia drew back at my words. I nodded. She looked and sounded so much like the character my mother wrote about in her Aunt Chloe poems. They were her set of poems about an older woman who, after leaving the chains of bondage, managed to learn how to read and write. My mother's poems touched the heart but what about fair pay for her labor?

"You aren't paid what you are worth, Lavinia."

"No. But we do what no one else will do. We proud of that. No shame or disgrace in it. Everyone knows Deborah is the best at what she does."

"I'm sure she's proud of her work. But there is no sin, and nothing in the Bible says she shouldn't be paid what she is worth."

They all sat there, in silence. That's how I successfully distracted them from their work and showed them how attending Atlanta Baptist Female Seminary could have been, and should have been, something more. The question was, how?

Gabriel—I mean Reverend Harmon—noticed how quiet I was later on. Once we dropped Miss Packard off to her boarding house, he spoke to me, still rigidly settled in the back. "No dinner for you today?"

"You cannot mean to tell me you get to have dinner at people's houses every day with that kind of fare?"

"Pretty much. There's not much more appealing to folks than an unmarried preacher man, you know."

"Is that why you decided to become a minister? So, you could eat for free on people?"

"No." Gabriel was serious. "I wanted to help."

That was not the answer I was expecting him to give me. Far from it.

"Yes. I understand." I told him about Deborah.

"What do you think you can do?"

"I have no idea. I'm glad to be here, but the thought that I will return to Milford in a few weeks without having helped her, or anyone else, doesn't seem right or fair."

"Then, it seems to me you can solicit help if you come with me on my weekly circuit to my parishioners."

"What? You want me to help you eat from others' tables?"

"That's not what I said. I said, you can come and talk to people I know. You'll eat better than Mrs. Turner's."

"Really? Will it be all right with them? To have an extra person at table?"

"What is the expression? To eat high on the hog, as it were? Yes, there will be plenty enough for you, Miss Mamie Harper. You bring an extra special grace to the table."

I could only see the back of his well-formed head, and the strain of his muscles as he drove the horse to take us to the next dinner spot. However, his expression grew on me so well, I almost felt comforted by it.

And that's how it all started. Perfectly innocent. Two souls engaged in an ever-present search for philanthropy from the best parts of colored Atlanta.

And getting it.

Driving around, I got the impression that, in spite of his different start in life, Gabriel knew well the life I knew as someone without a father. His tried to do for him by sending him to the best of the Negro circumstance, but still couldn't really be a very loving parent to him. I had none, but my mother, in her capacity of having to work and travel often, was a distant parent as well. There were many times I felt much closer to Mama Manda, March's mother.

Then, one day, it hit me. Amanda Smithson was a minister's wife who did as she pleased. We had just departed the Paulson house, where we had been fortunate enough to dine on roast capon with mashed potatoes and an assortment of cookies and salads.

"Is there something wrong?"

I quickly telegraphed my thought to Gabriel. "I never realized it before today."

"I have heard much of your school. How some schools in development here in Atlanta languished, but she made a success of something out there in the wilds of Georgia. It's quite a story."

"I wish I could talk with her. Milford seems so far away, just now."

"We can take a drive back for the holiday if you like."

I turned to him. "You would really wish to accompany me there?"

"Of course. If you wished it."

I thought of it for a moment, but then knew a trip of such short duration would not help me feel less homesick, nor help me to understand.

"The thought of you wishing to please me is kind, Reverend. Thank you. I'll consider it, but I would not wish to dislodge you from Atlanta or your circuit of meals."

"I wish I could see your face to tell you how much your happiness matters to me."

A silence fell between us then. His tender words were very persuasive and I knew he spoke from his heart.

Gabriel was not like any man I had ever known and I was proud to know him.

As a friend, of course.

ᔫ ᔫ ᔫ

Friday was the first day I noticed. Deborah did not attend the morning session. Friday was her delivery day for the wash. That was a task usually reserved for the children of the washerwomen. As I walked to school last Friday, I noticed children driving buggy wagons loaded with baskets of sparkling clean clothes. The sharp, acrid scent of lye hung around in the air and mingled with the sweet smell of starch, scented with lemon. It covered over the smell of summer in this part of town, where a lot of the washerwomen lived. A caravan of these buggies formed early as the children drove the wagons to north of Atlanta, where the customers lived.

I had been on the receiving end of the services from Deborah, who had washed my blue and green striped dress. She also cleaned and dusted my white boots. I hadn't worn them since my ill-advised, first day of course, but I had to marvel at her handwork.

I paid her double, of course, since that's what I thought of as fair. She didn't want to take the money, but then she did, and said it was against all of my clothes for the summer. And now, she didn't show up for school.

There were only two weeks left in the term. If she didn't attend, she would not receive her credit, nor would she receive the special certificates Miss Packard planned to give to each student who finished the job as a member of the inaugural class of the Atlanta Baptist Female Seminary.

Gabriel came for us as usual, but I told him I would walk. I needed to check on Deborah. He drove away with Miss Packard, looking quite concerned, but I assured him I would be fine.

"Here now. I cannot split you, nor deprive you of dinner with the parishioner of choice." Miss Packard had come to know of his practices. "I will take a cab."

"Are you sure, ma'am?"

"I am. After all, isn't Friday usually fish day? I know you wouldn't want to miss that." Those blue eyes twinkled at me as she hailed a cab. "Please. Check on Deborah. Sometimes this has happened before, but if she knows you care, it might importune her to return. But, Miss Harper, don't be surprised if she doesn't. We cannot possibly save all of them."

Gabriel reached down for my hand and I raised myself up to sit next to him on the buckboard. I watch the muscle in his arm ripple underneath his black broadcloth he always wore and I felt light in my head all of a sudden. I attributed to the heat of the day and turned from him, trying to be intent on focusing on the task ahead, and guided him close in on where Deborah lived.

The house seemed still, too still for my liking. The twins were gone, it seemed, but there should have been signs of life there if Deborah were within. At least, smoke from the chimney. Nothing rose from there, and there was not a sound.

Gabriel and I looked at each other. "Let's go."

He took me by the hand and laced his fingers with mine, trying not to feel fear at facing Deborah's fate. We had no choice but to face this circumstance together.

Please, Lord. Let her be okay.

CHAPTER 7

The inner part of the house smelled of the lemons Deborah used in her laundry mixture. I saw her slumped on a pallet in the corner. Bless her, the twins were the ones with bedsteads, tied tight in the corner and made up with some old looking quilts, but she slept on the floor. My knees were shaky when I lowered myself to look at her, and I was relieved to see she was sleeping. I shook her arm and called her name.

She startled, almost knocking me down, but then put a startled hand to her chest. "What you doing here, Miss Harper?"

"I was concerned for you when you didn't come today. I wondered if you had taken ill."

"Where are the children? What time is it? They aren't back yet?"

"No. I don't think. They aren't back yet."

"It shouldn't take them all day to get the money. Where can they be?"

Gabriel stepped forward looking like a hero out of a fairy book with his long black hair swept back from his forehead. "I can start looking for them. Tell me where they deliver."

"My customers are all along Peachtree Street. Up by 12th and south of there."

"I can ride up there. You stay here with Deborah." He patted my arm and I helped Deborah to stand.

"He can help, okay?" Deborah was the one shaking now and leaned on me. I put an arm around her. "Let's get you some food while he's going for the children."

"I didn't mean to sleep long, Miss Harper. I was up all night long finishing the wash. I wanted to come today. I hope I'm not in trouble cause I wasn't there."

"No, no. Come on and sit down. I can fix you something." I started opening up cupboards and saw, with not too little shock, how bare they were. There was nothing to eat.

Deborah smoothed her rough hair over with her hands and reached for a scarf, deftly twisting her hair up into the scarf with her hands. "Fridays is when I shop for food once the children have come back with the money. I don't have anything until they get back."

There was a handful of dried up onions in a basket. Not even any potatoes. "Well, we want to have something for them when they get back. I can go out and get something and we'll fix it for when Gabriel brings them back."

"I don't have any money to pay you, Miss Harper."

"That's okay. We need to get something together for all of us when Gabriel returns with the children. Will you be okay here?"

I knew where the local market was, since Deborah didn't live far from me. I rushed there and with my earnings for the week, bought some ingredients for a stew and hurried back to her house with them.

"We can make a chicken stew. Let's get it ready."

Her eyes grew large. "A stew. We haven't had anything like that for a time. I don't know how I can repay you. I can do more wash for you."

"Oh, Deborah. I appreciate it. Your clothes smell so much fresher than anyone else. Thank you."

We worked silently together, and soon, a fragrant stew was bubbling away on the cook stove.

"I don't have no bread or nothing."

"We can put some dumplings in there with the flour you have. It will be okay."

"I don't know how to thank you, Miss Harper. I really don't."

To my amazement, she burst into tears. I embraced her. "What ever is the matter?"

"I wanted to show you I'm a good student, and instead you see me so hungry and tired. Can't even provide for my children."

"Deborah, I don't think of you like that at all. We're just waiting for the children to return. Once they do, it will be okay. You'll be caught up again. Please don't worry."

"You are good people, Miss Harper. Thank you."

I stirred the stew several times to help it not develop a crust. I knew how to do that much, at least. Just as I was about to give it all up and try to encourage Deborah to eat, Gabriel came through the door with the children. The sun was about to set in the sky and I couldn't keep the words from my lips since I was concerned too. "Where have you been?"

Deborah gave a cry like I had never heard before and ran to the children. The way she clasped the children and greeted them made me wish my own mother had embraced me like that.

"What's that smell ma?" Pax said.

"Miss Harper. She been here with me and made you all something good to eat. Why were you gone so long?"

Streaks of white tear tracks traced down Serena's small, brown face. "We went to drop off the laundry and get paid like always, one day early, and they didn't give us the right amount. I tried to say they didn't give us enough, but they wouldn't listen and slammed the door in my face, ma."

Gabriel put an arm around the girl's shoulder as my insides took a dive to my practical boots. "They had called the police on her and I was able to explain I knew them and would bring them home. I got there just in time."

"Ma, we need the money. They have plenty and wouldn't pay. Our laundry is always good."

Deborah patted them. "I know, honey. I know. Give me what you got and go on and wash your faces to eat some of this stew."

Serena put money into her mother's hand and like the little mother she was, took her brother by the hand and out to the wash pump.

Deborah's hand shook as she counted the money. "A dollar and a half. Half of what I was supposed to get. What are we going to do now?"

Gabriel gave a sharp look at me. I had nearly emptied out my pockets to pay for the chicken and vegetables for the stew. I could get more but it would take time. "Sit down with the children and eat, please."

Deborah sat down at the meager table. "Please, Reverend. Say grace for us."

"Dear Lord, watch over this family. Help them to see the injustice that reigns in Your world isn't from You. We need to keep You close to us and help us figure a way to blessings. At the same time, Lord, help us to see the blessings we have in each other. Thank You. Amen."

When I opened my eyes, Gabriel's face had a closed look. "Please, stay to eat some of this stew. We can't eat it all." Deborah offered.

That might be true. In one sitting. But they could have it tomorrow. I looked at him, ready to suggest we go to Mrs. Turner's and be grateful for whatever burned goodness she had to offer.

But then he stepped forward. "We would be honored. Sit down and eat, Miss Harper."

I sat as he directed and choked out a small portion with a dumpling. Deborah, no doubt, felt relief to be able to eat a good meal with her children. Something was sustaining her into not worrying, while my stomach was clenched too tightly to admit many chunks of chicken or vegetables into my mouth. What could be done for Deborah and her family? What right did people have to not pay a good woman her due wages?

After the humble fare, Gabriel suggested to Pax that they wash the dishes while I went over the day's work with Deborah so that she didn't fall behind in her lessons.

Something triggered a hitch in my heart as I watched him work with the boy while I showed Deborah the necessary calculations on her board. Serena watched us, I believed, and Gabriel showed me it was true, that I learned something new today. I had to sort it all out.

୬ ୬ ୬

"Pax and Serena are very special children. I want to bring them to my church for the picnic." Gabriel intoned as he drove me home in the shay. I finally allowed myself to sit next to him instead of on the little seat behind.

"You would leave their mother behind?" I was a little shocked at his cavalier attitude as he drove me home, practically around the corner.

"No, but sometimes mothers need a little time to themselves."

"I guess that's why I was always getting left behind."

"What do you mean?"

"My mother. I was always getting left behind for her to appear in one place or another. I understood after a time, but I've always had to look out for myself. It made me think if I had children, I wouldn't leave them alone so much."

He dropped the reins from his beautiful fingers, now that we were in front of the boarding house. "That explains so much about what you wanted to do for those children. And their mother. It was wonderfully giving and compassionate of you. That's who I always knew you were."

His kind eyes regarded me. And I'm well used to being regarded, but his looking at me was another thing entirely. Tingles ran up and down my spine, almost as if they were preparing a pathway for Gabriel to trace those same fingers on me.

The way he was looking at me made me feel sorry I had let so many unimpressive boy-men kiss me before this. It also made me feel sorry that a kiss, a small harmless kiss, was all I could ever have of this kindly soldier for the Lord. But I had always sought to have my way, from a very young age. So, I was going to take it.

I leaned into him and tilted my face just so and for a split second. Just for an instant, I wondered. Was this his first kiss?

Something about the way he was tilting to me was not experienced. It was untried and an unseen hand pulled me back from him and I jumped down from the buckboard. "Good night, Gabriel." I shouted out over my shoulder and hurried into the parlor, into the safety of Mrs. Turner's house so I didn't have to ask him any more questions about anyone else who might have come before me.

I didn't want to hear about it.

CHAPTER 8

The weekend turned out nothing as I thought because some foolish man in Washington D.C. went and shot the president. As he promised, Gabriel brought his horses and shay and we all went to church at Summer Hill. Miss Packard didn't mind, and she gave me kind of a strange look when I asked her if I could attend his church once more. "Dear Hattie has improved, so I'm taking her with me to the church we will visit this weekend. And she will be in class with you on Tuesday."

After some indecision, they had decided not to have class on Independence Day, a fact that disappointed the students, but gave Deborah some happiness as we went to church together, heard Gabriel preach and joined in the fun at a picnic afterward. There was a newly created park just down the road from the church and we walked there to allow the children an outlet to expend their energy. Gabriel made for a great impromptu force to watch the children while Deborah and I linked arms and strolled to the picnic where all of the church ladies had set up a wonderful buffet.

Deborah spoke up in her direct way. "I'm sorry about Garfield, Lord knows. I'll be praying for him. But, Miss Harper, I'ma always be thankful for the blessing God gave me by putting you in my life. I'm sorry to see school end and to have you go."

"Well, we never know where life will take us. I'm open to all options." I patted her hand and smiled across to her.

"All of them, Miss Harper?" Deborah slid me a sly gaze.

Oh my. They say this happens to teachers. Sometimes your students teach you.

"Most of them."

"I think you should stay open to all possibilities, as you said. He's a good man. It would be a shame to see someone else of these church women get him because you were scared."

"Scared?"

"You're my teacher in the classroom, but I'm older than you. I've seen more. I've seen enough. That's a good man, and a handsome man, who is very interested in you. That's all I'm going to say. And I say, you need to stop being scared."

"I appreciate that thought, Deborah. Thank you."

"You welcome. And I think you need to have some chicken stew at the wedding this winter. You did a good job with it."

I patted her hand a little more sharply this time, as a reprimand.

Marry? Gabriel? I could see it, but I still had my reservations. I still wasn't sure my unorthodox ways wouldn't come to shame him in the end. And if they did, and it tore us apart, it would be sadder than I could ever say.

Watching him play hopscotch with the children as we walked to the park made hug myself against the warm July day.

Now was all I had to give him.

☙ ☙ ☙

Miss Giles sat in on the Tuesday morning session. She sat on a pew mixed in with the other students. I would not have known it was her, but for her pale face sticking out from the usual brown faces of my students. When they dismissed for lunch, of course, she remained behind and Miss Packard came to us with their lunch pail in hand. I brought forward mine and we sat on the benches with our sandwiches.

"Your energy is admirable, Miss Harper." Miss Giles said. "The students really enjoy how vivid you make the subject to them."

"I appreciate the opportunity to help. What will happen next for the Seminary?"

"When school ends, Hattie and I will head back to Boston to raise funds for next year. And hopefully a new building. It was good of Father Quarles to let us have this basement, but there has been some talk of sharing space with the Atlanta Baptist Seminary side."

"We don't want to merge schools, but rather compliment the male equivalent." Miss Giles insisted.

"I see. Well, I do have to go back to school myself, but if there is anything I can do to help, let me know."

"You have helped us so much, dear. If we had to close after this first session, I don't know how we might have carried on. You were a blessing. Your time in Atlanta proves how badly your example is needed. So, we thank you. I know Deborah thanks you as well."

"And Reverend Harmon." Miss Packard said, nodding.

Miss Giles giggled a little.

"Thank you, ma'am. That's all, well, up in the air now."

"You should determine to get him nailed down." Miss Packard put forward.

"Well, I supposed some time will determine what I should do."

"You're still very young. No need to rush it." Miss Giles held up a hand.

Miss Packard retorted. "But Reverend Harmon would be a very good prospect. Marriage is a crowning jewel in a woman's life."

Well, interesting and contradictory words from ones who had not elected to marry.

I wondered why.

But the students had started to filter back into the classroom so that question would have to wait for another day.

၉ ၉ ၉

The talk from lunch filtered back in with the students and made it hard for them to concentrate.

They were all in a bit of a distemper, so I asked them what was wrong.

Deborah spoke. "I'm not the only washer woman who has been getting cheated out of her pay."

Lavinia bristled. "I don't get what is happening. Why won't these people pay us our due?"

I shook my head. "That's truly a shame."

"I heard over at Fredonia Baptist they made a society," Lavinia spoke out.

I had to think of a way to get them focused on geography, but I was curious. "What society?"

"The washerwomen in the church banded together and said they could only pay them a certain amount or they won't wash."

"Not wash?" Deborah asked. "Can they do that?"

I shook my head and stepped to her. "There are work stoppages. I've heard of them up north. In some of the steel factories."

"What do they do?"

"They banded together. They refused to work. They got someone to talk to the people to let them know their terms."

The students liked the sounds of that. "Did it work out?"

"Sometimes it does. Sometimes people can get harmed."

"Some folks tried last year. It didn't work." Another student spoke out.

"I recall it." Deborah said. "But I would be a whole lot willing to join something this year."

"We need a meeting place and a way to get word 'round. We can ask Reverend Harmon."

"You mean you can, Miss Harper. He would listen to you," Deborah put forward and the students laughed.

The sound of laughter caused Miss Packard to look backwards toward us. "We better get on with the matter of the day, in thinking of geography matters." But given what had happened and that Deborah wasn't alone, a planned work stoppage might be in order.

I could hardly wait for the day to be over and to talk with Gabriel about it. When he came to pick us up, I fairly bounced into the back of the shay to tell him.

"So, we need a meeting place and I said I would ask you. Reverend."

"I'm not sure I have the authority to lease the church out for such a matter. I would have to ask the board."

"Ask the board? Deborah and her children need more money right now. It will take them forever."

"Miss Harper, you do have to keep in mind Reverend Harmon's position is temporary. We are certainly in sympathy with Deborah and the other washerwomen, but we don't want people to have to lose position and stature to help them."

I sat back and bit my lips down. That was something that had never happened before. I wondered what was stopping me from speaking out when I would have said something before.

Gabriel saw Miss Packard into the boarding house and returned to the shay.

"Come forth and sit next to me. I need to talk to you."

He reached up to me and helped me down and up again. I nestled next to him, feeling a little woozy at all of the handing over what had just happened.

"You cannot just burst forth with whatever and whenever, Miss Harper. I have already shared these concerns."

"Why not?'

"It might be Miss Packard has different interests. She may or may not be interested in seeing the washerwomen get better pay. You must learn to be more prudent."

I never thought of it that way. And I certainly didn't consider Miss Packard might be an enemy. But Gabriel had a point. If the washerwomen were paid better, they might want to stay in those jobs and not come to Atlanta Baptist Female Seminary. Oooh....

"Well I'm sorry. Is there some plan? Or can you tell me?"

He regarded me with what looked like half a smile on his face. "Are you laughing at me?"

"Far be it from me, Miss Harper, to laugh at you. No, everything you are about to me is all seriousness."

For some reason, his words made me shiver inside. Did I tell him again I didn't want to be a minister's wife? Why was this man so contrary and stubborn?

Still, even as I thought the words, they rang hollow in my brain and resonated between my ears. It seemed I had unfairly judged Gabriel and put him into a box where he did not belong. He appeared to me more in the way of a warrior for the unjust and I found his position extremely appealing.

"Yesterday's picnic was a cover for a meeting. There were about twenty washerwomen who decided to form a society. The next meeting will take place on July 17, after ABFS finishes for the term."

My mouth went from my lips pursed together to a rounded O. "Why was it all kept so secret?"

"We don't need everyone knowing about it. People might blab."

People. Oh. People like me. As I had just done with Miss Packard.

"Well, let me help in some way."

"Believe me, you will be called upon if you are needed."

"Well, I'm going to leave Atlanta when the term is over. I can help now."

"We have to wait for some logistical things, so there's not much to do now but wait. If you aren't staying in Atlanta much past the end of the term, then you may not be needed."

"I want to stay. I don't have to be back in Milford for any real purpose until the middle of September when the term starts."

"I will think about it. In the meantime, here we are. Dinner at the Dempsey's."

I rubbed my hands together. "And fried chicken with all of the fixings."

"Indeed."

He tied up the horse and came around on the other side of his shay and lifted me down with the span of his hands on my waist and as he let me down, he smoothed himself my torso in a most unseemly way.

Well, maybe being a minister's wife had some perks I didn't know about before. Like being married to the minister.

"I promise I will be more prudent from now on." I kept my hands on his arms and they felt nice and firm underneath the pads of my fingertips.

"I hope you will not force me to trickery to keep you quiet, Miss Harper."

"You may employ all of the trickery you like, Reverend."

"I thought you felt ill against my kind."

"You have improved yourself upon further acquaintance."

I stretched myself up to meet him and our lips met in perfect timing. Ahh. So he had done this before. I mean, I had of course, but I just wasn't sure how far back the ministerly conduct had gone.

Maybe not too far, since he wrapped his large hands about my waist, almost massaging heat into my back while he kissed my lips so I was suffused with heat all through me. I was literally filled up with July and nearly August by the time he pulled away.

"Do you resolve to keep quiet from your employers, ma'am?"

I almost had forgotten what the words yes or no meant, given how his dulcet lips kissed me. So I just nodded.

"Good. Tonight, the Dempseys provide fried chicken but the recruitment begins tomorrow. This may be the last good, hot meal you get for a while."

He took me by the arm and led me up the pathway. "That's okay," I declared. "Some of my clothes are a little snug."

"I like snug. Don't you, Miss Harper?"

I was about to open my mouth and tell him what I would like, but Mrs. Dempsey and her honey biscuits with hot fried chicken beckoned to me. I would not have stopped for anything less.

ℰℐ ℰℐ ℰℐ

So the recruitment for the Washing Amazons was on. And Gabriel was right. We had no time for luxurious dinners any longer. We had to go through some of the worst places in town to let people know about the Society. They had pulled together to provide a pot of money for the strike, so the washerwomen and their children didn't need to be hungry during the course of the strike.

Gabriel was chosen to be the one who would negotiate with the employers for the fee they set. People figured that with his heritage and coloring, he was closer to them and would know how to help them achieve their obstacle.

The time for the completion ceremony for Atlanta Baptist Female Seminary had come to an end. I wore an all-white dress to the occasion, as did all of the students. The service was held in the main part of the church so the students could see each other in the light now, as opposed to the darkness.

They were so proud of their accomplishments, and I was very proud I had been there to help them. Father Frank Quarles read an address and Miss Packard and Giles stood together to give the students their certificates. I almost cried when I saw the sun emerge on Deborah's face at her achievement. Serena and Pax sat with me and they both exhibited the right amount of pride at what their mother had done.

I was proud of what she and the other washerwomen were about to do by taking control of their destiny and taking a strike for liberty. I never expected, though, the next thing that would happen.

CHAPTER 9

It was New Hope Baptist's turn to have the next meeting the following day on Saturday. Gabriel offered to come by and pick me and Deborah up. The children would stay at home, since they had delivered Deborah's laundry on Friday. We were sure they would be bored by the business stuff to be included in the meeting.

Since it was Saturday, the day most others delivered wash, we expected an easy path to New Hope. But to our surprise, there appeared to be swarms of people who were making their way there. Gabriel started to be afraid there would be no room for the horses. And he was one of the featured speakers who had to go to the podium that had been erected the front on the church stairs.

He did find a place, but we had to walk a long way through crowds.

"Who are all of these people?"

Deborah had a smile on her face. "They like me. Washerwomen."

"Washing Amazons," I said, taking up the name the local newspaper tried to make up to hurt us.

I couldn't believe there were so many well-dressed women of the race who swarmed about us, looking fresh and cool in their best, in spite of the hot July day. "It's incredible."

"You all did a good job getting the word out." Deborah fairly jumped up and down, like she was a child with no cares.

I grasped Gabriel's arm, in spite of myself and Gabriel clasped my hand. "We did this. So many people!"

"Get up there, Reverend! Tell them what we've planned." I shouted at him. Clearly, I had no idea what I was doing.

Until.

He looked down at me and it was not anything like we had been surrounded by thousands of people. No. We were all alone in the middle of the crowd by ourselves.

"I need you up there with me. You helped, Miss Harper. I mean, Mamie. Please. Come."

"I'm…."

"Don't tell me you are shy."

I couldn't help but laugh. "No, that's not what I was going to say."

"You still don't like ministers."

"I didn't say that either."

"Well?"

"Let's get up there! The washerwomen need you."

"They need us."

He took me by the hand and led me through the crowd to some stairs on the edge of a building. I recognized some of the other ministers and greeted them.

New Hope's minister waved his arms and the crowd silenced. "Thank you! Washerwomen, we will not continue to accept just anything! They will come to see you and know of the valuable service you provide! Unite!"

The Washerwomen took up the chant. Chills ran up and down my spine at the way they made the chant ring out, and I knew I would never forget this moment. "We could do anything. We could conquer the world!"

"No one will go pick up wash on Monday. No one."

The crowd fell silent. This was it. They were about to do it. I stood silently next to Gabriel, our hands entwined together and me grasping on his powerful forearm.

"We will stay at home!" one woman shouted.

"That's right. If you see any sister washerwomen sneaking out, you must chase after her and convince her. This will not work unless we all stay out. Everyone. Each church has been set up with resources to help you through the strike. It may take time. It may take several weeks or days, but the washerwomen must be heard."

The women all clapped and shouted. I felt a strange wind at my left and I turned away from Gabriel to meet it and I saw some police officers approaching the stage. I grasped Gabriel's hand. "They are coming for us."

"We aren't doing anything wrong. Stand firm."

I gripped on to him tighter, but the angry looks on the men's faces didn't help me to feel calm.

"This here gathering is illegal. We are going to tell you coloreds one time to go home. Get on out of here."

No one moved. Not one bit. No one said anything. The minister of New Hope stepped forward. "We have the right to peaceful assembly."

"Get on home, I said." The man pushed at the minister, showing how low he was willing to go.

The minister pushed back. When a minister is willing to get mean, it's a sure sign of trouble. A sure sign chaos was about to break out. Sure enough, other police came in and started shoving at people, trying to get them to leave.

Gabriel took me in his arms and rushed off of the stage with me. Everyone was running everywhere and every which way. We ran into an alley way between some houses. "Where is Deborah?" I yelled back at him.

"I didn't see her, are you okay?"

"I'm fine. We have to find Deborah. She has to get back to the children."

He wrapped his arms around me and I hugged him back, feeling his large body over me, protecting me. "This is madness. It's like the way I felt when I first met you. I wanted not to respond to you, but Mamie, you bring me such joy. I need you in my life."

"Why are you talking this way while everything is so crazy?"

"I may not have the courage at another time. Or you will think of reasons to turn me down. I'm not listening to it anymore."

He lowered his face to mine, kissing my lips with such dizzying effect. Those wonderful kisses wiped from my mind all doubts about ministers as men. This was a man. Oh, yes.

Things quieted but for the most part, it was a peaceful dispersal. The stage area, still and quiet now, stood reminding me of all that had been said.

He guided me back up the street to where his horse continued to stand and we took the carriage back to Deborah's house. She was not there.

"You stay here. I will find out what happened to her."

Serena burst into tears and threw her arms around my middle. It was as if I had been smacked in the head. "Find her and bring her home."

"I will."

He stepped to me and kissed me on my hungry mouth once more. I didn't care what the children saw. I wanted to—no, needed to—transmit all of my support to him.

Once Gabriel left, I pulled Pax into my embrace as well. "She's going to be okay. I promise it."

What I really meant was, they would be okay. And I hoped their mother would know that, no matter what happened.

☙ ☙ ☙

Gabriel came back late at night to say Deborah had been arrested. "Lots of us left when the police said to leave, but Deborah and a handful of washerwomen refused. So they arrested her with some others. To make an example of them."

"That's awful."

"We can see to them on Monday, because they won't let us have access to them over Sunday. Nothing to do but go to bed." He stared down at me. "You cannot stay here alone. I'll make a pallet on the floor. You go sleep with Serena. She would want to make sure the children would be okay."

Once he said it, there was nothing else to be done. I squeezed myself onto the tied bed with Serena, while she slept. The poor girl's face was crusted over with tears.

The next morning, I made everyone some porridge for breakfast, and we all went to Summer Hill church together.

To be sure, our arrival, together with some other woman's children, was causing a stir, but I didn't care. Deborah deserved to be honored and Gabriel did when he preached a fine sermon, honoring the sacrifices of the Washerwomen. What a strange place I found myself in now, watching Gabriel proudly from the front of the church with a well-behaved child on either side of me. Watching us, one might think we were a little family of some kind.

But it was not going to be. Deborah's children would return to her and I would return to Milford. Gabriel would move on from this summer position and everything would be resolved.

Still, when I went to the back of the church to use the facilities, I overheard some of the Summer Hill women refer to me as the "teacher on the ant-hill."

I remembered Miss Packard told me, ant-hill was the mean name some had for the Atlanta Baptist Female Seminary school. The old cats were at it again.

Dazed, I made my way back to my seat, and put my arms around the children. It was one thing for me to believe I didn't suit as a minister's wife.

It was another thing for someone else to believe it.

CHAPTER 10

It took Gabriel three days to retrieve Deborah from jail.

"How is it going?"

"I guess Reverend Harmon told you about the washing license idea." I told her after she had the chance to have a bath and to restore herself from the ordeal of prison. Gabriel proposed the women have a license they would lease from the city to conduct their jobs, in exchange for higher pay. "It seems as if people are thinking about it. They aren't missing clean clothes yet."

"It's going to take weeks. Watch." Deborah's confident spirit seemed to be low. Maybe jail had done that to her.

"Lord, I hope not. I hope all is resolved when I have to return to Milford."

"Everything doesn't run on Milford time, Miss Harper. You will see. These people going to decide they don't need our clean clothes. And that's a shame because we were the one thing keeping most of them from the gutter."

I got an idea. Another one. "Maybe if we wrote a letter so that they could see it."

"Not we. You. You're a teacher. You need to write it, so we can all sign it. Let them know how we feel."

"You know I'm willing to help in any way."

I went to Mrs. Turner's myself to retrieve the pen and the paper. In the meantime, Deborah had gathered the women from the jail who had been incarcerated along with her. They were the leaders in each of the washing societies that had been formed, a special sisterhood in the same struggle, so I could certainly understand they had something to say. It was a little crowded in Deborah's house, but her face shone with joy at having the chance to be heard.

After a lot of thought and some verbal insistence, they had me write the following:

Mr. Jim English, Mayor of Atlanta, Washing Society

Dear Sir:

We, the members of our society, are determined to stand to our pledge and make extra charges for washing, and we have agreed, and are willing to pay $25 to $50 for licenses as a protection, so we can control washing for the city. We can afford to pay these licenses, and will do it before we will be defeated, and then we will have full control of the city's washing at our own prices, as the city has control of our husbands' work at their prices. Don't forget this. We hope to hear from your council Tuesday morning. We mean business this week or no washing.

Yours respectfully,

ભ ભ ભ

I thought it was a respectable letter.

Gabriel did not.

He was not very happy when he saw the letter in the Atlanta Constitution, after it had been pointed out to him. "Did you write the letter?"

There was no need to hide from him. "I did. Along with the leaders of the Washing Societies."

"It sounds like you. 'Don't forget this.' Indeed."

"Well, how else were they supposed to make it clear about no washing?"

"Sometimes people won't like it if these things are forced."

"Well, some action had to be taken. Children will go hungry if not."

Gabriel eyed me evenly. "It appears we have had our first disagreement, Miss Harper."

I eyed him back. "We have always disagreed."

"Is that your end opinion of me?"

I swallowed. "It would seem so."

"Well, once you learn to trust other people, the world will be a better place."

"It might indeed, Reverend Harmon."

We said nothing to one another in the thick silence of the hot July afternoon. When he dropped me off at the boarding house, he guided his horse away from me without so much as a goodbye. And there it was. Like I had always thought. I ruined it.

I always did.

ဢ ဢ ဢ

July became August. The mayor and the people were willing to pay the dollar per twelve pounds the woman wanted. We rejoiced in pure celebration.

Until the landlords all across Atlanta started to raise rents, thus offsetting any gain the women made in salary.

Poor Deborah and the other Amazons. They were—more or less—right back where they started.

As was I. What a failure I was. I had planted the seeds of rebellion in their bosoms. The seeds had taken deep root but had been plucked out by the enemy.

So, on a hot August morning, instead of taking myself to Summer Hill Baptist church, after packing my things and saying goodbye to the ones who cared for me in Atlanta, I took the train back to Milford to prepare for the upcoming term.

ဢ ဢ ဢ

I was very pleased when Mother and Mama Manda greeted me upon my return, with my mother declaring I must have grown an inch or two.

"You look taller, Mary." Her voice was like a warm bath, and touched me even more because she was saying something nice about me.

"I'm still short, by some estimation."

"Would that be by anyone's particular estimation?"

I opened my mouth to deny it. I found I couldn't. "My demeanor says it all. I suppose."

"Yes. You look very much like I did whenever I fought with your dear father, my Fenton. Are the wounds irreparable between you?"

"It would seem so. In any case, he lives there and I live here. I interfered where I should not have and he's angry with me."

"The anger need not be permanent."

"I'm afraid that it is. But it's fine." I squeezed her hand. "I'm glad to see you. I've returned to Milford, and I'll assist with the start of school in any way that I'm able."

My mother's demeanor was always one of control. I would have sworn that I saw a smile about her lips. If mother smiled.

There was much to do to prepare for the upcoming term, so I did not have much time to mope around and feel sorry for the lost love of Reverend Gabriel Harmon.

It came about as I always said. I would not have been able to spend my life fighting off the wounds and scars of being a minister's wife. He was much better off without me. All of Atlanta was. All I had done was cause chaos and difficulty. It was better I stay in the country.

ↄ ↄ ↄ

One morning, I helped Mama Manda sort papers in her office. She looked up from writing something and blotted her document, telling me, "I'm sure you will be interested to know Mr. Lewis has been promoted, and will help me with more official things this year."

Mr. Lewis was her son-in-law and my March's husband. The one who had dropped into her lap. "What a wonderful thing for him. And March."

My dear friend had just confided in me she was expecting a happy event to come to her next spring. Part of my heart soared for her. A precious babe. The first babe in the Milford College choir and a babe for Mama Manda to be a grandmother to. More family. Such joy.

I guess March had gotten it right in her approach. While I, the always impulsive Mamie, was left behind. Certainly, a raise in position and income was a nice thing for the Lewis branch of the Milford College family.

She held out the freshly-signed stack for me to put away. "That means that I have to hire someone to replace him in the classroom. We will have an additional fifty students. The school is growing by leaps and bounds."

Growth was always good, but was a challenge at the same time. "Will you be able to hire someone soon?"

"I will. A very promising candidate is coming by train. I wonder if you will go up to greet him while I finish my letter."

I stood. Ready to help as always. "Gladly."

"You may want to take your mother with you."

"My mother?" Mother was here to rest from her speaking circuit, not to greet strangers on the train.

"Yes. I believe my potential hire would be impressed to meet her."

"Of course." I should not be surprised. Wouldn't Mother mind being used as a selling point for the college? After all, she was not staying here.

I found her on the front porch of the old Milford home, relaxing. The old home was used as housing for teachers. She seemed unusually eager to take a walk to the train platform in the heat of the August day and more talkative than ever.

She linked her arm in mine and patted my hand. I chalked her happy spirits up to the news about March and I tried to smile in response.

"I see something troubles you, child. Why are you down, Mary?"

"I make trouble, no matter where I go."

"No. You stir hearts and change minds, where ever you go. Be proud. Believe me, I know, from years of trying. You were successful in a matter of weeks."

"But, the women didn't get more money to help their children."

She stopped me. I faced her. "Mary, the other domestic servants in Atlanta almost left their jobs behind. You gave them hope. You gave them a voice. Only you, my daughter, could have created such an uproar all over Atlanta. And it's a start. They know now. They matter. They don't have to be silent any more. That's something to be proud of."

It was hard though. Even though I was wearing my blue and green striped dress, there was not much that could make my spirits improve.

The sound of the train in Milford was a bit of an event, as the once daily arrival of the train meant deliveries, as well as new people to the small college town.

I stood on the platform, holding my breath against the muggy August day, and avoiding breathing in the cinders falling from the burned coal of the train, which powered the engine along.

The train stopped and the stairs were lowered, as was the usual custom. From the Jim Crow train, I heard the clapping of small feet against the wood of the platform and two small forces whirled off of the train, and launched themselves at me.

Serena and Pax wrapped themselves around me and against all good sense, I breathed out into the August heat. What were they doing here? In wonderful new clothes as well?

"Where is your mother?"

"There she is!" Serena yelled and pointed down the platform at the sight of Deborah in a pink dress being escorted from the Jim Crow car by Gabriel.

The Reverend Harmon and Deborah came up to us and now my breath was clean taken away. I embraced Deborah and stood back from Gabriel, not sure what to say.

"You glad to see us?"

"I am, Deborah. So happy to see you here. Are you in Milford for a visit?"

"No. We here to stay. I got a job here. This is a better place for me and the children anyway. Atlanta is too big and noisy."

"I'm so glad." I embraced her again, feeling the pricks of tears behind my eyelids.

"Ain't you going to ask about the Reverend?"

"Sure. If he wants to tell me what he's doing here."

He bowed to me, as heroic and handsome looking as ever with his strange nose. He looked down it. "Miss Harper. Mrs. Harper, I presume."

Mother shook Gabriel's hand. "I am. So nice to meet you Reverend Harmon."

"How do you know him?" I asked.

"I've heard about him. I've seen all about him, too."

I bit my lip from saying something that would have made me look like a child. My, I was coming quite a long way.

"Well, I'm here to interview for a teaching job here at Milford this year." Something made my heart beat so rapidly I was aware of it now. Oh, the ways the body betrayed.

"Oh. I see. Well. Welcome to Milford, Reverend."

"You aren't happy at that?"

"Do you believe I should be?"

"I thought the prospect of me as a teacher would be more appealing to you than to me as minister, Miss Harper. Now you are free to be as impulsive as you wish. I was offered some other opportunities elsewhere. Some offered better money. But when the chance came up to come here, to where you are, and to see something of this place that made you, Miss Harper, the wonderful person you are, I could not pass up the chance."

I stood back a little from him, in complete shock at this speech.

He stepped forward, closer to me. "In truth, I have come to escort Deborah and the children here and make sure they are comfortable in their move. I have not yet interviewed for the position. If you do not want me here or feel that my presence would be an imposition in some way…"

I stepped forward to him, away from my mother's side, and raised myself up as I knew how to do, kissing those dear lips. He wrapped his arms around my waist and held me snug to him, kissing me in return, neither of us caring about the wind whipping around us in the wake of the departing train. "I wouldn't mind having you here, Reverend Harmon."

"Dearest Mamie, you must know I'm in love with you. And I appreciate the welcome here. I know what it means to be welcomed into your world.

Trust and believe." He placed me back down on the platform, gently.

I thrilled to hear those words from his dear lips. Before I could respond in kind, he squeezed me around my waist.

"Now, if you will guide me to where I might meet my new employer, Miss Harper, I would be grateful."

Gabriel took my arm in his and tucked my hand under his arm, where I knew I belonged.

"Follow me." I said.

The warmth of his hand was the perfect shield I needed to protect me from any other harm I might endure. It was so sweet of him to think he could do something else for his career. Maybe he wouldn't like teaching, but that was fine. What mattered more, more than having to face entire churches full of spiteful old cats, was that we were together.

With this man by my side, I was home, in one place, where I had longed to be. Forever.

THE END

AUTHOR'S NOTE

Mary Frances Harper was a real person. However, in spite of how famous her mother, (Frances Ellen Watkins Harper) was in the 19th century, all we know about her is her birthdate in 1862, her death date in 1908 and that she taught Bible class. That's all. I wrote this story to give her a narrative and a privileged viewpoint from which to observe the Black Washerwomen's strike of 1881. I credit her with writing the letter to the newspaper in the story. The letter is real, but its author is not known.

The Atlanta Baptist Female Seminary, also real, was founded in April of 1881. The Black Washerwomen's strike took place in July of 1881. I believe that in some way, these events had something to do with one another. When Sophia Packard and Harriet Giles decided to open their school to educate Black women, starting with a population of older women who just wanted to read their Bible, they sowed seeds.

The strike was the occasion when these women found truth. If they banded together, they had power. More than three thousand took part and, as the story suggests, gave ideas to other domestic workers for higher pay. The establishment figured out a way to quell them. Within ten years, the washerwomen's work had been taken over by better technology. Still, their strike allowed them to think of what was possible.

Labor scholars credit this strike with inspiring other workers about the power to strike. So, in the name of fair and better working conditions, we all owe the washerwomen a debt of gratitude for their strength, conviction and insistence to be seen as human beings with families to support.

Miss Packard and Miss Giles returned to Atlanta and continued to operate the Atlanta Baptist Female Seminary. While on their tour to the north to raise money, Miss Packard and Miss Giles met John Rockefeller who emptied his pockets and asked them if they were serious about their school. When they said yes, he started a fund to help them construct a building to get out of the subpar church basement. Within two years and hundreds of students later, they moved to a location a few miles away into renovated army barracks.

In gratitude, Miss Packard and Miss Giles wanted to name the school after John Rockefeller. He declined but requested that they name the school after his wife's parents, who had been long time abolitionist activists. So in 1884, The Atlanta Baptist Female Seminary became Spelman Seminary and in 1924, changed names once more to Spelman College, the college where I teach.

I have much to thank Miss Packard and Miss Giles for in persevering with their vision. If they had not, I would not be in a position to teach young women what is now Spelman's tag line and central belief, "A Choice to Change the World." I like to think that's what Mamie would have believed in as well.

Here are some sources I used in writing of "The Washerwoman's War:"

• Boyd, Melba Joyce. *Discarded Legacy: Politics and Poetics in the Life of Frances E. W. Harper 1825-1911*

• Guy-Sheftall, Beverly. *Spelman: A Centennial Celebration.*

• Hunter, Tera. *To Joy My Freedom.*

• Jenkins, Candice. *Private Lives, Public Freedom.*

• Watson, Yolanda and Shelia Gregory. *Daring to Educate*

ABOUT THE AUTHOR

Piper G Huguley, named 2015 Debut Author of the Year by Romance Slam Jam and Breakout Author of the Year by AAMBC, is a two-time Golden Heart °finalist and is the author of "Migrations of the Heart," a three-book series of historical romances set in the early 20th century featuring African American characters, published by Samhain Publishing. Book #1 in the series, *A Virtuous Ruby*, won Best Historical of 2015 in the Swirl Awards. Book #3 in the series, *A Treasure of Gold*, was named by Romance Novels in Color as a Best Book of 2015 and received 4 ½ stars from RT Magazine.

Huguley is also the author of the "Home to Milford College" series. The series follows the building of a college from its founding in 1866. On release, the prequel novella to the "Home to Milford College" series, *The Lawyer's Luck,* reached #1 Amazon Bestseller status on the African American Christian Fiction charts. Book #1 in the series, *The Preacher's Promise* was named a top ten Historical Romance in Publisher's Weekly by the esteemed historical romance author, Beverly Jenkins and received Honorable Mention in the Writer's Digest Contest of Self-Published e-books in 2015.

Her new series "Born to Win Men" will debut in December 2016 with *A Champion's Heart* as Book #1.

She blogs about the history behind her novels at http://piperhuguley. com. She lives in Atlanta, Georgia with her husband and son.

A Radiant Soul

Kianna Alexander

In 1881, Sarah Webster is returning home to Fayetteville, NC to celebrate her mother's milestone birthday. Having spent the last two years working as a pastry chef in a Cheyenne hotel, she's a very different person than she was when she left. Her efforts towards women's suffrage, unknown to her family back home, are near and dear to her heart.

Carpenter Owen Markham, charged with building the gazebo that will serve as Mrs. Webster's birthday gift, is intrigued by the middle daughter of the Webster household, whom he's never met before. Her father has decreed that he and Sarah are suited, but when he hears her unconventional stance on women's role in society, he's not so sure a love match can be made.

For my nieces: Alexandra, Bria, Briana, and Erin. May you grow into the warrior women I know you can be.

"It has been said that unsettled questions have no pity for the repose of nations. It should be said with the utmost emphasis that this question of the suffrage will never give repose or safety to the States or to the nation until each, within its own jurisdiction, makes and keeps the ballot free and pure by the strong sanctions of the law."

Inaugural Address of President James A. Garfield

March 4, 1881

PROLOGUE

May, 1881

~Cheyenne, Wyoming Territory~

Sarah Webster arranged her freshly baked tarts on a tray with measured precision, smiling as she went about the task. Her workday neared its end, but she wouldn't leave until the dish was just right. Focusing on the presentation of her pastries helped her drown out the noisy chaos of the kitchen. Within a few minutes, she had filled the tray.

"Sarah, where are my strawberry tarts?"

In response to the shouted question, Sarah shook her head. Grabbing the small, cloth bag filled with sweetened whipped cream, she quickly dropped a dollop onto each of the dozen confections. "On the way now, Chef!"

Grasping the edges of the tray, she moved to the other side of the bustling kitchen, where her superior waited to inspect the finished product.

Chef Robert, a black man of fifty years of age, stood with his hands laced behind him. His short, barrel-shaped frame was draped in black trousers and white chef's coat that matched her own. The traditional white cloche sat atop his balding head. He swept his dark-eyed gaze over the tray, scrutinizing the tarts. Moments later, he gave her a curt nod, the signal that he found her work satisfactory.

"Thank you, Chef." Sarah sidled away, handing the tray of tarts off to one of the waiters, who'd been quietly observing the exchange. As the waiter slipped through the swinging doors, Sarah released a pent-up breath. She dearly wanted a moment off her feet, but she knew she had a couple of hours left before her shift ended.

Feeling Chef Robert's eyes on the back of her neck, she turned and went back to the pastry station. Once there, she washed her hands in the basin and started work on her next order: a triple–berry, lemon cake for a wedding later that day.

While she mixed the batter, Sarah mused on her situation. At twenty-two, she knew what an honor it was to hold a position at Cheyenne's beautiful Inter-Ocean Hotel. Barney L. Ford, the black founder of the hotel, had founded several businesses around the west, and had opened this property in 1875. The Cheyenne Inter-Coastal had gained national fame as the first in the country to have electric lighting throughout.

As a proprietor, Mr. Ford was known for his discerning tastes when it came to hiring employees. Sarah knew how lucky she was to have snagged the position, especially considering how she'd come to the area. She'd answered an ad that had appeared in the *Fayetteville Observer*, her hometown newspaper. It had been a longshot, but the chance she'd taken had led to her becoming the youngest chef in the hotel's history.

Once the batter reached the proper consistency, Sarah began the delicate task of adding berries to the mixture. The idea was to incorporate them well, without smashing them. Whole berries made for a more pleasant presentation, and beyond that, smashed berries released juices which could ruin the consistency of the final product. Mindful of that, Sarah used a wooden spatula to gently fold the batter over the plump blueberries, raspberries, and blackberries. She'd learned the technique from Rosaline Rhodes-Pruett, the baker whom she'd apprenticed under for three years.

Once the cake layers were safely tucked into the oven, Sarah set about making the creamy lemon glaze that would top the cake. Citrus fruits were hard to come by in the Territories, but Chef Robert had connections to a grower in Florida, who sent shipments of oranges, lemons, and limes twice a year. This cake's glaze used a bit of fresh lemon juice, but got most of its bright flavor from dried lemon zest. Sarah zested lemons whenever a shipment arrived, and kept some carefully preserved, along with the other spices on the rack above her station.

"Sarah. You're free to go, my dear." Chef Robert approached her station with an easy smile. "Good work today."

She set down her pastry bag, admiring the freshly frosted triple-berry cake. "Thank you, sir. I hope the couple and their guests enjoy it."

He nodded. "I'm sure they will, assuming it tastes as wonderful as it looks."

"Thank you again, Chef." Sarah smiled. She much preferred this version of her boss. He was a very serious person during the workday.

Once the day's orders were completed, he visibly relaxed. Sarah supposed she understood that. After all, Chef Robert ran a very efficient kitchen.

"I'll see you tomorrow." Chef Robert tipped his cloche in her direction as he disappeared through the swinging doors.

With a smile and a wave, Sarah moved to the basin to wash the remnants of her latest creation off her hands. Then she moved to the small pantry adjoining the kitchen to strip off her chef's coat. Turning it over in her hands, she could see the purple stains left by the blueberries she'd handled. Resigned to take the coat home and wash it, she folded it and tucked it into her handbag.

The absence of the coat revealed her attire: a blue blouse with a white lace collar, and a pair of denim trousers. As she dusted a bit of flour from the legs of her denims, she giggled at the thought of how the genteel Southern ladies of her hometown might react to her wearing such unconventional clothing. In North Carolina, most women wouldn't dare to wear trousers outside their own homes. Here in Wyoming Territory, however, things were very different. Women here wore what they pleased, lived the lives they wanted, and perhaps most importantly, they had the lawful right to vote. That precious right was one the ladies back east simply didn't possess.

Securing the strap of her crocheted handbag in the crook of her elbow, Sarah left the pantry, strolled through the kitchen and then the hotel's dining room, before she passed through the lobby on her way out to the street. As she stepped outside, she saw the hotelier climbing out of his chauffeured coach.

Stopping, she offered a smile. "Good day, Mr. Ford."

He returned her smile. "And a good day to you, Miss Webster. Headed home?"

She nodded. "Yes, sir, after I've seen to a few errands."

He tipped his hat to her as he entered the hotel, and she went on her way.

Navigating the busy street, Sarah made her way to the telegraph office. She took care to avoid the buggies, buckboards, and folks on horseback as she walked. She nodded greetings to a few of her acquaintances who passed her on foot, all the while keeping close to the road's edge to avoid the pounding hooves of other folk's horses, and the waste the beasts left in their wake. The cacophony, consisting of the hoof beats, wagon wheels rolling over the rutted dirt road, and the many conversations, provided a backdrop to Sarah's thoughts. The noise provided something of a soundtrack to her daily life.

When she stepped into the telegraph office, she was relieved to find it nearly empty. Only one other person stood between her and retrieving her messages, so she stood a respectable distance away and let the man finish his business with the clerk.

After the man left, Sarah approached the tall, wooden counter. "Afternoon, Tillman. How are you?"

Tillman Sutter, the telegraph clerk, busied himself scrawling notes on his pad of paper. When he looked up, a smile broke over his olive-skinned face. "Why, Miss Webster. I'm just fine, and how are you?"

"I'm well. Any messages for me?"

Tillman, seated atop a stool behind the counter, swiveled to his left to open the wooden box containing his incoming messages. "Yes, ma'am. You've got two. One came in from Washington yesterday. The other came from your folks back east this morning." Fishing two slips of paper out of the box, he handed them to her.

She accepted the offered slips. "Thank you, Tillman." She turned her head toward the sound of the door opening, and saw two more people enter the office.

Backing away from the desk to allow other patrons access, Sarah took a seat in one of the chairs lining the back wall of the office. Her eyes grazed over the two messages. The one from her father requested her presence at her mother's forty-fifth birthday party in early July.

The other telegram was from the United Women's Advancement Society in D.C., with whom she'd been corresponding. The women of the society had extended an invitation to their upcoming conference, to be held the second week of July. A smile spread over Sarah's face as she realized she now had good use for the vacation days she'd been saving up.

Excitement coursing through her and she hurried out of the telegraph office, intent on going home to start making her travel plans.

ε‹ ε‹ ε‹

~Fayetteville, NC~

Running the plane over the section of log for a final time, Owen Markham stepped back to assess his work. The piece of pine was to be part of a sitting bench ordered by the Goodman family, and he knew they demanded the highest caliber of craftsmanship. Checking the piece to be sure it was completely straight and flat, he lifted it from its spot atop two sawhorses, and carefully added it to the pile of planks he'd already made for the project.

Tugging the old handkerchief from the pocket of his denims, he dragged it around his hairline, then across his neck to banish the perspiration there. Even with the windows of his small woodshop open, the heat could become oppressive during the middle part of the day. Adding his non-stop work for the last few hours to that, and he felt downright exhausted.

Easing through the open door into the yard that lay between his shop and his small cabin, he went to the pump. Setting the bucket below the spigot, he worked the handle to fill it, then scooped up and drank several dippers full of the sweet, cool liquid. He hauled the remaining water in the bucket into the house, where he used it with a sliver of lye soap to wash away the sweat from the morning's labors. Refreshed after the cleansing, he slipped into a clean pair of denims, but chose to forgo a shirt due to the work that still lay ahead.

He fixed himself a sandwich with a few pieces of leftover ham. He added some dried apple slices and a cup of lemonade, then sat down for a late lunch.

After he'd eaten, he returned to the woodshop, ready to assemble the four benches the Goodmans had ordered to place around their property. He'd just begun hammering when he heard a knock behind him. Turning toward the sound, he set down the hammer.

In the doorway stood George Webster, the city's premiere haberdasher and shoemaker. "Afternoon, Owen. How goes the work?"

He smiled, walked over to shake his hand. "Hard as ever, but I don't mind it. Come on in, Mr. Webster. What can I do for you?"

George eased inside, taking a seat on one of the low stools by the drafting table. "Came to see if you can fit me in for an order. I know you're busy by Liza's birthday is coming."

Owen knew George referred to his wife, Elizabeth. Mrs. Webster was a seamstress by trade, and worked with George in his business, serving his female clients. "Sure, I'll make some room for you." Owen sat down on the other stool, sliding up to the drafting table. Opening his project ledger, he grabbed a pencil. "What do you need?"

"A gazebo."

Owen blinked a few times. "Big project. Gonna take me a while."

"I know. Liza's been asking for one for years, and what better time to give it to her than her milestone birthday?"

He nodded. "I see. And when would you want it finished by?"

George looked a bit hesitant. "Well, her birthday's July second, so..."

Owen held back his groan. "So, in about four or five weeks, then?"

George nodded. "Yes, if you can do it. I'm willing to pay a bit extra for the quick completion."

His eyes scanning over the other projects already in the ledger, Owen searched for a gap that would allow him to fulfill Mr. Webster's request. "Hmmm. I think I can fit you in, but I'll have to start right away."

"That's fine. How soon should we have the area ready?"

Owen jotted down Mr. Webster's name in the ledger. "Depends on the design. Let me show you my sketches. Got three different gazebos you can pick from." Reaching into a crate he kept beneath the drafting table, Owen extracted a sketchbook. He opened it, flipped to the pages showing his gazebos, and handed it to George.

After perusing the three sketches for a few silent moments, George pointed out the middle of the road model. "This one. I think it'll suit her nicely."

Owen made a note of the model number in the ledger next to George's name. The gazebo he'd chosen had lattice on all but one side, which was left open for entry. The interior wraparound bench provided comfortable seating, and the shingled roof would provide protection from the sun, rain and wind. "Good choice, Mr. Webster."

"So when will you need the yard ready?"

"About a week. It'll take me that long to get the wood and to trim the pieces down. Any particular wood in mind, something she likes?"

"She's partial to cherry."

Owen nodded, noting that in the ledger as well. "Good choice. Stands up well to the elements. I've got a little cherry on hand, and I can order some more from the mill. Going to add an extra few days to the timeline, though, so let's stay I'll start first week of June. How's that?"

"Sounds good. Gives me time to have the yard trimmed. The store has been so busy, I've neglected the yard, and it's starting to look like a jungle back there." He chuckled.

Owen joined in George's laughter. "Hopefully, you'll have tamed the savage weeds by the time I come in with my lumber and tools."

"How much do I owe you?"

Owen quoted the price, and without hesitation, George wrote him a bank draft for the amount.

Then he stood and shook Owen's hand again. "I've got to get back to the store. Thanks for your help, and send someone around to the house if you have any messages."

"I will. And thank you for your business."

With a wave, George slipped out the shop door.

After he left, Owen spent a few minutes making notes in the ledger, including the amount of cherry wood, linseed oil, and pitch he'd need. Knowing he'd need to purchase more nails, screws, and other hardware, he made mental note to visit the general store later in the day. Closing his ledger, Owen returned to the center of the shop and continued assembling the first of the Goodman's benches.

By the dinner hour, Owen had finished assembling, sanding, and staining all four benches. Setting aside his brush, he wiped his brow again and locked up the shop. Returning to his cabin, he scrubbed the stain and sawdust from his hands before donning a clean shirt and heading to town for dinner.

Hitching his horse to the only free post between Dottie's Eatery and Mac's Barbershop, he entered the restaurant. After he'd eaten a simple meal of roasted chicken, fried potatoes and green beans, he went into Mac's for the evening's meeting.

Owen nodded to Mac, who was busy trimming the mustache of a white patron. Few local whites patronized Mac's shop, since it was black-owned, and as Owen passed the chair, he smiled.

I wonder if that white man would be here, if he knew about the back room.

Owen took a seat on the west wall of the shop, perusing the pages of the *Fayetteville Observer* while Mac and his client made small talk. Once the man had paid his bill and departed, Mac looked his way.

"The boys are already back there." Mac jerked his head toward the back wall.

Setting the paper aside, Owen marched over to the wall, giving it five sharp raps. After a beat, the wall opened, and he slipped inside, shutting the false panel behind him.

In the small room, the other eight members of the Sons of the Diaspora sat around a small table. They were all men of color, who sought the enforcement of the fifteenth amendment to the Constitution, which granted them the right to vote. They were still fighting every day for the rights extended to them with the amendment's passing, eleven years prior. Black codes, poll taxes, and other nefarious plans to keep them from exercising their rights were always afoot, but the Sons remained resolute.

Looking out over the faces of his compatriots, Owen smiled. "What are we getting into this weekend, boys?"

CHAPTER 1

Late June, 1881
~Fayetteville, NC~

Sarah stood outside the Fayetteville train depot with her valise at her feet. Her summer-weight, tan skirt and white blouse offered her some respite from the heat of the Carolina sun, as did the covered roof of the depot platform. She'd donned a small, simple hat and a pair of low-heeled slippers for ease of movement before she'd left home in Cheyenne. Now that her week-long train trip had finally ended, she was eager to get home to see her family. Due to the cost of the trip, and the scarcity of her vacation time from her work at the hotel, she hadn't visited home in almost a year.

Watching the flow of mid-day traffic moving down Franklin Street, Sarah scanned the faces of the drivers. When she saw the familiar face of her older sister, seated behind the reins of their mother's buggy, Sarah could feel the smile stretching across her face.

Mary matched her smile as she navigated the buggy to the road's edge. Parking the vehicle, she set the handbrake and hopped down, catching Sarah up in her arms. "It's good to see you, troublemaker."

Sarah grinned as she returned her sister's embrace. "I missed you as well, warden." As the oldest sibling, Mary had often taken on the role of a second mother to her younger sisters during their formative years. The memories of those days were still fresh in Sarah's mind, and obviously still lingered for Mary as well.

Stepping back, Mary stooped down to pick up Sarah's valise. "Is this all your luggage?"

She shrugged. "I travel light."

With a shake of her perfectly-coiffed head, Mary slung the valise up into the back of the buggy. "Come along, Sarah. Mommy, Daddy, and

Kate are eager to see you." She returned to the driver's side and climbed aboard.

Sarah hoisted her skirt and launched herself up onto the wooden seat. Once she and her sister were in place, Mary got hold of the reigns, and with a skillful snap, got them underway. The buggy merged into the flow of traffic, heading toward the northeastern edge of town and the Webster family home.

As the buggy rolled along the hard-packed earth of the road, Sarah watched the familiar scenery scroll by. "How are Hubert and Emily? Did they come down from Virginia with you?"

Mary smiled at the mention of her husband and young daughter. "They're well, thanks. Emily is at the house, but Hubert couldn't take time off the mill."

"I can understand that. It takes quite a bit of effort for me to get days off from the hotel." Sarah genuinely liked her brother-in-law, and while she was disappointed that she wouldn't get to see him this time, she was glad she'd get to see her young niece. "How old is Emily now?"

Mary navigated the buggy around a bend in the road, making a left turn. "She's two, almost three. Talks all the time, though most of it's gibberish. Cutest darn thing you ever saw."

"Heavens. They do grow fast." Sarah could clearly recall Emily as a chubby infant who was attempting her first steps the last time she'd seen her.

"And how are things in the Territory? Still wild and untamed out there?" Mary accented her question with a chuckle.

"Cheyenne is a lot more civilized than you think, Mary. The air is fresh and sweet, folks are courteous. And even though I come home every day bone-tired, I love my work."

"I can relate. I feel the same way after I've been on my feet all day, taming heads. But I wouldn't trade it for any other job." As a teenager, Mary had discovered her innate talent for hairdressing. As she'd moved into adulthood, she'd made it her career.

By now, they were on Webster land. The two sisters lapsed into silence and Sarah could feel a lightness coming over her as she scanned the comforting familiarity of home. The rolling slopes of grass-covered land, four acres of it, surrounded the two-story farmhouse in which she'd been born. Seeing the house growing closer and closer as they drove made Sarah's heart do a somersault in her chest.

Mary parked the buggy and stabled the two horses, then she and Sarah climbed the four steps up to the wide front porch.

Kate, the youngest Webster child, swung open the screened door. "Sarah!" She hugged her sister tightly.

"How are you, Kitty Kat?" Sarah stepped back, tapping her index finger on the bridge of her baby sister's nose as she called her by the childhood endearment. She stepped into the cool interior of the house and placed her valise on the floor near the coat rack.

As Mary entered behind her, shutting the door, Sarah could hear her mother's voice coming from upstairs. "Katherine? Are your sisters here yet?"

"Yes, Mama," Kate called up, even as she rolled her eyes at being called by her proper first name. "They've just arrived."

Sarah's gaze swung to the top of the stairs, and Elizabeth Webster appeared there. A broad smile graced her bronze face. "Sarah Jane. It's so good to have you home, baby." She descended the steps as she spoke, and the moment she got close enough, pulled her daughter into her arms.

Wrapped in her mother's tight hug, Sarah chuckled. "It's good to be home, Mommy."

When her mother released her, and she stepped back, Sarah was again reminded of the strong maternal resemblance she and her sisters had to their mother. Elizabeth, or Liza as most folks called her, had a petite frame, bronze skin, and light-brown eyes. Her hair was dark, nearly jet black, and bore the deep waves of her mixed Occoneechee and African ancestry. Kate and Mary were like copies of their mother, except Kate wore her hair in a short cut while Mary was rarely ever seen without a fancy up-do.

Sarah, the middle child and the odd one out in so many ways, stood a few inches taller than her mother and sister. The demands of her job left her with little time for coiffing, so she wore her long hair in a single plait trailing down her back.

She moved further into her mother's parlor, taking in the familiar sights. A beige settee occupied the center of the room, and short legged oak table sat in front of it. Two small, round tables, each with a gas lamp atop it, flanked the settee. Two dark green wingback armchairs, as well as two matching armless upholstered chairs, were arranged in a semi-circle around the settee.

"Where's Daddy?" Sarah posed the question as she looked around the lower level of the house, seeking any sound that might indicate his presence.

"He's out in the backyard," Kate volunteered as she dropped her skirt-clad bottom onto the settee.

"Overseeing my gift, I'm sure." Liza gestured toward the kitchen, where the back door stood propped open. "Go on out there and speak to him. I know he'll be glad to see you."

Sarah walked through the front parlor, then the kitchen, and stepped out onto the back porch. From there, she could see her father, George, in profile. She smiled at the familiar salt and pepper of his close-trimmed hair. He stood by what looked like the beginnings of a small structure being built in the center of the yard, and carried on a conversation with the builder.

Her eyes swung to the other man. Tall, shirtless, and well-built, the man held a hammer in one hand. The stranger's skin was dark, the color of fine mahogany. His hair was in short, thin dreadlocks that barely grazed the hard line of his jaw. He wore a pair of snug-fitting denims that sat low on his hips, and his bare chest glistened with perspiration.

He swung his deep brown eyes in her direction then, and as their gazes connected, she could feel the heat stinging her cheeks. From her spot on the porch, she saw his full lips open as he spoke to her father, who then turned her way.

"Sarah! Come on over here, sweetheart, and meet Owen." George waved her over with his hand.

Swallowing, Sarah willed her feet to move, careful not to trip as she stepped off the lip of the porch. If she fell over her own feet in front of this gorgeous man, she swore she'd die of embarrassment.

Once she was safely on the ground, she pasted on a soft smile. Looking at the handsome stranger made her feel strange and out of sorts, so she looked at her father instead.

With measured steps, she moved across the yard toward the man who'd raised her and the tall, striking fellow standing beside him.

ↄ ↄ ↄ

Owen dropped his hammer to the ground as he watched George's middle daughter glide toward him. Having only live about eighteen months in Fayetteville, Owen had never had the occasion to meet Miss Sarah. Taking in the sight of her now, he regretted that misfortune.

Sarah was taller than her mother was but just as strikingly beautiful. She was a vision of amber-hued skin, full, pink lips that looked as soft as petals, and a slender figure that was still full in all the right places. She moved with grace, and when she paused near her father, she assumed the typical stance of a young woman in mixed company. Clasping her hands in front of her, she angled her head up, looking to George.

Owen watched her, entranced. Her demure posturing only served to enhance her femininity in his eyes.

At first, her attention was on her father, but after she hugged and greeted George, she turned her intense, copper eyes on him.

When their eyes met, something moved through him. A tremor shot through his body, and he shifted his weight from one foot to the other. The sensation was unlike any he'd ever felt before.

Reaching for her hand, but never dropping his gaze from her face, he smiled. "I'm Owen Markham. Nice to meet you, Miss Webster."

"Please, call me Sarah." She allowed him to grasp her hand.

He lifted her delicate hand up to his lips and kissed the back of it. "Whatever you wish."

George cleared his throat, momentarily breaking the spell. "I've got things to attend to inside the house, so I'll leave you two to get acquainted. Sarah, I want to hear all about the happenings in the Territory when you come in."

Reluctantly, Owen let her delicate, soft-skinned hand slip from his grasp. She moved nearer to her father. "Yes, Daddy." Sarah gave her father another peck on the cheek, and then the older man disappeared into the house, letting the back door swing shut behind him.

Sarah, looking a bit nervous, gifted him with a gentle smile. "I see you're working, I don't want to disturb you."

He shook his head. "It's no trouble at all. Did I just hear your father say you came from the Territory? Whereabouts?"

"Wyoming. I work at a hotel in Cheyenne."

He scratched his chin. "Sounds interesting. How long have you lived out there?"

"Since the summer of '73."

He nodded. She'd left only a few months before he first arrived in Fayetteville. "Your father tells me you're an unmatched chef when it comes to sweets. Is that true?"

She giggled, covering her mouth with her fingertips as if to stifle it. "I don't know if I'd say all that, but I'm not surprised. Daddy is always boasting on his daughters."

"And why shouldn't he? You're obviously very capable, and beautiful on top of that." He hadn't intended to be quite so forward, but the words had tumbled from his mouth. Now that he'd said them, he couldn't take them back.

Her cheeks reddened again, and this time she directed her gaze away from him. "You flatter me, sir."

"Please, call me Owen." He winked at her. She was just as beautiful as her father had professed, and even more so. All the Webster women were lovely, but for whatever reason, this plucky middle child seemed to suit his fancy most of all.

He watched her, letting his eyes rake over her beauty for a few silent moments. The bright sun shining overhead illuminated her delicate features, allowing him full view of her smooth-skinned loveliness. The coy way she diverted her eyes from him fired his blood.

She seemed to sense his scrutiny. The slightest of smiles touched the corners of her mouth as she took a small step back from him. Pointing at the unfinished structure, she asked, "Is this going to be a garden shed?"

Doing his best to shake himself free of her spell, he shook his head. "No, ma'am. It's just a foundation right now, but when I finished, your mother's gonna have a top-quality gazebo."

Her eyes widened, the smile deepening. "Oh, that's lovely. Mommy's always wanted one. What a thoughtful gift for Daddy to get her."

"He picked a real nice design, too. Brought my sketchbook." He gestured to the small ironwork table a few feet from where they stood that he'd set the book on. "Fancy taking a look at it?"

She clapped her hands. "Oh, I'd love to."

He retrieved the book, opening it to the proper page. By her side again, he pointed out the chosen design and let her see it. "Good seating inside it for nice days. Lattice walls there, come in handy if your mother decides to plant roses or ivy or any other creeping vine."

She beamed as she perused the design. "It's lovely. I can't wait to see it when it's finished."

Owen rubbed his hands together, noting how genuinely pleased she seemed with his work. "Thank you, Miss Sarah. It'll be done in time for your mother's birthday party." Closing the book, he tucked it beneath his arm.

"I know she's going to love it. I can just picture her, sitting out here reading in the mornings." Her smile softened, becoming wistful. "She works so hard around the house. She deserves it."

Touched by Sarah's admiration for her mother, he nodded. "I'll do my very best work for Mrs. Webster."

"Oh, I don't doubt it." She gave him a sidelong glance, her eyes sparkling beneath a fringe of dark lashes. "Thank you in advance."

He blinked. If he didn't know any better, he'd say Sarah was flirting with him.

She exhaled through parted lips, long and slow. Slipping her hand into her skirt pocket, she pulled out a fan. Snapping it open, she began working her wrist to stir up a breeze. "Heavens, it's hot out today."

Watching her, he could feel the heat rising within him. Instinctively, he knew the fire in his blood was fueled by this woman, not the weather. Did she feel the same way? He could see the small beads of perspiration beginning to form around her hairline. "I don't want to keep you out in this heat, Miss Sarah. Why don't you go on in where it's cooler?" Even as the words left his lips, he knew he'd be bereft after her departure.

She nodded, tucking the fan away. "I should let you get back to your work. It was nice to meet you, Mister—"

He looked at her pointedly.

"I mean, nice meeting you, Owen."

"Likewise."

With a wave, she turned and made her way back to the house.

When the door closed behind her, Owen looked on for a few moments more. Could any woman really be that appealing? Surely she had some disagreeable quality, though none were obvious to him at the moment. Their first meeting had left him with nothing but positive impressions of Miss Sarah Webster.

Smiling, he retrieved him hammer and set back to work. Between now and Mrs. Webster's party, he planned to exercise every opportunity at his disposal to learn more about her daughter.

Chapter 2

Late June 1881
~Fayetteville, NC~

With her mother's old feather duster in hand, Sarah climbed the last two steps into the attic of her family home. The small, circular windows on either side of the space let in a good bit of early morning sunlight, giving the attic a soft glow. Coming into the room, she stooped a bit until she cleared a low beam, then stood between two of the ceiling beams. She'd have to keep to the space between those beams if she wanted to stand up fully.

Once Sarah had moved out of the doorway, Kate entered, followed by Mary. All three Webster sisters were dressed similarly: old trousers and shirts of their father's, cinched and tied to fit them. Each of their heads were tied up in a scarf or wrap, to protect their tresses from the swirling dust.

Today's work of gathering their mother's good tablecloths and fine china from among the numerous dusty crates promised to be dirty. Elizabeth had trained her girls from an early age on how to most efficiently go about cleaning, and the first order of business had always been to prevent the sullying of their gook skirts and gowns by dressing appropriately for chores.

The three of them moved to different areas of the room, pulling back tarps to locate the items they'd come for.

"Lord, I can't remember the last time Mommy brought down her good china." Kate tossed aside a tarp to search the contents of a crate.

Mary snapped an old sheet, sending a cloud up a cloud of dust. As it fell over her, she sneezed.

"Bless you," Sarah and Kate said in unison.

"Thank you." Mary set the old sheet aside, squatting to search her crate. "I think the last time Mommy used the china was…"

"My nineteenth birthday." Sarah completed her sister's sentence. "Remember, Kate? I'd finished my apprenticeship with Ms. Rosalie a few weeks before that."

Kate, now leaning over the crate with her forearms buried inside, nodded. "Oh, that's right. Don't know if they would have been feeling so celebratory, if they'd known you were going to move so far away."

Sarah, having found the crate containing her mother's crystal glasses, set it aside. "Don't start with me, Kate." Her younger sister was still a teenager, and Sarah tried to remember that, lest she be pulled into her manufactured drama. Kate had always been the one to stir up confusion. As the baby of the family, she never lacked for attention, but she also never seemed to get her fill of it.

"All right, you two." The comment came from Mary, in her usual role as peacemaker between her two younger sisters. "We all know Mommy and Daddy want Sarah closer to home. No need to revisit that now."

A small voice from the second floor broke into their debate. "Mama? I want Mama!"

Mary set aside her crate. "Emily's calling me. I found the silver, I'll take it downstairs and we'll polish it later." Taking the small wooden box into the crook of her arm, Mary returned to the attic door and descended the steps.

Left together in the attic, Sarah and Kate continued the task. Sarah watched her sister Kate pulled tablecloths out of her crate, then handed them over to Sarah. Turning them over in her hands and holding them up to the light, Sarah checked them for stains and damage in the manner their mother had taught them.

After a few idle moments, Sarah turned her focus back to the crate of crystal punch cups she'd found. She'd need to get them downstairs to be washed free of dust and checked for cracks or chips.

"I didn't mean to start anything."

Kate's soft confession caught Sarah's attention. "It's all right, Kitty Kat."

Kate sighed. "It's just that ever since you left home, Mommy and Daddy are always after me about something. I wish I could have the freedom you two have."

Sarah took care to move the heavy crate closer to the door, and then came over to where Kate knelt. Squatting down, she draped an arm over her shoulder. "I understand that. I remember feeling the same way when

Mary left home. Don't fret, Kitty Kat. Your turn'll be coming along before you know it."

Kate sighed. "I know, I know. That's part of my worry. I remember how they reacted when you took that job out west. Seems the only way I can make them happy is to stay close by."

Sarah gave her sister a squeeze. "You've got a whole year before you graduate to figure it out. And when the time comes, choose what's going to make you happy. I promise, we're all going to love you, no matter what." She punctuated her words by placing a kiss on her sister's forehead.

Kate smiled. "Thanks, Sarah."

She shrugged. "Just looking out for my baby sister. Now come on and help me carry the crystal downstairs. It's a two-person job."

"All right. We'll have to come back up for the rest, I guess."

The two women climbed to their feet, with Sarah carefully avoiding the ceiling beams. Near the door, they hoisted the crate of crystal, squeezed close together to fit into the narrow stairwell, and started their slow descent.

Once they'd taken the crystal to the kitchen and left it on the table, Sarah and Kate returned to the attic. As they moved the crate of tablecloths, and another crate containing the six crystal punchbowls that went with the cups, Kate went over to stand by the window facing the back. "Owen's already out there working, I see."

Sarah, setting a crate aside, joined her younger sister at the window. Casting her gaze down on the yard below, she saw Owen there. The hour was still early, but he was already hard at work.

"Does he ever wear a shirt when he's here?" Sarah posed the question to her sister, never taking her eyes off the hard line of his muscular arms as he raised a center beam atop the gazebo's base. He was easily the most solidly built man she'd ever laid eyes on. His muscles rippled beneath his deep-brown skin as he worked, and she found it difficult to look away from his rugged handsomeness.

"Nope, and I can't say I mind. He is a handsome devil, isn't he?" Kate ribbed her sister.

Sarah pursed her lips. "Simmer down, Kate. I'm betting he's too old for you."

Kate scoffed. "But he's just right for you, Sis." She winked.

Sarah could feel the heat rising into her cheeks. Parts of her agreed with her sister's assessment, but she wasn't about to admit it. "Cut it out. Let's get this stuff downstairs. We've got a lot to do."

Sarah tried her best to keep her mind on the task at hand as she and her sister got back to work.

It took the better part of the morning, but all seven crates of tableware for the party finally made it down from the attic. The sisters stacked the crates in the pantry adjoining the kitchen, so the family could have breakfast at the table.

Sarah made dough for biscuits while her mother fried bacon in the cast iron skillet. For an added treat, she sprinkled a handful of chopped walnuts and plump raisins into the dough before dividing it into small rounds.

Liza smiled. "Raisins and nuts in the biscuits? You're always trying something new."

She slid the pan into the oven, closing the door. "Trust me, they're wonderful. We serve them at the hotel, and they're very popular."

After the cooking was done, Sarah enjoyed scrambled eggs, bacon, and her biscuits with her parents, sisters, and her young niece. Mary held her daughter in her lap, cleaning her small face whenever she saw remnants of food clinging there. Watching the interaction made Sarah wonder what it would be like to be a mother, and be responsible for filling another person's every need.

With the remnants of the food and the dishes cleared away, Sarah started polishing crystal in the kitchen, while her sisters went back upstairs to mend a few torn tablecloths.

She carefully lifted one of the crystal punch bowls from its crate, holding it up to the light with both hands. Turning it left, then right, she inspected if for cracks that might cause punch to leak out of the vessel.

The back door swung open, startling her. She spun to see Owen standing there, in all his shirtless, muscled glory. Her breath hitched in her throat at the sight of him, so close to her. She swore she could feel the heat rolling off his body as it touched her own.

Lord, what a handsome man.

As her upper body completed the pivot, she lost control of the bowl.

Sarah watched in horror as her mother's crystal punch bowl crashed to the floor, the glistening shards scattering across the sun-dappled wood.

Owen grimaced. "You all right?"

She nodded, feeling the tightness enter her neck and shoulder. "For now, but I won't be once Mommy finds out about this."

As if cued, her mother's voice called from upstairs. "What was that ruckus?"

Drawing a deep breath, Sarah uttered a very unladylike curse.

Owen crossed over to where she stood, placing a fleeting touch against her shoulder. "Don't worry."

She mustered a small smile at his attempt at reassurance, but she knew her mother would not be so charitable.

☙ ☙ ☙

Owen squatted down to survey the shimmering mess on the kitchen floor, just as the lady of the house swept into the kitchen.

As she tossed a quick glance at the floor, Mrs. Webster's pretty face folded into a frown. "Good heavens. Is that one of my punch bowls?"

Sarah started to open her mouth.

Owen cut her off. "My apologies, Mrs. Webster. I knocked it off the table." He let his gaze quickly slide to Sarah, lingering long enough to see her wide-eyed surprise, before placing his full focus back on her mother.

Mrs. Webster sighed. "It's all right, Owen."

"I'll be sure to deduct the cost of it from my fee for building the gazebo, ma'am. Will that be acceptable?"

The older woman's expression softened noticeably in response to his offer. "Thank you, Owen. That's very nice of you."

He gave her a bow. "I'm at your service."

Now Mrs. Webster smiled. "Oh, you. Sarah, could you help Owen clean up this mess? I wouldn't want anyone falling and getting cut."

"Yes, ma'am." Sarah moved across the kitchen to the small pantry, returning with a broom.

Seemingly satisfied, Mrs. Goodman left the room. When she was gone, Sarah turned his way. "Why did you do that? Why did you take the blame for me?"

He shrugged. "You looked pretty scared of what your mother might do to you. I harbor no such fear, so I took responsibility."

Using the broom to gather the brilliant shards into a pile, she shook her head. "And the offer to take the price of the bowl out of your pay?"

"Seemed reasonable." He shrugged again. Inside, he felt somewhat amused by her confusion. "It isn't often a man has a chance to rescue such a fair damsel."

She pursed her lips. "The 'fair' part may be true, but I'm no damsel in need of rescue."

His brow hitched, because he hadn't expected the level of annoyance projected in her tone. "It wasn't meant as an insult."

She released a sigh as she stooped to sweep the shards of the punch bowl onto a flat sheet of metal. "I'm sorry. I'm just annoyed with myself for being clumsy. Thank you for your kindness."

"You're welcome." He watched her walk, taking in the graceful sway of her steps as she tossed the remnants of the bowl into the refuse bin.

She set the broom aside, turned back his way. "Did you need something?"

"I came in for a cool drink." He rubbed his chin. When he'd first entered the house, he'd been seeking a cup of Mrs. Goodman's tart lemonade. Now, he thought the presence of her middle daughter might refresh him just as much.

She went to the icebox. "There's just a little of Mommy's lemonade left. I'll get it for you."

Moments later, she handed him a cup of the cold, sweet drink. Taking a long draw, he looked at her. She'd taken a seat at the table, and had set about polishing the crystal dishes scattered all over the tabletop. Anyone could see she had a lot of work ahead of her, and he had a gazebo to build. But something about her kept him glued to the spot. Rather than getting back to the work waiting for him, his mind was busy thinking of reasons to remain in her presence.

To break the silence, he asked, "What's it like out in the Territory?"

"Why do you ask?" She rubbed her cloth against one of the remaining punch bowls.

"From what I heard, it ain't the safest place in the world. Especially for a woman alone."

Her brow hitched, but she kept her gaze on the crystal. "And how do you know I'm a woman alone?"

He shifted his weight from left to right. "Your Pa told me."

That didn't seem to sit well with her, because her jaw tightened up. "Good to know Daddy is telling my business. Anyway, it's not that much different from living here, except for a few things."

He took another draw of lemonade. "Like what?"

"Beautiful land out there. Wide, open spaces, folks farming and raising cattle. General stores, hotels, all of that."

He tried to conjure up a picture in his mind's eye based on what she described, but had little luck. "What are the folks like out there? Any hostile Indians?"

She shook her head. "I haven't met any 'hostile' Indians. That's just a dime novel myth, far as I'm concerned."

"Then tell me what they're really like."

"There's a lot more of the races mixing out there. Folks ain't so proper and concerned about what everybody else thinks. And," she paused long enough to turn her eyes up to meet his, "women can vote."

He drained the last of the lemonade, set the cup on the butcher block near the basin. "Really? I heard about that, but I didn't think it would apply to colored folks."

She pursed her lips. "Things are different out there. Everybody can vote, no matter what they look like or where they come from. You're twenty-one, you can go and vote. Just the way it ought to be."

He frowned. "I don't know about all that."

Her eyes narrowed. "What do you mean?"

He shrugged. "I'm not sure I agree that women ought to be voting. Not when the government doesn't bother to enforce the fifteenth amendment." He and the other Sons had discussed this very issue at their last meeting. As of late, women all over the country had been getting their bonnets in a bunch and demanding that they should have the right to vote. Owen, along with most of the Sons, agreed that the women's suffrage movement was a detriment to the voting rights of men of color.

She set the cloth aside, fixing him with a hard look. "How can you say that?"

"It's what I believe. The constant squawking of your fellow woman about suffrage only serves as a distraction from the real issue."

She folded her arms over her chest, shielding her bosom from his view. "And what, pray tell, is the 'real issue'?"

"No more rights should be granted to anyone, until the government enforces the rights they already gave out. Men of the race should be able to vote freely."

"And I suppose we women should just be content to wait around until then?"

He shrugged. "Why not? You waited this long, haven't you?"

She blinked once, then again. Her expression held all the welcoming charm of an angry hornet. "Mr. Markham, if you don't mind, I'd like to get back to my work." Snatching up the cloth, she began furiously scrubbing another piece of crystal.

He wanted to chuckle, but thought the better of it. With a shake of his head, he opened the back door and slipped out.

CHAPTER 3

June 30, 1881

Sarah stood by the parlor window, taking in the sights outside. The sun was making its slow but steady journey toward the horizon, and she could see the flickering glow of a few fireflies as they passed.

Returning to her seat at the sewing table, she lit a lamp. She still had to finish repairing the lace collar of her summer-weight party dress, and she knew that the waning light of day would be long gone before the task was completed. Gathering up the waves of sunny, yellow fabric, she positioned the lace and the collar beneath the foot of the sewing machine and began making her lock chain stitch.

A half an hour passed, with only the sound of the machine to break the silence. She'd removed the finished collar from the machine when she heard footsteps descending the stairs. Looking up from her stitching, she saw her father approaching.

"Did you finish your dress, dear?"

She nodded. "All that's left is to tie off the stitch. Should be ready in time for the party Saturday."

He waited, silently watching while she tied off the stitch.

"Something you need, Daddy?"

He stroked his salt and pepper beard. "Yes. Did you know Owen is still working?"

"I can hear him hammering, but I haven't been back there today." And she hadn't. She'd been too busy getting the house prepared for her mother's party. Even after all the preparations she and her sisters had made, she still felt they had a million more things to do.

"Take him a sandwich and a drink. It's the least we can do, with him working so hard to finish in time." George had settled into his favorite armchair, with a copy of the *Fayetteville Observer*.

Without being asked, she lit the lamp next to her father's chair so he could read by the soft glow. "Yes, sir." Regardless of the fact that she didn't want to be bothered with Owen, she knew better than to question her father's edict. Leaving the two lamps lit, to be sure her father had enough light, she moved into the kitchen.

Since the rear of the house faced westward, she had the remaining sunlight to aid her in putting together a simple sandwich for Owen. She laid a few slices of roast chicken from the icebox between two slices of her mother's stoneground wheat bread, and placed it on a plate. Adding a cup of the lemonade Mary had made this morning, she took the simple meal outside.

As her father had indicated, Owen was still working on the gazebo. His shirtless silhouette moved against the darkness as his powerful arm swung the hammer, striking a series of nails to fuse two sections of cherry wood together.

At her approach, he stopped swinging and set the hammer down. Looking at the offerings she'd brought, he smiled. "Why, Ms. Sarah. That's mighty kind of you."

Shaking off the warmth that his smile set off within her, she handed him the items. "Daddy asked me to bring it. And I'm certain he's watching, since he has a clear view out the back window from his armchair."

Owen chuckled. "Noted, but thanks just the same."

With a curt nod, she turned to go back inside.

"Wait."

The single word, spoken in his deep, silken voice, made her stop in her tracks.

She swiveled her head and upper body toward him. "What is it, Mr. Markham?"

"I said something you didn't like. I can tell, because you've gone back to being formal with me."

She could feel her face tighten up. "I'm not too keen on your views on suffrage, but there's no reason that should matter."

"Sit with me." He took up a spot on the grass next to the unfinished gazebo. "You can sit on this flat rock so you won't sully your skirts."

She stood there in the growing shadows for a moment, looking back and forth between him and the back door. *Why in the world would he want to sit with me?* "What are you about?"

"Just don't cotton to eating alone, if I can help it." He patted the rock. "Please?"

Swallowing, and mindful of her father's watchful eyes, she acquiesced. Soon she was seated on the flat rock next to Owen, her hands in her lap, fingertips laced together.

A warm breeze swept through the yard, rustling the leaves of the magnolia and crepe myrtles planted around the property.

"Want a piece?" He offered her some of the sandwich.

She shook her head. "I'm still stuffed from dinner." She sat in silence, content to entertain her own thoughts as he polished off the sandwich and set the plate aside.

"I didn't mean to rile you. About the suffrage issue."

She said nothing, unsure of the right words. He was a man, and she didn't think he could ever truly understand what it meant to be a woman, let alone a woman of color, in a world that so often tried to crush your spirit.

"I believe what I believe, but I shouldn't have been so brusque about it." He drank some of the lemonade in his cup.

"You're right. You shouldn't have."

He frowned, but said nothing.

"My aunt Gert is an agitator. She's marched for the vote, for black men, for women, for the natives and the immigrants. She wants us all to have equal rights. Not just men."

He looked as if he wanted to say something.

She fixed him with a glare. She hadn't come out here to lecture him, but thinking of her mother's older sister, the warrior Gertrude, fired her resolve. "Aunt Gert has taken fists to the face, been threatened, and jailed because of her work, but none of that has stopped her. I learned from her what it means to fight."

His eyes widened.

"She's the bravest person I know, man or woman, and I have the utmost respect for her."

"Heavens. I didn't know any of that."

"Well, now you do. And I'll thank you not to disrespect my views, even if you don't agree."

"I'm sorry, Sarah. I'll try to do better in the future." His expression showed that he'd been properly chastised, and wasn't too pleased about it.

A sigh escaped her. "You did rescue me from my mother's wrath, so I suppose we're even."

"Good. Pax, then." He stuck out his hand.

She shook it. The moment their hands touched, she felt a shiver of electric excitement shimmy up her spine.

Instead of letting go, he lingered, drawing the contact out.

In that moment, she felt an odd sensation sweep through her. Her body tingled, and the feeling seemed to radiate out from their joined hands. *What's happening to me? Why does he make me feel so out of sorts?*

"I work for suffrage." She blurted the words, unable to stop them from tumbling out.

His brow creased in confusion. "I thought you worked in a hotel restaurant?"

"I do. But I've been working for suffrage for the women of this country since I left home. I write essays for different publications on the topic, and occasionally, I lecture. I've been corresponding with an organization in Washington, D.C. as of late."

"Hmm." He scratched his chin. "Do your folks know about it?"

"No." She looked down at her hand, still encased in his. "With all that's happened to Aunt Gert, they'd never approve."

"I'm not going to tell them, if that's what you're fretting about."

She looked up to meet his gaze. "Honestly?"

He nodded. "I may not agree with the concept, but it's not my place to interfere. You're an adult, after all."

Full darkness had begun to fall, and she could barely make out the lines of his face as he watched her. "I appreciate that."

A nonchalant shrug came in response.

Aware of the hour, and of the perceived impropriety of their being alone together, she stood. Brushing bits of grass from her skirts, she turned to him. "I have to be going. It's getting late."

He picked up the cup and the plate and handed them to her. "Thank you for the meal."

She gave him a polite nod. "Thank you for the conversation."

She started her walk back to the house, all the while turning their encounter over in her mind. For whatever reason, she trusted that he'd keep his promise not to tell her family about her suffrage work.

As she stepped up on the back porch, she saw a figure standing in the back window over the kitchen basin. Soft lamp light illuminated the figure, and she smiled.

Entering the house and closing the door behind her, she asked, "How long have you been standing there, Daddy?"

"Plenty long enough," he quipped, giving her shoulder a squeeze. "You and Owen are good together.

Shaking her head at her father's matchmaking, Sarah leaned up to give him a kiss. "Goodnight, Daddy."

And before he could say anything more, she slipped out of his embrace and went upstairs to seek her bed.

೧ ೧ ೧

After Sarah's departure, Owen took a few moments to gather up his tools and supplies. Once he'd filled the wooden toolbox he kept everything in, he donned his shirt and grabbed the box by the handle. Then he set off on foot for the trip home.

His small cabin and workshop were located about a half mile south of the Webster property, so he hadn't bothered with his wagon beyond the first few days of the job, when he'd been hauling wood to the worksite. Now that all he needed were his tools, he walked to work each day, using the time and solitude to collect his thoughts.

As he strolled alongside the dirt road, he thought back on his conversation with Sarah. She probably feared he'd give away her secret to her parents, but he would never do such a thing. Aside from being a man of his word, he knew firsthand what it was like to work in secret for a cause you believed in. That was the very crux of his work with the Sons of the Diaspora.

The Sons worked in the shadows, meeting in the evenings after the barbershop closed. In an effort to secure the franchise for men of the race, they raised funds for travel and to cover poll taxes that might be levied by corrupt county party bosses. Those among them who could read, like Owen and Mac, tutored those who were illiterate. From time to time, when the Sons could procure a literacy test, they studied long into the night with their brothers, to prepare them for the exams. Whatever barriers stood between Black men and the ballot box, the Sons meant to tear them down, brick by brick if necessary.

He entered his cabin a short while later, closing and locking the door behind him. He set the toolbox on one of the low bookcases near the front door. After he'd lit a lamp to illuminate the cabin's interior, he stripped off his shirt and denims, tossing the sweat-damp fabric over the back of a chair. He'd need to visit the laundress in town over the next day or so, to drop off his dirty things and get a pile of his fresh shirts and denims from her.

Nude as a newborn, he darted through the house and out into the yard between the cabin and his woodshop. There, he pumped up a good bit of cool water, and used it along with a small bar of lye soap to cleanse the grime from his body. Bathing outdoors, in the summer, made sense to him. It was less messy and less troublesome than hauling water into the house. Luckily, the location of his home afforded him the privacy he needed to do so. Beyond his woodshop was a wide swath of tall pines and spruce, their branches stretching toward the sky. The forest extended for a good mile and a half around his home on three sides.

Clean and cooled off, he returned to the house and donned a pair of linen pants. He looked around his one-room cabin. It wasn't fancy by any stretch. It held only two chairs, a table, and the roughhewn bed he slept in. He had the basics of a kitchen on one end: a fireplace, a basin, and a few cabinets. His "parlor" consisted of a couple of crates he'd fashioned into a long, bench-like seat, covered with a simple burlap cushion. The only indulgence he had were bookshelves. He'd built four of them, about hip high, to store his massive collection of books. When not working, he loved to read, everything from the Bible, to Shakespeare, to books on woodworking.

Above his bed, he'd hung the lone decorative piece in his home: a quilt. The small quilt had been sewn by his mother's mother, Ethel, and placed with him in the bassinet upon his birth. Their little family, consisting of Owen, his mother, Myrtle, father, Curtis, and Grandmother, Ethel, had lived the large balance of his life in the Great Dismal Swamp on the border of North Carolina and Virginia. Like many other escaped slaves, his family had taken refuge there. His mother had been heavily pregnant with him at the time she ran.

He slipped between the sheets, settling in for the night. Pushing aside the jumble of thoughts to seek rest, he let his eyes slide shut.

A vision of Sarah awaited him in his dreams.

CHAPTER 4

July 1, 1881

A yawn escaped Sarah's mouth before she could cover it. Trudging into the kitchen, she lit two lamps and placed one on either side of the window ledge. The sun had yet to rise, but she had a very large triple-berry, lemon cake to attend to for her mother's party. So risen she had.

Tightening the belt of the cotton wrapper covering her nightgown, she stifled another yawn as she set about making a pot of coffee. If she wanted the cake to come out right, she need to be fully awake and in possession of her wits. While the coffee brewed, she went to the basin to wash her hands, and started gathering the items she'd need.

By the time Sarah sat down with a hot mug of coffee, cut with a bit of cream from the icebox, the sun was fully up. Taking a sip of the life-giving brew, she sighed contentedly into the silent kitchen.

Moments later, the silence was broken by the tinkling laughter of her young niece, Emily.

Turning, Sarah saw Mary entering the kitchen, holding her daughter's tiny hand.

"I smell coffee." Mary glided over to the stove, where the still warm pot rested. "Emily, say good morning to Auntie Sarah."

"Ga' moan'in, auntie!" Emily launched her tiny, gown-clad body up into Sarah's lap, and tossed her tiny arms around her neck.

Sarah smiled. "Good morning, sweetie. You didn't come for coffee, did you?"

Emily frowned. "Mama say coffee for gwown ups."

Shaking her head, Sarah giggled. "That it is, Em." She kissed her tiny brown forehead.

Mary soon joined them at the table, with her own cup of coffee.

"Getting ready to make the cake?"

She nodded. "Why else would I be up this dang early?"

Emily began to bounce on her lap. "Cake! Cake! Cake!"

Mary shook her head, placed a steadying hand on Emily's shoulder. "Calm down, darling. Cake is for grandma's birthday tomorrow, remember?"

Her tiny bottom lip shot out, but Emily nodded somberly.

Elizabeth, Kate, and George entered the kitchen then, all headed for the coffee pot. Mother and daughter were still in their bedclothes, but George was fully dressed.

"Going down to the butcher house. Ainsley's got some fine beef for the party." George downed some of the coffee, and then kissed his wife before heading out the back door on the way to town.

Sarah, still seated with Emily on her lap, looked around at the kitchen full of all the women she loved. "You all have to get out. I'll need the whole room to properly prepare my cake."

Emily resumed her bouncing. "Can I help, auntie?"

She shook her head. "No, sweetheart. Not this time."

Mary scooped up her baby girl, hoisting her onto her hip. "Come on, baby. We'll go upstairs and try to tame that hair for the party." Mary eyed her daughter's cockeyed pigtails and shook her head. "These just won't do."

Once her mother and Kate had had a shot at the coffee pot, the other women filtered out of the kitchen, leaving Sarah alone. Rising from her seat, she went to the large mixing bowl she'd set out earlier. Adding a heap of flour, she began the process of making heating the oven for the cakes. With the wood tucked inside and the fire lit, she opened the back door and the window to allow the cool morning air in. Then she turned her focus to her cake batter.

With the coffee flowing through her, she made short work of the batter. In less than an hour, she had the six cake pans full and ready to go into the oven. This cake would be about the same size as the one she'd made for the wedding several weeks ago at the Inter-Ocean, but here at home, she lacked the benefit of a large oven. Therefore, the cake layers would have to be cooked in two batches.

She leaned over to slide the first three pans into the oven. When she stood again, she saw Owen walking up to the gazebo, toolbox in hand. It was the first time she'd seen him in a shirt. It was a simple, soft blue with short sleeves and buttons down the front. He wore the shirt with a pair of denims. While she had to admit her disappointment at having her view of his chest obscured, the shirt did nothing to detract from his rugged handsomeness.

With the first cakes in the oven, she had nothing pressing to do, since she planned to make the glaze when the second batch went in. So, she leaned against the basin and watched Owen work.

First, he attached the last two beams to the main frame of the gazebo, using a hammer to drive the nails. With that done, he fit beautiful lattice panels to four of the five sides of the gazebo, attaching them with nails as well. He disappeared around the house, and returned with a short ladder.

Sarah watched as he climbed the ladder and fit the roof, which he'd already assembled, atop the gazebo. She had to admit, the finished structure was very impressive, and a beautiful gift to celebrate her mother's milestone birthday.

I could watch him work all day long.

There was something appealing about watching a man work with his hands. She couldn't recall ever being so enraptured by the sight of any other man doing physical labor. He eyed the gazebo with a smile, running his hands over the wood in a way that mimicked a caress. She wondered what it would feel like to have his strong hands slide over her skin that way. The thought made the corners of her mouth tip up into a smile.

Scandalized by the direction of her thoughts, she inhaled deeply, hoping to return to her mind to purer musings.

The smell of the cake touched her nostrils, and she remembered the layers in the oven. Scurrying to retrieve the potholders, she pulled out the three pans as quickly as she could manage. Examining them to be sure they weren't burnt, she breathed a sigh of relief. While the edges were a bit brown and crispy, the main portion of the layers was fine. Resolving to trim away the edges, she set the cakes on the table to cool and slid the other pans into the oven.

When she looked to the window again, she saw Owen slowly dragging a paintbrush over the gazebo. With each stroke, he left a glossy, dark patina, which allowed the color of the wood to show through. He obviously worked quickly, because most of the structure was already covered with stain.

She turned around, intent on trimming the first three cake layers of their overcooked edges.

A moment later, Owen swung open the back door, and stuck his head inside.

"Morning, Sarah. Can you tell your folks to stay away from the gazebo until the stain dries?"

She nodded. "I will."

He looked as if he was going to go back out, but stopped, inhaling deeply. "What is that heavenly aroma?"

The compliment brought heat up into her cheeks. "It's my present to Mommy. Triple-berry, lemon cake for the party."

He eyed the cake layers on the table, easing farther into the house.

She could feel his unspoken request flowing between them. "Yes, you can taste the trimmings."

Clapping his hands together, he fully entered the kitchen, letting the door shut behind him.

❧ ❧ ❧

Amazed by his good fortune, Owen moved closer to Sarah and the offered pan of cake trimmings. They were a little burnt, but if the cake tasted anywhere near as good as it smelled, he felt sure it wouldn't matter.

He picked up a bit of the cake and pressed it into his mouth. Instantly, a groan escaped him. "My Lord, Sarah. Everything your father said about your baking skills is true."

She blushed, directing her eyes toward the floor. "Oh, go on, Owen."

"No, really. This is the best cake I've ever tasted." He went back for another bit of the heavenly confection. "Just don't tell my mother I said that and we're square."

"Thank you for the compliment." She looked up then, mirth dancing in her dark golden eyes. "I'm flattered."

He let his gaze sweep over her, taking in her attire. She wore a thin wrapper of blue cotton. The hem of a matching gown peeked from beneath the bottom of the robe, nearly covering her bare feet. To some degree, he felt as if he were intruding. After all, it wasn't proper for a man to see a woman who was not his wife in her sleeping attire. Nothing about her demeanor communicated discomfort, so he didn't bring it up. As he swallowed a mouthful of the sweet, crisp cake trimmings, he forced his mind away from thoughts of what she might have on beneath her nightgown.

Setting down the empty plate, he took a step nearer to her. "You have flour on your face."

She tensed a bit. "Where? It may be confectioners' sugar."

It would be easier to just brush it off than try to explain it to her. Before he could stop himself, he reached out. Using his fingertips, he brushed the white dust dotting her jawline away.

She trembled at the contact, her eyes closing.

"It's gone now," he said softly. He knew he should move his hand away, but he couldn't. Instead, he drew his fingertips along her satin jawline once more.

Another tremble. Her eyes slowly opened, and she looked up at him. "Owen, what are you about?"

Still touching her face, he shook his head in wonder. "I'm not entirely sure. All I know is it feels natural to touch you. It feels...right."

Her lashes fluttered in a very endearing way. "Owen, I...we..."

"I'm not going to hurt you. I would never." He took another step, placing his body flush against hers. His free arm draped loosely around her waist.

She didn't back away, didn't show any sign of protest. Her expression only communicated wonder and a bit of virginal trepidation.

Still, he would not let this encounter rest solely on his assumptions. "If I'm making you uncomfortable, I'll leave. Just tell me."

Her answer came with a slow shake of her head. "No. It's like you said. It feels...natural. What does that mean?"

The innocence in her eyes, and in her question, made his heart pound in his chest. "I don't know. But I can't wait to find out."

He dipped his head, readied his lips to touch her cheek.

"Auntie Sarah?!" A tiny voice shouted from the depths of the house.

Owen released Sarah abruptly, and they had only a moment to put space between them before the youngest member of the household raced into the kitchen, peals of laughter coming with her.

She ran right up to Sarah, clutching her wrapper. "Auntie, help now?"

Sarah seemed to think it over for a moment. "Okay, honey. Help Auntie make the glaze, okay?"

The little one nodded and clapped in delight.

Owen smiled at the scene. Once day, Sarah would make a fine mother to the child of some very lucky man. Thinking that man might be anyone other than himself made him very annoyed.

Returning to the door, he announced. "I'll let you attend to your work. Please remember to tell everyone about the stain."

She looked his way. "I will see you at the party tomorrow."

"See you then." With a nod, he left the house. As he gathered his tools and started home, he wrestled with his inner questions of what might have happened between him and Sarah, had the little one not appeared when she had. He'd been about to kiss her, and he'd sensed she was agreeable to that. Now that he'd missed the chance, he had no idea when the next opportunity would present itself.

Sarah was untried; she wore her virginity on her sleeve and he would not be the sort of man to take advantage of that. He would, however, seek to court her properly. Her father had already expressed his desire that Sarah marry and move back to Fayetteville to settle down. Owen could sense something growing between the two of them, something that might get George Webster his wish.

There was still the matter of Sarah's views and her work for women's suffrage. He wasn't sure he could abide by those things. She thought women ought to be able to vote, but he disagreed. Women wanted too much, in his mind.

They wanted the franchise, wanted to work outside of the home, and more. And when women sought employment, they wouldn't be content with being nurses or teachers. If women were to do everything men did, what was to separate the sexes? He didn't know the answer to that, nor did he have a solution. All he knew was that he wanted to see Black men able to cast a ballot, without fear of reprisal.

Sarah was much more headstrong than the women he usually found appealing, but she appealed to him just the same, in a way no woman ever had before.

Thinking on Sarah, and the conundrum she presented, he set his feet to the road and headed toward home.

CHAPTER 5

July 2, 1881

Sarah pushed her empty plate toward the center of the table, looking toward her father. "I'm stuffed. What a breakfast, Daddy."

George, seated at the head of the table, smiled. "I simply made a meal befitting the special occasion." He turned loving eyes on his wife. "Happy birthday, my love."

Sarah, along with her sisters and niece, all directed their eyes to the opposite end of the dining room table, where the birthday queen sat.

Elizabeth's cheeks reddened. "Thank you, dearest, but that's the fifth time you've said it today." A swipe of her napkin across her mouth momentarily hid her grin from view.

George winked. "And the day is only beginning, Liza."

Sarah couldn't help smiling at her parents' interaction. They'd been married twenty-five years, yet still carried on like lovesick adolescents at times. Watching them as they made doe eyes at each other from opposite ends of the table made her wonder if she'd ever have something so special in her own life.

Little Emily tugged on the arm of Sarah's nightgown, dragging her out of her own thoughts.

"What is it, Emily?"

"Upstairs. Mama gonna fix your hair." Emily pointed a chubby finger toward the staircase.

Sarah looked up to see her mother and sisters climbing the stairs. Realizing she'd been so lost in her own thoughts that she hadn't even noticed them leaving the table, she got up to follow them.

Stopping, she looked to her father, who busied himself stacking plates. "Daddy, let me help you clear the dishes."

"Grab those water glasses and bring them in the kitchen."

Sarah did as her father asked, and followed him into the kitchen. There, they placed the dishes in and around the basin.

"I'm going to the pump for some water." George made his way toward the back door, with a water pail in hand.

Sarah turned to go upstairs, but stopped when she heard her father call her name. "Yes, Daddy?"

"How are you getting on with Owen? He's a nice man, isn't he?"

Sarah knew better than to tell her father what she really thought. "Yes, Daddy. He's very nice." She kept the statement and her face neutral, so as not to give her matchmaking father any false hope.

That seemed to be enough to appease him, because he smiled and went on outside to the pump.

Shaking her head, Sarah went upstairs to join the other ladies. Everyone had gathered in their parent's bedroom, and when Sarah entered, her mother was nowhere to be seen.

"Where's Mommy?" Sarah asked as she took a seat in her father's old rocker.

"In the bathing room, soaking." The answer came from Mary, who stood behind Kate as she sat on their mother's vanity stool. Mary was currently combing Kate's hair up into some intricate style.

Emily had taken up residence on the braided throw rug by the bed, and was quietly playing with her beloved rag doll.

Sarah looked toward the partially open door of the bathing room and released a little sigh. Her small place back in Cheyenne had indoor plumbing, thankfully, but her bathing room only had a shower. She envied her mother's ability to climb into the big claw foot tub and enjoy a hot, soothing soak.

"So, what's going on between you and Owen?" Kate folded her arms over her chest in anticipation of the answer.

"Yes, do tell." Mary chimed in as she slid yet another pin into Kate's hair.

"There's nothing to tell. I know Daddy is out to yoke us together, but I'm not so inclined."

"So you say." Based on her tone, Kate seemed wholly unconvinced.

That made Sarah roll her eyes. "I do say so. I've just met the man, for Heaven's sake."

Her lips pursed around a few hair pins, Mary spoke again. "You were comfortable enough with him to be alone in the yard with him. After dark, even."

Sarah frowned. "Daddy sent me out there, to bring him a meal since he was working late."

"I'll bet Daddy didn't tell you to stay until after the sun went down."

In response to Mary's pointed statement, Sarah could only look away. She wasn't about to admit that she'd stayed simply because Owen had asked her to, or that she'd been far more comfortable than she should have been in the presence of a man she barely knew.

Kate giggled, clapping her hands together. "I knew it. Look at her face. Something's going on between them."

Laying back in the rocker, Sarah blew out an exasperated breath. "You two are as crazy as loons. I just met the man a week ago, and already you two have decided we're destined mates."

"Your sisters may be on to something."

Sarah's eyes shifted toward the bathing room door again, shaking her head as she realized her mother had been listening the entire time.

"After all, Mary was married at nineteen."

Mary's expression was a mixture of smugness and pride.

Sarah wanted to gag. Instead, she called back, "Yes, Mama." All the while, she thought about how tired she was of being compared to her older sister. It seemed everything she did was immediately measured against Mary's achievements, and in most cases, Sarah just didn't feel she measured up.

She looked to Kate, the baby of the family. Not only was she the youngest, and thereby incapable of wrongdoing, she was also the "pretty" one. From where Sarah sat, between the industrious, intelligent Mary and the beautiful, cooperative Kate, things always seemed a bit...intense.

"Come on over, Sarah," Mary called. "I'm done with Kate."

Sarah watched Kate rise, and took in the beauty of her pin-curled up-do. "Wow. That looks amazing." Sliding onto the bench Kate had vacated, Sarah looked at her reflection in the oval mirror mounted on the vanity.

"I've got something similar in mind for you." Mary gently turned Sarah's head from side to side.

"Sorry I didn't get a chance to take my braid out." She patted the long single braid, which had been intact ever since her arrival home.

Mary waved her off. "It's okay. Won't take me but a minute." True to her word, Mary used the bone comb to work Sarah's hair free of the braid in less than a minute.

As the thick mass of dark waves fell around her shoulders, Sarah smiled. Her hair was one of the few things she felt confident in. While her other features might be considered plain, her hair was as thick and rich as her mother and sisters, and even a bit longer.

Mary splayed her hands through Sarah's hair. "Your hair is in good shape. Who's been minding it for you out west?"

"I've been doing it myself. I do purchase tins of orange oil from the mercantile. They get shipments of it from back east."

"It shows. Your hair looks and smells wonderful." Mary used the tail end of the bone comb to make a slanted part. "By the time I'm finished with you, Owen won't be able to resist you."

Kate chuckled, as she admired her own hair in her mother's silver hand mirror. "He's as good as caught, then. He'll be our brother-in-law soon enough."

As had been the case since she'd first laid eyes on him, Sarah's pulse quickened at the mention of Owen's name. Her sister's outrageous declarations aside, she wouldn't mind dazzling the handsome carpenter, not one bit.

Settling into the padded seat of the bench, Sarah winked. "All right, Mary. Work your magic."

ↄ ↄ ↄ

Owen entered Mac's Barbershop, letting the door swing shut behind him. Removing his bowler, he exchanged nods and words of greeting with the men inside. About ten gentlemen of varying ages occupied the shop at the moment, as was to be expected. Anyone visiting Mac's on a Saturday morning could expect the place to be crowded. With today's celebration at the Webster place, Owen had known to come early and anticipate a long wait.

Snagging the last empty chair along the west wall, Owen settled into the seat. It was a steamy, hot July morning, and he'd donned an old but clean plaid shirt and denims, knowing he'd change clothes before the party.

McLean "Mac" Grant, a tall, barrel chested man of the race, was nearing his sixtieth year. He'd been trained as a barber by his master during his enslavement, a skill his master prized, since Mac was his head houseman. After the war and word of Emancipation, Mac had gone south in search of his beloved wife, who'd been sold away from him years prior. Returning to Fayetteville with his wife Hazel by his side, he'd opened his shop in '75.

Mac and Tim, the young apprentice barber he brought in to help him serve the Saturday crowd, both had men in their chairs. Eight other men, Owen included, were waiting to be served.

"It's a damn shame," Mac declared as he took his shears to the beard of the man in his chair. "The law gives us the right to vote, and some folks just won't let us be."

Owen looked around at he faces of the men in the shop. All were of the race, and three were members of the Sons. He assumed Mac felt comfortable speaking on the subject, due to the current dynamic in the room.

"It's been over a decade," added Will Pruett, the town's shipbuilder. "I don't have much hope that the government is going to step in at this point."

"Garfield's platform seems promising. I think he's got the best interests of freedmen at heart."

Owen thought on that statement, made by an older man he didn't recognize. President James Garfield had taken the oath of office just this past spring, and had been president only a few months. He could easily recall reading the new president's inauguration speech in the pages of the *Fayetteville Observer*, courtesy of the Associated Press. President Garfield had spoken passionately about the rights of the Negro race, so much so that Owen was inclined to agree with the stranger's assessment.

Tim, young and nearly always a contrarian, raised his voice in dissent. "I don't believe nothing these politicians say, until they do it. We'll see what's been done by this time next year."

Mac shook his head. "We'll see. But if the women keep agitating for their vote, who knows." He shrugged, and then tapped his client on the shoulder. "You're all done, sir."

Owen sat back in his chair, eager to hear what the other men thought about that topic. Opinions flew back and forth, until one voice rose above the din.

"Bottom line is, women are too addled, too foolish to be given the vote." Tim clapped his hands together, as if applauding his own genius.

Owen looked at the boy, who couldn't have been more than seventeen but seemed so sure of his stance. Several weeks ago, he probably would have agreed with Tim. Now, having met Sarah, he couldn't say that so readily.

That gave him pause. Was he really letting a woman, one he'd only just met, alter his way of thinking? What was it about her that had him so out-of-sorts? She was beauty, and she made one hell of a cake. But what else did he really know about her, other than that she was stubborn, headstrong, and would likely put a man through his paces with a smile on her face?

He imagined Sarah was spending the morning with the other women of the house, putting on their finery for the party. He wondered how she would style her long, thick mane of hair, which he'd only so far seen fashioned into a single plait hanging down her back. Would she paint her face like the other young women of town were apt to do? Don some low-cut summer gown that would display the rounded tops of her breasts and accentuate the feminine curves of her body?

"Owen, you're mighty quiet. What you think?" Mac's question dragged him back to reality.

Unsure of what to say, Owen offered a shrug. "I don't spend too much time thinking about what the women are up to. I'm just concerned about casting my own ballot in peace."

"Here, here." Will nodded his agreement. "That's just where our focus should stay."

Mac skillfully redirected the conversation by asking, "Who's excited about escorting your wives to the Webster's party today?"

A mixture of laughter and groans rose from the assemblage. Owen could only smile when he saw the wide-eyed look on Tim's face. Unable to resist teasing the boy, Owen chided, "Our Tim looks a little nervous. Coming to call on young Miss Katherine?"

Tim swallowed hard. "I...uh...well, I'll be at the party, if that's what you're asking."

Mac, positioned a few inches to Tim's right, ribbed the boy. "Come now, Tim. We all know you've set your cap for the youngest Webster sister."

Tim said nothing, but his expression spoke volumes as he made a show of dusting the hair clippings off his client's shoulders with a handheld sweeping brush.

Owen chuckled to himself. George Webster was a big man, easily twice Tim's size. Mr. Webster also had a reputation for being fiercely protective of his daughters. Owen supposed that meant he should be flattered that George thought enough of him to try to yoke him to his middle daughter. Smiling to himself, he grabbed up a copy of *Harper's Magazine* and opened it, content to pass the time reading until his turn in the chair.

Men filtered in and out of the shop, rotating between the waiting chairs and the barber chairs, until Owen got into Mac's chair.

"What you looking for, Owen?"

He regarded his reflection in the wall-mounted mirror for a moment. "Just trim my mustache and neaten up my beard."

"You got it." Mac swung the canvas cape over Owen's torso, fastening it with the ties in the back.

Twenty minutes later, a freshly groomed Owen bid the men in the shop goodbye, and mounted his horse for the ride back to his cabin.

CHAPTER 6

July 2, 1881

When Sarah stepped out the back door in her party dress, she could see that the yard had already been outfitted in celebratory finery. She scanned the scenery with a smile, noting how everything reflected her mother's favorite color. Festive yellow bunting had been hung along the top edge of the old wooden fence that marked the boundary of the yard. The trestle tables filled with food had yellow tablecloths. And the new gazebo, the centerpiece of it all, had been draped in yellow ribbon. Sarah instinctively knew her mother would love the setup.

The time was ten minutes until one, and the party was to begin on the hour. Elizabeth Webster thought of punctuality as a virtue, and that was a well-known fact in town. Most of the party guests had already arrived, and were scattered around the yard. People sat in pairs or stood in groups, carrying on various conversations as the warm Carolina sun shined down on them. As custom dictated, the food hadn't been touched. No one wanted to be rude by eating before the guest of honor made her appearance.

Sarah moved off the back porch and into the yard, greeting her friends and neighbors. It was nice to see everyone dressed in their best clothes, and she complimented a few people on their attire as she made her way toward the gazebo.

Her father, in his best summer-weight suit, waited there with her sisters, who'd donned their party dresses. Mary's dress was a high-necked creation in a soft shade of green, while Katherine had chosen a soft-lavender gown with a square neckline and cap sleeves. Sarah brushed a bit of dry grass from the skirt of her own dress, a pink, off–the-shoulder ensemble, and took her place next to the rest of her family.

As the clock chimed the one o'clock hour, Elizabeth stepped out of the back door. She looked resplendent, and far younger than her forty-five years, in her daffodil-yellow party gown. The sweetheart neckline, edged in lace, provided lovely framing for the gold necklace her daughters had given her as a gift.

A smiling George left the gazebo to escort his wife off the porch and into the yard. As Sarah and her sisters looked on, their parents began making the rounds of the assembled guests.

"Mommy looks so pretty." Kate made the remark.

"Indeed. Mrs. Alston must have spent weeks making that fancy gown." Mary clasped her hands together.

"Well, ladies, Mommy wouldn't approve of us standing around the gazebo." Sarah stepped down off the platform into the summer brown grass. "Let's go greet the guests."

The three of them parted, fanning out across the yard to speak to the fifty or so people positioned around the yard.

Seeing shipbuilder Will Rhodes enter through the open gate brought a smile to Sarah's face. Knowing his wife and daughter could not be far behind, Sarah hastened toward him.

"Miss Sarah. Good to see you." Will stuck out his hand to her.

With a smile, she shook with him. "Mr. Pruett. Good to see you again, as well."

Rosaline Rhodes Pruett entered the gate just behind her husband. Clutching Rosaline's hand was the couple's three-year-old, adopted daughter, Milly.

Seeing Sarah, a smiling Rosaline wrapped her in a tight hug. "Heavens, it wonderful to see you. It's been so long since you were home."

Sarah returned the embrace of her mentor, the woman who'd taught her the finer points of baking. "It's only been a year and a half. But I'm glad to see you too, Miss Rosaline."

Releasing her, Rosaline gave her young daughter's hand a squeeze. "This is my friend Miss Sarah. Milly, can you say hello?"

The shy little girl, wearing a ribbon around her little afro, offered a small smile. "Hello."

Sarah stooped down to touch Milly's shoulder. "Pleased to see you again. The last time I saw you, you were just a baby." Standing to her full height again, Sarah scanned the yard for her older sister. "If you can find Mary, I'm sure my niece Emily won't be too far behind. I think she and Milly will get along famously."

Rosaline craned her neck a bit, squinting despite the shade provided by her wide brimmed, flower festooned hat. "I see her. Find me later, because I want to hear all about your job in the Territory." Rosaline gave Sarah's hand a squeeze, and then she, Will, and their daughter strolled off.

Watching the small family depart, Sarah released a small sigh. She loved the Pruetts dearly, having known them most of her life. Seeing them was always a pleasure, but today, they served as a reminder of the staid, conventional life her father wanted for her. He'd love nothing more than to see her return home, marry, and settle into a life of running a household and raising children. She loved her father dearly, but she didn't know if she could ever be happy fitting her life into the mold of his desires for her.

The grumbling of her stomach reminded Sarah that she hadn't eaten breakfast. The party preparations hadn't left time for it, and now, she eyed the buffet. People were already beginning to gather there, so she set her feet in that direction.

She got in line behind the seamstress, Mrs. Alston. Just as Sarah finished complimenting the woman on her work on her mother's party dress, she felt someone tap her on her shoulder.

Swiveling her head, she came face to face with a smiling Owen.

"Afternoon, Miss Sarah." He tipped the bowler he wore in her direction.

Dazzled by his bright smile, and by the dashing figure he cut in the crisp white shirt and tan broadcloth trousers, she stammered a bit before getting herself together. "Good afternoon, Mr. Markham."

He clasped his large hand around her fingertips, raised her hand to his lips. Before she could react, he kissed the back. "Please, call me Owen."

Mindful of Mrs. Alston's watchful eyes, and the knowing, amused expressions of the ladies serving the food, Sarah pulled her hand away. Feeling the heat licking at her cheeks, she nodded and hastily turned her attention back to the vittles.

When she and Owen had been served, he pointed in the direction of one of the few remaining empty spots in the yard. "Care to sit with me?" He gestured to the blanket tossed over his forearm.

Not trusting herself to say anything coherent, she offered a nod and smile, then followed him to the spot. There, beneath the shade of her mother's willows, he spread out the blanket and they took seats. She sat a bit away from him, both to make space for her voluminous skirts, and to avoid anything that might be perceived as impropriety.

While they ate, they made small talk. Owen spoke of some of the jobs waiting for him at his woodshop, and Sarah spun a few tales of her life in Wyoming Territory. All the while, she noticed how natural and comfortable it felt to talk to him.

"I'm curious. Is your aunt Gert here for the party?"

She nodded, pointing to where her aunt sat. "There she is, in the gazebo with my mother."

He looked that way. "That's her in the blue gown?"

"Sure is."

"Why, she's a tiny one."

She assumed he was speaking on Gertrude's petite figure. "What she lacks in height, she makes up for in fierceness."

"Based on your description, I wouldn't risk riling her." He winked.

She rolled her eyes. "Hush, Owen."

"Do you know what was happening here last year, during the election?"

She shook her head. "No, what do you mean?"

"There's a group of whites out of South Carolina, called the Red Shirts. Don't know if news of them has traveled to the west yet."

She frowned. "I've never heard of them."

"They're affiliated with the Democrats, and their sole purpose is to keep men of the race from voting. While you were tipping to the ballot box, men like me had to deal with intimidation, threats, and worse from the Red Shirts, simply because of our race."

A sigh slipped from her lips. "I'm sorry to hear that. I agree with you that the law should be enforced to protect your franchise. But I still think women's suffrage will complement that, not take away from it." He scratched his chin. "I'm still not certain. But if women like you and your aunt are willing to fight on the behalf of others, I may have to rethink my stance."

She smiled. "See? I'll convince you yet, Owen."

"We're getting on like old friends, Miss Sarah." Owen drank from his cup of lemonade as he made the remark.

She nodded. "It seems we are. What do you suppose that means?"

He shrugged. "Perhaps it means your father will get his wish." He winked after making the statement.

Shaking her head, Sarah directed her gaze away from her handsome companion, looking out over the yard spread out in front of them. She could see that a few latecomers had shown up, but one in particular caught her attention. Her brow scrunched together as she tried to figure out why a boy of fifteen would be at the party, without his parents.

Wondering aloud, she said, "What's Quinton doing here?"

 espsps

Owen scratched his head in response to Sarah's somewhat cryptic question. "I don't know. It is a party, though."

By now, Sarah had set her half-eaten food aside. Rising to her knees, she continued to peer into the distance. "Yes, but Quinton shouldn't be here alone. Unless..."

"Quinton. Quinton." He repeated the name, hoping to jog his memory as to why it sounded familiar. "The telegraph clerk's son?"

Now on her feet, Sarah nodded. "Yes. And since he's alone, I'd bet eight bits that something has happened. Something big."

Owen climbed up from the blanket and rested his hand on the small of her back. "Something big and good, I hope."

She turned her gaze to meet his. "I don't know." She looked back across the yard again.

He followed her gaze, and he saw the boy. Quinton stood just inside the gate, his hands waving as he spoke excitedly to Mr. Webster, who had his back to them. Quinton's expression was one of excitement, but it didn't convey anything that made Owen think the news was positive.

Quinton finished what he was saying, and ran off. With a nod, Mr. Webster turned and trudged toward the back porch, his expression grim.

Sarah's hand flew to her mouth. "Oh my heavens. I've not seen my father look that way since he broke the news of our grandmother's death."

She started walking, taking wide steps, and he followed, matching her pace. While they moved toward the porch, he saw Mr. Webster raise his hand and call for everyone's attention. Soon the entire assemblage of party guests had gathered at the foot of the porch, awaiting whatever the man of the house had to say.

Taking a deep breath, George began. "Young Quinton has just informed me that..." he hesitated a moment before continuing, "President Garfield has been shot in Baltimore."

A collective gasp rose from the party guests. Folks drew their spouses and significant others close to them, clutched the hands of the children.

Owen instinctively reached for Sarah's hand, capturing it in his own. Dread rattled through him like a buggy careening down a rutted dirt road. *How could this have happened?*

He thought back to the morning's conversation in the barber shop, and the hope some had expressed for Garfield's administration. What would become of that now? Would the president, who'd been in office for only a few months, ever get the chance to fulfill his promises?

Looking around, he saw Will. As the two men's gazes met, Will shook his head, his expression grim.

She clamped her other hand over her mouth, covering a sob.

George continued his speech, as his visibly shaken wife joined him on the porch. "We thank all of you for coming out to celebrate Liza's birthday. But in light of these events, we'll have to cut the party short."

Near the gazebo, an older woman fainted.

Kate, who'd been standing nearby, rushed over, shouting, "Somebody get the doc! Mrs. Carlton swooned!"

Chaos followed that announcement, as people rushed to and fro. Will, who'd stepped forward to alert the doc, ran to saddle one of the Webster's horses.

Sarah squeezed his hand, then moved her hand up to clutch his arm. "The whole world has gone mad. And all of this on my mother's birthday." Her soft voice shook with emotion.

"I know." He said nothing more, not knowing what words, if any, would comfort her.

She tugged his arm, began moving toward the open gate. "Let's go."

"Where?" He asked the question even as he allowed himself to be pulled along.

"It doesn't matter. I just need to get out of here, away from this chaos."

He didn't respond, but continued to move alongside her. Their pace gradually increased until they were both jogging. Even as they left Webster property and started down the road on foot, he remained silent and resolute.

Out on the road, he asked, "Will you come with me? Where we can have some privacy?"

She looked into his eyes, nodded. "Yes."

He had no words to tell her how he felt, or to explain his actions. How could he tell her that hearing of the president's demise had frightened him, had spurred him to action by reminding him of his own mortality? Impropriety aside, he desperately wanted to be alone with her. Perhaps once they had some privacy, he could better convey his thoughts.

He thought she might ask more questions, but she didn't, and that gave him some degree of comfort. Knowing she trusted him enough to run off with him this way, to an unknown destination, felt wonderful. He would be sure to do nothing that would violate that trust.

Slowing down some, so as not to exhaust her, he kept his steps moving toward his home.

CHAPTER 7

As Sarah moved along the road with Owen, she soon found herself growing tired of the solemn silence they'd lapsed into. Aside from that, she wasn't keen on wandering in the woods with him, and at the moment, she had no idea where they were going. So she turned her curious gaze on his face. "Owen, where are we going?"

"To my cabin."

Her breath hitched in her throat, but rather than stop in her tracks, as logic told her she should, she continued walking. "Why?"

"I know that everyone will begin to gather at the telegraph office, to await news from Washington."

Her brow furrowed.

As if sensing her confusion, he continued. "I'd really like to spend some time with you, Sarah. I know it's not the most proper thing, and I'll walk you back home if you like, but..." he cast a hopeful gaze in her direction.

Before her good sense could make her tell him to take her home, some strange force inside her made her bob her head up and down in the affirmative. "It's all right, Owen." Even as she spoke the words, she wondered what had gotten into her.

"Good. At least the sun is still up." He shrugged his broad shoulders as they strolled into his front yard. "Maybe that makes it less improper."

"I suppose." She mumbled the words as they walked past his cabin. Then she stood by his side, watching him turn his key in the lock on the front door of his woodshop. Moments later, he ushered her inside.

"This is where I do my best thinking." He made the remark as he sat on a short stool near the door. Gesturing to the stool's twin, he waited for her to sit.

Sarah knew that the hem of her party dress had likely already been befouled by the sandy soil along the road, but habit forced her to sweep up the skirts anyway to avoid the thick layer of sawdust covering the floor. Gingerly, she took her seat on the stool, taking care to spread her skirts properly as she did so.

"You've told me about your life in the Territory. Anything you want to know about me?"

She scrunched her brow in thought for a moment. "Where are you from? If you were born and raised here, I would have known you."

He shifted a bit on the stool, as if seeking a more comfortable position. "I'm from the Great Dismal, near Edenton."

Her brow hitched. It was common knowledge that the Great Dismal Swamp, which lay across the border between North Carolina and Virginia, had been home and haven to a large population of runaway slaves. Her next question was the most logical one, at least to her mind. "Where did your people run from?"

"Little town called Blairsville, in the northeastern part of Georgia. Ran before I was born."

Intrigued, she settled in as best she could on the hard wooden seat. "Do you know much of the story?"

A wistful smile crossed his handsome face. "Sure do. My grandmother has told the tale since I was old enough to remember. When my Pa found out my Mama was carrying, he vowed he wouldn't let his child be born a slave. So he and his brother, my uncle, started plotting. Grandma was in on it, too, and when the four of them ran, my mother was heavy with child. I'm told my Pa carried her in some places, but she made the journey without a single complaint."

She could feel her eyes widening. "Your mother fled slavery while carrying you? You should be proud to come from such a strong woman."

His smile broadened. "I am. My mother is incredible, and I can never repay her for what she did to assure my freedom."

"You know, your mother would fit right in with the women I know. What's her name?"

"Myrtle."

"Well I'd love to meet Mrs. Myrtle Markham. She sounds remarkable."

He looked her way, as if her words had given him pause. "You want to meet my family?"

She shrugged. "Sure, why not? From everything you've told me, I'd be honored."

A moment passed in silence, as his expression turned thoughtful.

Rising from the stool, he grasped her hand. Tugging her to her feet, he said, "Come here. I'd like to show you something."

She followed him to a large, flat table centering the room. The table, constructed from a large, thick piece of wood balanced atop three old sawhorses, had an odd looking tool resting on its surface.

"Tell me about your upbringing." His large hand wrapped around the tool as he posed the question.

"It was typical of a girl of color growing up in this area, I suppose. That is, except for my mother's literacy work."

Now, he began to glide the tool over the surface of the wood, producing spirals of pulp. "Literacy? What kind of work did Mrs. Webster do?"

"Back in those days, many of the new freedmen didn't know how to read or write. My mother was part of a ladies literary society that educated them in those vital skills."

"Mrs. Webster was free born, then?"

She nodded. "Yes, in New York. But my father was not. He purchased his freedom from his master in South Carolina before migrating here."

"I see." He stopped moving the tool, looked in her direction. "Do you know what this is?"

She shook her head. "I have no idea."

"It's called a plane. In carpentry, it's used to level the surface of a piece of wood."

Curious, she ran her gaze over the newly planed section. "Where did you learn your carpentry?"

"From my father and uncle. That was their function on the plantation they ran from. Both of them were master carpenters in the master's woodworks. During my raising in the Great Dismal, they passed their knowledge on to me."

Listening as Owen revealed a part of his past to her, she couldn't help feeling her heart opening up to him. She sensed an undercurrent of determination in him, a palpable drive to succeed.

As if giving voice to her thoughts, he spoke again. "My father insisted that I learn, so that I could be my own master, as he said. As long as I have my skills, I'll always be able to support myself."

"In a way, that's how I feel about my baking." She moved close to where he stood, drawn there by his honesty, and by an unknown force that seemed to propel her to his side.

He grasped her hand. "Would you like to try?" He gestured to the plane. She answered with a slow nod.

He placed her hand on the grip, and then laid his own large hand over hers. Guiding her movements, he helped her move the plane along the surface of the wood. She was surprised at how smoothly the tool moved, gliding over the wood as it cast off the curly shavings.

What surprised her more, however, was how much she enjoyed his touch. The warm sensation of his hand covering hers made her feel safe, and possibly a bit reckless. Wanting to break the spell, she pulled her hand away.

"Thank you for teaching me," she blurted. "I suppose I owe you a lesson in baking."

He looked a bit confused, but didn't press as he set the plane aside. "Can you teach me to make apple pie? It's my favorite dessert."

"Then that's what I'll teach you." A smile lifted the corners of her mouth.

He smiled back. "There is something else I'd like to teach you, if I may be so bold."

"Oh?" She looked up into his eyes. "What is that?"

By the time she'd spoken the last word, he'd draped an arm loosely around her waist. "Have you ever been kissed by a man, Sarah?"

Her heart thumped in her chest. "Once or twice, but I've never been… moved by it."

That seemed to please him, because a light danced in his dark eyes. "Then you're overdue for a lesson."

Without another word, he tilted her chin up and let his lips brush against hers.

℘ ℘ ℘

He kept the first kiss brief, in case she became uncomfortable. With his face inches away from hers, he asked, "Do you want to learn, my sweet?"

"Yes." Her answer came out in a whisper.

Letting his gaze meet hers, he brushed his knuckle over the supple line of her jaw. "You're aglow, Sarah. You have a radiant soul."

"Oh, my…" came her breathless reply.

He leaned back in, pressing his lips to hers again. This time, he drew her body as close to his as possible, and relished the feeling of her wrapping her arms around his neck. Using the tip of his tongue, he gently parted her lips and let his tongue slip inside.

She moaned low in her throat as the kiss deepened.

He took things slowly, aware of her inexperience. When he felt her body tense, he broke the seal of their lips and eased his mouth away. As his kisses moved to the column of her throat, she trembled.

"Owen…" she whimpered his name.

Flicking his tongue over her collarbone, he smiled. "How much do you want to learn?"

Her breaths were heavy and thick. "As much as you will teach."

Heat swirled through his body. "Come with me." With one arm still draped around her waist, he led her toward the door.

Only the evening songs of the birds and insects greeted them as they moved across his backyard. As they reached the back door of his cabin, he unlocked it and led her inside.

Later, Owen held Sarah's clammy hand within his own as he walked her home. He could not remember ever having felt so awkward in the presence of a woman.

The sun had sunk low on the horizon, less than hour of daylight remained. As they moved along the worn path, he watched her face, noting her expression, which was so serious it bordered on solemnity. While he watched her, she kept her eyes straight forward.

Unable to bear more of this odd silence, he spoke. "Sarah, please." The two simple words pained him to say, but he needed her to speak.

"What am I to say, Owen?"

He gave her hand a squeeze. "Whatever you want to say. Just don't look so sullen."

"It isn't sadness you see on my face." She hazarded a glance in his direction. "It's shame."

Her gaze fled.

He blew out a long, slow exhale. "Come here." Deviating from the path by a few feet, he gently tugged her hand, leading her to stand with him beneath the shade of a tall pine.

She dropped her gaze, as if counting the blades of tall summer grass beneath her feet.

He crooked his index finger and used it to lift her chin. As her lovely face came into view, he could see the unshed tears standing in her eyes. "Listen to me. You have nothing to be ashamed of."

She blinked, as if to stave off the tears, but one fell anyway. "I shouldn't have let you…"

"Give you pleasure? Is that what you feel so badly about?" Owen drew her closer to him, draped his arms loosely around her waist.

She pursed her lips, her jaw tightening.

He considered that her soundless agreement with his statement. "Your maidenhood is still intact. I would never sully you."

"What we did was so..." A deep shade of red filled her cheeks.

"Good? Delightful? Pleasurable?" He would hold on to his memories of what they'd shared for a lifetime. He had used his hands and lips to bring her to completion, and everything about her reaction said that she'd never been there before.

"My parents would never approve."

"I don't plan on telling them. Do you?" He smiled, hoping to lighten her mood.

Her smile didn't match his, but her expression did soften. "You're outrageous."

He leaned in to place a soft kiss on her brow. "You are beautiful, Sarah. Beautiful and passionate. I would be lying if I said I didn't want to go further tonight. But I would never bring dishonor on you."

Her dark lashes fluttered in time with her rapid blinking. Softly, she replied, "Thank you, Owen."

He brushed his knuckle over the satin line of her jaw. "Thank you."

The sound of pounding hooves and someone calling Sarah's name broke through the silence of the forest. Knowing someone was probably looking for her, Owen released Sarah from his embrace. "Go. Seems someone has come after you."

"What about you?"

He waved her off. "I'll walk home after you've left. Don't worry yourself."

She offered him an appreciative smile as she left the shelter of the trees and returned to the main road.

Owen faded into the brush, crouching by the road's edge.

There, he saw Sarah's older sister Mary, approaching on horseback. Mary reined her mount to a stop. "Sarah, where have you been all afternoon? Papa sent me out after you."

"I...uh...just needed some time alone." Sarah's vague, non-committal answer stuck in Owen's craw to a degree, but he knew why she'd said it. After all, it was the same reason he was currently hidden away in the brush.

"No matter. Another telegram came. President Garfield's alive, but badly wounded." Mary patted the saddle, scooting her body forward. "I'll tell you all about it on the way home."

Taking her sister's cue, Sarah approached the beast.

Owen watched as Sarah slipped her foot into the stirrup and hoisted herself, fancy gown and all, onto the horse's back, behind her sister. Once she'd hooked her arms around Mary's waist, Mary clicked her heels against the horse's sides.

Rising to his feet, Owen stood by the road and watched as the horse galloped off.

Once they were out of sight, he turned and headed back to his cabin.

ℭ ℭ ℭ

The next evening, Sarah approached the front door of Owen's cabin. She had a basket resting in the crook of her left elbow, which contained everything she'd need for the evening's lessons. Reaching the small stone stoop, she raised her fist and rapped on the door.

He opened it a few moments later. He wore a pair of denims, belted at the waist, but his upper body was bare. Surprise filled his eyes as he looked at her. "Sarah. What are you doing here?"

Doing her best not to stare at his chest, she gestured to the basket. "I promised you a lesson on apple pie baking, remember?"

He nodded. "I do, but you want to do it today?"

"Since I'm leaving for Washington tomorrow morning, we don't really have a choice." She paused. "That is, unless you want to wait until my next visit home. I don't know when that will be."

He stepped aside. "Come on in."

She entered the cabin, moving over to his table to set the basket down. She eyed his kitchen setup briefly, as he stood close behind her.

"I don't have an oven, I'm afraid. Since I live alone, I've never had need of one."

She looked into his fireplace, seeing the iron rack sitting inside. "It's not a problem, so long as you have an iron skillet with a cover."

He moved past her, opening a cabinet and reaching inside. "Like this?" He extracted a good sized skillet and its lid, holding them out for her inspection.

She nodded. "Yes. Those will do nicely." She set the cookware on the table, near her basket.

"So, where do we begin?"

She chuckled. "At the pump. We need to wash our hands."

"Right this way." He gestured for her to walk ahead of him out the cabin's back door.

A few moments later, they returned to the table with freshly washed hands. "It's best to start the fire now, so it will be nice and hot when we've readied the pie."

She stood by and watched as he placed the wood and kindling beneath the grate. He stuck a match, tucking it beneath the pile. As the flames started to appear, he used a small bellows to awaken the blaze fully. When he was satisfied with the fire, he returned to her side.

"All right. We begin with the dough." Lifting the lid of the basket, she extracted the ingredients that she'd packed in mason jars: flour, salt, and a portion of chilled butter that was melting rapidly in the July heat. "Fetch a bowl, please."

He did as she asked, returning with a white ceramic bowl.

"First, we prepare our surface." She sprinkled an empty section of the tabletop with flour. "Next, let's mix the ingredients to make the crust." She poured the remaining flour and salt into the bowl. Using a wooden spoon she'd brought with her, she stirred the dry ingredients together before handing the spoon off to Owen. "Add the butter into this, and mix it well."

He unscrewed the lid on the jar containing the butter, and added the soft lump to the flour mixture. As he attempted to mix the ingredients, she slipped into the space between him and the table. Once there, she placed her hand over his to show him the proper technique.

"You want to cut the butter into small pieces, then work it into the dry ingredients." She spoke softly, feeling the effects of having their bodies so close together. His hard body rested comfortably against her back.

"You are an excellent teacher," he remarked, nuzzling his stubble-dappled cheek against hers. "I'm enjoying my lesson immensely."

Heat swept through her, and she knew the warmth didn't originate from the fire. "Focus, now. We need to get in here with our hands and work this into dough." She took the spoon and tossed it back into the basket. When she placed her hands into the bowl to work the mixture, his hands soon followed.

For a few silent, sensual moments, their fingertips played and dallied in the soft, damp mixture, often brushing against each other's. By the time the ball of dough was formed, she'd broken out in a sweat.

Needing to break the spell, she grabbed the dough ball and split it into two pieces. "I've some diced apples in another jar, so that will save us the work of cutting. I've already put in the spices I use: brown sugar, cinnamon, a bit of nutmeg." As she spoke, she placed the two dough balls on the floured surface and began flattening them out.

"Let me help." He placed his hands atop hers, assisting with the process of flattening the dough into two large circles. "There."

The intense heat still flowed between them, along with memories of how they'd behaved the last time they were alone in the cabin. "You know, there is some similarity between making a pie and carpentry. If you think of the structure of it, I mean. The bottom crust is like a foundation, and the filling is like the inner structure…"

"And the top crust is like the roof." He interrupted her rambling, fixing her with a knowing look. "There's no need to babble, Sarah. Your virtue is as safe as you wish it to be."

She twisted around to look into his eyes. In that moment, wasn't sure she cared about her virtue anymore. With him holding her against his bare chest, she knew she was liable to have a lapse in judgement at any moment. "Let's at least start the pie to baking, Owen. Then we can see what happens."

"Fair enough." He backed up, gave her a bit of space.

She turned her attention back to the pie. She emptied the remnants of melted butter from the jar into his skillet, spreading it around with her fingertips.

He grasped her hand and drew it to his mouth. She gasped in delight and surprise as he sucked the traces of butter away. The action was bold, sensuous, and downright wicked.

"You build the pie. Put your skills to work." She drew the hand away, tucking her tingling fingertips into the pocket of her skirt.

He chuckled, then assembled the pie under her watchful eyes. First one crust, then the apples, then the top crust. She showed him how to pinch the two crusts together, then placed the lid on the pan.

He set it on the iron grate in the fire place. "How long will it take to bake?"

She shrugged. "About an hour or two, if the lid is left on."

He took a seat in one of his armless chairs, gesturing for her to sit on his lap. "Come. Let's pass the time."

Shaking her head, and knowing she should go sit someplace else, she eased into his lap anyway. "Do you mean to corrupt me, Owen Markham?"

"No more than you wish to be corrupted, my sweet."

He pulled her in to his kiss, and as their lips met, she found she no longer cared.

CHAPTER 8

July 5, 1881

Sitting on the hard seat of the buggy next to her older sister, Sarah watched the passing scenery as the vehicle rolled down the rutted dirt road. The day had finally returned for her to leave her parent's home, and return to her own life. As the buggy bumped along, she tried to push away the sense of melancholy that had been hanging over her ever since that morning, when she'd wished her mother, father, and Kate a tearful goodbye.

"You're awfully quiet over there. Thinking of all the things you have to do when you get back home, I imagine." Mary glanced her way, but only for a moment, before turning her attention back to driving.

She offered a nod. "Yes, a busy time is approaching." The statement wasn't untrue; there would be plenty of work awaiting her at her destination. What she didn't say to her sister was the same thing she'd withheld from the rest of the family: she was not bound for Cheyenne. No, if anyone had seen her carefully guarded train ticket, they would know she'd booked passage to Washington D.C.

Mary navigated the buggy around the familiar bend in the road, and the train depot came into view. "What time is your train again?"

"In a couple of hours." She kept her answer purposefully vague.

Once she'd parked the vehicle on the edge of the road near the depot and set the handbrake, Mary hopped down from the driver's seat. Sarah followed suit, dusting off the skirts of her pink traveling costume once she achieved firm footing.

Mary handed her the single large valise she'd brought. "Are you sure you don't want me to wait with you? Mama will only make me do chores if I go back home."

She shook her head, accepting the bag. "No, Mary. Go on back.

I've been trying to finish this book for weeks now, and this will be the perfect opportunity." She held up her copy of Hawthorne's *The House of Seven Gables*.

"All right. Finish your book then." She leaned in to give her a hug, then a peck on the cheek.

"When are you and Emily headed back to Richmond?"

"Day after tomorrow." She stepped back, then walked around the buggy and climbed back up into the driver seat. "Safe travels, troublemaker. I love you."

She blew a kiss in Mary's direction. "I love you, too. I'll send Papa a telegram when I'm safely home."

With a nod, Mary slapped the reins, guiding their parents' old buggy back toward the Webster home.

Sarah watched her sister disappear around the bend. Then, clutching her small handbag and her valise, she entered the train station.

Long, polished wooden benches provided a place to sit inside the station, and Sarah quickly found an empty spot to inhabit. Tucking her valise beneath her skirt, and her handbag onto her lap, she glanced at the big clock on the wall. She had a good two and half hours to wait before the northbound train arrived to whisk her to D.C. Taking out her copy of the novel she'd been telling her sister about, she settled into the seat and opened it to the red ribbon she used as a bookmark.

She'd read about a chapter or so when she started to nod off. The early hour, coupled with the sleep she'd lost over the last few nights, conspired to make her eyelids heavy. The moment she closed her eyes, she could see Owen's face.

She hadn't spoken to him in the two days since her mother's birthday party. That day had held so much excitement and anxiety, she still hadn't recovered.

In her semi-conscious state, she found herself back in his cabin. Just like that fateful evening, she was sitting across his lap, with the bodice of her gown pushed down, baring her breasts to his touch and his kisses. She could feel the warmth of his mouth in the hollow of her neck and surrounding her nipples; she could feel his bold, questing hand teasing her feminine warmth as he played beneath her skirts. Her breath piled up in her throat, until it came out in gasps. His hands, his mouth, they were all too much. She could feel her blood heating, feel the magical sensation rising from between her thighs...

"Sarah, darling."

She heard him call her name. A smile touched her lips.

He spoke again.

"Wake up, Sarah."

She sat up with a start, her eyes popping open to the bright, sunlit interior of the train depot. She was confused for a moment, because she knew she'd heard Owen's voice.

"You must be tired, to fall asleep on this hard bench."

She let her gaze drift to her left, and saw him sitting next to her on the bench. All the heat that had filled her body during her dream went directly to her cheeks. "Owen. How long have you been here?"

"Only a moment. I hope I didn't startle you."

She shook her head, even as she blinked a few times to let her eyes adjust to this brightly lit reality. Hoping her face didn't look as red as it felt, she asked, "What brings you here?"

He clasped her hand. "I wanted to remind you that you didn't do anything shameful the other day." He kept his voice low, even though there wasn't anyone else in the depot but the two of them and the ticket agent.

Time had helped her feel less ashamed, but she sensed that wasn't why he'd actually come. "So you've said. But why are you really here?"

He drew a deep breath. "I want to ask you to do something for me."

Her brow hitched. "What's that?"

"Don't go to D.C. If you can't stay, I'll understand. But please don't go to Washington."

She studied him, hoping his expression would give her some clue as to why he'd be concerned about where she went. "Owen, I told you that I was headed to Washington when I left here. You're the only one who knows. Why would you try to stop me now?"

"Things were different then."

"How?"

"When you first told me where you were going and what you planned to do there, it sounded like you were going through some rebellious stage against your father's wishes."

She furrowed her brow, being sure not to hide her distaste for his assessment. Still, she held her tongue, curious to see what he would say if she allowed him to keep talking.

"But now, with the President being shot—" he hesitated, his expression growing even more serious. "It's foolish and dangerous to go up there."

She folded her arms over the bodice of her traveling costume.

"And you think that by coming down here and calling me foolish, you'll stop me from going to do something I've planned to do for weeks?"

His eyes widened, as if he were surprised. "Sarah, darling, I..."

"Don't 'darling' me, Owen." She resisted the urge to wag her finger, but didn't plan to mince words with him. "No matter what my father wants, you aren't my husband or my keeper. You have no right to come here and insult me, or tell me what I can and cannot do."

His jaw tightened. "I didn't come here to insult you, Sarah. I'm only concerned for your safety."

"And why is that? We aren't yoked together." Deep inside she knew that wasn't entirely true, based on the encounters they'd shared. He'd given her something called "completion", something no other man had ever given her. Even though she was new at this, she sensed the experience somehow tied them together.

He drew back. "What we shared meant something to me. But apparently it meant nothing to you."

His words stung, but she refused to let him see her pain. "Goodbye, Owen. I'll send a wire to my father when I'm home. You can check with him, since you're so concerned for my safety." She made a show of turning her gaze away from him, choosing instead to look out the rear windows of the depot.

She heard his growl of frustration, and then his retreating footsteps as he left. When she turned back, he was gone.

A tear slid down her cheek, and as the sound of the approaching train began to fill the space, she stood to gather her things.

ɔ ɔ ɔ

July 6, 1881

Wednesday morning, Owen got up with the rooster and drove his old buckboard deep into the forest along the winding banks of the Cape Fear River. He carried along nothing but his axe and his canteen.

His encounter with Sarah the day before had left him frustrated, angry. He'd gone to the train station with his mind set on protecting her, only to be rebuffed. Even though dismissed him and his concerns, he still couldn't help being worried about her.

Worse still, in the few brief days she'd spent in Fayetteville, he'd become...attached to her. Somehow, he'd become consumed with the idea of her as his, so much so that he hadn't thought twice about trying to stop her from going to Washington. Knowing that she'd affected him this way—that she'd managed to work her way into his heart—only increased his irritation.

In the silent forest, where only the birds and animals dwelled, he let his feelings have their head. Draining some of the water from his canteen to quench his thirst, he stripped off his shirt and approached a stand of young pines. The trees were ripe for use; not so young that they were still flexible but not so old that they were brittle.

Soon the sound of metal splintering wood filled his ears. With each swing of the axe, he felt some of the bitter feelings leave him. By mid-morning, he'd felled seven trees and cut them down into sections to haul back to his shop.

Driving the buckboard down the worn road, he inhaled deeply of the fresh morning air. As soon as he unloaded the wood into this shop, he looked forward to making himself a cup of hot coffee and a tall stack of flapjacks running with butter and syrup. His stomach growled loudly at the thought, and he urged his mule on toward home.

When he pulled the board up next to his woodshop, Owen was surprised to see George Webster sitting on a half barrel by the shop door. Wondering what Mr. Webster might need, he waved to the older man before setting the hand brake. After he'd stabled his mule, Owen returned to the shop, his keys in hand. Opening the door, he said, "Good morning, Mr. Webster. What can I do for you?"

"Good morning, Owen. I just came to ask you something."

The two men were now inside the cool, semi-dark interior of the shop, and had taken seats on the two stools inside.

Noting the serious expression Mr. Webster wore, Owen felt his own brow furrow. "Is there a problem with the gazebo?"

"No. My wife is enjoying it as much as possible, considering the tragic events that marred her birthday." George paused, as if choosing his next words with care. "I came to ask you about my Sarah."

Owen bristled, but did his best not to show it. "I'm not sure what you mean, sir."

"I'm sure you do. I told you before her visit that I wanted you to pursue her. That she was ripe for courting, and that I approved of her being courted by a fine gentleman like you."

Owen swallowed, thinking back to his memories of Sarah, perched half-dressed atop his lap in the cabin just a few days ago. Knowing her father would never place his behavior that night in the "gentleman" category, he kept it to himself. "So, don't you have anything to say?" George's eyes were locked on Owen's face.

He shook his head, pushing his thoughts aside for the moment. "Mr. Webster, I tried. I truly did. But your daughter is the most headstrong woman I've ever met, and I'm not sure she wants to settle down with anyone, least of all me."

He sighed. "Headstrong is a fair description. She's been that way since she was a little girl. Always wanted to do everything for herself. Insisted on learning to ride a horse when she was barely eight." He chuckled, as if the memories amused him.

Owen couldn't help smiling as he imagined Sarah as a feisty little girl, wagging a tiny finger as she made some declaration or other. "Knowing that makes me feel somewhat better, but it's still a defeat."

"I don't think it has to be. You just have to ask yourself, how far are you willing to go for her?"

That gave Owen pause. He looked to his elder, unsure of what to say next.

George asked, "Now that you know my daughter, how do you feel about her?"

He didn't hesitate. "I care for her. Deeply, actually."

George smiled. "Then start thinking on what you're going to do to convince her that you belong together."

Raising a hand to scratch his chin, Owen could feel the gears of his mind turning.

"Be warned, she will make you work for it. She takes after Liza. But if you are willing to work for her, to prove yourself, you'll win the greatest treasure you could ever hope to possess." He stood, gave Owen a firm slap on the shoulder. "Buck up, young man. You've got me in your corner, and that's a start."

"I appreciate that, sir."

With an easy smile, he headed for the door. There he stopped and turned back. "Call me George. After all, if you do this right, I'll be your father-in-law." Whistling, Mr. Webster made his exit.

After he left, Owen sat in the shop for a few long moments, thinking on what he'd said. As his growling stomach reminded him that he hadn't eaten breakfast, he went into the house to whip up the flapjacks.

The wood, and his conquest of Sarah's heart, would have to wait until after he ate.

CHAPTER 9

July 8, 1881
Near Washington, D. C.

Sarah walked through the well-appointed foyer of the home of Mrs. Crenshaw, her hostess. Mrs. Crenshaw's home, just outside of the city proper of Washington, was the largest house Sarah had ever been in. Even the home of the Goodmans, the well-heeled black family back in Fayetteville, and that of her boss, hotelier Barney Ford, seemed somewhat small in comparison.

Mrs. Amira Crenshaw was tall, slender, and had skin the color of rich mahogany. Her black hair was carefully coiled low on her neck, and held in place with several pearl-accented hairpins. Dressed in her fine, white-silk blouse, edged in lace, and a dark skirt, Amira moved quickly through the house. "The Capital Suffrage Society ladies are all seated in the parlor. They're eager to hear from you, Miss Webster."

Tamping down her nerves as best she could, Sarah nodded. "I hope I won't bore them." This was only her third speech before a group, so she aspired to keep them awake so she could arm them with information.

"Oh, nonsense. You live in the Territories. To a bunch of eastern ladies like us, that in itself is interesting."

They turned toward the open door of the parlor, and Sarah could hear the myriad of female voice seeping out of the room. Seeing the long, oval-shaped mirror mounted on the wall just outside the parlor, she stopped to check her reflection. "I'll be in momentarily, Mrs. Crenshaw."

With a nod, her hostess disappeared through the doorway.

Regarding her reflection in the mirror. She straightened the collar of her yellow blouse, and then smoothed a lace gloved hand over the navy blue skirt. Touching her hair to be sure her bun was secure, she then reached into the pocket of her skirt and extracted an extra hat pin. Using the pearl-tipped pin, she secured her hat, a flat blue disk adorned with yellow flowers. Satisfied with her appearance, she slowly made her way into the parlor.

As she entered, she saw the members of the Capital Suffrage Society for the first time. About thirty well-dressed ladies of various hues, heights, and ages were seated in the room. Sarah was somewhat surprised by the makeup of the audience; she hadn't expected to see such a diverse group in the room. Most of the women were black, but there were also quite a few who were white, or Oriental, and even one who appeared to be Native.

She knew from her correspondence with Mrs. Crenshaw that the group affiliated with the American Women's Suffrage Association. AWSA founder, Lucy Stone, advocated for racial harmony and encouraged the efforts of women of all races toward suffrage. This was in direct contrast to Elizabeth Cady Stanton and Susan B. Anthony's National Women's Suffrage Association, whose leaders had opposed the passage of the fifteenth amendment.

All the seats in the room were positioned to face a lone, empty armchair. A smattering of applause greeted Sarah's entrance, and as she took her seat in the chair, the room quieted.

"Good afternoon, ladies. My name is Sarah Webster, and I was invited by Mrs. Crenshaw to speak to you about my experience voting in last year's presidential election, and my life in the Wyoming Territory."

A female voice called out, "Good show, Amira!"

Mrs. Crenshaw, seated up front, waved off the praise with a bright smile.

Sarah shared in the smile, and then continued. "As you know, women were given the right to vote in Wyoming Territory in eighteen sixty-nine. I felt very fortunate that, after moving to Cheyenne to take a position at a hotel, I was able to cast my vote for president this past November." She paused, gauging the somber mood that descended over the room. "I voted for President Garfield, and like all of you, I was shocked and saddened to hear of the tragedy that befell him. I truly believe he will advance the cause of suffrage, and the rights of people of color, if he survives this terrible ordeal."

"We must all pray for the president's recovery." Amira's sage words were followed by murmurs of agreement from all over the room.

Sarah spent time speaking about her experience at the polls, and her passion for submitting essays to eastern newspapers on the topic of suffrage for all.

Amira announced, "I contacted Sarah after I read her essay in *The Christian Recorder*."

After that, Sarah chatted about her life in Cheyenne. She did her best to quell the persistent myth of "The Lawless West," and paint a more accurate picture of the bustling town she'd come to love, and to consider a second home. She spoke of the famous Inter-Ocean Hotel, where she was employed, and of some of the other institutions and businesses in the city. The women's eyes widened as she described some of the places she passed by on a daily basis: St. Mary's Cathedral, the Union Pacific Railroad Depot, and the vistas of the Rocky Mountains rising in the distance.

Her speech ended to rousing applause, and she smiled in response. Amira stood then, calling everyone's attention with several sharp claps of her hand. "Now that we've heard Ms. Webster's story, let's put our thinking caps on. What can we do to further our cause here on the East Coast?"

The Native woman said, "Yes, let us think on it. If women having the ballot in Wyoming Territory have not led to famine and pestilence, why can't we have good results here as well?"

A few laughs rose in the room in response to the woman's sassy remark. Looking around at the assemblage, Sarah knew she liked these women. They were from all different backgrounds, but their passion for the cause of suffrage united them to each other, and now, it seemed, to her.

The women rose from their seats, rearranging the chairs until they were all in a circle. Once seated again, they all spent another hour or more spouting ideas.

"What about a bake sale to raise funds for our travel fund? So we can protest in other cities?"

"We should form a committee to paint signs and keep a ready supply on hand for marches."

"Let's start a petition for suffrage. If we can get enough signatures, those lazy men in Congress will have to address it, won't they?"

Sarah waded in with her own suggestion. "If you want to get the attention of Congress, I suggest a letter writing campaign. Bombard them with so much mail that they'll have no choice but to hear our demands."

Amira turned her way. "You are truly a gem, Miss Webster. Thanks for coming."

Speaking truthfully, she replied, "It was my pleasure."

"You'll make some lucky gent a wonderful wife someday." Amira winked at her before turning back to the conversation at hand.

The mention of marriage set Sarah's mind in motion again, but this time, her thoughts were not focused on advancing the cause of suffrage. No, her traitorous mind wandered to thoughts of Owen. Despite his stubborn ways, there was something about him that called out to her. Being with him had made her feel safe, whole. And now, as she thought of him for the first time in two days without becoming angry, she realized something.

She missed him.

Why had she lashed out at him the way she had at the train depot? He'd gone out of his way to come there, to try and stop her from coming to Washington. She'd been so angry and so determined to go her own way, she'd missed the whole point of his words. He was worried about her. And if he were worried enough about her to go there and try to stop her from leaving, that meant he cared about her.

Amira touched her hand, drawing her back into the present. "Are you all right, dear? You look rather stricken."

Drawing a deep breath, Sarah nodded. "I'll be fine."

And she knew she would be, once she set things right with Owen.

⅌ ⅌ ⅌

July 8, 1881

Fayetteville, NC

After the lunch hour, Owen made his way to the telegraph office. Hitching his horse to the post outside, he entered the place to find it as busy as he expected it to be in the middle of a workweek. Removing his hat, he stood at the back of the line to await his turn.

A quarter of an hour later, Owen stepped up to the counter and was greeted by Marla Jackson, the assistant telegraph clerk. "Afternoon, Owen."

"Afternoon, Marla. What's the latest on the President?"

She shook her graying head sadly. "No improvement. They say the doctors can't find the bullet that lodged somewhere in his middle."

Owen shook his head as well. It was tragic to think of any man suffering through such agony, and the fact that the man was the President of the United States made it even worse.

Marla announced, "You got a few letters, and a telegram. Came in about an hour ago." She handed over a stack of envelopes and the telegram slip. "Sorry for your loss."

A somewhat confused Owen took the stack from her, and moved away from the counter so the next person in line could be served. Taking a seat in one of the old wooden chairs by the door, he set the envelopes aside to read the telegram. His mother had sent the message from the Edenton office.

Owen. Grandmother has died. Come home soon for burial. Love, Mother.

Reading the message made his heart clench in his chest. His grandmother Ethel had been one of his closest confidantes throughout his life, and he'd loved her fiercely. Knowing that she'd slipped away to be with the ancestors, and that he hadn't been at her side to hold her hand, pained him. What had happened? Had she been ill? And if so, why hadn't his parents told him? He had so many questions, and he knew the best way to find the answers would be to do as the telegram had instructed. He had to make arrangements to wrap up his last order and close his shop, and get home to his parents as quickly as he could.

With a wave to Marla, he pocketed the telegram and his letters, and replaced his hat atop his head. Then he returned to his horse. Once he was astride his spry gelding, he clicked his heels and turned the horse toward home.

As his mount sailed across the countryside, he thought of his grandmother and how he hadn't had the chance to tell her that he'd fallen in love. Yes, he loved Sarah, and he was willing to admit that to himself now, as well as to her.

But telling her would have to wait. For now, he needed to be with his family.

CHAPTER 10

July 11, 1881
Washington, D.C.

Sarah gave Amira Crenshaw one final, tight hug. The two of them were at the New Jersey Avenue Station, where in a few hours' time, Sarah would board a train that would take her back to her life and work in Cheyenne.

"God speed, Miss Webster. I hope you'll write me, and please know you're welcome in my home whenever you find yourself in Washington."

"Thank you for everything." Sarah spoke the words into her hostess' ear before releasing her from the hug.

With a wave, Amira departed, leaving Sarah on the platform with her valise, her handbag, and her wandering thoughts.

Before leaving the Crenshaw's home, she'd again donned her pink traveling costume. Mrs. Crenshaw had been kind enough to have it cleaned and pressed in preparation for Sarah's long journey home, so it looked as clean and fresh as the day she'd purchased it.

Moving away from the road as Mrs. Crenshaw's carriage departed, Sarah contemplated going inside the station to await her train. As she glanced around, though, she noticed a small cafe adjacent to the station. The front window displayed an array of pies and pastries that looked so enticing that Sarah started walking in that direction.

Soon, she was seated in the cafe, enjoying a steaming cup of café au lait and a heavenly berry tart. She tucked her valise beneath the small table for two to keep it out of the way of anyone who might need to walk past. While she lifted the silver fork—loaded with buttery crust, which overflowed with strawberries, blueberries, and raspberries—she kept her gaze focused on the scene outside the cafe window.

Traffic was heavy, as would be expected on a warm summer day in the nation's capital. People rushed to and fro on foot, mounted on horseback, and seated behind the reins of various buggies and carriages. The city was alive with activity, even as the president convalesced in an undisclosed location, while the doctors tried to figure out if his life could be preserved. Everything she'd heard pointed to President Garfield's immense fortitude and will to live, but she still worried that his injuries might not be curable.

She sipped from her coffee, minding the time as displayed on the big clock hanging about the pastry counter. She still had a good hour before her train was scheduled to arrive, so she settled in and turned her attention back to the window.

Is that Owen?

She squinted, thinking her eyes must be tired. But as she looked again, she saw him striding down the walk, passing the cafe window. He wore a well-fitting pair of denims and a crisp, white shirt with the sleeves rolled up to expose his powerful forearms.

As if he sensed her watching him, he turned and looked directly at her. Stopping in his tracks for a moment, he touched the glass with his open palm.

She placed her hand against the inside of the window, as if to touch his.

A smile broke over his face, and he moved swiftly to make his way inside.

Moments later, he was at her side. She stood, and the two of them stared into each other eyes for a long, wordless time. She hoped her eyes conveyed her feelings, but if they didn't, she would tell him later.

Suddenly, he reached out and pulled her into his arms. As he held her against his chest, she sighed. Being in his arms felt marvelous and welcoming—like being home. And while she was curious to know what brought him here, she decided that could wait until she'd had time to enjoy the feeling of him holding her.

ɞ ɞ ɞ

Owen felt the smile stretch his lips as he held Sarah's trim, feminine form against his own. Holding her like this made him feel whole and fulfilled, and he never wanted to let her go.

He'd been intent on reaching the train station, where he'd assumed she'd be waiting for her train to Cheyenne. He'd come to Washington as soon as he'd completed his business with his family for his grandmother's burial. He'd been heading for the station when something made him glance into the cafe. Seeing her there, in that fancy pink getup with the black lace trim, had made his heart skip a beat.

When he felt he'd squeezed her sufficiently, he released her and stepped back. "I've never seen a lovelier sight."

She blushed prettily. "Heavens, Owen. What are you doing here anyhow?"

"I was looking for you. I've been in town since last night. I remembered that today was the day you'd return to Cheyenne. So, I checked the train schedule and headed for the station, thinking you'd be there."

She offered up a sweet smile. "Well, now that you've found me, what is it?"

He grasped both her hands in his own. "Sarah, I love you. I couldn't let you go back to the Territory without telling you that."

Tears began to well in her beautiful brown eyes, but she blinked them back. "I…love you, too, Owen."

No sweeter words had ever been said to him, and he leaned down to kiss her. Mindful of their surroundings, he settled for a chaste brush of his lips against her forehead.

Suddenly, she pursed her lips. "Oh, goodness. Have you come to stop me from boarding my train?"

"No, darling." He shook his head. "After the way that played out last time, I don't plan on ever doing that again."

Her smile returned. "Good. But speaking of that, I apologize for being so flippant with you."

"You were right. I had no claims on you, and no right to tell you what to do. I'm sorry I was so bullheaded." He'd come to Washington knowing that if he could catch her before she boarded her train, he'd have to apologize to her. And it wasn't simply to get back in her good graces. That day, he'd let his worry cloud his judgement so much that he'd been unable to see the truth in her words. The many days he'd spent without her had shown him the error of his ways.

"Wait. If you're not going to stop me from going back to Cheyenne, how are we to properly court? Are you coming with me?"

"No. I'm not cut out for life out West. Plus, my business is established in Fayetteville."

She sighed. "I love my parents and my sisters, but I don't want to move back home."

He caught her hands again. "Sarah, we'll set that aside for now. Your train will be arriving soon. When you get home, write me. I promise we'll iron all this out. For now, all that matters is that I love you."

"And I you." She leaned up, kissed his jaw.

Then, he helped her retrieve her valise from beneath the cafe table, and carrying it for her, escorted her to the train station.

Epilogue

Thanksgiving Day
November 1881
Fayetteville, NC

Taking care not to drop anything, Sarah moved slowly across the dining room, balancing her mother's ceramic gravy boat in one hand, and a crystal butter dish in the other. Finally setting the items down in the one remaining empty space on the table, she took her seat and breathed a sigh of relief.

Seated next to her, Owen clasped her hand beneath the table. "Well done, my love."

She rewarded his complement with a soft smile. Returning her gaze to the table, she let her eyes sweep over the feast laid out before them. Sarah had spent the last two and a half days in the kitchen with her mother and sisters, toiling over the meal. Now, as she looked out at the fat, roasted turkey, cornbread dressing, fried potatoes and array of vegetables, she felt proud at what they'd accomplished.

Seated around the table for the meal were the entire Webster family, including Mary's husband and daughter. In addition, Owen's parents, Myrtle and Curtis, were also present. This was their first meal together as an extended family, and while Owen and Sarah were still courting, everyone safely assumed that marriage would eventually take place. The two of them had been exchanging letters for months now, and Owen had even gone out to visit Sarah in Cheyenne in early September.

George said the blessing, and everyone began digging in to the meal. While they savored the food, they conversed about what had turned out to be an eventful year.

"It was so sad the way President Garfield passed," Myrtle commented.

"Eighty-one long days of suffering."

Curtis shook his head sadly. "No one should have to leave this world that way."

Elizabeth added, "I'm sorry to say this, but I think our hopes as colored folks may have died with him."

Kate, staring into her glass of lemonade, remarked, "President Arthur just doesn't care about us the way Garfield did."

Sarah had to agree. Since Arthur had taken office, following Garfield's death in September, he'd been focusing most of his efforts on civil service reform. She hoped the Arthur administration wouldn't lead to a lack of progress toward goals for Blacks, but there was no way to know that now. She sincerely wished Garfield hadn't been shot, and that he'd live to carry out the agenda he'd spoken of in his inaugural address. Sadly, fate had made a different determination.

When the meal was finished, Sarah slipped away into the kitchen to help her mother and sisters with the clean-up. By the time that was done, the moon hung high in the autumn night sky. Donning a wrap over her bare arms, she stepped out the back door and onto the porch. Slipping away to her mother's gazebo, she sat there in the quiet, enjoying the call of the crickets and the soft night breeze.

Owen appeared, taking a seat next to her. "I was in the kitchen looking for you, darling. Kate said you'd come out here."

She smiled, gave him a kiss on the cheek. "You're welcome to sit out here with me."

"Actually, I had something else in mind."

Sarah watched with wide-eyes as Owen knelt before her, dropping to his knees on the wooden floor of the gazebo. "Will you marry me, Sarah? I don't ever want to know a life without you again."

Her hand flew to cover her mouth as he opened a small box to reveal a sparkling band of gold. Tears sprung to her eyes.

"What do you say?"

Unable to speak around the lump of emotion in her throat, she nodded.

He slipped the ring onto her finger, and by her next breath, he'd swept her up into his arms

The sounds of cheering drew her attention, and she turned toward the ruckus. There, on the back porch, stood their whole family. Even Sarah's little niece Emily stood there clapping, though she probably had no idea what was happening.

Turning back to Owen, she asked, "Wait? Where are we going to live?"

"I've been thinking on it. How do you feel about Baltimore? It's a large enough city that I'm sure I can establish my carpentry business there. It's less than a day's train ride from here, and it's very close to the Capital."

"I could join the Capital Suffrage Society, and start doing more work for the cause." She could feel her excitement building. "Unless my future husband objects."

He shook his head. "I will never object to anything that makes you happy Sarah."

She lifted her hand to touch his cheek. "Then it's settled. I love you, Owen."

"I love you, darling."

And to show her just how serious he was, he tilted her chin and kissed her right on the lips.

THE END

Author's Note

I truly enjoyed writing A RADIANT SOUL. As a history nerd, it allowed me to indulge my natural curiosity. Additionally, I relish any opportunity to work with Alyssa, Lena and Piper, who are sisters of my heart.

I'm particularly interested in US presidential history, and this story allowed me to spin a yarn that intersects the events around the assassination attempt on President James A. Garfield and the suffrage efforts that were going on during his brief administration. While Sarah is fictional, there were many women of color like her, contributing to the effort to obtain the franchise for women in this nation. Some of their names may not have been recorded by history, but I hope to honor them in some small way through this work.

If you're looking for the recipe to Sarah's cake, I'd suggest you visit Julia's Blog, where I found the inspiration for the dish. I'm not much of a baker, but who can resist a great slice of cake? Here's the link: http://juliasalbum.com/2012/10/triple-berry-blueberry-raspberry-blackberry-bundt-cake-recipe-kefir-buttermilk-lemon-glaze/

I appreciate you taking the time to read my work, and I hope you've enjoyed it.

ABOUT THE AUTHOR

Like any good Southern belle, Kianna Alexander wears many hats: loving wife, doting mama, advice-dispensing sister, and gabbing girlfriend. She's a voracious reader, an amateur seamstress and occasional painter in oils. Chocolate, American history, sweet tea and Idris Elba are a few of her favorite things. A native of the TarHeel state, Kianna still lives there with her husband, two kids, and a collection of well-loved vintage 80's Barbie dolls.

For more about Kianna and her books, visit her website at: http://authorkiannaalexander.com/

LET US DREAM

ALYSSA COLE

Harlem – 1917. After spending half her life pretending to be something she's not, performance is second nature for cabaret owner Bertha Hines. With the election drawing near and women's voting rights on the ballot, Bertha decides to use her persuasive skills to push the men of New York City in the right direction.

Chef Amir Chowdhury jumped ship in New York to get a taste of the American Dream, only to discover he's an unwanted ingredient. When ornery Amir reluctantly takes a job at The Cashmere, he thinks he's hit the bottom of the barrel; however, working at the club reignites his dream of being a force for change. His boss, Bertha, ignites something else in him.

Bertha and Amir clash from the start, but her knowledge of politics and his knowledge of dance force them into a detente that blooms into desire. But Bertha has the vice squad on her tail, and news from home may end Amir's dream before it comes to fruition. With their pasts and futures stacked against them, can Amir and Bertha hold on to their growing love?

ACKNOWLEDGMENTS

Many thanks to Mala Bhattacharjee and Farah Ghuznavi for their help with the linguistic and cultural aspects of the story. Also, Colleen Katana, Derek Bishop, Krista Amigone, and my anthology mates for their invaluable feedback.

Applauding youths laughed with young prostitutes
And watched her perfect, half-clothed body sway;
Her voice was like the sound of blended flutes
Blown by black players upon a picnic day.
She sang and danced on gracefully and calm,
The light gauze hanging loose about her form;
To me she seemed a proudly-swaying palm
Grown lovelier for passing through a storm.
Upon her swarthy neck black shiny curls
Luxuriant fell; and tossing coins in praise,
The wine-flushed, bold-eyed boys, and even the girls,
Devoured her shape with eager, passionate gaze;
But looking at her falsely-smiling face,
I knew her self was not in that strange place.

Claude McKay, "The Harlem Dancer"

"They come with their laws and their codes to bind me fast; but I evade them ever, for I am only waiting for love to give myself up at last..."

Rabindranath Tagore

CHAPTER 1

October 1917
Harlem, New York

"Hold your ear down, 'less you wanna get burnt again." Nell's accent, cultivated in the rich soil of the Deep South, slipped through the racket of the hair salon on a Saturday afternoon. Her voice was warm and sweet, like a peach right off the tree, and Bertha closed her eyes at the feeling of home it stirred in her. It reminded her of that brief happy time where she'd awoken in the same bed every morning and helped her mama with the cleaning before heading off to school or dance lessons.

Strains of different conversations swirled through the Glossine-scented air of the salon: Negro boys getting sent off to fight in France, and maybe to die there too; the latest show put on by the Lafayette Players over at the theater; and, of course, the upcoming elections.

"My man barely wanted to let me come to the shop for a few hours. He ain't thinking about letting me near a ballot box," one woman said. Laughter circled around the shop, the tense kind that happened when a joke wasn't really a joke but you either laughed or despaired. Bertha didn't laugh; she kept clear of entanglements with men because she was now in a position to do so, and they still controlled most aspects of her life. Even she couldn't muster the fake joviality to laugh at what these women, who had a fraction of her autonomy, faced.

"You want that ear or no, Miss Hines?" Nell asked.

Bertha pulled her ear down flat with her index and middle fingers, remaining stock still as the heat of the metal comb warmed the oil on her scalp and the sensitive skin on the backs of her fingers. She stared down at the brown skirt peeking out from under the protective sheet Nell had draped over her before commencing to straighten Bertha's long, thick hair. She was wearing the dowdiest dress she owned; long, drab, high-collared. It was yet another costume, this one designed to cover up instead of reveal. Something told her the crowd at Colored Women's Voting League wouldn't go for the sequins, bangles, and silk that made up her usual nightly wardrobe.

"You learned from your mistake last time," Nell chuckled, placing the comb down on the metal warming plate and running a brush through Bertha's hair. "Still as a statue."

"You're the one who burned my neck last time, so I think you're the one who learned," Bertha reminded her. "You had everyone in the Cashmere thinking I had a love bite."

She lifted her head the slightest bit to cut her eyes at Nell's reflection in the mirror.

Nell made a sound between a laugh and a snort of disbelief. "A love bite at the Cashmere is about as common as a spot on a leopard."

Nell was only teasing, but her words plucked at Bertha's already taut nerves. She straightened her spine to its usual rigid alignment and lifted her shoulders back. "There's nothing common about it when we're talking about *me*."

She used the tone that had gotten her through the last few years, the one that reminded people of exactly who she was. Of course, she had been exactly nobody when she first started using it, but people didn't want to have to think too hard, really—they believed what you presented them with.

Girl, people see what they want to see; they take the path of least resistance. We just got to lead them down the path that benefits us. Ain't nothing wrong with that, hear me?

Her father had been many things, but foolish wasn't one of them. Bertha gifted people with the idea that she was not to be treated lightly, and they responded accordingly. No one had thought a poor Black whore audacious enough to bend the truth in such a way, and she had benefited from it, plain and simple.

Nell paused in the intricate chignon she had begun creating and caught Bertha's gaze in the mirror. Her eyes were wide in her toffee-toned face, and her mouth hung slightly open as she realized that Bertha hadn't appreciated her jab.

"You know I don't mean nothing bad, Miss Hines."

"Nell, you heard anything from your cousin who applied at the hospital?" Sandra, a local washerwoman who was getting a conditioning treatment in the chair next to Bertha, interrupted, either out of rudeness or to head off any awkwardness. Bertha was glad, whatever the reason; she didn't want to embarrass Nell if she could help it.

Nell's fingers flexed against Bertha's scalp as she resumed her work, grabbing up long hanks of hair, twisting and pinning. "Yes, ma'am. She got the job. Got her a nice white uniform hanging in her closet. Used so much starch I don't know how she gonna bend over!"

"Well, good!" Sandra beamed, slapping her thigh beneath the sheet covering her clothes. "I didn't believe it when they said they was hiring Negro nurses now. My sister can come up from Charlotte and get a job here when she done with school."

Bertha thought of how she'd come to New York with hopes of a good, respectable job, too. How so many women, fleeing the restraints of the South, had. She thought of telling Sandra how a chunk of the White nurses had resigned, rather than work with Negro women. But Sandra was looking at her expectantly, so she smiled and nodded benevolently—she was a performer after all. Her daddy had once told her that pretending was a full-time job. Bertha had thought him full of it, but wasn't she her father's child now?

"Well, wouldn't that be something!" she said, flashing a grin at Sandra. "I bet she'll snap up a position in no time."

The door to the salon opened and the cool autumn air danced through the scent of flower-infused oil, miracle growth conditioner, and singed hair, carrying in the smell of roasted nuts from the vendor down the street. A young boy entered, straightening the lapel on his too-large suit.

"Anybody got numbers for Miss Queenie?" The expression on his still-round face was comically serious, a replica of the older number runners who posted up on corners and visited businesses throughout the day, taking people's money and leaving them with a bit of hope.

"Boy, get in here and stop letting out all the heat," one of the other hair dressers called out. "And give me my usual numbers, boxed."

She handed the boy some coins and he noted something on a slip of paper before stuffing it in his pocket.

"Oh, I had a dream last night. My mama told me to go to building seven-three-one. I'm gonna play that," another woman said. The crowd in the salon voiced their support of the idea.

"What about you, miss?" the boy asked. He had wide, innocent eyes—

too innocent to be caught up in the numbers racket already. But Bertha knew all too well that age didn't mean anything once money was involved.

"Not for me," she said.

He nodded and jogged out the door, running off to pick up more bets and carry them back to the number hole.

"All done," Nell said, whipping off the protective sheet and dusting off the back of Bertha's dress. Bertha stood and examined her hair in the mirror for a minute. It was unremarkable, which was exactly what she wanted. She handed Nell her due, plus a good tip to make up for getting high and mighty with her. She liked the woman—and Nell hadn't been wrong.

"You sure look nice," Sandra said, eyeing the high-necked brown dress and matching jacket. "You goin' to church or somethin'?"

Bertha smiled. "Something." She took a look at the women crowded in the shop: hair dressers, laundresses, domestics. She was doing this for them. She pinned on her wide-brimmed brown hat, took one last look in the mirror, and then headed out onto the street.

It was Saturday afternoon, and if she hadn't known already, she would have as soon as she turned onto Lenox Ave. The traffic was bumper to bumper, and the line of trolleys, horses, and Model Ts made her glad she had decided to walk off her nervous excitement. The sidewalks were packed with people strolling, out showing off their autumn outfits as they walked slowly up and down the street. The clusters of people she navigated through grew and shrank as people drifted away from conversations with one group and into them with another.

She had no time to stop and talk, either with acquaintances or with strangers in the mood to chat, as she headed for the meeting. She went over her planned speech in her head.

We need the vote, and I have a plan, you see...

"Hey, Miss B!" She was pulled from her planning by a familiar voice—and the familiar scent of chicken and collard greens. The mix of tangy and savory aromas brought her back in time, to when mama would make dinner and the family would all eat together, back before her father discovered his surefire moneymaking venture and pulled her away from family and school and into his obsessive scheme.

Your mama's too dark, and she don't got good hair, like us...

"Hey, Mary." Bertha slowed but didn't stop, as she walked by the woman's bizarre portable stove tucked into a baby carriage. Well, there were two carriages now—Mary's business was expanding along with the rest of the neighborhood. "Still no chance I can lure you to my kitchen?"

Mary laughed. "The Cashmere too fancy for my simple cooking. Don't tell me you got folks in there eating chitlins in their fixy dresses!"

Bertha laughed. "One of these days, I'll change your mind, just to have that cornbread of yours in my kitchen every day," she said with a wink.

Mary looked down, bashful. "This corner ain't glamorous, but I like being my own boss woman. You know how that is."

"That I do, Mary. Good afternoon!"

Bertha walked away with renewed purpose. Women like Mary needed her to do this, too.

She arrived at the Colored Women's Voting League building, following the other women who entered without the slightest hesitation. She could tell from their clothes and their hats and the way their eyes were a little wary as they greeted her, even in her nice dress and make-up free face, that these were *good* women. Upstanding, pillars of the community, and all the things she wasn't.

Her stomach tightened but she pulled her shoulders back and lifted her chin.

You belong here just as much as them. Act like it.

She felt a sense of calm come over her as she eased into the role. She was a businesswoman, looking to protect her interests and those of the women who worked for her. These uptight suffragettes might look down on her, but they *would* hear her out.

A woman in a dress that looked like something fit for a funeral—to be buried in, that is—stepped onto the stage. She was light bright and tight-lipped, wearing no make-up, her hair brushed back into a simple bun. A preacher's daughter, if Bertha had ever seen one.

Bertha tried not to be critical of her, but she knew exactly what women like Delta Henderson thought of her. It was instinctive for her to size them up, look for weak spots, and, once discovered, to be ready to point them out the moment they dared talk down to her. Some men walked through dangerous territory with their guns cocked and ready, and Bertha did the same with her words. It had been the same on the road with her father, the same when she took over the Cashmere after her husband Arthur had died, and she wouldn't treat these women any differently, though she wished she could.

"Sisters, thank all of you so much for joining us at this important meeting," Delta said. She looked around, her eyes lit up with the kind of ridiculous hope that made Bertha roll her own. Hope wasn't going to get them the vote; it was time for action.

"One of the most important elections of our lifetimes is coming up one month from now," Delta said. "On that day, the men of New York state will be voting on whether we, their sistren, will finally be afforded the God-given right to vote."

Applause broke out in the room and Bertha joined in. The press of emotion in her throat at the possibility that lay before them annoyed her; it seemed hope was catching, like cooties. She cleared her throat and folded her hands in her lap, waiting for the applause to die down.

"Now, they had the same opportunity two years ago, and they did not make the correct decision."

Grumbling broke out amongst the women.

"I know. It's frustrating." Delta held out her hands and then lowered them, modulating the volume in the room like the conductor of a big band. Bertha grinned. Definitely a preacher's daughter.

"But we've made great strides since then. We've organized with the National Women's Voting League, the Women's Suffrage Union—too many wonderful groups to name—and the suffrage movement is more united than it has ever been."

Bertha was tempted to ask why they needed a separate organization—and a separate building—for Negro women if there was so much unity, but that would have been low. Besides, she knew why. They all knew why.

"But now we're in the last stretch of the race and we need to apply pressure," Delta continued, pressing the fist of one hand into the palm of the other. She looked out over the crowd with determination shining in her eyes. "We have to convince the men to vote yes. Speak to your husbands, brothers, cousins. Speak to your fellow congregants at church. To the brother lodges affiliated with your women's clubs. By now, we all know that we deserve the vote, but they need to know it too. They need to give it to us."

Raucous applause littered with "Amen!" broke out, but Bertha was no longer clapping. She was standing, one hand raised in the air. Delta Henderson's vibrant gaze slid over her once, twice, three times, her fierce smile faltering a bit with each pass.

"The time for questions is at the end of the talk, sister," she said, raising and lowering her hand, as if Bertha could be bidden like the chattering crowd had been a moment before.

Bertha remained standing.

She had planned to be genteel, placid, nonthreatening—the way women were supposed to act, even when demanding a simple acknowledgement of their humanity. Instead, she pitched her voice loud, projecting to the back of the room as her father had taught her. Years on the theater circuit meant her enunciation was crisp and sharp enough to cut to the heart of the matter.

"That's well and good, but I think I'll ask mine now, thank you," Bertha said. "You mention church and clubs and lodges and leagues, but what of the women who belong to no such organizations? What of the poor laundress, the illiterate maid, the downtrodden prostitute?" A gasp went through the crowd then, as if that last word had sucked the respectability out of the room.

"Well, our first priority is making sure that the people in a position to influence the upcoming election know what to do," Delta said. There was challenge in her tone, as if Bertha was ruining everything just by asking to be seen. "We have limited time and resources and where we direct them is of the essence."

That's that, then.

Bertha had been looking at Delta, but now angled herself toward the crowded auditorium, making eye contact with several women as she continued. "These women need the protections the right to vote will provide more than anyone. They should be a priority." She realized her righteousness was leading her off track and tried to get back to what she had come to say. She'd had a plan. "Disregarding women who aren't seen as rich, or smart, or respectable enough is a miscalculation. How can their skills be harnessed? How can they be included now, so they aren't left behind later?"

The women in the audience looked anywhere but at her. The floor, the stage, or at the women beside them as they whispered behind their hands.

"This is really not the forum for such matters," Delta said, her color high. "Once we win the right to vote for all women, we'll be able to better use our power to uplift—"

"Uplift? You mean the same patronizing lies women have been fed by men for generations? That we've been fed by Whites since the end of the war?" Bertha let out a bark of a laugh as she began making her way out of her row, her skirts grazing the knees of the scandalized women closest to her. She didn't know why she had wasted her day trying to fit in with these women.

She got to the aisle and turned back to the stage. "Keep your uplift, Mrs. Henderson. I wasn't asking how you could help these women, but how they—we—could help you. If you couldn't figure that out, then we have nothing else to discuss."

She didn't march out of the room, but walked slowly, confidently, her hips swinging slightly too wide for good taste. As she was heading out the door, one person began clapping. Her head swiveled in their direction to meet their derision, but when she saw who it was, she realized it wasn't mockery. Seated in the back row, wearing a full-length fur coat and a smart hat that Bertha was sure cost more than she could imagine, was Miss Q, reigning queen of the numbers game. Miss Q hadn't dressed to accommodate the sensibilities of the suffragettes. When you were as powerful as her, you didn't have to.

Miss Q spoke out against social injustice and unfair conditions, and she didn't mince words. Anyone who had seen her ads demanding police reform and community improvement in the Negro newspapers knew that. Bertha nodded in the woman's direction as she passed through the door, and Miss Q nodded back, a smirk on her face.

Bertha kept her same measured pace as she walked out of the building, and as she walked blindly down the crowded streets, tilting her head at people who called out her name. She was perfectly calm and pleasant, save for the helpless anger that was only expressed in the exaggerated sway of her hips, and how tightly her gloved fists were clenched.

The sun was lowering in the sky—her entire day had been lost to the beauty salon, all to make herself presentable, but flat hair and a stuffy dress hadn't changed who she was. There was no time for rest, either. It was straight to the Cashmere to begin preparing for the Saturday evening crowd. She would have to make sure the performances were lined up perfectly to give the audience the best bang for their buck, that the food orders had come in, that the Gallucci's had delivered the ice blocks for the night, and the cops had been paid off. That her bouncers had an updated list of which men not to let inside, no matter what they said— the Cashmere had a rep for keeping its girls safe now that Bertha was in charge, and that was something she wouldn't slack on.

After doing all that, she would have to prep for her own performance. It had once been comforting to slip into her old, familiar stage persona, but just the thought of it fatigued her now. She wanted nothing more than a finger of scotch and her bed, but that wouldn't happen until the sun came up.

She entered the Cashmere through the alley that ran behind the building, using the back door that led into the kitchen.

Her chef, Cora, was already at work prepping everything she would need for the night. The woman's huge stomach poked out from beneath a now too-tight chef's jacket, reminding Bertha that she would soon need a new cook in addition to a new dishwasher.

"Has anyone stopped by, Cora?"

"Only Officer O'Donnell, looking for his envelope." She sucked her teeth. "You would think the police didn't have a payroll how often they show up here with their hands out."

Shit.

She pulled her pocket watch out and checked the time. The new dishwasher should have arrived already. When the merchant who provided her dance costumes had visited the day before to deliver a new skirt, he'd said he had a man for her. Mr. Khan was usually reliable, but if he didn't come through she was going to be in a hard spot.

"Miss Bertha?"

She breathed a sigh of relief at the sound of Ali Khan's distinct accent, a mix of Southern drawl and the lyrical cadence of his native country. She turned, allowing the brown-skinned, older man the slightest hint of a smile as she inclined her head toward him.

"Mr. Khan, how are you?" She shook his hand, as she did everyone's: brief, fast, and with enough pressure to pre-empt any they might exert on her's.

"Good, good. Heading back to New Orleans tomorrow," he said. His face lit up, and she envied him the brief burst of happiness that came from knowing he would see his wife and children soon. The man only stopped by a few times a year, but she knew everything about his family.

"I'm sure Sable and the boys are looking forward to your return."

Ali chuckled. "Sable is looking forward to having help running the shop! And maybe my esteemed presence, yes. But before that, I have another delivery for you. *Asho*, Amir."

She heard a sigh come from the proximity of the back door, and not a wistful one. It was a sound of deep aggravation, the same she emitted before sitting down before a pile of paperwork or, lately, before donning her skirts and smile and stepping onto the stage.

The door, which had been left ajar, pushed open, and Bertha felt her control drop for just an instant. She'd expected someone young and ridiculous, or older and fatherly; just about anyone other than the dark, brooding man who stepped into the doorway with a scowl on his face.

His hair was inky black, longish and thick. It was brushed back from his face, revealing sharp cheekbones shaded by five o'clock shadow and full lips—dusky pink against his golden brown skin. His eyes were a deep, dark brown, with long lashes that seemed at odds with the intensity of his gaze. Said gaze passed over her, then away disdainfully, reminding Bertha that if she didn't constantly lay down the path for how people, men especially, treated her, they'd see her as the path itself and walk right over her.

He said something in their language to Mr. Khan, then his gaze drifted from her face to the door behind her shoulder, as if looking for someone else. She'd seen that look before; he was expecting a man to come out and talk to him.

She pursed her lips and made a show of stepping closer to him, walking a circle around him and inspecting him like a cow at the market—the same way she'd been inspected by men with promises of work when she'd shown up in New York, ready to put her past behind her and start fresh. Audition after audition, each rejection more stinging and each theater more low brow until she'd landed at an uptown cabaret, with the manager licking his lips and saying he thought she'd fit in just fine.

But that was the past. This was her joint; she was the boss now and any man who worked for her would respect that.

"Does he speak English, this Amir?" She stopped in front of him and met his gaze, letting hers dip just a bit when his lips pulled to the side in annoyance.

"He does, this Amir," came the reply, in an accent entirely different from Mr. Khan, sharpened with a crisp British enunciation. "And this Miss Hines? *Apni Bangla bolte paren?*"

"Amir," Ali said, shooting him a quelling look. "Miss Hines is a fine woman. *Bhadrobhabey kotha bolo onar shathey.*"

"Are we going to have a problem?" she asked. She could have asked herself the same thing. Her interest in men had been primarily business, even now that her business had become selling drinks and entertainment instead of her body. There had always been a sort of detachment, even when she fell apart in a man's arms—even when the men weren't paying. She had stopped dating entirely since taking over the Cashmere. Nights on the town had developed a different edge of tension; she'd often felt like a plump chicken out with a hungry farmer, never sure when he'd reveal his knife. She didn't need a man trying to cut in on her business, and she'd had more than enough of being told what to do. The only men who interested her now were the Cashmere's customers and the dead presidents on the scratch they handed her.

This Amir, though. The fact that she hadn't yet kicked him out proved she would have to be very careful with him.

That tempting mouth of his pulled up into a smile, but his eyes were still as hard as stone. "You won't have any problems from me. Just tell me what I need to do—in English—and I'll do it."

"I'll hold you to that," she said. She took another step toward him, just to see him frown again. They weren't close enough to dance, but she felt a pleasant tingle go through her at even that proximity.

Careful.

"Will you have a problem handling any particular food products?" she asked. "Beef?"

His brows went up a little, then receded back down into his glower. "I'm Muslim, not Hindu. I can't imagine eating pork is a job requirement, so as I said, no problems from me."

His response was curt, his shoulders and neck tensed as if he were straining against some challenge. She tried not to take it personally. Men always seemed to think she was challenging them, just by operating in a world outside the one located under their thumb. She kept her expression bland, letting her gaze flick over him assessingly as the silence dragged out one beat, then another.

"Well, let me know ahead of time if you need accommodation for fasting, prayer, or anything else that might come up," she said. Something struck her then. "You know what this place is, yes?"

He opened his mouth and closed it, and his gaze dropped to the ground.

He knew.

"It's a business," she continued, "and if you have a problem with any aspect of my business, let me know now. I don't want to be out a dishwasher in the middle of dinner service if you suddenly find your feathers ruffled by a girl in a short dress."

His gaze came up to meet hers, and there was that burning, insolent look again. "I need work."

"And I need a worker. It seems we have come to an agreement."

She held out her hand and he took it; he didn't try to crush her hand as she imagined he might, but waited to see how much pressure she exerted and exerted the exact same amount back. Warmth surged through her at the press of his palm against hers, delicious, unexpected, and unwanted. She squeezed a bit harder, then pulled her hand away, embarrassed at the sheen of sweat forming on her upper lip. It must have been the heat from the stove.

"Cora can you show him what to do real quick?" she asked.

"Sure," Cora said, breezily. "Not like I have a busy night to prep for."

"I have some bangles for you to look at before I go," Ali said, drawing her attention back to him. "They're very nice, and reserved for my clients in New Orleans, so you can be the only woman in New York with them!"

"You bring me the most exciting things," she said, glancing at Amir. He turned to face Cora. "Come to my office and let's see what you've got."

Ali talked about something or other as they made their way through the club and then the hall that led to her office, but Bertha wasn't listening hard. She was busy hoping the fact that her hand still tingled something fierce didn't mean a damn thing.

Chapter 2

Amir didn't know why he'd let Ali talk him into this. He'd told the man he was done with restaurants, after being fired from his last three jobs. He loved working in a kitchen, but it seemed employers didn't like it very much when you pointed out the unsafe, unfair, or indecent ways in which they treated their employees. The British officers aboard the *Kandahar* hadn't liked it, and the head chef at the Drake Hotel had liked it even less.

Amir stepped back as dishwater sloshed over the side of the sink, then sighed. He had always been considered *theta*, and his parents had warned that his willfulness would get him in trouble one day. His willfulness had gotten him to America, and if this country wasn't trouble, he didn't know what was.

He felt swindled, like a child who had listened to *rupkatha* before bed and come to believe the stories were real. But Amir now knew that virtue wasn't always rewarded and evil sometimes did win the day. He'd witnessed it as his family's land had diminished, plot by plot, victim of East India Company law. He'd seen it in Calcutta, in the faces of the poor on the street and the illiterate sailors who filled the boarding houses.

America was supposed to be different.

You should just go back. Like a dog, with his tail between his legs.

When he'd left his village for the port city of Calcutta, drawn by the possibility of work on a British steamer and tales of adventure and prosperity in far-away places, people had expected that he'd soon return humbled and ready to take a wife and settle on the family farmland. It wasn't that they wished him ill. It was simply that they'd seen so many of the other men who spent years in Calcutta, building up debt to the *ghat sharengs* who housed them and the *sharengs* who were the key to getting hired for an outgoing crew, return in the same manner.

But Amir hadn't been deterred. He'd grown up with stories from Raahil *Chacha*, who had made Amir study English grammar and learn about men with strange names like Marx and Engels while his cousins played. His uncle had left Bengal for adventure, despite the academic success that had already laid the foundation for a promising future. His family had considered it a betrayal, but Raahil had seen places like Morocco and Portugal and England with his own eyes, tasted their foods and mingled with their people. He told Amir all kinds of stories, except for the ones that would explain the burns on his arms and why he sometimes went quiet for days. Raahil's stories had driven Amir from his town in search of more.

In Calcutta, he'd gotten a job in a restaurant near the docks and immersed himself in the community of seamen, first teaching the illiterate men at his boarding house the basics of reading and writing and eventually, in a series of events composed of happenstance and Allah's will, organizing against unfair conditions. He'd fallen in with a group of young Socialists, drawn to them by the ideas that his *Chacha* had instilled in him. He hadn't meant to get involved in such activities, but watching the injustice that surrounded him everywhere in the crowded port city spurred him to help where he could. After two years of such work, he'd been assigned to the crew of the *Kandahar*, likely so he would no longer be a bother to the *ghat sharengs* as they grifted money from desperate men.

They certainly don't seem to mind that you never came back. While the *sharengs* did not seem to feel his loss, his family did. His cousins with no land of their own had taken the management of his, but the longer he stayed away, the murkier the situation became. In the last few weeks, Amir had begun to wonder if perhaps it wasn't time for him to return.

When he'd jumped ship in New York, fed up with the hellish conditions the British thought suitable for their Indian crewmen, he'd thought he'd make something of himself in America. He'd been on the ships for three years, and each time they stopped in New York he'd felt the city thrum in his blood. To a village boy raised on a smallholding farm in Bengal, the tall buildings and seething streets had been like walking through a dream he hadn't remembered having, even after the glorious hustle and bustle of Calcutta. He had been sure that New York was a place where he could make something of himself— outside the bounds of the British imperialist box—and return triumphant. He would buy back the plots of land his family had been forced to sell in increments as the zamindars collected their debts, and use his American-made wealth to thumb his nose at the *sahebs* and their rules.

But here he was, two years later, working the lowest job possible in a place of ill repute. The women passing in and out of the kitchen in their make-up and revealing dresses were certainly selling something more than drinks, and music and shouts filled the entire place, growing louder as the night progressed. Bertha had stopped in and told him if any strange White men tried to enter through the back door to come get her immediately, leaving him on edge and worried about raids that could have him on a boat back to Bengal. What had he gotten himself into?

One who goes to Laanka turns into Ravaan, his neighbor had chided at the celebration before he left for Calcutta, and his aunties had agreed. If they could see the company he kept now, they'd quickly join his parents in the afterlife, just to pass on news of his shame.

"Chicken fried steak, order up!" Cora called out. He looked over at the cook as she wiped sweat away from her brow and moved on to the next dish, her belly bumping the plate she'd set on the counter. Perspective coated the burn of his irritation, calming him. It chafed to be demoted to a dish scrubber while the tools of his trade were at hand, but at least he wasn't carrying a live, kicking thing in his belly while doing the work. Besides, he needed the money.

He'd been steadily building his savings, despite a few setbacks, after the last of which his enraged boss had threatened to report him as an undocumented alien—the recent immigration act had given many men a trump card over him, something Amir resented keenly. He had left Bengal to find himself and America had told him what he was: "undesirable." In the eyes of the American people, he was no different than a criminal or beggar. An exotic disease that might infect the country from within. He couldn't vote, own land, or naturalize; his life was dependent on people deciding not to report him or taking the risk of hiring him. He thought back to the way Bertha had looked down her nose at him, though he'd felt something other than resentment stir in him then.

Na, Amir. There was no point in thinking about her full lips pressing together as she'd inspected him like one of the British officers before he'd boarded their ships. When Ali Khan had told him what kind of place the Cashmere was and that it was owned by a woman, he'd expected someone frivolous, gaudy; it hadn't even registered to him that the woman in the kitchen could be her. He'd thought her just another witness to his shame. But Bertha Hines had wasted no time in correcting his misconception; she had been sharp, all business.

Except for the way she looked at your mouth. Remember that?

Amir did remember. He also remembered the way she had been so close that the scent of her hair had enveloped him, heavy floral musk tucked up primly under that hat of hers. And though he had balked at the way she brought up his religion—as if it would stop him from doing his job—in retrospect, he realized that she was the only employer who had even taken it seriously. He ran his hands over his apron, feeling a different kind of shame at how he'd taken each question as a challenge and reacted accordingly.

Patha! Stubborn ram, always looking for something to butt his head against. His father had roughed a hand through Amir's hair each time he repeated what became a common saying in the family, even after he'd needed to reach his hand up to do it. Amir missed that, even though he'd often jerked away, indignant.

His flatmates called him Pintu, but it wasn't the same. No one in America knew that *daak naam. Patha* was buried with his parents.

Across the kitchen, Cora huffed and put a hand to her stomach. She had been frowning in concentration since the dinner service had started a few hours before, but now a smile illuminated her face.

"Strong kicker?" Amir ventured. Her head whipped in his direction, but then she dropped her hand and went back to work. She'd eyed him suspiciously since he'd interrupted her training for the Maghrib prayer, making Amir wish he'd asked Bertha where he could do so in private when she had offered. He sighed and sloshed another pan into the soapy water.

"Feels like he's tryin' to kick me to the moon sometimes," Cora said after a long silence.

Amir smiled, remembering when Sabiha Auntie had been pregnant with his cousin and let him feel the baby move beneath his hand. Amaan was all grown up now, working in the fire room of a British ship, last he'd heard. On the *Kandahar*, one fireman had gone mad from the heat and attacked one of the officers, who'd tried to force him back into the inferno of the engine room. It had made Amir wonder about those days when Raahil Uncle had sat slack-mouthed and blank-eyed, staring into the distance.

"That means he's anxious to get out and show the world what he can do," Amir said as he scrubbed. "He'll be a go-getter, as they say."

Cora chuckled. "If he's anything like my husband Darryl, that's a sure thing. Fried chicken and greens, order up!"

They worked in silence for a bit, Amir scrubbing glasses and shoving them into drying racks as Cora bustled about the kitchen. Each time she passed him, he felt a bit more like an ass. He dropped the last glass into the rack and wiped his hands on his apron.

"I have experience working in a kitchen. Tell me what to do, and you can rest for a bit. Do you need anything prepped?"

She narrowed her eyes at him, and he could tell she was struggling with giving him even a bit of control over her workspace. He'd never been able to do it in his kitchens, but Cora had extenuating circumstances that he'd never had to consider.

"I was a cook back home, and on a ship, and since I've been here in the States," he said. "I learned at the side of a man who would not think twice about throwing a hot pan in your direction if you made a mistake and I won't even tell you how strict my grandmother was. I won't make a mess of things, if you tell me how you want it done."

Cora bit her lip, then glanced at the pile of greens beside the cutting board. "You ever made collards?"

Amir smiled; his flatmates would get a laugh out of a Bong being asked if he could cook *shak*. Slightly less insulting than asking if he could cook fish. He still remembered following his *Nani* through the market each morning, as she bought whatever was cheap and in season, and then into the kitchen as she decided the best way to prepare it. He'd learned at the knee of a master culinary improviser. But Cora had no reason to know that, and he had jumped to enough conclusions for one night. Besides, a good cook was always looking to improve.

"Can you show me?"

∞ ∞ ∞

Amir watched the plate the waitress carried out of the kitchen with more than a bit of pride. He was an accomplished cook, but this Southern style food wasn't something he'd tried before. Cora had tasted the fried chicken and collards herself, giving him a nod of approval, and then sat down and eaten some during her break. Amir had a small plate of the *shak* at her urging, and was proud of his attempt. The greens were tender and tangy, infused with a hint of the smoked turkey neck Cora had told him to add for flavor instead of the ham hocks that were part of her own recipe. The chicken was crisp, the combination of spices a perfect complement to the succulent meat beneath. It wasn't halal, but Amir's philosophy held that Allah was more forgiving of certain transgressions. On payday, he would head to the kosher butcher, the closest thing to halal, and make a feast for his flatmates. With a bit of *panch phoron* mixed into the seasoned flour coating, the chicken would be even better.

He was contemplating variations on Cora's recipe when a sound that seemed distinctly out of place at the Cashmere reached his ears. He still wasn't used to the loud music, but most of it had been enjoyable enough that it had him tapping his feet or moving his head in time. He hadn't expected this.

He stood, drawn toward the main section of the club by the familiar sound of fingers plucking skillfully at the taut strings of a sitar, the blows of palms against a tabla setting a driving percussive beat. Those were the sounds of home, coming from the stage of this Harlem hole in the wall.

He got to the door and stopped. Dishwashers weren't allowed out front at most places, and he was sure the Cashmere was no exception.

"Go ahead and peek," Cora said. "Nobody gonna be looking this way now. Not while Miss Hines is up there."

He pushed the door open a crack and was surprised to see some White faces in the crowd, along with the varying shades of brown. That was no small thing, given the way segregation was so strictly enforced in the States. Cora was correct: the women with their sleek hair and the men in their sharp suits, all of them were staring toward the front of the club, enraptured. He pressed the door open a bit more so that the stage came into view and he saw exactly why.

Cora had said it was Bertha on the stage, but for a moment Amir knew she had to be wrong. A woman clad in an elegant sari stood there, her long, dark hair falling over her shoulder in waves and her arms curving up and over her head. Her stance meant that her cropped choli was lifted perilously high, revealing bare brown skin from her waist to approximately three rib bones short of *Jannah*. Beneath the flowing fabric of her loose skirt, one dainty foot was on point. Her knee was bent and pressing against the skirt in a way that somehow made you quite aware that it was bare skin pressing against smooth fabric. She just stood there, drawing it out until Amir found himself willing her to move.

When the tension in the room was about to teeter into unbearable, she turned her head abruptly toward the audience, teasing, just as her hips began to sway. Her eyes were lined with dark kohl, making them seem large and enticing. Her lips were red, luscious, but the smile that rested on them was relaxed and mysterious.

Jewelry was draped over her hair and encircling her forehead, sparkling gold to match the earrings that dripped from her ears, the temple necklace that circled over her collarbones, and the bangles that lined her wrists.

The plucking of the sitar strings began to pick up pace and Bertha launched fully into her dance. Amir watched, annoyance, amusement, and something dangerously close to lust swirling in his mind as she whirled before him. The dance was delicate and feminine and powerful all at once, but more than anything it was seductive. What it was *not*, was an actual Indian dance.

Most classical dance was rooted in Hinduism, but Amir's village had been one in which religion had generally been no barrier to friendship and community; he had learned classical dance from neighborhood festivities and annual celebrations with friends, and this wasn't it. There were bits and pieces mashed together—she completed some mudras, striking the hand poses fairly accurately; others were things he supposed she had created on her own. He could see hints of ballet in the way she jumped and swayed, and he supposed other styles were mixed in too. Her arms moved languidly, and her feet followed familiar patterns—to an outsider she looked like she knew what she was doing. Her shoulders jumped and her bangles shook in time to the music. But the way she moved her hips was something entirely American.

The day before Amir had boarded the *Kandahar*, he had come across a street performance near the docks in Calcutta. An old woman beside him had huffed, "Nachinir lajja nei dekhunir lajja." *The dancer isn't ashamed, but the onlooker is.* He was definitely not ashamed as he watched Bertha, though other sentiments stirred in him. He should have been offended at yet another bastardization of his culture, but he felt a kind of wonder as she whirled and swayed. Perhaps it was because the woman on the stage was so open and free, compared to the stiff-backed woman he'd met in the kitchen.

He'd seen *baiji* women perform their dances for the *sahebs* in Calcutta, had also seen the *sahebs* demand to be taught in one breath and decry the dances as repulsive and lewd with the next. He scorned the British for taking every bit of his culture and steeping it in their own ways until it was to their taste, dashing out what wasn't. But watching Bertha elicited something else in him. Something that made his heart race and also hit him with a wave of homesickness stronger than the sea churned by the rage of a monsoon.

He felt Cora come stand beside him but he couldn't tear his gaze away from the woman on the stage. The same woman who'd talked down to him like he was a cur who had wandered in from the alley, begging for a scrap of meat. Amir considered that perhaps he had been wrong to be offended by her show of superiority earlier: he and every other person in the audience were quite ready to prostrate themselves before her as she whirled toward the finale of the song.

"She don't perform as much anymore since she took over the place," Cora whispered. "But I sure love when she does."

Bertha spun into a dramatic pose, back bent, hands supplicant, dark-rimmed eyes turned towards the heavens as if she begged for redemption. The music stopped and the audience went wild, cheering and hooting, begging for an encore.

Bertha finally left her pose and graced the crowd with a smile. Someone handed her a microphone, and she spoke in that velvety voice of hers that had stroked over Amir during their first encounter.

"Thank you, everyone, for coming to the Cashmere tonight. We've got a ragtime group from Louisiana up after this intermission, so I hope I'll see you all dancing yourselves. Especially you over there, with those rubber legs of yours." Amir couldn't see who she extended her arm toward, but low laughter rumbled through the crowd. "I do have a special message for all of the men in the crowd, tonight," she said. Her voice dropped low, husky, and every man in the crowd leaned closer, as if she were talking to him and him alone. Amir did, too, then leaned back, annoyed that he could be taken in by her ploy. He watched the hungry expressions of the men closest to him, and felt a serpentine motion inside of him that had nothing—or everything—to do with how Bertha's sinuous hips had entranced him.

"Fellas," she said, voice intimate like she was speaking to her lover across a pillow. "Did you enjoy my dance tonight?"

The crowd broke out into more hoots, hollers, and whistles.

"Why'd you make us wait so long for it?" a man called out, followed by a chorus of agreement.

She smiled, her gaze slipping in the direction of the outburst, then to the ground, all coyness. Amir felt himself leaning toward her again, and he didn't fight it this time.

"Oh, you want me to dance again?" she asked.

More shouts, more applause, and then she lifted her head and pinned the crowd with a look that made Amir's throat go tight and his pulse race.

"Remember that when you go to the ballot box one month from now. Because I've got a hankering to vote and the only one who can help with that is you men. Vote yes for women's suffrage, because until she gets the right to vote, this nautch girl is retired."

She capped her statement with a wink, and then sauntered backstage, ignoring the incredulous shouts interspersed with laughter that followed in her wake. Men jumped up in their seats and women reached across tables to touch fingertips with their friends as they shared knowing looks. Amir simply stared at the curtain that had closed behind her.

"Ain't she something?" Cora hooted, slapping Amir's shoulder.

"Yes," Amir responded. "Something, indeed."

Chapter 3

"I still don't understand why we have to be here today. I'm still exhausted from Saturday." Janie crossed her arms on the table directly in front of the stage and rested her head on it. Her face was clean, make-up free, reminding Bertha that she was younger than she appeared when she was glammed up and working the crowd. Janie was always exhausted, but that was to be expected when a girl had a movie star face and an hour glass figure to match. Her services were always in demand, both at the Cashmere and with the sugar daddies she had in rotation outside the club's walls.

"We're here today because the vote is happening less than a month from now," Bertha said, pacing back and forth on the stage. "I'm glad you decided to show up this time. I got up early the other day and you all stood me up."

Wah Ming, who went by Jade to the men at the club who were flummoxed by two simple syllables, brushed her blunt bangs out of her eyes before lighting the cigarette Janie had just rolled for her. "That's because you scheduled it for the morning after a party with all the Tammany big-wigs. We were beat!"

"That you all are invited to these kinds of parties is one reason why I'm giving these courses," Bertha said. "Look, I've told you already, the vote will be here before we know it. Any man who isn't absolutely voting yes has to be convinced otherwise."

From the corner of her eye, she saw the kitchen door open half way. Amir's head popped through and he held up a hand in greeting. She'd asked him to come in and do some repair work if he wanted to take home a bit more money. He'd been obliging, shockingly so, considering the way he'd squared off with her when he first arrived. After that first day, he'd been reserved with her but not sullen. Cora seemed sweet on him after a few shifts together, a first for the Cashmere kitchen. He was a good worker, and that was all that mattered, anyway; everyone knew Bertha Hines didn't play in her own yard, or anyone's yard, when it came down to it.

Some said she did it to keep men panting after her, which was partially true. Men wanted nothing more than what they couldn't have, and if that kept them coming to the Cashmere, that was fine with her. But after years of being groped up and put down, Bertha mostly wanted peace of mind.

She chucked her chin in Amir's direction to acknowledge him and he slipped back into the kitchen.

"I'm no suffragette," a woman from the back called out, saying the word the same way most suffragettes would refer to her profession. She received grumbles of approval from the small crowd of girls Bertha hired as waitresses—and rented her back rooms to for their other work, with the offer of protection.

Bertha sighed. "Do you want laws that protect you from the police officers who hit you up for bribes? From the people who won't hire you for jobs and never gave you the opportunity for schooling?"

There was a sulky silence in the room but no dissent, and Bertha smiled. "Then you are suffragettes. We need to get this vote and we need to know what to do with it once we have it. Today we'll be going over local government and a few recent laws that have had a negative impact on you."

"Like the hotel law?" Janie asked sleepily. The law had been passed to make it harder for prostitutes to rent rooms, meaning more women had to hustle on the streets or give up their earnings to pimps.

"Yes, like that. We'll examine who voted for the laws and what political parties they come from." Bertha felt the slightest spark of hope. "Now, none of you are fools. I've seen you hold conversations with every type of man in the Apple, from shoe shiners to senators. There's no reason you shouldn't have some say in what happens in this city and this country."

"No one cares what we think," another woman, Cathy, called out. "Half these suffragettes think we dragging down the race. Way they tell it, if we just dressed nice and stopped whoring around, people would treat us right."

"And I still won't be allowed to vote, even if women get suffrage," Wah Ming added. "Remember? My kind isn't wanted here." She stubbed her cigarette out into an ashtray.

Bertha understood their frustration; when the decks were stacked against you, playing felt futile. "Many people would be glad if none of us in this room existed, and if we never got the right to vote. That would work out real nice for them, wouldn't it? If we never had the chance to take them to task for treating us like shit?"

She took a deep breath. Cussing aloud wasn't part of the image of control she tried to project, but it had many of the girls sitting up and paying attention.

"But what if we get the vote and nothing changes?" someone asked. The voice was so quiet it could have been the nagging one that kept her up at night. Bertha looked at the women before her; some were happy with their lot in life, some were not. The majority had not been given much of a choice. All had lived with disappointment as a constant companion; such was the fate of any woman in the United States, and especially ones born some shade darker than porcelain white.

"If we get the vote, everything will already have changed," Bertha said. "And once we have it, we'll keep voting until we get every damn thing we deserve from this country." She let the words hang there. "We fight in a hundred ways just to get through every day. Let's see what happens when we try fighting one hundred and one, okay?"

Bertha looked out at the women, not sure if she'd let her natural flair for the dramatic push them too far, too fast.

"You know, I used to pull some good grades before I had to leave school," Janie said. "I guess a couple more lessons wouldn't hurt none."

"Good. Let's get started."

છ છ છ

Later that day, Bertha sat at her desk reading through the local Negro newspapers she hadn't had time to peruse earlier in the week. Her office was decorated in soothing colors: warm pink and yellow fabrics, souvenirs from her time spent on the road. None of the familiar objects worked to calm the tension that mounted as she read. A letter from her mother in Chicago, with news of her brothers and step-father, had already left her feeling sad, an emotion she generally pretended didn't exist. Then she'd seen one of the regular ads from Ms. Q in *The Age*:

> To the Black citizens of Harlem: On Tuesday, October 5, 1917, three women were beaten and robbed by officers of the law. This was carried out in plain daylight and nothing will be done because these women also sell their bodies. Those of you who look down on such things will say they deserved it, while your husbands will be wondering if it was one of the women they are stepping out on you with. Regardless of what you think of their profession, these women have rights. To the men reading this, stop spending your time scheming to get women in your bed and think on how to get them to the ballot box. Give women the right to vote against politicians who allow things like this to happen unchecked.

Bertha was glad for the ad, written in Ms. Q's signature style, but distressed about what it reported. When she turned the page she was met with even worse news. Two more clubs in the neighborhood had been shut down over allegations of prostitution and racial mixing. One was going to reopen, and the owner of the other remained jailed. She dropped the paper down onto the pile of invoices and receipts that constituted the afternoon bookkeeping, pushing her palms into her eyes as frissons of panic ran through her body and coalesced at the back of her neck.

Why can't they just leave us be?

When the Commission of Fourteen had started, their primary goal had been stopping "White slavery," or what they called White prostitution. Now, seemingly bored after helping drive Negroes up the length of Manhattan all the way to Harlem, the vice squad had decided to target them, too. Not out of any desire to stop "Black slavery"—she was sure many of the men working that beat weren't put out by that particular moral failing—but for two reasons: to shut down Negro businesses and to stop White folks from patronizing them. A couple of them had come sniffing around the Cashmere over the past few months, and unlike the beat cops, they seemed immune to bribery. Bertha could almost laugh; between the suffragettes and the vice squad, the primary function of morality seemed to be as a thorn in her side.

Most of the other clubs had already put in strict "No Whites" policies. While it should have been slightly edifying to be able to wield such power, it wasn't done out of hatred. It was the only surefire way to avoid investigation, and for their owners to avoid jail time.

It was all so ridiculous.

Bertha, perhaps more than most, understood how subjective a thing race was. She looked up at the framed poster on the wall beside her desk and sighed.

THE RAJJAH BEN SPECTACULAR

FAR EASTERN MYSTICAL MAGIC NEVER SEEN ON THESE SHORES! MIND READING, SPIRIT SUMMONING, AND OTHER ACTS OF LEGERDEMAIN! HINDOO DANCING, AND MORE!

A knock at the door cut her moment of pity short.

All for the better, she thought.

"Come in," she called out, straightening in her seat. The door opened and Amir stepped through. He wore a simple tan shirt, tucked neatly into dark trousers paired with suspenders. His sleeves were rolled up to his elbows, and Bertha tried hard not to stare at the sleek, dark hair that dusted over his forearms and peeked out of the neckline of his shirt.

"Can I help you, Amir?"

"May I sit?" he asked.

She nodded and he settled into the seat in front of her desk. She tried to read his expression to determine whether he was going to quit, demand a raise, or try to give her some friendly advice, as men were wont to do.

"I listened to your talk earlier," he said, then stopped abruptly. She waited for him to go on, but he shifted in his seat and began looking around the office.

"Is there some reason you feel compelled to tell me about your eavesdropping?" Her voice came out low, flirtatious, even though that wasn't what she intended at all. It made her feel a bit strange to know he'd been listening, which was ridiculous because performing on stage was second nature to her. But she hadn't been performing, really. She'd let her guard down for a moment, as she joked and traded information with the women, who had by the end seemed as excited with the project as she was.

"It's just…why are you doing this?"

She would have been offended if the expression on his face hadn't been so direct. There was no judgment or, worse, disgust, but you never could tell. Maybe it bothered him to see women learning about politics. That would be more likely than him supporting it, given most men she'd encountered.

His dark gaze was fixed on her with the same intensity as their first meeting, but without the frustrated anger—she realized now that's what it had been. Her face heated under his scrutiny.

"Well, I want the women to be prepared when we get the right to vote," she said. "It may not happen a month from now, but it will happen soon."

She didn't mention how she knew so much about the law. As they'd traveled from state to state and city to city, her father had always made sure they knew the local and federal ordinances that could help or hurt them in case things went sideways. What was allowed for Negroes, what was allowed for women, what the local government and police forces were like.

Gotta know the lay of the land before you take the shortcut, Bertie.

"No. *That* was incredible. I understand why you teach the class." He leaned forward in his seat. "I'm asking why do you do *this*." He spread his arms expansively. "I admit I don't know very much about politics here, outside of certain specific things I've learned the hard way, but you know so much. Why run this club? If you are interested in helping these women, why allow them to sell themselves?"

The words pelted Bertha like fruit thrown from a balcony. She pursed her lips as she tried to gauge how much she felt like explaining the ways of a woman's world to a man, and found she didn't feel like it at all.

She leaned back in her seat. "I won't be questioned about my business by a dishwasher. You can go."

She picked up the paper on her desk and stared at it, eyes blindly scanning. After a few moments of silence, she glanced up over the edge of the paper to find him watching her. His gaze swept her face, as if trying to figure her out; she'd seen him look at a clogged drain with the same pensiveness. Bertha didn't take to being puzzled over.

"You've been dismissed, Amir."

"I think perhaps there has been some misunderstanding," he said. "I asked because I want to know, not as an insult. I apologize for hurting you."

"You should apologize for thinking someone like you *could* hurt me," she said, letting the paper flop onto her desk ever so casually and smiling at him as if that were the silliest idea she'd ever heard.

That was usually enough to put a man in his place, but Amir didn't even flinch.

"So if I told you your dance the other day was a sad imitation of the real thing, it wouldn't bother you in the least?" he parried, his smile just as benign. It quickly faded, as did Bertha's brief hit of pleasure from taking a jab at him.

She'd been insulted in many ways, but never about her dancing. That had been the one thing that no one—not her father, not the racist audiences, not the theater directors who had deemed her style "unpolished" during audition after audition—had been able to make her doubt. To most people, her dance had been some exotic fantasy and she had excelled at it; Amir knew better, and he found it *sad*. She would have taken anything else: ungainly, graceless, lewd. Sad? Bertha had been ambivalent about her dancing lately, but she still had her pride.

He stood up suddenly, scrubbing a hand over his face. "I shouldn't have said that. You know, I came in here because I thought maybe we could help each other, but obviously I was wrong. I finished the repairs to those chairs like you wanted. Good day."

"Wait." Bertha was standing now, too, fingertips pressing into the edge of her desk. He'd apologized for his words, but that was different from saying he didn't mean them. "It's rude to offer a blanket critique and then run away. Tell me specifically what you found so sad."

He exhaled through his nose. "Well, I suppose this won't be the strangest way I've ever been fired," he muttered, shaking his head. "You dance wasn't sad. I was being spiteful because you made me angry."

"You'll agree that's one thing I seem to do well."

He let out a short laugh, and Bertha realized that he had a deep indentation in each cheek. It was the first time she had noticed, and she hoped it would be the last given the sudden flush that went through her body.

"I wanted to suggest a trade," he said. "I know your class is for your women, but I wondered if I could listen in from the kitchen during each session. I learned a lot, things I don't learn from my flatmates—we're usually talking about the politics back home."

He paused, pressed his lips together in the way stubborn people did when forced to give up something they didn't want to. "I came to America for the opportunity. Then I got here and everything I see is oppression. I have no rights and no hope of them unless something changes. I need to learn."

It was the yearning in his voice that got her. The hopeless desire for more that got stomped out of every American with any good sense after a while, replaced with hatred or defeat or going along to get along. Bertha had just discovered that yearning again, and she wasn't going to be the one to kill it in Amir.

"You can listen without offering me anything in return. Good day." She sat down, sighing around the lingering sting of his insult. It would fade, as all bruises did.

"I don't take charity," he said, shoving his hands into his pockets. "I can teach you some things about dance in exchange."

He was looking down at her, a glint in his eyes that made her neck go warm, again. Being closer to Amir was the last thing she needed and dance lessons would necessitate exactly that.

"A dancer and a dishwasher, how remarkable," she said. "No thank you."

"For someone who just got done telling those women not to let the world look down on them, you seem very preoccupied with the position you hired me for," he stated calmly. "I'm sure you know this, but power dynamics rooted in social status are a system designed to separate people instead of bringing them together for the greater good."

Bertha raised a brow. She didn't feel shame at the reprimand; derision was often the only weapon she had. She had the uncomfortable feeling that Amir might understand that.

"My very own Bolshevik," she said, tilting her head. "Isn't that the bee's knees."

"There are worse things I could be," he said. "A Democrat. Or is it Republicans who push these restrictive laws on Colored people? If only I had someone to instruct me in such things."

His thumbs slid behind the straps of his suspenders and he looked at her in a manner she figured was charming, if you liked dimples and full lips and raised brows.

She picked up a stack of papers on her desk and began leafing through them. "The next lesson is in two days. You can tutor me directly after."

CHAPTER 4

Amir had spent the morning before the first lesson pretending it was just a regular day, but his flatmates had sensed something amiss, peering at him curiously as he sipped his *cha* and read letters from home, updating him on family friends, his land, and local politics.

"What is it?" Fayaz had finally asked, his dark brows drawn together as he rubbed a palm over the morning stubble covering his round cheeks. He'd pulled off a bit of the puffy wheat *luchi* Amir had made and dipped it into the fragrant *aloo dum*, using it to scoop up the potatoes, onions, and garlic that comprised their simple breakfast. "Did the Hines woman finally kick you out on your bottom? You have more than enough savings to get by, don't worry so much."

"No, no. It's something else," Syed had cut in, getting up to stand next to Amir and lean in close, examining him. "Starched shirt with a clean collar. He's got *pomatum* in his hair, he's shaved, and he doesn't smell like a donkey's behind for once. Hmm…"

Amir swatted at Syed, who jogged just out of reach and pointed at him, eyes wide and brows raised. "He's going to see a woman!"

Amir downed the rest of his tea and stood up, ignoring his laughing friends as he carried his cup to the sink. "I have an assignment at work today. I criticized my boss's dancing, see"—he waited for the groans and recriminations of his flatmates to subside— "and then I told her I could teach her a thing or two."

There was silence behind him as he washed his cup, and he braced himself for a barrage of jibes and jokes at his expense. When he was done washing and drying and the jokes hadn't commenced, he turned to find Fayaz and Syed staring at him.

"You're going to dance?" Syed had asked.

"We could barely get you to dance *jari* last month," Fayaz had said. "I thought you were so shy, and now you're teaching someone?"

"A female someone, who had his brow creased like old *roti* the morning after he came back from his first shift," Syed had added. He and Fayaz had chuckled conspiratorially.

"It's nothing. She's teaching me what she knows about politics and I'm teaching her what I know about dancing. It's a mutual exchange of skills, nothing more. I thought you both were socialists, *na?*"

Both flatmates had burst out laughing and Amir had grabbed his coat and headed for the Cashmere. They were right; he was more of a wallflower than a dancer. He spent his time at festivities in clusters of likeminded people railing against British imperialism. That didn't mean he couldn't dance; young people dreaming of revolution were not exempt from family and religious events.

Amir had lied to Syed and Fayaz though. It wasn't *nothing*; for the first time in a long while, he had found himself looking forward to a dance. And for the first time since he was a child, he was nervous about it.

Rupe Lakshmi, gune Saraswati. That's what he had thought when he'd heard Bertha teaching the women in her employ. *Beautiful as Lakshmi, learned as Saraswati.* He worshipped neither goddess, but he wasn't sure he could say the same of Bertha if he got too close to her. And he was supposed to teach her to dance.

Now he sat in the kitchen, seat pulled up to the door as Bertha circled the stage, explaining the different branches of local elected government and what their roles were. Her hair was twisted back into two rolls that met at the nape to form a bun, leaving her strong jawline and swan-like neck exposed. Her loose blue blouse was tucked into black trousers, wherein Amir's problem laid. Her skirts were never ridiculous and frilly, but those trousers left nothing to the imagination. They clung to the curve of her behind, highlighted the flare of her hips and the taper of her thighs. Amir paid attention to her words, but while his ears were compliant, his eyes were following another course of study.

While her hips were curved, her posture was straight as a mainmast. There was no bend to her there, which was perfect for the kind of dancing he would assist her with, but his mind strayed to the more carnal ways in which she might lose that rigidity.

Thamo. He was leering after her like a pervert stalking women at market. While he was no stranger to lust, he'd thought himself better than that. He shut his eyes and exhaled.

Allah, keep my thoughts respectful and proper.

"Okay. I see some of you are falling asleep, so we'll finish here for today," Bertha said.

"Can we talk more about electing judges next time?" Janie asked. She was Amir's favorite because she always asked for explanations that he couldn't ask for himself. "Because these cops are a problem, but it's the judges who want to throw the book at you. I want to vote for someone who doesn't pretend he don't got a pecker."

Amir suppressed a laugh, but he must have made a sound because Bertha glanced at him. The corners of her mouth raised by a few degrees, and the shift in latitude did something to Amir. He lost his equilibrium for a second, like those first days onboard a ship when his body hadn't yet adjusted to the vessel riding the dips and swells of the ocean.

His will power was going to require more than a quick request for divine help, it seemed.

"Of course," Bertha said, turning back to the women.

"When I went to night court last week, I told the judge that the cops stole from my apartment and he said I was lying," a waitress named Eve said. "I bet they get a cut of what they steal from us."

"Maybe. One day when you're able to vote, you can help vote him out," Bertha said. "Okay. Those of you working tonight, be back at eight o'clock."

The women got up and filed out, some of them peeking through the propped-open kitchen door. When they had all gone and he could dawdle no longer, Amir stood and walked toward the stage, but Bertha had stepped down.

"Are we not going to...exchange now?" Amir asked. The possibility disappointed him more than he expected.

"We're going to practice in my apartment," she said.

"Don't want to be seen cavorting with the dishwasher, eh?" That possibility disappointed him more than expected, too.

"Okay, I earned that," she said. "My apartment will give us more privacy. Unless that makes you uncomfortable."

Her hand went up to her earlobe to finger the pearl set in gold that hung there, and in that motion he glimpsed something incongruous with the Bertha he'd come to know over the last few days: vulnerability. She wanted privacy because she didn't want anyone to see them, and not because of him. It did something to him, seeing that flash of uncertainty in her. It was as if she'd shared a secret with him, had revealed the soft spot she kept hidden from a world always probing for one. He cringed in memory of his arrogant appraisal of her dance.

"That's fine," he said. "But before we start, I need to make something clear."

"What's that? That you don't want me trying to sully your virtue?" The right side of her mouth lifted up, and it was so striking he was glad she hadn't deemed him worthy of a full smile. His head went fuzzy for a moment, like when he was working in a hot kitchen and forgot to eat or drink.

"I was a sailor, Miss Hines. I have very little virtue left, and you're welcome to it."

That got a light laugh from her, as if his answer surprised her.

His grin faded as he tried to broach the uncomfortable topic that had to be tackled before they began. He didn't know if it was necessary for her, but it was for him.

"Spit it out, Amir."

"Dancing can be a very personal, spiritual, cultural thing for some. It isn't for me. I can teach you some basic technical aspects, but I'm not going to be your guru." He would have had to be Hindu to be a guru anyway, but the American craze for all things "exotic" didn't care much about differences in religion, language, or caste.

She didn't say anything and he tried again, softening his words. "I meant no offense. I know there are people paying good money for a brown man to teach them Eastern spirituality. I can't do that for you."

She let out a short, sharp laugh. "Oh, trust me, I know what people are willing to pay. Dance is all I want from you."

He resisted offering up his virtue again; she was his boss, even when she teased him. He followed her through a hallway that branched off the dance floor to its end, where she unlocked a door that led to a flight of stairs. At the top was another door, which opened to a large apartment—large compared to where he lived, at least. He slipped out of his shoes at the threshold of the door, ignoring her confused expression, to take in the space where she lived.

The furniture was all dark wood and sharp angles, which might have meant the previous owner had been a man but could just as easily have been Bertha's taste. Framed images adorned the walls, and shelves lined with books. He spotted something familiar and realized it was a variation of the poster he had seen in her office.

"Rajjah Ben," he read aloud.

She was bent over the graphophone already, a round black disc balanced delicately against her fingertips, but she paused, head tilted and eyes wide as if the dance practice had already begun and she was striking a pose.

"'Come see the mystic of the Far East and his dervish daughter,'" he continued. She dropped the disc down onto the turntable but didn't move the needle.

"Well, I guess it's best you know, especially given your little speech downstairs. I've spent half my life doing this kind of dance and still haven't added up to more than a sad imitation. Story of my life." She said the words on a faux sigh, as if they were a joke, but Amir knew better than that. There was a bitterness there that resonated in him, the same thing that vibrated in his marrow and bones when he joked about tea time or wearing his shoes in the house.

He kept his eyes on her, on that back so straight it might buckle from the strain. "If you were the dervish daughter, then Rajjah Ben was your father."

She walked over to the couch and sat, began working at the laces of her boots. "Yes. He was a very talented musician, and a charlatan. Long story, short: he met an Indian man while performing in New Orleans, a trader like our Mr. Khan, and asked about the turban he wore and what it represented. The man told my father it represented freedom; he only wore it so Whites would leave him be when he traveled selling his goods. It was a ruse that people accepted because of the very little they knew about Indians. My father became obsessed. With the culture, with the music, with the fact that a man darker than him could travel wherever he pleased just because he was neither White nor Black."

Amir studied her face, and the careful absence of expression that told him just how deeply her father's decision had affected her.

She shrugged. "One day while traveling for a show, he bought a strip of linen, wrapped it around his head, and entered a restaurant that served Whites exclusively. He nearly sweated the thing through, way he told it, but when the manager came up to him, he asked him if he was a dignitary instead of telling him to get out. Rajjah Ben was born that day. He acquired fancier turbans, elaborate robes. An accent that would make you cringe. I'm sorry." She glanced at him to catch his reaction. Amir's neck tensed, but how could he blame her for her father's obsession? "His dervish daughter joined him a few years later, once she'd finished primary school and the dancing lessons he'd set up for her."

"And your mother?" he asked.

"My father thought she was too obviously Negro to pass, and she refused to pretend to be otherwise anyway." She shrugged. "He kept me on the road for months at a time, the stretches getting longer as I got older. One day she wrote to say she'd found a new man, one who didn't want her to be something she wasn't and who didn't pretend he was either."

The wistfulness in her voice was faint, but knowing her, it only hinted at the true depth of her pain.

"They live in Chicago now. They came to see our show with their two little boys during our final tour a while back, and I brought the boys—my brothers—onstage to participate. It was nice."

She looked at him. Amir didn't know what to say. He knew America was not fair—his own attempts to get citizenship had proven that. But the desperation that led to the creation of Rajjah Ben, and to Bertha's loss, was not unfamiliar to him.

"Back home, the change began slowly, they said," he said. "I was too young to notice, but my father railed against the men wearing British trousers and their ridiculous hats. 'Next they'll paint their faces white!' he said." He looked down. "Have you noticed my accent? How it's different from Ali Khan's?"

She nodded.

"When I got to Calcutta, a drunk saheb bumped into me. I told him to watch where he was going and he mimicked my accent, roaring with laughter." His face still heated, thinking of how ugly and shameful his words had sounded spat back at him. "I spent months getting rid of it, trying so hard to sound like the people I hated. Because I knew there was opportunity in erasing the parts of me that they found laughable."

There was a noise as she stood from the couch. Her heeled boots were gone, and it surprised him, how small she really was. Bertha didn't feel small.

"I know some people find psychoanalysis stimulating, but I'm not one of them. Shall we dance?"

Her voice was so silky smooth that it took a moment for the slap of her words to hit him. He'd never told anyone that about himself and she had brushed it away. Then he looked at how her chest rose and fell, at the way her lips pressed together, and remembered that to a ram, butting against a wall was less painful than a blow to the flank that took it unawares.

"I had an accent once, too," she finally said when he didn't respond. Then she raised her arms and cupped her hands, as if waiting for the rain to come and fill them. "Shall we dance?"

It was an order this time, but a gentle one.

He took a deep breath. "Of course. Show me what you've got."

CHAPTER 5

"Okay, lift your shoulders, *then* turn your hands like...so. Yes, like that. Press your fingers together harder. Make sure your feet hit the floor three times. Like this."

Amir executed the move he was explaining, and Bertha nodded, but mostly to the thought that was running through her head.

He's gorgeous.

This was their fourth session and it was getting harder to fight those kinds of thoughts, the ones at odds with the standards she had set for herself once she took over the Cashmere. Once she'd regained control of her own life. But Amir's shirt was off, thrown over the arm of her settee, and he stood there in his undershirt, suspenders hanging down over his trousers, and a fine sheen of sweat on his arms and face.

She tried the move again, finishing in the pose of invitation, but already knew she hadn't done it quite right by the expression on his face. He wasn't demanding, or exacting—his expression was one of indulgence. It was *kind*. She hated it.

She didn't know exactly why she had agreed to the lessons; she supposed that like Janie, she couldn't turn down the chance to see what could have happened if she'd been given proper tutelage. That, and she couldn't pass Amir every day and live with the knowledge that he'd found her lacking.

"Here, let's try this." He turned and reached into the pocket of his jacket and pulled something out, then came and knelt before her. "Put your foot on my knee."

She looked down at his thick black hair, at the whorl in the middle that would not be tamed by his pomade. She had never seen a man from this angle, she realized; she'd been with so many, but she had always been the one kneeling. An unwanted arousal bloomed in her as she lifted her bare foot and rested it on the curve of his bent leg. His kneecap poked into the sole of her foot as he shifted his weight and she let out a soft gasp. She wasn't one for soft gasps, so when he looked up at her, she was sure he saw that her brows were raised with surprise at herself.

"Ticklish?" he asked, grinning. His two front teeth were a little too large, but for some reason that only made Bertha think of how they'd feel pressing into her inner thigh.

Don't think it.

She tried to school her thoughts, but her resistance to the images flashing in her mind didn't stop the heat dancing in her belly like Salomé. She found that she was still able to blush, after all this time.

"Just a little," she choked out.

"Then I'll be more gentle," he said. He opened his palm, which she had felt on the flat of her back or at her wrist or on her shoulders over the last week, and revealed two strings of tiny silver bells.

"Is this so you can hear me approaching when you and Cora are gossiping in the kitchen instead of working?" she asked. Jokes were good. Jokes distracted from thoughts that had nothing to do with Congress or the Cashmere and everything to do with how his hair would feel beneath her fingers. She wasn't one to miss an opportunity to take what she wanted, though...

She wobbled a bit, making sure not to overplay the quick jerky motion, then laid her hand on his head to steady herself. His hair was thick and silky and the warmth of his ear pressed into her hand; there was something strikingly intimate about feeling that delicate shell against her palm. She was about to pull her hand away, when she was distracted by the unintended consequence of her ruse. There was a jingle as his hand darted up and cupped behind her knee to steady her, but this touch was different from the light taps and corrective nudges of their lessons. It was his fingertips pressing into her skin through the thin material of her pants, his palm and digits exerting strength to grip and hold her in place.

Bertha swallowed hard and shut her eyes against the quick, sharp longing that lanced through her. He was completely still, unmoving save for a racing pulse where her palm met his ear. She couldn't tell if it was hers or his. Amir didn't move for a long moment, then released his grip on her. It wasn't a quick motion, but a slow caress that sent a tremor through her.

"You don't need bells to announce your presence," he finally said as he tied the string around her ankle. His voice was lower than it had been, the air around them a bit more charged, like the feeling in a room right before she launched into her dance.

Bertha was so focused on his touch and her response to it that, for a moment, she forgot what he was talking about.

His fingertips grazed the skin and bone of her ankle as he tied, each touch sending little shocks through her that marched steadily towards her apex like the soldier boys parading down Fifth Avenue.

His shoulders rose and fell on a sigh, then he looked up at her and grinned, and it wasn't until his dimples sank deeper—an indication of growing amusement—that she realized what he wanted. She switched the foot that rested on his knee and reminded herself that she was indifferent to his presence as he tied the second string. That his touch did absolutely nothing at all to her. He was just a man, and one in her employ at that.

"There," he said, standing. There was only the slightest darkening across his cheekbones, and in his eyes, to show he'd felt even a fraction of what she had. "This is a bit of baiji—natchni, a form of the kathak we were already doing."

"Like nautch?" Her voice came out smooth, no breathiness, no husk. She couldn't let him see that he'd affected her any more than she had already revealed. Once a man knew he affected you, he started getting ideas, and in Bertha's experience those ideas were never good for her in the long run. Getting the Cashmere from Arthur had been a stroke of luck— cunningly executed, but luck all the same. She couldn't go all soft-headed over a man now.

"Yes. A version of nautch is what has been exported to Britain and the US." He had enough tact not to show his disdain.

She'd occasionally gone to nautch shows to pick up new techniques, when it was allowed; sitting in the Colored section of the theater as a White woman whirled to Indian music.

"Traditionally, a natchni would travel with her husband, or master, and dance and sing while he played. After the performance…" He looked away from her. "Nevermind."

Something about his expression pricked at her. She knew very well what happened after performances, no matter the country or culture. Men wanted what they had just seen, and if there was a "master" in the mix, he likely profited from that. Her father had never done so, and had gotten into brawls when admirers pushed their luck. Arthur had been a good egg, but he hadn't been possessive; men offering the right price had been able to indulge their fantasies of Bertha in nothing but her bangles.

You don't mind, do you? You know we got bills to pay…

"I'm going to clap, since we have no drum here," Amir continued, and

Bertha shook away the thought. "For each clap, step firmly once so that you match it with a jingle."

He began clapping, looking at her expectantly, and irritation tugged at her like a rough john. She held up a hand, but not to dance.

"First answer this: in addition to people from the expanded Asiatic Barred Zone, what other group is no longer allowed entry into the US effective February fifth of this year?"

He cocked his head to the side, eyes turned up as if he searched for the question on her ceiling. "Apart from madmen, criminals, and any other bogeyman politicians could think of? Apart from people like me?" He met her gaze then. "Illiterate people. People over the age of sixteen must take a literacy test before being allowed entry. The same way Blacks in your Southern states are given tests before being allowed to vote."

Bertha raised her brows. "Very good. You're right, with the exception being that there's a chance of passing the test immigration gives foreigners, whereas the tests for Negro citizens are generally not passable."

He nodded, then worried his bottom lip a little like he did when he was turning something over in his mind. "Does it make you hate your country? Knowing such things happen and no one stops it?" He ran a hand through his hair and Bertha's fingers flexed. "I felt a kind of hate in my heart before I left home, and I thought it was for my country, for what the British had made it. Now I don't know."

Bertha had felt that churning, directionless rage. Every time her father forced her to straighten and curl her long hair because an Indian girl wouldn't have the naps that even her "good hair" didn't hide. Every time someone directed bile at her because they knew she was Negro, and every time they fawned over her because they fell for the lie that she wasn't. Every time she felt glad when she was allowed something that America generally kept from citizens like her because she had tricked others into thinking she was foreign.

Girl, people see what they want to see.

"I don't hate America." She resumed her position, arms raised. "If I hated it, that would be admitting they'd broken me. We can both clearly see that I'm not broken."

She stood with her back straight, and her gaze trained on the wall behind him. It was how she had stared into the back of the crowd before beginning her dance so she wouldn't have to see the anticipation for the whirling, spinning lies she was about to create.

She pursed her lips. "You said you were going to clap."

He let out an indulgent sigh and then bought his hands together hard. Bertha closed her eyes, listening to the jingle as she stepped her feet in time.

ℭ ℭ ℭ

Later that evening, she swept through the club, knowing all eyes were on her. Her dress was scarlet and so were her lips. The dress was loose fitting but still managed to cling to her curves, and the hemline brushed well above her knees. Her hair was pulled back into a heavy bun; she looked longingly at the younger women with their chic short cuts that didn't require hours of straightening and pinning and curling and wondered how freeing it might be to simply walk into the salon and tell Nell to cut it all off.

She was dressed a bit more revealingly than she had since taking over the club; before, when she had been one of the girls smiling at patrons and hoping to hook one to take to a back room, Arthur had insisted she wear as little as possible.

"Show them thick thighs of yours," he'd say, grabbing and squeezing. She'd acted like she enjoyed his rough touch because there had been no other option and, hell—sometimes she hadn't been acting. He'd been the source of power and protection in her world, and if he took a cut of her earnings and felt entitled to her goods, her lot was still a sight better than most women in her position. And she had no regrets; eventually, Arthur had gone from pimp to husband. Then he had passed away. She'd slipped into widow's weeds and cried—that hadn't been an act either—then held out a will with had her name listed as inheritor while her eyes were still rimmed with red. The Cashmere was hers, and now the girls didn't have to offer their bodies to anyone they didn't see fit to.

She had reminded them of that earlier in the night. "We want the men to vote yes. But the rules still apply; don't degrade yourself, unless that's the kind of thing that gets you steamed up."

The club was bumping as she passed through; cigarette smoke swirled through the air like steam rising from a manhole in the dead of winter. The scent of food and cologne and sweat permeated the air as people danced; she spotted Janie grinding on a flustered looking White man she was fairly certain was a local union big wig. Wah Ming was sitting on the lap of a brother who had connections with the Tammany drive to recruit Negro voters to the Democrats. Her throaty laugh mixed with the dolorous trill of a trumpet as Bertha passed the group. As she was walking, a hand shot out and grabbed her by the waist, pulling her down onto a firm lap.

Her neck stiffened and she jumped up, whirling in the cloud of smoke and bourbon scent.

"Do that again and you'll lose a hand," she warned, then her stomach plummeted as she recognition hit her. The man seated with a smug smile on his face was that combination of brown skinned and light eyed that inflated a man's ego, and between his political victories and his prowess in the sack, Bertha grudgingly had to admit that he wasn't completely full of hot air.

"Oh ho!" Victor held his hands up. "Still off the market? I thought you might make an exception for an old friend after all this time."

His eyes roamed over her body, as if mentally comparing her with the younger version of herself from a few years back. He knew her body about as well as any man, so he'd be a fair judge.

"You pay for the company of all your friends?" she shot back, lifting a hand to her hip.

"I'm a politician, baby," he replied with a shrug and a smile, and Bertha had to laugh at that. She appreciated when a man was honest about his faults.

She'd liked Victor; his fixation on her had been exhilarating at a time. An older, sophisticated man who treated her like a lady instead of a whore—most of the time. Sometimes, after a few drinks, he'd wanted her to do things he'd deny in the light of day, but he'd been good to her. After Arthur had died, Victor had learned very quickly that Bertha had no use for a man's relative goodness once she had her own power. Politics had pulled Victor to Albany shortly after that, immersing him in the political theater outside of the city, and she hadn't seen him since.

"What are you doing back in town?" she asked.

"I have a meeting with some of the men running for office," he said. "Tammany is looking to shore up the Negro vote. There's hope of getting more of our own into office this year."

"Oh, I wouldn't know about such things since I'm not allowed a ballot," she replied blithely. Victor looked around, then stood up, motioning for her to follow him. He maneuvered through the crowd, taking them to a dimly lit alcove where there was a bit less noise.

"I heard about your little challenge to the men," he said, his straight teeth flashing bright as he grinned. "I'm disappointed I won't get to see you dance while I'm here. I miss that."

Bertha's throat went tight. She felt like she was back in her office,

Arthur's office back then, immediately after his death. Victor was using the same cajoling tone he had then. *I can take care of you, baby. You really think you can just step into his shoes?*

"Well, you'll just have to come back to town once we get the vote," she said. "Nice seeing you, but I've got business to attend to."

His hand went to her wrist, and it was nothing like Amir's warm touch—the only male touch she was used to now, she realized. Victor's grasp was urgent, possessive.

"I can help you," he said. "I've got sway with the state's most prominent Negroes, and many of the Whites too."

She looked at him, unsure of what was expected of her. "I'm sure your parents are very proud," she said, then tugged at her wrist. His grip tightened. It wasn't menacing, but he was making clear that she was going to listen, whether she wanted to or not.

"I know you're not naive, Bertha. Stubborn, but not naive." He gave her wrist a quick tug, pulling her against him. She'd once pretended she enjoyed that, but she no longer had to pretend, and the discordance froze her for a moment. His mustache brushed her ear as he spoke, and she shivered.

"You want men to vote yes," he said. "I can *get* men to vote yes."

She should have been pleased, but she knew he wasn't offering out of the kindness of his heart.

"What do you want?" she asked.

"A private dance, like you used to give before you got too uppity for it," he said.

Ah. There it was, a hint of anger belying the suaveness of his tone. She was too good an actress, it seemed, or he was too gullible. She'd presented herself as a woman not available at a man's slightest whim, and that was somehow a personal affront. He didn't just want a dance—he wanted her on her knees again.

"I don't do private dances," she said. "I don't do private anything."

"I'm traveling all over right now talking to groups about the upcoming elections. I've been asked to write an editorial for the Union League, explaining whether I'm for or against women having the vote," he said. "They say that men listen to me, that I'm good at changing minds. It will be published in all the papers, be seen by every man of consequence."

Bertha felt ill. She felt ill like the first time she'd let a man use her mouth and she'd gagged and almost been sick on the floor. She'd learned what to do since then, which Victor knew all too well.

"So you want sex from me in exchange for your word that you'll convince a significant number of men to vote yes?" She hoped laying it out before him would make him see how insulting his offer was.

"You've sold yourself for less." He wasn't trying to be cruel, but her hand went to the wall to hold her up. Her back was still straight, though.

He wasn't wrong. She was asking her girls to use their wiles; what would that make her if she said no? Just another pimp.

"You know there are men out there already spreading the word. Du Bois and the other race men are willing to do the same—what's right—without asking for anything in return."

He shrugged. "I'm a politician, baby."

She didn't laugh this time.

Don't degrade yourself. But hadn't she told herself she'd do anything? Well.

"If that's the only way you can get your rocks off, sure thing. Write your little editorial, show me proof that men have responded to it, and I'll make you forget whether you're coming or going. Just like old times."

The words came out sultry, velvety smooth, how she'd reeled in her customers night after night when she worked the floor searching for johns. They'd never known when she was faking it because she was always faking it.

"Is there a problem, Miss Hines?"

She turned, this time tugging her wrist away. Amir stood behind them, brows drawn and scowl lines pulling at that mouth of his.

"Nothing I can't handle," she said. He didn't move though, just stood there looking at her as if he'd strip his shirt off and pummel Victor if she gave the word. As if he could protect her. Her eyes filled at the foolish earnestness of it all and she blinked away tears that had sprung up out of nowhere. "Thank you for checking."

Victor harumphed, looking at the dishtowel in Amir's hand. "You can go back to the kitchen, boy."

She whirled on him. "And you can go back to your table." She tilted her head toward his party, who were laughing and carrying on. "Scram."

"I always loved that temper of yours," he said as he backed away. "You'll hear from me soon."

She stared him down, even after his back was turned. Amir moved to stand next to her, but he didn't touch her. Had he seen the tears before she caught herself? No one was supposed to, most especially not him.

"Can you come to the kitchen for a moment?" His voice was level, as if he hadn't witnessed anything, making her all the more sure that he had. "I want you to try something."

"I'm working," she said. Her voice was harsh, but not more so than necessary given what had just passed.

"Brilliant. This is work related."

His elbow bumped hers playfully as he turned, as if beckoning her to follow him, and she did. She couldn't go back onto the floor just yet; couldn't have Victor looking at her as if she were a prize he had already won.

She smelled it as soon as she walked into the kitchen: a rich, tangy spice that made her mouth water.

"Cora?" she asked. Cora knew her way around the kitchen, but if she'd been hiding a recipe that smelled this good from her, they were going to have to have words.

Cora was sitting with her feet propped up on an empty box and a bowl of steaming food in her lap, looking content. She shook her head as she finished chewing. "I was craving fish stew yesterday and Amir said he'd cook me some. I make some good fish stew, so I can say with authority that this is some good fish stew."

She tucked in again, a radiant smile on her face.

"Try some," he said, grabbing a bowl.

"Why do you need me to try it?" Bertha asked. She leaned back, eyeing the pot suspiciously.

He laughed. "Because you didn't eat before practice this afternoon and I don't think you ate after, and you're going to be on your feet all night," he said as he ladled up the stew. "I told you it was work related. Here."

She took the bowl from him, and a spoon, schooling her face into a mask of annoyance to hide that inside she felt soft as kitten fur. She often worked so hard that she forgot to eat, not realizing it until a drink went to her head too quickly or she collapsed into bed as the sun came up. How had he noticed?

She scooped up a fragrant spoonful and made a sound of pleasure when it touched her tongue. Tangy, hot-sweet, lush—it was delicious. She said nothing, scooping up spoon after spoonful until the bowl was empty. The stew was rich, but she felt lighter somehow having eaten it.

"Thank you." She handed him the bowl. He took it with a grin and moved to the sink. "You better watch your back, Cora," she teased.

"I can't see my toes, let alone my back, but I'll try," Cora said.

Bertha laughed and moved to head back out onto the floor. It wouldn't do to be gone too long, though as she heard Cora and Amir chat she wished she could stay and sit with them. But she was the boss, and that was how she liked it.

"Let me know if you need anything else," Amir called out as she was going through the door. She looked back at him and his grin was gone. There was tenseness in his shoulders and jaw that belied the easiness with which he'd led her into the kitchen. His gaze flicked toward the door and then back to her. "Anything."

She should have said something cutting to remind him that she was in charge and she'd never need his help. That was how she made it through each day; reminding others of who she was and where they stood in relation to that. But she sheathed the cutting jibe and simply nodded.

Because while she hadn't needed his help, the taste of his food and the slant of his frown served as a counterbalance as she sauntered onto the floor, helping to pull her shoulders back and her head high, the better to look down her nose as she passed Victor. He winked at her as she walked by. She ignored him.

The election needed to be over, and fast.

CHAPTER 6

"Practice again today, Pintu?" Fayaz asked as Amir pulled on his coat, a shabby thing left behind by the flatmate he'd replaced. The autumn had been on the warmer side, but cold winds and dropping temperatures had descended to remind him that another interminable New York winter awaited him. His walk to the Cashmere would leave him chilled if he didn't get a new jacket.

If you're there for that long. He couldn't very well work as a dishwasher forever, could he? If that was the case, he'd be better off returning home and tending to his land, like Sabiha Auntie begged him to in her letters. He'd been giving it more and more thought, especially as his savings grew. He would be a peasant back home, but a well-educated, well-traveled one. He could tell stories to his children about the time he lived in a city far away, like Raahil Chacha had with him. Unlike before, Amir wasn't able to conjure up an image of a doting wife. Instead, he thought of sitting on the couch beside Bertha as they did after each lesson, sipping *cha* and talking politics.

"They *practice* every day," Syed said, drawing an annoyed glance from Amir as he struggled with the buttons on his coat; the previous roommate had been a slimmer man than him.

Syed peeked up from the letter he'd received from his mother, updating him about his wife. "You'd think they were planning to take the stage with all this *practice*."

Amir rolled his eyes before slipping into his shoes and heading through the door. "Keep this talk up and you can get someone else to cook for Azim's wedding. *Khoda hafez.*"

"Eh, don't be so sensitive, Pintu!" Fayaz called out as the door closed.

It was hard not to be sensitive. The mere mention of Bertha twisted something in him that should have been straight. She was his boss. That was it. But Syed was right.

Although he learned something new during each of their political talks and her lessons, Bertha had learned enough from him by now. It wasn't as if he was some grand master of the art form—she was a far better dancer than him. He simply had more technical knowledge by an accident of birth. Her dancing had been more than fine when he'd first seen it. It was better now, but who would really know apart from the two of them? But instead of decreasing the number of practices, they now met every day, even when she wasn't teaching her citizenship classes. She was surely getting *something* from the meetings if she kept scheduling them, but he didn't know what, and that was why any mention of her from his friends was no joking matter for him.

He knew what he was getting from their lessons, and it wasn't just the finer points of American politics. Amir had gone to the fire rooms that fueled the *Kandahar*, had felt the heat of the great coal-fed engine, but that was nothing compared to the way he felt as he stood behind her and watched her hips move. His focus should have been the tips of her fingers or the angle of her shoulders as they rose and fell—not that those weren't distracting, too—but Bertha had made up for a lack of actual knowledge by moving in a way designed to ensure the audience paid no attention to the finer details.

Amir had fancied a woman before. He'd dreamed about his neighbor Nazia for years before an arrangement was made and she had been married to a man from another village. Once he'd made it to Calcutta, there had been Nita, the widow who rented out rooms and occasionally took her tenants as lovers. After her was Piyali, the café owner's daughter who had smoked cigarettes, worn British-style trousers, and spoken of revolution as they lay sweaty and sated in her bed.

But he fancied Bertha in a different way. Yes, every time he repositioned her arm or ankle during their lessons he imagined what it would be like to touch her everywhere. To kiss and lick her everywhere. But he also fancied her intelligence, and her toughness, and how she was the first person he'd butted heads with who'd butted right back, and with a smile.

Her smile. He thought of the look of pleasure on her face when she'd tasted the stew he'd prepared and his chest clenched. It had felt right, seeing her smile like that and knowing he had been the cause.

The thought warmed him against the cool autumn wind that snuck up under his jacket. The tumult of excitement and joy and apprehension that roiled in him each time he approached the alley leading to the back door of the Cashmere began to build. Those feelings were abruptly cut short when he turned the corner to the alley and saw a White man standing there, smoking a cigarette. Alarm bells went off in his head, louder than the calls to prayer that echoed across Kalinga Bazaar.

He's just having a smoke, Amir told himself. *He's not here for you.* He resisted the urge to turn and run. The man had already seen him, and running would give him reason to pursue. Amir hated that he had to plot his next move like a criminal, simply because a few sahebs had gotten together and decided they didn't want his kind around.

He kept walking, against his will, ready to flee if the man reached for him.

The man leaned against the wall, taking another pull of his cigarette but leaving room for Amir to pass. He tried to remain calm, to act as if he was just your average, every day, legal American citizen reporting for work. His apprehension began to decrease as he passed the man and heard no sign of pursuit.

"Hey."

Amir froze, a preliminary before taking off at a sprint. Then the man continued.

"You know any clubs around here a guy could go to for a good time?"

Amir turned and looked at the man. He had a thin, drawn face, and eyes like he'd spent too long squinting into the sun. He didn't look very much like a man searching for a good time, but then again, Bertha had explained that many of the Whites came to the club to gawk and stare, to "see the Negro in his natural habitat," as she'd put it. He'd told her about the sahebs and their wives walking through the slums of Calcutta holding handkerchiefs to their noses as they looked about, like they were at a zoo exhibit.

Oh my, they eat with their hands!

Although the Cashmere catered to a mixed crowd, Amir wasn't the one who got to decide who was allowed and who wasn't. He also had the sinking feeling that the man was more interested in him than in the club. "No. Only Negro clubs around here, sir."

He cringed at how the honorific slipped out. Why should he call some White man lounging in an alley like an urchin "sir"? The only power that the man held over him was the color of his skin, but that was all that was necessary in America, it seemed. Back home, too, now.

"Negro, you say?" The man didn't hide his appraisal of Amir as he continued to squint at him, or his skepticism. "Huh."

I don't want to go back. The panicked thought came out of nowhere, a sudden truth that bowled him over with the weight of it. He missed his neighborhood, his land, his people. But if he left he would miss the busy Harlem streets and the confusion that was America. He would miss Bertha.

"That's too bad," the man said, then looked away. "I know men who pay good money to find out about places like that."

He took a lazy drag of his cigarette.

Amir said nothing more, just turned and continued on his path toward the Cashmere. He used the key Bertha had given him for the back door and pulled it open, not looking back. As he passed through, he peeked through the crack left between the door and the wall by the hinges it turned on. The man was looking right at the open door, then turned and walked out of the alley.

Amir released a breath and told himself it was just a coincidence. Wouldn't an immigration agent have arrested him without preamble? The man had just been looking for a good time, and he'd find someone else to help him achieve that goal. He pulled the door closed hard behind him, making sure it was locked.

"Amir?" Bertha's voice called out.

"Coming," he replied. He tried to leave his paranoid thoughts and his disgust at his reaction, at the door. He had enough real life worries, like reminding himself that a dance was just a dance and Bertha was well out of his league.

℘ ℘ ℘

Bertha was behind the bar, looking through her ledger. Amir was stocking glasses he'd brought out from the kitchen. They'd practiced for a bit, his non-encounter with the man in the alley causing him to lose his train of thought a few times, and then they'd sat and talked. It had been comfortable; her on the couch with her legs tucked up under her, Amir beside her. The length of a cushion had separated them, and though he'd just been nearly pressed against her as he'd instructed her, he wondered if he'd ever be able to cross that gap on the sofa. It may as well have been the distance from his sleeping quarters in the bowels of the Kandahar to the officers' quarters above.

Then they'd gone downstairs, and his opening duties had brought him out to the bar and hers had brought her into the kitchen. Neither of them acknowledged the fact that the bartender would have stocked the glassware when he arrived or that Cora preferred doing the kitchen inventory herself. They'd done the same the previous day, and the day before that. They were performing a different kind of dance now, seeking each other out and then retreating, but he wasn't sure she noticed. It could be that she just needed a friend; she had men after her all the time, and Amir wouldn't be one of them.

"What did men do for pleasure while out at sea?" she asked abruptly. She didn't look up from her book and continued making notes as she moved her pencil down the column.

Amir fumbled a glass and almost dropped it, catching it at the last moment. "Pardon?"

She glanced at him. "I'm just wondering. What do men do, stuck out in the middle of the ocean with no woman around for a thousand miles? I'm sure some of them have no need for a woman and do quite fine for themselves, but what of the others?"

"Is there anything in particular that prompted you to ask this?"

"It's just that you mentioned how long your journeys were when we spoke earlier. Every night, I see men acting like goddamned fools because there are women around that they might have sex with. I wondered what they do with that energy when there aren't."

Amir placed a highball glass down on the shelf, carefully, and tried not to think about the word "sex." Allah give him strength, he didn't need to think of that any more than he already did when it came to Bertha.

She looked at him innocently, but the very primness of her expression— brows raised, mouth a contemplative pout—tipped him off that she knew she was toying with him.

"It depends. The officers did…officer things, I suppose. Sitting around, looking important while they smoked pipes." Her lips twitched at that. "With the lascars, some men prayed a lot more. Some kept themselves busy with work. Some were too tired to do much of anything. I imagine they thought about sex a lot, and…relieved themselves when the opportunity arose."

"And you?" she was looking at her book once more, but he could feel her attention directed toward him. "How did you pass the time?"

"When I wasn't cooking or helping around the ship, I read in my bunk," he said. "A lot."

"Mm-hmm."

He moved beside her to stock the water glasses and she turned and leaned on the bar, her body facing him.

"Do you still read a lot?" she asked, a smile on her lips. She was flirting with him, and even though he knew it was a rote act for her it still made his heart pound in his chest like waves smashing against the hull of a ship.

"I'm rather private about my reading habits," he said, leaning his hip against the bar to mirror her stance. "So I'll refrain from answering that."

"Mm-hmm." The same two-syllable sound, but this time it came out low, almost a purr. Amir leaned toward her, not thinking but following the pull of the hum in her tone.

A crash and a cry of pain from the kitchen made his heart lurch in a different way, and had them both spinning and jogging toward the door.

"Cora?" Bertha called out as they entered, and then they saw her.

She was hunched over, hand gripping the edge of the counter hard. Shards of glass were scattered around her feet, but he had a sinking feeling that the liquid on the ground had another source.

"I think he got tired of kicking and wants to take the natural way out," she said. Sweat beaded at her hairline and she pressed her lips closed against another shout.

"I thought you weren't due for another month," Bertha said. Her body was tense, all trace of flirtatiousness gone. "You can't have the baby now."

Cora shot her an annoyed look. "Maybe you should tell him that."

Amir touched Bertha's arm.

"Can you go ring an ambulance?" she nodded and rushed back toward her office. He knew she must have been terribly frightened because she didn't push back against being given something resembling an order.

Amir grabbed a pot and filled it with water. He placed it on the stove top, flame high, and dropped the heavy shears Cora used for kitchen work inside. Just in case.

"Cora, I'm going to bring you out to the main room. We can have you lie in one of the booths until help arrives."

He placed an arm around her for support and she gripped his arm tightly. "Guess I won't get to try that aloo stuff you promised me," she said as they walked. She was trying to make light of things, but her voice shook and her eyes were bright with tears.

"I'll bring you some at the hospital. Surely it will be better than the food there."

She made a keening noise as they approached the closest booth. Amir pushed the table away and laid her down on the vinyl-covered seat.

"I don't think he's gonna wait," she said, eyes wide.

Amir's heart thumped hard. He was afraid, too—afraid for Cora and her baby—but he'd learned on the ship that in any given situation one person had to take charge, and this time it would be him.

He grinned. "That's right. He's a go-getter. He's not going to wait around for a bloody doctor to make his debut."

Cora tried to smile back, but faltered. "Back home, there was a woman who was the best at catchin' babies. They said Miss Junie was a hundred years old and had caught a thousand babies at least. Even if the baby came out blue and quiet she could breathe life into 'em." She closed her eyes and tears streamed down her face and into her hair as pain gripped her again. "I should have never left. I want Miss Junie. I want Darryl."

Amir felt the panic rising in her; the same that was in him, but multiplied by all of Cora's incalculable hopes and dreams for her child.

"Cora, look at me." He heard the sound of Bertha's return but kept his gaze on Cora.

Cora opened her eyes.

"You don't know me so well, but you know Bertha. Do you think she would let anything happen to you and your baby in the Cashmere?"

Cora's chest rose and fell. "No. Not if she could help it."

"Exactly right. Nothing here happens without her say so."

He glanced up at Bertha then and didn't have to guess at how the call had gone. Her expression was pinched but she inhaled deeply and drew her shoulders back before striding over. "Of course not. And I say this baby is gonna be fine. He's gonna be perfect."

"Is the ambulance coming?" Cora asked.

She nodded, then shook her head, then nodded. "It might be a while. There was an accident with a car and a trolley. They said it would be best if we could bring her in. Said labor usually lasts for hours."

She walked over and knelt beside Cora.

"Do you think you can make it to the hospital?" she asked.

Cora shook her head in frustration. "I don't know. I don't know anything. This is my fi—AAAghh!" One hand gripped the wood running along top the booth and the other the cushion. "No. No, he's coming now."

"Shit. Shit." Bertha sat planted where she was.

Amir tried to catch her gaze. "Bertha."

She didn't move.

"Bertha, love." Her gaze finally flicked to him. "Can you please go get the hot water and the shears from off of the stove? And a stack of kitchen towels? And bring them here?"

She let out a shaky breath. "You sound like you know what you're doing."

"I've heard the story of my birth from my father enough times. There was a heavy rain and he was too scared to leave my mother alone so he had to deliver me himself." His father had always said it was his proudest achievement. It wasn't until after his father had passed that he'd realized that his father had meant him, Amir, more than the birth itself.

His stomach lurched at the enormity of what they were about to do, but then Cora cried out and there was no time for fear.

Bertha nodded, galvanized by having a task to achieve, and headed for the kitchen.

"I…have to check if the baby is coming," Amir said. "We can wait for Bertha to get back."

Cora laughed around a grunt. "Miss Bertha like to pass out if she peeks under my skirt. Just look. I don't care as long as this baby comes out safe."

He checked, not quite certain what he was looking for but sure it wasn't there. "Not yet," he said, wishing his father had gone into a bit more detail about the logistics of his delivery.

Bertha returned with the requested items. After placing them on the table, she slid onto the bench so that Bertha's head was in her lap. She wiped at Cora's brow with a damp cloth, her face drawn with worry. Amir held Cora's hand as she breathed through contractions, and they both offered her encouragement.

"I'm gonna push," she said eventually. Her eyes were wide with fear but there was determination in her grip on his hand. Amir looked at Bertha and she shook her head, so he moved down between Cora's legs. He knew some people would think it shameful, but sordid thoughts were the last thing on his mind as the crown of the baby's head became visible. Amir just stared for a moment, unable to move as he realized that there was no going back. Cora and her baby were depending on him.

"Okay, breathe and push. I think," he finally said, trying to keep his voice calm.

"Yes, that's right," Bertha said, holding Cora's hand. "Breathe and push. Push and breathe."

He was sure she had no idea what she was talking about either, but Cora needed guidance and she was providing it.

It went on like that for who knows how long, Cora working, Bertha and Amir talking her through the pain. Finally—finally—the baby's head and shoulders pushed through and Amir grabbed and pulled, wrapping the slick bundle in a towel. There was silence in the club, and Amir gently patted the baby's back. It didn't react for a tense moment, then he felt the baby's chest expand against his wrist and a scream pierced the air.

"Yes!" he shouted, leaning forward to pass Cora the bundle. "Alhamdulillah."

Praise God.

He moved beside them, grabbing the shears. Tears streamed down his face, mixing with the sweat, and when he looked at Bertha she was wiping her eyes. He quickly cut the cord and tied it. His father had emphasized that, at least.

"It's a girl," Cora said, her voice hiccupping from her sobs.

"She's beautiful." Bertha wiped at her cheeks. She looked at the baby and her eyes filled again. Amir's heart was full of wonder and joy, surging in him like a river with no outlet, and he did the first thing that came to mind. He leaned in toward Bertha, and when her head swiveled in his direction he kissed her.

It wasn't a lustful kiss, simply a chaste press of mouth against mouth, but it hit him with a force that nearly stopped his lungs from working. Then Bertha leaned in closer, pressing harder as if she needed more from him. He gave it to her.

The kiss deepened to something sweet and rough, just for an instant, and then she pulled away. Her gaze snared his and she let out an exhilarated trill, as if they'd just crossed the finish line at a race.

That was it; they were sharing in a victory and nothing more. She looked back down at Cora, who was entranced with her little girl.

"I'm going to go hail a cab," Bertha said. "We should get you to the hospital."

"Darryl is at work," she said. "Over at Baker's." Her husband stocked shelves at a local market.

"I can go tell him to meet you," Amir said. "I just need to wash up. "He was wiping his hands with a towel, his gaze traveling between Bertha and Cora and the baby.

"Harlem Hospital," Bertha said, and he nodded.

He headed toward the water closet, the thrill of new life—and the feel of Bertha's mouth—suffusing him with an emotion that made him sure he was glowing like an electric light.

"I have a name for her," Cora called out after him, and he turned to her. "Amira. Sounds nice, huh? I think Darryl will like that. Amira."

She looked down at her child again.

"I'm partial to it," he said, his voice thick.

His hands shook as he washed them, and he stopped for a moment and gripped the edge of the sink as the terrifying wonder of all that had just passed fully struck him. Wonder wasn't the only thing he was feeling; Bertha's mouth had been warm, inviting, and he tried to push away the image that had lodged in his mind during their kiss and refused to budge. Bertha, sweat-damp and happy, holding a brown baby who had his eyes and her nose. Men weren't supposed to imagine such things, *na*? Daydreams of babies and happiness were as naive as believing the streets in America were paved with gold and all people were welcome with open arms.

Amir buried the flash of envy and jogged into the cold evening air to tell Darryl the good news.

CHAPTER 7

"Wait, Cora had her baby in *this* booth?"

Janie and Wah Ming jumped out of the seat where they'd been lounging against one another with matching looks of disgust on their faces.

"Ya'll know you both came from your mama's nethers, right?" Eve asked.

"Well, Cora ain't my mama," Janie shot back, examining the back of her dress.

Wah Ming's face relaxed and she shrugged and settled back into the seat. "I've seen worse than childbirth happen in this booth, if we're being honest. I've done worse, too."

She winked.

Janie sighed and sat back down beside her.

Bertha waited for them to settle down. "As you all know, Amir has taken over the cooking temporarily."

"Why temporary? The man can cook!"

A burst of agreement broke out from the group.

"I thought he was handsome, but after eating that fried chicken he made last night, I'm wondering if he's got a wife back home or if I can lock that down," Janie said.

Wah Ming nudged her.

"What? I'll share my chicken with you," Janie said. "Maybe not the chicken. You can have some of the greens though."

Bertha felt the tickle of something unusual at the back of her neck. She didn't like the idea of the girls discussing Amir's matrimonial status or joking about changing it. She wasn't jealous, though. And she certainly wasn't thinking of how his mouth had felt against hers, or the happy shock that had gone through her when he kissed her. She hadn't felt that way since her first kiss; behind a venue in Gary, Indiana with a boy who had come to the show three nights in a row and presented her with flowers the second two.

She'd imagined Amir's mouth against hers many times—many, many times—but her fantasies had leaned toward what she knew of men. Amir grabbing her by the arm and backing her against a wall, or some other louche situation. That his actual kiss had been so sweet and full of joy ruined the illusion. She couldn't imagine that he'd kissed her driven by lust or some baser emotion. His mouth had been warm and firm and decisive, and he'd laughed against her lips like they had accomplished something together. She would've fallen into that kiss if Cora and Amira hadn't been there, in need of immediate help. She almost had anyway.

That was a problem.

"Does anyone have a real question?" she asked. "Unrelated to Cora's delivery?" *Or Amir?*

A girl named Lucie raised her hand. She was a quiet one, though she did well with the men who liked to hear themselves talk.

"Why does voting matter?" she asked. "I'm just thinking about how Du Bois and everyone got all hopped up over getting Wilson into the White House. Wilson talked a lot of stuff about making things better for us, about justice and kindness, and look! Things are worse than ever with him in office. More segregation. More injustice. Hell, forget Wilson; the suffragettes didn't even want us at that parade of theirs." Lucie caught her voice rising and sank down in her chair a bit, folding her hands in her lap. "It just seems like voting isn't as hot as we're making it out to be."

Bertha looked at the woman, at the way none of them were meeting her eyes now.

"I see it like this," she said. "One time, a long time ago, I met a john who talked so sweet. Looked rich. Smelled good. Came in here telling me I was the prettiest thing he'd ever seen, begging me to put it on him, all that nonsense." There was a ripple of knowing laughter among the girls. They'd heard it all before. "I thought he was swell. Classy. Let him convince me to go back to a room with him."

The laughter stopped.

"That man threw me on the bed and started trying to get crazy. Thought because he was paying for it, he could do whatever he wanted. But I screamed and the man running the hotel bust through the door and pulled him off of me."

Bertha looked at the girls, and knew many of them had been there before, too, and some hadn't been so lucky. "What I'm saying is, I bet on that man. I thought he was the best choice of the pickings that night. I thought he was gonna do right by me. And I was wrong. That didn't mean I didn't go back to work the next night. That didn't mean I never got fooled again. When you're trying to survive, sometimes you're gonna encounter liars. Politicians are the worst of them. But there are good ones too. You take your chances there like anywhere else in life because the only other option is giving up. That make sense?"

There were a few shaky head nods in the group. Bertha felt a bit shaky herself. Had Amir heard that? She wasn't ashamed, but she still wondered how he might react.

A movement at the front of the club caught her attention.

"The club isn't open yet," Bertha called out. She'd told the last girl in to lock the door behind her, but of course whoever it was had forgotten.

"Well, good, because I've got a headache and I'm not in the mood for that ragtime noise right now."

Bertha startled when the person came into view from behind a column. She already knew who it was from the accented voice, but when the fur coat swept into view she was certain. Miss Q. She hadn't seen the woman since that day at the suffrage meeting, and she'd only been into the club a few times over the last couple of years. Rumor had it that she was mobbed with suitors angling for a slice of her numbers kingdom, and she wasn't having it. She held court in her own lavish apartment, hosting the finest minds of Harlem, ranging from musicians to artists to businessmen.

A flurry of whispers erupted from the girls.

"You can all go now," Bertha said, already stepping down from the stage. Miss Q had made herself right at home in a booth, and looked at her with a bemused expression as she approached.

Bertha slid in beside her. "Can I get you a drink?"

"No. Though I hear this Hindu chef you've got in the kitchen is maybe worth venturing here late night for."

He's not Hindu.

Several people had commented on the food in the days since Amir had taken over. Cora had been no slouch, but Amir had taken her recipes and made them into his own, incorporating spice mixtures close to those of his home country into the familiar down-home food Cora excelled at. The man knew his way around a kitchen.

"You should come try it some time," Bertha said.

"Oh, I will. I don't have time now, though. My driver is waiting outside.

I wanted to talk to you about these classes you've been having."

Bertha tried not to show her surprise. "You know about the classes?"

"Girl, I have number collectors running these streets every day. When they're done with their routes they come back to me. They hand me the money and the numbers, and they tell me things they hear along the way. I know most everything."

She gave a meaningful look around the club and then looked back at Bertha. "Everything."

Bertha's heart slowed and her palms went sweaty. Could she know? About the forged will? About what she had done to survive?

Miss Q smiled. "But I also know how to mind my business. That's the most important thing." She leaned back in her seat. "I like what I hear about you, and what I hear you doing with these girls, even before the classes started."

"I just treat them like they should be treated," Bertha said with a shrug. She was still trying to figure out Miss Q's angle. Was she there to threaten her? To force her way into the business? She knew Arthur had borrowed money from the woman once, but that had all been paid up before he passed, or so he had told her. He had been cheap, but not a welcher that she knew of.

The thought of losing the club made her head spin. The Cashmere was her life.

"You say that like it's normal." Miss Q pulled out a long thin cigarette and lit it, moving idly as if Bertha weren't on pins and needles waiting for her to get to her point.

She inhaled deeply, then exhaled. "You saw what happened at that suffragette meeting. People act like just because you ain't in church or washing some White child's ass that you don't amount to nothing. But there are a lot more people who don't count than do, if that's the case." She shrugged.

"Is there something you want?" The question was rude, but Bertha was on edge. If Miss Q even suspected what Bertha had done with Arthur's will, Bertha would be under someone's thumb, yet again. Everything in her rebelled at the idea.

Miss Q laughed. "I like you. Direct and to the point. I don't want anything really, except to add some girls to your class. Few of the street girls who work over by me. And some of the money counters."

Bertha waited, but Miss Q didn't talk further.

"That's it?"

"That's it. You have smarts to share. I have girls who need more smarts."

Bertha's life had been full of strange bargains lately: dance lessons with Amir, classes with her girls, and a piece of her soul with Victor. But those all had clear cut rules. Miss Q certainly must have wanted something else.

"I can take a few more," Bertha said carefully. "I've been feeding my girls though, and I can't offer that to everyone if the group gets too big."

It was the truth; she was a businesswoman, not a saint.

Miss Q nodded. "I'll pay for food and drink for 'em. You're doing work, and you should expect to get paid."

Bertha held out her hand and Miss Q shook it. "Let's keep things straight—I'm not going to be in debt to you for any of this," she said. "Don't expect that a month from now you can show up and suggest I open a craps room or give you a cut of anything."

She held Miss Q's gaze, preparing for the worst. Bertha respected the woman but, like most people with a lick of sense, she feared her. Miss Q regularly crushed ruthless men who tried to cut into her territory under her heel like insects; Bertha had no doubt the woman could make her life uncomfortable if she so chose.

Miss Q released her hand. "I wondered about how you got this place out from under Arthur. You don't take shit."

"Now I don't," Bertha admitted. The set of her shoulders relaxed the slightest bit. "One day I just couldn't stand another minute of it. Of being told what to do and how to do it and that I'd better do it with a smile."

Bertha had never admitted that to anyone—it was the kind of confession that raised questions she didn't want to answer—but something in the way Miss Q regarded her made her think she might know a thing or two about that particular feeling.

"And then old Arthur ended up dead and you ended up with the Cashmere, huh?" She let out a low laugh.

"I didn't kill him," Bertha said. "God and a bum ticker took care of that."

Miss Q exhaled, her lips pulled in a not quite smile. "We do what we have to in a world that tells us we don't deserve even a bit of power. But if you say you didn't, then that's none of my business."

"Tell your girls to be here at two on Monday," Bertha said.

Miss Q nodded and got up to leave. She walked away, her fur coat trailing behind her, then turned. "I know I just said I was good at minding my business, but..." She glanced toward the kitchen door. "What do you know about this Hindu fella?"

He's not...

Bertha's stomach flipped. She'd thought the crisis had passed, but it seemed Miss Q had waited to hit her with a doozie.

Bertha's back teeth gritted against each other. "You also just said you valued directness. Whatever you have to say, say it."

"One of my guys says he saw your guy talking with one of them cops that've been hanging around here trying to act like they don't stick out like a sore thumb. Same as the one who showed up in The Romper Room before they got shut down."

No. No no no. She thought of Amir's soft touch against her wrist, her ankle. Of the way his dimples deepened like pools of mirth when she told him stories, and his dark brows furrowed when she explained about the electoral process and the rights of citizenship.

"He wouldn't," she said. "There must be some misunderstanding."

"You of all people should know a man can and *would* do anything," Miss Q said with a delicate shrug. "My guy didn't hear anything, just mentioned what he saw to me. And now I'm mentioning it to you. That's it."

Bertha nodded. "I'll look into it. Two o'clock Monday then."

The sound of Miss Q's heels clicked in the silence of the club, followed by the sound of the door opening and closing. Bertha knew she should feel anger, but instead she felt a deep sadness that spread over her body. It weighed her down, like the kudzu that had clung to the trees in her childhood home, eventually toppling them when their weight grew too much to bear. If her life had taught her anything, it was that people always left and men weren't to be trusted. There was no reason the thought of Amir ratting on her should have been particularly hurtful, and yet...

She got up and walked to the kitchen. From inside she heard Amir singing as he worked, his voice so low it was almost a hum.

She girded herself and walked in.

He was at the stove, as he always was now, his shoulders marking the rhythm to which he matched his song. He stirred something that smelled like heaven, and then lifted the spoon, swiped a finger across, and stuck it into his mouth. His eyes closed as he savored it, teeth scraping over his bottom lip to catch the last traces of the sauce, and Bertha felt a raw wave of want go through her, like a ripple going over water, expanding toward the horizon.

"Is it really that good?" That was easier than asking if he had betrayed her.

His eyes fluttered open and seemed to darken as they settled on her. No, Miss Q had to be wrong; men were low down snakes, but Amir was no actor. He couldn't fake the way he looked at her, and he couldn't look at her like that and then run to the police.

He insinuated himself into your life so easily. He's closer to you than anyone. Bertha began to tally the time spent with Amir over the last few weeks: hours and hours. Talking, getting to know each other. Being set up?

No.

He walked over with that slightly bowlegged stride of his that should have been ridiculous but made him seem confident instead.

"Want to taste?" he asked. His voice was rough, not at all how it had been as he sang to himself.

She nodded and reached for the spoon, but he held it aloft. Bertha was slightly ashamed but a tight heat bloomed between her legs, and when he slicked his index finger over the curve of the spoon she swallowed hard.

He lowered his glistening finger toward her lips.

"Are you fooling?" she asked.

"No one touches my cooking tools but me," he said, thick brows raised. "Do you want a taste or not?"

Dammit, he knew she wouldn't resist a challenge; she doubted he knew that this was one he would regret.

"Okay," she said. She leaned forward and traced her tongue over his fingertip. The sauce was delicious, but not enough to justify what she did next. She gripped his wrist with both hands, flattening her tongue to give his finger a few strong licks, then sucked it into her mouth. Amir should have known that playing with her was a losing game.

Maybe he wants to lose.

"Bertha."

Her name was a plea for help, or for more. She glanced up at him as she sucked once, twice, three times, loving the way his lips parted and his eyes went dark and intense. She released the digit with a pop and he squeezed his eyes shut.

"You're right. It's quite good," she said, dropping his hand. "I'll put it on tonight's menu. Be a doll and write out the name and description for me."

He didn't say anything; his breath was coming out ragged and his pants were tented at the groin, an intriguing hint that almost tempted her to continue. Almost. But it also meant he wouldn't be thinking straight and now would be the best time to catch him unprepared.

"I need you to ask you something." Her voice was cool now, bordering on harsh. "Have you spoken to anyone about what goes on here at the club?"

His forehead wrinkled, and she hoped his confusion wasn't only at the abrupt subject change.

"Just my flatmates," he said. "It isn't every day one delivers a baby."

Was he playing dumb?

"And no one else? Has anyone approached you?"

His shoulders rose and fell. "There was a man in the alley the other day. I thought he was from immigration."

There was fear in his expression now, something Bertha hadn't seen before. She usually ignored the fact that he was not here legally, that he could be taken away and thrown on a ship at any moment. It seemed absurd, the thought of such a thing happening, but she knew as well as anyone that people always left. That knowledge didn't make her feel any better.

"Why didn't you say something to me?" she asked.

"Because I was ashamed," he said. He turned to the stove and went back to work, his gaze locked on the pan before him. "I nearly ran from that man. Why? Because I was afraid that he would put me on a ship and send me home. In that moment, I was not Amir the chef, or the sailor, or the dishwasher. I was an alien and a criminal, all because my skin is brown and I hail from Bengal."

Bertha knew that gut churning feeling, of being forced into shame not because of anything you did, but who you were.

"Just...things are tense right now. Be careful who you speak to," she said.

He nodded and kept stirring.

She reached out a hand toward him, rested it on his shoulder. "Amir—"

"What are you doing tomorrow during the day?" he asked abruptly.

"I have nothing planned," she said, then realized that was a lie. "Apart from our next lesson."

"I have something to do, so I can't come tomorrow."

"That's fine." Maybe she did need to be more careful with him. She shouldn't have felt such a childish sense of disappointment that he was canceling their unspoken plans. It was just as well; their lessons had become more tea and talking than dancing these days.

And the talking is what you will miss tomorrow.

"Since you have no plans, I can pick you up at ten."

"What for?" she asked.

"So you can put our lessons to the test," he said. He moved to the cutting board and began chopping a large onion.

"I said I wasn't dancing until women got the vote," she replied.

He stopped chopping and glanced at her. "This is a private event, not a show. The dancing will be optional, in fact. I just thought it would be nice to do something. Together."

"Oh."

Bertha was nonplussed. Doing something outside of the Cashmere made whatever it was between them more real. Like he was courting her. Bertha had never been courted before, really; men had taken her out on the town, but only because they were getting their money's worth.

"Fine," she said. "Now you get to prepping. We're expecting even more folks tonight, since people have been spreading the word about your cooking."

She headed for her office to do the day's administrative work and told herself that the funny feeling in her stomach was from Amir's food and not the fact that she'd just been asked on a date.

CHAPTER 8

Bertha perched next to her office window, staring at her pocketwatch. She had debated going outside to wait, but hadn't wanted to stand out in the street. What was she supposed to say when neighbors asked what she was doing? That she was waiting for a man?

She had been so taken aback at being asked to go somewhere outside the comfortable confines of the Cashmere that she hadn't realize the ramifications of it. She had been publicly off the market since she'd taken over the club; it was part of her mystique. She wasn't quite sure how she felt about stepping out in public with a man again, and with Amir being that man.

She was good at lying, but not to herself. Not about something this dangerous. She desired Amir. When he wasn't around, she wished he was; when he was, she wished he was closer. And it was more than desire. When she was with him, she felt the same foolish flame of hope that had flickered during her years on the road and her first months in New York, when she thought she'd become a famous dancer, before being extinguished. She wasn't a cold woman, but she had gone a long time without that particular warmth. Then Amir had strode in, arrogant and rude, and then arrogant and sweet, and Bertha was fairly certain she was going to be burned however this shook out. That didn't stop her from wanting to step closer, to hold out her hands toward the dancing light.

A truck pulled up in front of the Cashmere and she stuck her watch in her pocket and squinted through the window. The truck had "Cohen's Deliveries" written across the side, but when the passenger door swung open, it was Amir who hopped out. He looked up at the window, as if sensing her presence.

"Hey!" He waved up at her and she felt a little shock go through her.

The wind tousled his thick black hair, and a wide smile graced his face. Beneath his open jacket he wore a bright-hued, short-collared shirt that went down to his knees, with slim trousers poking out from beneath. He looked like a handsome prince come to rescue her from her tower. Bertha didn't need rescuing, but it was hard to turn it down when it showed up looking like that.

He waved again and her lips pursed. No matter how dashing he looked, he was still a man standing in the street calling for her like she was a doxy. Well, Bertha *was* a doxy, but no one treated her like one. Not anymore.

She raised the window and leaned over the sash.

"I'll be down in a moment," she said.

"Yes, come on!" He did a little dance while looking up at her, playful and flirtatious, and it moved her so much that she was tempted to slam the window shut and lock herself in her office.

That was when she noticed it from her peripheral vision; the way traffic slows when there might be an accident worth checking out. The street was packed with people strolling on a Saturday morning. Many of them had already swiveled their heads or stopped to see what was going on. She could already hear the gossip mill churning up a current stronger than in the East River. *The former whore and her foreign lover. Bossy Bertha finally beds down.*

She slammed the window down and adjusted her dress. If she didn't go, there would be even more talk.

People see what they want to see.

She locked up and headed out to the street, slowly sauntering toward Amir, who was leaning into the driver side window talking to the man she assumed was Syed.

"Miss Bertha Hines, nice to meet you," the man said cheerfully, but his smile faded into an expression of confusion as she ignored his hand stuck through the window, pushed Amir aside, gently, and pulled the door open.

"Pleasure to meet you, Syed. Please move over."

"But—"

"Bertha, what are you doing?" She didn't have to look at Amir; she knew his brow was furrowed and those frown lines were showing. She should have stayed in her office. She should have said no to begin with. The excitement that had woken her up early to prep and pamper herself faded, and she felt silly for thinking things could turn out any other way but bad.

"What am I doing?" she asked tightly. "I might ask the same of you, calling at the window like you were raised in a barn. Look around."

His gaze moved away from her, took in the clusters of pedestrians who had stopped to stare.

"So? People are looking. That's what people do." She could see the hurt, the anger, there, but it didn't matter.

She sighed. "People also talk. If it gets around that I'm getting hollered at and driven around by strange men, the respect I've worked so hard to build up will be gone, just like that."

How could he not understand that?

Amir's expression grew thunderous. "Strange men?"

"You know what I mean," she said.

"I know exactly what you mean, Miss Hines," he said, then turned and stalked off to the other side of the truck cab. Bertha shut her eyes, but didn't flinch at the slam of the door.

This was why she had sworn off men.

"Ready?"

When she opened her eyes, Syed had moved over and was patting the seat. She climbed up, allowing him to pull her inside when her skirt hampered her movement. Amir remained silent, facing resolutely forward.

Bertha pulled the door shut, waved at her neighbors and the others who had stopped to gawk.

"Look at you, Bertha," her neighbor Delphine called out.

"Never too late to learn to drive!" Bertha replied in a voice that was two parts cheer and one part sass. Delphine laughed. Bertha had created the story, and no one would doubt it now. Amir would forgive her, wouldn't he?

Would you forgive him?

Bertha's stomach flipped and her eyes stung. She turned to Syed and gave him her best smile. "I really don't know how to drive."

Amir hissed something in Bangla and Syed replied in a placating tone.

"We can do this. No worries." Syed showed her how to start the car and took over the pedal control, blushing furiously when his legs touched hers, as Bertha controlled the wheel. After a block and a half, they stopped and exchanged seats. Amir faced out the window, and Bertha supposed that she had been foolish to think stepping out with a man who wasn't paying could have gone otherwise.

They had a long afternoon ahead.

೮ಾ ೮ಾ ೮ಾ

Amir stalked about the kitchen of the hotel where the wedding was being held, growling orders at the men who had volunteered to help with the preparation of the buffet. It was a beautiful venue, the use of it a favor to the groom, who had worked there for a few years now. The kitchen was large and clean, with the nicest stove top he'd ever seen, but even that couldn't lighten his mood. Syed smoothed over Amir's rough orders with smiles and song, keeping the mood jovial as the men finished the preparation of the *walima* feast.

Bertha's theatrics shouldn't have surprised him, but they had, and that surprise had turned into a simmering anger that wouldn't leave him, like a too-hot chili whose burn lingers on the tongue. It wasn't just any anger; it was the foul, sullying rage that came with the humiliation of being reminded yet again that, here, he could not be seen as just Amir. He was a "strange man," as Bertha had put it. He was something to be ashamed of. And that she was the one who had reminded him...

Amir thought of the letter from Sabiha auntie that had been awaiting him the previous night. The one that was crinkled and stained, with half his name smudged off because the letter had been rained on at least once on its journey from Bengal to Harlem.

How are things over in New York? Last you wrote, things were not so well. You didn't say it of course, but I know you well enough even if I have not seen you for some years. I ask because it is time for you to come home. When you left for a short while, your cousin agreed to manage your land, and when he married, I did what I could. But now my Khoka is going to be a father, and I am going to live with him and his wife to help with the baby. That leaves the problem of your land. I don't know what will happen if you don't return; the land of your father and grandfather will likely be lost. I've asked before but now it is no longer a question: you must come home. Don't you want to come back, find a wife, and settle down? Or will you wait until something breaks you as it did Raahil? You are stubborn, but you know what you must do.

The letter had kept him up all night, the tug of home and the possibility of a life in the States twisting him into knots. That and thoughts of Bertha, of the undeniable attraction between them, and the possibilities it held. Her civics lessons, and their talks, had made him think that perhaps there was a place for him in America. That once he knew how the system worked, he could begin to change it. And then he had pulled up with Syed and she had looked at him how a zamindar looks at peasants come to beg for a few days' leeway with their rent.

"Azim and Maria are arriving soon," Syed said as he settled beside Amir, his tone gentle instead of teasing. Amir swallowed the mean-spirited response that popped into his head. This was a wedding celebration and he needed to rid himself of any bad feelings—like anger, or jealousy—that could taint the auspiciousness of the day.

He nodded.

"Try not to take it personally, Pintu," Syed said clapping him on the shoulder.

"What other way is there to take it?" Amir asked in a low, annoyed voice.

Syed rolled his eyes. "*Boka.* Always getting so worked up. Have you even said anything to Miss Hines about your feelings for her?"

"There are no such feelings," Amir said stubbornly, then crossed his arms over his chest. "She should know how I feel."

"The same way you 'know' that she intended to insult you earlier today?" Syed asked. "And how she knew that you meant to take her down a notch by making a scene? *Ak daley dui pakhi.* You two are a perfect match, truly."

"You're supposed to be *my* friend," Amir growled.

"Yes, and it is a friend's job to offer guidance when your head is stuck in your behind," Syed said. "Perhaps instead of scowling your way through the rest of the day you could try talking. You do enough of it at the flat, keeping me up at all hours with your socialist clap trap."

Syed laughed and Amir couldn't resist cracking a smile.

"You always want to understand every little thing," Syed said. "I'm not as smart as you, but I am not confused by what is happening with you and Miss Hines. Think with your heart and not with your ego."

Syed removed the apron covering his suit and left the kitchen, but Amir dawdled. He was still angry, but then he remembered Bertha's expression as she had marched toward the truck. Her mouth had been tight, but her face a mask of relaxed superiority. It had been the same look she wore when he'd found that man holding her arm and speaking low to her in the corner of the club.

Nothing I can't handle, she'd said flippantly when he'd arrived, ready to defend her honor. Bertha didn't need defenders though; she did it well enough herself. And him showing up as he had, calling her out into the street, had given her a whole new set of things to defend herself against.

Bloody hell.

He stopped in the bathroom to clean up, realizing that he didn't know where Bertha was. He'd brought her to a strange place and abandoned her in a fit of pique. So much for showing her a good time.

She was easy to spot when he stepped into the hall, despite the bright fabrics that had been hung to bring life into the room that was normally sedate in shades of beige and brown. She was a beacon of forest green velvet, calling to him from across the crowded room. Her dress could be called modest in its cut and length, but the way it hinted at her curves without revealing too much of them was just as distracting. Amir wasn't the only one who thought so.

She was surrounded by a group of men, smiling and talking animatedly with them, as if she was catching up with old friends. Fayaz, Syed, and several of the lascars he'd met since jumping ship were amongst them; all seemed enraptured by whatever it was Bertha was saying. He'd thought she would be upset, but she seemed to be in good humor. She said something saucy—he could tell by the way just the right side of her mouth curved up—and the men around her laughed. She wasn't flirting, but she was certainly enjoying the attention.

Did you expect her to cry at your absence?

He walked over, expecting Bertha to acknowledge him and the group to part, but she continued talking and no one else appeared to notice him. He stood on the edge of the group feeling like he was the one who was a newcomer.

"They are here!" someone called out and the group broke up. Some of the men scrambled towards instruments that had been set up beside a dais. Amir approached her, feeling a tremor of apprehension that settled in his shoulders.

"All done setting up?" she asked politely. She wasn't cold, or rude, but her words still sprung up in front of him like a brick wall. There was no intimacy, nothing to indicate that they were anything other than co-workers. He didn't think she did it to punish him. He had put her in an untenable position then lashed out when she reacted accordingly; she was likely trying to make the best of things.

"I'm done in the kitchen. And I'm sorry," he said.

She reached out and tapped his shoulder. "There's nothing to be sorry for. I got to drive a truck and I've spent the last hour chatting with some nice men who told me all about how Azim and Maria met. Thank you for inviting me."

That was when Amir began to worry. Her tone, the cadence of her words, the calculated movements: she was playing a role. She was pushing him away, retreating behind her ability to laugh and smile and say just the right things. She was treating him like the girls at the Cashmere treated their johns, and she would only do that if he had treated her how johns treat their girls.

"Bertha." He reached out and took her hand. He'd never held her hand for longer than a brief touching of palms as they danced before. It was soft—surprising, given how hard she worked—and not much smaller than his. And it was shaking.

A man he had met at past religious gatherings came by and guided them to a table as the band began to play. They took their seats and the door opened, and a beautiful bride walked in. She wore a traditional Western white wedding dress, simple and lacey, but her veil was a long, rich rectangle of fabric from back home.

It wasn't until his hand tightened on Bertha's, and hers tightened in response, that he realized they were still holding each other. He wasn't sure what it meant, but if she was willing to allow it, he'd hang onto her for as long as he could.

CHAPTER 9

Bertha now understood why the bride's veil was so long. It was draped over both bride and groom for this last portion of the ceremony, creating an intimate space for them even as they sat before a crowd of spectators. The groom held a small, ornate mirror in his palm.

"What do you see?" the man leading the ceremony asked. She wasn't sure if he really held any religious position or was simply stepping in, playing the role required of him in a place where so few of the comforts of home were available to men like Amir and his friends.

"I see my future," the groom replied in a voice strained by emotion.

He handed the mirror to the bride, and even through the thin fabric Bertha could see how their fingertips brushed and then lingered. The question was repeated.

"*Veo mi corazon*. I see my heart."

The groom leaned in and kissed her then, and there were shouts of excitement and joy in the crowd, followed by applause.

Bertha finally pulled her hand away from Amir's to clap, each slap of skin jolting something inside of her. She wasn't one to get emotional at weddings; she hadn't even cried at her own to Arthur. In a way, it had been another business transaction. But seeing Azim and Maria had ushered her into a corridor lined with possibilities she hadn't thought within her reach, possibilities that beckoned her to throw caution to the wind and explore them. The feel of Amir's warm hand in hers had beckoned as well.

"That was lovely," she said as the band picked up again. The guests, mostly men dressed similarly to Amir and Syed, got up, some to dance and some to help set up the buffet of delicious smelling food. "Thank you for inviting me."

"I'm glad you came," he said. He placed his elbows on the table and folded his hands together. Then that dark gaze, the one she'd avoided since he'd stepped into the banquet hall, had her in its grip. "Even if I didn't behave like it after you got into the truck."

"I apologize for hurting you," Bertha said with a blithe smile, throwing his words from that first day he'd come into her office back at him. She couldn't resist the reminder that this wasn't the first time he'd had something to apologize for.

"I'm just grateful you know you have the power to," he replied. His tone was low and urgent. "More than anyone."

Bertha's breath caught, and the mask she had donned during their silent truck ride began to crumble at the edges, to lift away and reveal the emotions swirling beneath. She couldn't have that.

"Excuse me." She stood and bustled away from the table, sliding through clusters of men lined up to congratulate the newlyweds and those heading for the food. She stumbled into the hallway and entered the first door she saw through a haze of tears warming her eyes.

Why?

Bertha knew she had power over men, one that had resided in her swaying hips and her clenching pussy and now rested on her denial of them. But she also knew that wasn't what Amir was talking about. She didn't want to think of what it was that drew him to her, or vice versa, because it frightened her. She'd never wanted a man for anything other than his power and Amir had none: not wealth or political capital or street cred. That didn't stop her from daydreaming about their kiss, or from feeling an odd emptiness in her apartment when she stumbled in after closing up the Cashmere and he wasn't there.

Foolishness. She had more important things to think of. *The vote. The vice squad.*

Neither of those things had driven her running into strange rooms on the verge of tears, though.

There was the *click* sound of the knob turning, then the door opened slowly.

"Were you in desperate need of a tablecloth?"

Bertha looked around and realized she had hidden in a linen closet. "I wouldn't say desperate, but I thought I'd stick my head in and see what kind of linens a quality establishment uses." She rubbed her hand over a pile of whites stacked beside her. "Very luxurious."

"I'm sure they wouldn't notice if you borrowed a few," he said. He tugged on a small chain hanging from the ceiling, illuminating the space, then shut the door behind him and leaned back against it.

A tremor passed over her skin, raising the tiny hairs, as she took in the tilt of his head and the jut of his hips as he leaned.

"Neither of us can afford to be arrested for theft," she said. She was still stroking the tablecloths because she didn't know what to do with her hands. Well, she knew what she *wanted* to do with them: cup Amir's face, run her hands over that broad chest, slide her fingers up the nape of his neck and into his hair. When she wanted something, she generally took it, but she wasn't sure how to take this, or even what *this* was. It was more than desire, more than wantonness, though she very much wanted to be wanton.

Amir kept his eyes on her. "I'm guessing you didn't run in here because you hate me, but now I'm going to ask because I think we need to make some things clear. Do you hate me?"

"You wouldn't have made it over that threshold if I hated you," she said, rolling her eyes.

He pushed off of the door and took a step forward. "Well, perhaps you fancy me then?"

"I think you skipped a few rungs on the emotional ladder," she replied.

He came toward her then and didn't stop until he was nearly up against her. His hand rested on top of hers to stop her nervous petting of the linen. In the silence, the music from the band filtered into the closet.

"I invited you here to dance," he said in a low voice. "Do you want to go back out there?"

"Will it upset you if I say no?" she whispered.

"Only if you say no to this, too." He raised his arms, moving them in time to the music. He continued his dance, expression patient, and she realized that during all of their lessons they had never truly danced together. He'd shown her a move and she had repeated it for him, but they had never moved as one. She extended her arms, taking her position, and he smiled.

They didn't have their full range of motion in the small space; arms brushed as they rose and fell; shoulders knocked as they turned, and when she finished her spin facing away from him it was natural when her backside brushed against his groin. They swayed like that as the song ended, and didn't resume their starting positions when the next song began. Instead, his hand went to her arm and turned her so she was facing him.

"I know a man fancying you is nothing new but—" he dipped his head so she couldn't see his eyes "—I do. Quite a lot."

She'd seen Amir when he let his quick temper get the best of him; they'd gone toe to toe more than once. But that head dip, and the hesitancy in his voice, told her more than his words had.

"Amir?"

His head lifted and his gaze clashed with hers. She didn't even have to say the words that were on the tip of her tongue before he was following through on them. His head dipped again, but not in uncertainty this time. His decisiveness had returned, and there was no hesitation as his mouth covered hers. This kiss wasn't sweet, like the one they'd previously shared, despite the fact that he tasted of spiced honey. His lips were firm and demanding, and when he slid a hand up the back of her neck to hold her in place, heat raced through Bertha's body.

The spark she'd felt during their celebratory kiss hadn't been a one-off. Her body was humming from his touch, and she wanted it to sing. She slid her hands around his waist and flattened her palms against his back, feeling his muscles tense under her touch through the fabric of his shirt. She took his bottom lip between her teeth as she moved her hands, worried it a bit, but then his grip on her tightened and his tongue pressed into her mouth and Bertha moaned with pleasure.

They kissed until her lips felt raw and bruised, hands running over each other's bodies. She could feel his hardness pressing against her, and she forced her hand between them, down low so she could stroke his length through his pants. It had been too long since she felt this rush of emotion: fear, pleasure, curiosity, and desire, all tumbling around in her belly, creating an ache that only Amir could soothe.

His hands slid to the front of her dress and Bertha felt the release of pressure as he undid the buttons holding the fabric tight against her breasts. Then there was a different kind of pressure as his fingers found her nipples, teasing them as his mouth passed rough-gentle over hers, only moving away in the brief instances when he needed to breathe.

Bertha had never been what people would consider impulsive—her life had been committed to weighing and measuring what she could get away with for as long as she could remember—but it seemed Amir had changed that. She began gathering the material of her skirt, lifting, with one mad idea in mind. It seemed the madness had gripped Amir as well because he was raising his long suit shirt. She pulled one hand away from her skirt to run her hand over the furred ridges of his stomach and the waistband of his pants. Her fingertips delved into the waistband, then his hand clamped around her wrist.

"Look at me," he said, and for a second she wished she had disobeyed him because his eyes revealed everything. Adoration and adulation, tinged with something darker and deeper. "I've screwed for fun before. This isn't fun, if we do this." A bit of the seriousness left his face then, replaced with a cocky grin. "Not just fun, that is."

She slipped her hand into his pants completely, circling thumb and forefinger around his girth. "I've screwed for profit before, and I have to say I think we'll both profit from this. We'll have fun, too. But there's not *just* anything between us." She squeezed him tighter, stroked, perhaps to distract from the fact that she was going to reveal something of herself. "There hasn't been since you walked into my kitchen."

He thrust up into her hand and at the same time pulled her into a kiss, and after that there was no more talking. His hands moved down to grip her thighs and his thumbs stroked rough circles against her sex. She pumped her fist around him with short, tight jerks. When they were both panting and muffling groans, he turned and bent her over the stack of tablecloths. The sweet pleasure of him pushing into her was tempered with the briefest flash of doubt.

Not like this.

Then he stopped, suddenly leaving her empty.

"I want to see you," he panted, switching places with her so he was sitting back on the linens. She lowered herself onto him, watching his pleasure at her clench express itself in the arch of his brow, and the way his eyes slammed shut and then opened. For a moment, she exaggerated her pleasure, threw her head back and bit her lip; habit was hard to break. Amir leaned up and kissed her again, then rested his forehead against hers as she rode him.

"I want to see *you*," he groaned. His hands cupped her face, stroked her neck and clavicles, as he pumped up to meet her downstroke, but his gaze never left hers. Heat built in her as he watched her, and annoyance.

What did he want?

But he'd just told her.

She placed her hands on his shoulders and instead of meeting his gaze in challenge, she simply watched him. She didn't fake a damn thing, just moved, and then she felt it. It was as if something in the way Amir watched her, and held her, allowed her to feel her passion in a new way. Each stroke within reverberated through her body. The soft brushes and hard squeezes of his fingertips drove her closer to the edge. Even the friction of her bunched dress against her skin sent tremors through her. And when he began pumping wildly into her, eyes still locked on hers, Bertha bit back a scream as ecstasy filled up every bit of her and searched for release. She turned her head and bit down on the meat of his hand as her climax took her, and then he arched into her, surrendering to his own.

As Bertha drifted down from her bliss, she could hear the music in the background once more, reminding her of where they were. She touched his face gently, and he kissed her fingertip.

Yes, this Amir was going to be a problem.

CHAPTER 10

Amir lay back on the couch in Bertha's apartment, watching her as she dressed for the pre-Election Day party. The blood was only just starting to flow back into his brain; he'd been the one to pull her down onto the couch, but she had rendered him useless when she crawled onto his lap. The week since Azim's wedding had been a blissful blur. Bertha and her girls handing out suffrage pamphlets to men in the streets of Harlem. Amir bringing in Syed to be his line chef during the busier dinner hours as the number of guests exploded. And every free moment that hadn't been devoted to the vote or to the club, they'd spent with each other: touching, tasting, mapping each other's bodies with fingertips and tongues.

It seemed they couldn't get enough of each other. Amir had even started to spend the night, after making a show of leaving if anyone else was around, of course. Now he knew that she tossed and turned in her sleep, as if all the brisk energy that carried her through the Cashmere still flowed through her even when she tried to rest. He knew the taste of her in the morning, evening, and afternoon.

Nothing else mattered when he was with her, which was a dangerous thing. Another letter had come from his aunt about his land, and he would have to make a decision that didn't involve choosing between Bertha's soft lips and softer thighs. That didn't involve her sharp wit and the way he felt an actual pain in his heart, like he'd eaten too much *jhal-lanka*, every time he looked at her.

"Can you zip me up, baby?" she asked, looking back over her shoulder and Amir felt something that was startlingly close to anger. Not at her, but at even the possibility that he would have to leave her. He missed home— sometime the ache caught him unawares, triggered by the most ridiculous things—but thinking of a life without her sharp words and soft smiles singed like a hot pan that he had taken in his hand and couldn't let go of.

He lifted himself from the couch and moved to her, sliding his hand into the back of her dress and splaying it over her skin.

He looked at her face in the mirror and took in their reflection. Her eyes were closed and a gentle smile tugged at her lips. This was his Bertha, the one he was sure no one saw but him. It did something to him, to know that some part of her was reserved just for him. He hoped she knew that it was the same for him; though they still butted heads over some things, he also backed down instead of pushing, a feat his family had never thought could be achieved. He told her his hopes and his fears, though not all of his dreams for his future. Possibly *their* future. He was impulsive, but knew that telling her the idea he'd been mulling over would be pushing her too fast. If she didn't feel the same way...

"I wish I could stay like this sometimes," she said, voice low. "The way I am when I'm with you."

"Like what, love?" he asked.

"Like...myself," she said in a soft tone. Then shook her head and opened her eyes. "Tonight's a big night. Zip?"

And just like that, his Bertha was gone and Bertha the boss was back. He hoped that version of her was his, too, but he couldn't claim either version until he had decided what to do about his land.

"Are you nervous?" he asked as he zipped. "About tomorrow?"

"I just want the election to be over with," she said, giving herself a final glance. "I was silly enough to let myself start getting hopeful, and that never leads anywhere good."

It didn't take a leap of imagination to conclude she was talking about more than voting.

"What about you?" she asked, shifting the subject away from herself. "How will you feel tomorrow if I can vote and you can't?"

He knew why she had to ask; the very first time he'd heard about the suffragettes his reflexive response had been a resentment that surprised him. He'd considered himself more evolved than most men, had worked side by side with women in his political groups back home, and his instinct had still been to think that his own interests should be addressed first. "Well, I guess I'll have to get better at our political debates and try to win you over to the socialists."

She smiled and kissed him on the cheek. "I do look good in red," she murmured before swaying out the door. Amir followed. He couldn't argue with that.

They headed down into the club and as soon as they stepped on the floor business tugged them apart. There were glances and the occasional touch, but Amir was sweating in the kitchen with Syed, chopping and prepping, frying and sautéing. She was on the floor, managing the girls, the bar, the bands, the stage, and the surge of people who had shown up for the special event.

Once he got into the zone in the kitchen, there was nothing but the orders and fulfilling them, making sure each plate was perfect because this night was important to Bertha and she was the most important thing. Hours went by and eventually the orders started to slow.

Amir took a drink out of a pitcher of ice water, used a kitchen towel to wipe his brow. Syed dropped onto a stack of milkcrates.

"I hope that was the last of it," he said. "I can't even see straight right now, Pintu."

The doors swung open and Bertha strode in. She flopped onto a chair beside Syed. He'd known things were busy out on the floor, given the number of orders that had rolled in, but it was the first time Amir had ever seen her sit on the job.

"I'm starting to wonder if you're sprinkling something extra in the food," she said. "Or if it's just election fever."

"Maybe a bit of both," Amir said.

"Modesty doesn't suit you," she said. She was looking at him with that heat in her eyes, despite her fatigue, and for a moment he wished they were alone.

"Maybe going back home won't be so bad," Syed said, scratching his side. "You can open a restaurant and make your Bengali American food. You'll be the star chef of Calcutta by next year."

Bertha had been slack in the chair, but Amir saw the moment her neck went stiff and her mouth went tight. She eased her way up as the slouch left her back.

"You have plans to go back to Bengal?" Her voice was casual, in the way a shard of ice could casually slide off of a sloped roof and slice you open.

Amir's throat tightened. He hadn't known how to tell her about the letters; all the talking they did and he'd managed to avoid bringing it up. If he didn't go back, she had no need to know, and if he did...

"There's a problem with my land and I might have to go back," he said with a shrug. "It hasn't been decided."

"It hasn't been decided? Is someone else making the decision for you?"

He tensed at her tone. "Look, I'm trying to figure this out. It's not your problem, so don't worry about it."

He knew it was the wrong thing to say as soon as the words left his mouth.

She stood up and adjusted her dress. "I guess I won't then."

Amir bit back against the frustration building in him. "Bertha wait—"

"For what? People leave. It's what they do." Her expression was hard but her eyes were glossy; he had hurt her. Again. "I'm needed back on the floor."

She swept out of the room and he whirled on Syed, who held up his hands.

"Don't get mad at me, Pintu. You've been practically living with her for the last week. If you didn't tell her, I'm not the one you should be mad at."

Amir growled and threw his towel across the kitchen; it landed in a bucket of dirty water. Frustration pulsed through his veins. "I meant to tell her. I just hadn't decided what to do."

Syed raised his brows.

"What?" Amir snapped.

Syed raised his brows higher. "You know I have a wife at home," he said. "When I got on the boat and when I hopped off the boat, it was both of our decisions. You wanted this lady to bloody fancy you and once she does you pull something like this."

Syed shook his head and Amir knew what he was thinking.

Always making a mess of things.

He had messed up. Again. And he didn't know how to fix it this time. He hadn't just kept something from her, he'd kept the biggest thing from her. He hadn't wanted to admit the truth to her because he could hardly admit it to himself.

I don't want to go back.

How could he tell someone that his homeland no longer felt like home? That the only place he wanted to be was at the side of a woman who had no use for him in a country that didn't want his kind? He'd always thought he would go back and change things for his people; what kind of man did it make him if he didn't? And how could he have told her about the letter without heaping unspoken pressure on their new relationship?

"I'm going to talk her," he said.

Syed nodded. "Go on. I'll come get you if an order comes in."

Amir walked out into the club, which was busier than he'd ever seen it, though it was very late. A man sat at the piano, his fingers flowing over the keys so quickly Amir could hardly see them. A woman at the mic sang a suffragette anthem in a husky voice, jazz style, and the crowd nodded along. He scanned the smoky room and didn't see Bertha anywhere, so he made his way into the hallway towards her office.

He sensed she wasn't alone before he turned toward the already open door. Bertha sat on the edge of her desk, her crossed legs exposing smooth skin all the way to her upper thigh—exposed, save for the hand that rested on her knee.

The man who'd had Bertha in the corner that night that seemed so long ago sat comfortably in a chair, his fingertips caressing her knee until he followed her gaze and saw Amir.

"Can I help you, Amir?" she asked. Her face was perfectly composed as she lifted the man's hand away.

"I wanted to talk to you," he said, trying to remain calm. He'd already driven her away with his words, and if he couldn't contain himself he would lose her for good. Even a stubborn ram exercised caution when it met a worthy opponent.

"Well, as you can see, I'm busy." She flashed her saucy smile, but her eyes were shuttered, dousing the effect.

"I don't mean to insist, but I think it's rather important." He didn't have to try to keep his voice calm anymore, because he was so beyond anger and despair that he seemed to be operating on another plane. His hands hung limp at his sides; he couldn't even manage a fist. He felt disconnected from his body, disconnected from the possibility that Bertha had already written him off, and that he'd managed to plummet from *Jannah* to *Jahannam* so quickly.

"Oh, so now it's important." She nodded, several tight jerks of her head, but he knew it wasn't because she agreed with him.

"Get in line, buddy," the man beside her said. He touched Bertha's knee again, like he had the right to. "There's enough to go around, if the price is right."

Bertha started saying something to the man, but Amir didn't hear it because his numbness had lifted and anger rushed into him, pushing him toward the man in three quick steps. It didn't matter if he'd already lost her, or even if she had chosen this man over him. He grabbed the man by the lapels of his fine jacket.

"Apologize to her. Now."

"For what?" the man asked. He wasn't afraid, and in fact seemed to find the situation amusing, if anything. His gaze went back and forth between the two of them and then he let out an abrupt laugh. "Ohhhhhhhh, I see. This is why you're trying to renege on our bargain. You're his woman now?"

What bargain?

It didn't matter. Amir gave the man a shake. "Bertha is her own woman."

The man laughed again, then pried Amir's hands away more easily than Amir would have imagined.

"You got a funny way of showing that," he said, straightening his shirt. "Shit, Bertha, never would have pegged you for that kind of sister, but I don't need to force a woman. I'll call in this debt some other way."

"What debt?" Amir was angry and confused but neither of them acknowledged him.

"You'll be repaid with my vote, if I get it—and if you earn it," she said, then inclined her head toward the door. "Beat it, Victor."

The man chuckled ruefully as he walked out. "Good luck, buddy."

"Are you going to explain what just happened?" Amir asked.

"No." She walked around the desk and sat down. "You're leaving, right? So it doesn't matter. None of what happened matters."

The words were forced, as if she were telling herself at the same time she was telling him.

"I don't know if I'm leaving," he said carefully.

"Well, you didn't think it important enough to tell me either way, so the point still stands."

"Not important?" Amir ran his hands through his hair in frustration. "This is the most important thing, Bertha."

You are.

He walked over to her desk and turned her chair so that she was facing him. He couldn't talk about this with her desk between them, the way they discussed food deliveries and the nightly menu.

"How was I supposed to tell you why I might have to go back to Bengal without explaining all the reasons I cannot?"

She looked down, refusing to meet his eyes, so he dropped to his knees and looked up at her.

"What was I supposed to say? 'Oh, by the way, even though I'm here illegally and can't get a well-paying job or even my citizenship, I think I'm going to give up my family land because I'm in love with you and want to stay here'?"

Her eyes widened. "What?"

"You can't even be seen in the street with me without feeling compromised and I'm supposed to put the pressure of my future on you? I couldn't do it without feeling like I was forcing your hand, and I didn't want to be just another man trying to make you his," he said. "I was wrong, and I made a mistake, but not because you aren't important. If you don't believe anything else, please believe that."

Her hand went to his face, and he closed his eyes as her fingertips brushed against his stubbled cheeks.

"Maybe I'm too good at this acting thing," she said softly. "If you thought I wouldn't want to hear that."

Relief rushed through Amir. He hadn't meant to tell her *that*, but he had and she hadn't spurned him.

"I'm sorry," he said again.

"Don't think you're getting off that easy. I'm still mad enough to spit nails," she said. "I felt like my legs got knocked out from under me, and I don't handle that well."

"I know," Amir said, turning his head to kiss her palm. "I'm the same way. You may have noticed."

She sighed. "Looks like we're gonna have a bumpy road ahead."

"I'm a village boy. I'm used to bumpy roads."

She laughed, not too loud but it seemed like it, and that's when Amir realized the music had suddenly stopped.

"What—"

There was a commotion in the club and it wasn't because someone was blowing hot on the stage. Bertha jumped up and peeked through the curtains.

"Shit."

A chill went down Amir's spine as she whirled away from the window, and the sound of falling chairs and the scrambling patrons reached him at the same time. She was boss Bertha again, and she snatched his sleeve and pulled him to his feet as she marched toward the door.

"Cops are here," she said. In the hallway, the sound of people screaming and glass crashing could be heard more clearly. Instead of heading toward the noise, she pulled him in the opposite direction, toward her apartment door. She turned the key and pushed him into the hallway that led away from the club. "Go up to the apartment. If they try to get in through this door, go out the front door and head up to the roof, then cross over to one of the connected buildings."

Amir wasn't quite comprehending what she was saying or how she could say it so calmly.

"What? What about you?"

"This is my club and the girls are my responsibility. Now go."

"I can't—"

"You can't do anything down here but get in the way and get your ass hauled onto a slow boat to India. If you meant anything you just told me, you'll go. Now."

He wanted to argue, to butt heads, but instead he pulled her into a kiss. It was brief, but he put every bit of his love into it. And when she pulled away and ran into the fray, he locked the door, went up to the apartment, and did the only thing he could. He knelt and he prayed, hoping Allah was truly as flexible as Amir believed Him to be. If not, he might lose Bertha for the second time that night.

CHAPTER 11

"This isn't quite how I imagined I'd be spending Election Day," Bertha said, examining her nails instead of the décor in the sterile office she had been marched to. Her eyes were gritty from lack of sleep—the jail cell hadn't been the most comfortable place she'd spent a night, but not the least either. Worries about her girls, her club, and, most of all, whether Amir had been taken had kept her up, staring at the ceiling of the dank jail cell until daylight had begun to filter in through the barred windows. She was exhausted and scared, but she couldn't let the man across the table know that.

He pulled out a file and opened it, calmly flipping through the thick stack of papers. He had such a benign face, like a white-haired grocer you forgot as soon as he handed you your change, but Bertha wouldn't be put at ease by it. Gregory Barton was the head of the Commission of Fourteen, meaning he had taken up the mantle of purifying the city of whores, drugs, and race mixing. That he even saw the latter as a vice didn't bode well for her.

"Miss Hines, your establishment has been a hotbed of immoral activity for some time. Lewd dancing. Women selling their bodies. It says here that the act of fellatio was observed more than once, carried out in bathrooms and alcoves."

"Oh dear. Is that so?" She raised a hand to her mouth and widened her eyes. She wondered who had relayed this information, mentally running through a list of regular patrons in her mind, but it could have been anyone. She knew that the commission paid well, and not everyone who came into the club was in a position to turn that down.

Barton glanced up from the file. "Don't get cute, Miss Hines."

"Well, I can't help it, sir. I was born this way." She batted her lashes, though she was sure her make-up was a mess. The urge to be sick pushed at her throat. She could not, would not, let him see that.

He didn't smile, but he didn't frown either, and Bertha counted that ambivalence as a win. Some people would be groveling or lashing out, but she was trying to toe the line that led to her getting out of jail with her body, soul, and business intact.

"Patrons of different races were allowed to co-mingle." He looked up at her.

"My club is strictly Negro, sir. If anyone else got in, I wouldn't know, as I'm color blind." More lash batting.

"And on top of all these offenses, you personally spearheaded a push to influence male voters in your establishment on the issue of suffrage."

Bertha tilted her head to the side, unable to hide her surprise at that. "Is voting a vice, sir? If that's the case, I can direct you to several locations where men are brazenly engaging in that very act today."

Barton dropped the file to his desk, the wrinkles on his brow deepening. "It's undignified behavior for a woman. And for your kind, it's unseemly."

She hoped that the men heading out to the polls were more enlightened than the one before her. She hoped Amir was somewhere warm and safe, not being detained in a place certain to be more frightening than the bland office she was in. She wouldn't know the status of either hope unless she was released. Inside, she was fuming, ready to flip the desk over and make a run for it, but she couldn't show that. She would play this cute and flirty; if she kept things light even in face of his ignorance she might have a chance.

"I know what's unseemly—not getting to choose who represents me as a citizen, or who fills well-paying positions like the one you currently occupy."

Well so much for playing it light.

The man's lip curled.

"You have a lot of mouth for someone facing jail time," he said.

"First amendment. Read it sometime, fella."

Too much?

"Since you're so keen to talk, how do you answer to these charges?"

"Fifth amendment. Try that, too. I recommend it."

The man closed the folder and stared at her. "This isn't a joke Miss Hines. I know your crowd is all for a good time, but I have the power to make your life very uncomfortable."

She leaned toward him. "Every man has that power, snowflake. Why do you think I'm even here?"

"Ms. Hines, you go too far." His face went red and he stood abruptly. Bertha felt dread run through her. She'd played it all wrong. Should she have been more demure? Have shed a few tears? Men always liked that. She had pushed her luck and now—

Barton sat back down with the cigar he had grabbed from a wooden box and pointed it at her. "Because this is your first offense, and because someone has vouched for you, I'm going to let you go with a warning and a fine. But as for the Cashmere, that's it. I know you think you can do what you want, but we're watching you now. Next time, and there will be a next time if you think you can engage in these immoral acts, I won't be so lenient. No whores, no miscegenation, no funny business. You won't find prison life so amusing by half, I guarantee you that."

He shoved the cigar in his mouth and chomped on it, staring her down with a look that made her insides quail.

Bertha had no more smart-aleck remarks. She nodded, holding back the anger and frustration that churned in her chest and sought release. Her mind was already clicking ahead, trying to think of how she would get around this. She had to, didn't she? The Cashmere couldn't just close down. She couldn't give up on it that easily.

"You can go," he said.

Barton looked down, dismissing her, and she was escorted out into the main office, drawing leering looks that reminded her she was still dressed for a night in the club. She walked out into the chilly November afternoon and shivered. She'd lost track of time in the jail cell, but the sun would set soon. She had no money for the IRT or trolley, so it would be a long, cold walk back to Harlem.

The honk of a horn from the curb in front of the station got her attention, and she looked over to see Miss Q sitting in the back of a car that had been shined up like a pair of new dance shoes. Her driver got out and opened the door, motioning for Bertha to get in.

She climbed in and accepted the shawl Miss Q handed her. "I take it you were the one who vouched for me?" she asked through chattering teeth.

"An envelope full of cash was all the vouchsafe they needed." She lit one of her cigarettes.

"Why?" Bertha asked as the car pulled into traffic. "Why would you do that for me?"

Unease roiled in her stomach. She owed the woman for real now, and that was no small thing.

Miss Q took a long, slow drag, holding Bertha's gaze as she did. "Why did you teach those classes?" she asked, her words dressed in wisps of smoke. "You expect all those girls to give you something back for the time and money you put into it?"

"No, but—"

"Girl, how do you think I got where I am? I came here from an island no one's even heard of, barely spoke English, and thought I would die in the gutter." Miss Q shook her head. "We help each other. Whenever we can, however we can, using whatever means we got. You got the Cashmere and your knowledge. I got money. If I have to choose between another coat and a sister in need, you best not think you're gonna see me in a new coat come Sunday service."

She took another agitated draw of the cigarette and Bertha felt her throat close up. Not from the smoke, but because Miss Q was right. She thought about the girls trading shifts when one was sick, chipping in to raise money for Cora and her family even though Bertha had already made sure they were comfortable. Women helped each other in ways small and large every day, without thinking, and that was what kept them going even when the world came up with new and exciting ways to crush them.

"Thank you," Bertha said.

Miss Q sucked her teeth in response and looked out the window, but then she nodded her acceptance. "The club was ripped apart. You should know before you get there."

Bertha nodded numbly. "That can be fixed. My girls?"

"Most got away while everything was topsy turvy. Those who were arrested are out now, that I know of."

"And Amir?"

"The cook? Haven't heard anything about him."

"He's not here legally…if they caught him…" Bertha's heart constricted.

Miss Q just looked at her like she was a fool, then shrugged. "If they caught him, they're probably saving you trouble down the line, but I hope for your lovesick self that they didn't."

"And the vote?"

She almost wished she hadn't asked. She couldn't take one more bit of bad news. If the club was ruined and Amir was gone *and* women hadn't won the vote…she just might crack up.

Miss Q exhaled. "Nothing official yet, but it seems like the YES votes are adding up, according to my guys. I don't believe in counting my chicks before they hatch, but we might be at the ballot box next election."

Bertha sagged back against the leather seat and stared out the window, focusing on her relief as the tall buildings and crowded streets of Fifth Avenue passed by. She choked back the emotion blocking her throat and, for just a moment, let herself feel a bit of pure, one hundred fifty proof hope. It was a heady thing.

They would have the vote. Women in New York State would have the vote, and then across the country, because once a change like this started, it wouldn't stop.

The world wouldn't become her oyster overnight. She knew there was still a long road ahead—for women, for Blacks, for Asians, and all those downtrodden people who'd had their rights stripped away while being told they should just be glad they were allowed to call America home. But she knew a thing or two about performing; America had been pulling one over on a good number of its citizens for all these years, and it couldn't do it forever. No one was that good of an actor, not even her. Women winning the vote showed that the Land of the Free had been telling lies since its inception, just as Emancipation had shone light onto truths that many would have preferred stayed hidden. Maybe one day, all the pointless lies would be done with, and everyone could get to that Dream folks liked to talk about so much.

"What're you gonna do now?" Miss Q asked when they pulled up to the Cashmere.

"That depends," Bertha said.

"On a man?" Miss Q asked.

"On *my* man," Bertha said. "On my country."

"And here I thought you was smart." She shook her head in disappointment, but winked at Bertha as the car pulled away.

Bertha took a deep breath and entered the club. She had to push the door hard because debris was piled up behind it, blocking her path. She took a step inside and all the exhaustion she had been fighting slammed into her. It was destroyed, like a twister had gone through, taking everything of value and making sure it was good and broken. Wall hangings were ripped, chairs and tables in splinters, and glass had been crushed into shards that spread across the floor like sand at Coney Island. She couldn't tell what had been broken when patrons had made a run for it and what the police had gleefully destroyed, but the Cashmere was a shambles.

She clutched her hands to her stomach against the nausea working its way up through her system, trying to fight it down. She'd been building this place up for years, from even before Arthur had passed, giving him ideas and making him think they were his. Slowly crafting it into the place she'd wanted it to become until she'd been in control of it completely. And now it was ruined. She might win the vote once everything shook out, but it seemed she had lost everything else.

Something dropped in the kitchen and she jumped, the echo of the sound through the empty club getting her pulse racing. She started toward the door cautiously; no one knew she had been released, and people might have decided to pick the club over in case she wasn't coming back any time soon. She took up the broken leg of a chair and hefted it in her hand before striding into the kitchen with it raised over her head like one of the batters in the Negro league.

She walked in and found Amir at the stove, humming as he cooked, as though there weren't glass shards at his feet and flour and spices covering the walls. She realized she hadn't expected him to be there. She'd thought that it wasn't possible for her to have the vote and have him, too.

"Amir?"

One second he was stirring and the next he was stalking toward her, pulling her into his arms. He held her tightly and swayed with her, repeating a word over and over until she could make out the sound of it, even if not the meaning.

"Alhamdulilah. Alhamdulilah. You're safe." After that he began murmuring in Bangla, and she only understood the word Allah and her name.

Was he praying for her? She couldn't say the last time she'd appreciated someone doing that, but she let his fervent words wrap around her.

"I saw them take you away," he whispered, his hand sliding up to caress the back of her neck. "And I was so frightened I would never get you back. Anything could have happened to you."

Bertha took a deep breath, and released it.

"Of course nothing happened. I told the coppers I had something good to come back to," she said, turning to kiss his dimpled cheek.

"The club is wrecked, though," he said, leaning back to look into her face. His expression clouded with regret. "I'm sorry."

She swatted his arm. "I meant you, fool."

She watched as the realization hit him, the smile that stretched across his face, but also the hesitancy in his eyes.

"What is it?" she asked, trying to fight the dread rising to the surface of her skin. Even with his arms around her, she couldn't help but wait for the other shoe to drop.

"I have to make a decision about going home to deal with my land," he said solemnly. His throat worked a moment and his head dipped. "I want you to help me make this decision, but I don't know how to do it without being another man asking you to do something you don't want."

Bertha shucked off the dread like an old snakeskin and lifted her hand to his chest, laying her palm flat.

"The fact that you're even worried about that is a good first step," she said. "Now spill it."

"I did a lot of praying last night, more than I have in a very long time. I couldn't think of what might have been happening to you after seeing the police lead you away. So instead, I asked Allah to keep you safe. And I asked how we could be together. Here."

She couldn't have hidden how his words affected her, even if she tried.

"And did He have any great insights?" she asked in an unsteady voice, unable to resist teasing him.

He took her hands in his. "Actually…"

EPILOGUE

Five years later

"Okay, catfish curry and fried eggplant, order up!"

Amir glanced over at the plate Cora had made and grinned at her. "Remember all those years ago when you said you weren't sure you'd get the hang of this?"

"I don't know what you're talking about," she said. "I said I wasn't sure I *wanted* to get the hang of this. You're lucky Bertha is a smooth talker."

Amir removed his apron, having handed over the dinner shift to Cora. He could either bound upstairs and shower or spend a bit of time with Bertha before heading out to his meeting; the shower lost by a long shot. "I'm lucky for many things," he said.

"Most especially a friend willing to work in this hot kitchen without complaint?" Syed asked.

"Na, I have no such friends," Amir said, and Syed grinned. "But speaking of luck…"

He headed out of the kitchen and onto the restaurant floor. He had been worried when he'd proposed his idea to Bertha: the night of the raid, after he'd come down from the apartment and seen the damage, he'd realized she would have to rebuild from scratch. He had some savings, and if he sold his land back home to his cousin or a neighbor, he might have a little more. He'd proposed investing as a partner in her business, handling the restaurant portion while she took care of hosting and entertainment.

She'd been excited, but worried about how to make it work and how to keep her girls safe. He'd given her time to think, but she'd accepted his offer when Janie and Wah Ming had told her they were opening their own private club, run out of an apartment so it drew less scrutiny from the vice squad. They hadn't wanted to disappoint her, but they'd been inspired to strike out on their own. Bertha only had herself to blame for it; the girls—women—had realized they could stand on their own two feet, even if people tried to kick them out from under them.

Building up the business hadn't been easy. Acquiring funds, in addition to Amir's savings and the money from the sale of his land, and Bertha's matching contribution. Coming up with a business plan that suited both of them, which was no easy feat for two stubborn rams. But in the end, 'Bertha's' had finally opened—to little acclaim. But they had worked hard, strategized together, and eventually their sheer will to succeed had bloomed into success. Between the men from the Continent looking for a taste of home, those who had migrated from the South seeking the same, and people just looking to try something different, they were doing quite well. Amir knew that the restaurant business was as temperamental as the sea, but he was just glad he could weather the ups and downs with Bertha at his side.

Amir walked over to the hostess stand after surveying the dining room, not bothering Bertha as she talked to a customer making a reservation. Instead, he peeked down over the side of the wood panels that enclosed the stand.

"Abbu!" Pure happiness filled Amir as his son's eyes grew wide with surprise. Raahil threw his head back and laughed, mouth open wide to reveal the two new teeth that had recently come in. Was that a third, pushing through? His boy was growing up so fast; each new stage of growth pushed Amir to work harder in his fight against injustice. Raahil would soon be old enough to understand the sundry ways his family was seen as less than, and Amir wanted to be sure he never doubted his worth.

"Eh! What's so funny, my shonar chele?"

Done with their customer, Bertha turned around and picked up Raahil, making a silly expression as she pressed her face close to his, which made the boy laugh even more. Then she glanced at Amir, a soft smile still on her face. "We ran out of catfish again. Let's go over sales for the last three weeks tonight and figure out how we need to adjust the next food order. I also need your input on a couple of bands that want to play the Friday night show. And to discuss how to get around these ice distributors bleeding us dry. And…"

Many in the local restaurant group had assumed that having a baby would soften Bertha; after all, wasn't she on her way to becoming "respectable?" He knew they had wished it to be so because she ran circles around the majority of them when it came to business. However, they'd been mistaken; Bertha could now give orders in the same breath as baby talk, and still make sure you knew that the work had better be done fast and to her standards.

"Oh, I love it when you talk figures and food orders," he said, leaning onto the counter and squeezing Raahil's socked foot. "But tonight is the meeting of the Bengali factory workers, love. I'm slated to discuss labor laws and petitioning against the Barred Zone Act."

The right corner of her mouth pulled up.

"And I love it when you talk unionizing and naturalization," she said. He had been joking, but he knew she was not. His heart sped up; she could still do that to him with just a look, even though he had once worried that the sweat and screaming matches of running a business together might tear them apart.

"Will you save me a dance? Later, after Raahil is asleep?"

"I only dance once a month, Amir," she said, then her gaze dropped to his mouth. "But I might be convinced to make an exception."

He wouldn't kiss her in front of the early dinner crowd that had already begun to fill the tables—she was better with public affection than she had been all those years ago, but she still took her roll of boss Bertha very seriously, and so did Amir. Instead, he leaned forward to kiss Raahil's cheek.

"Ami tomake bhalobashi," he whispered in her ear as he pulled away, giving her hand a squeeze.

"I love you, too," she said. She bounced Raahil up and down, but in that moment her gaze was all for him. His Bertha.

Amir walked out into the streets of Harlem. He wasn't sure if he was living the American Dream—things were often hard, and people harder. But the love he had, real, pure, and unshakeable, and the life he had built—they had built—maybe that was better than streets paved with gold. It certainly felt like it to him.

THE END

Author's Note

Some of the books most helpful in the writing of this novella are as follows:

•   *African American Women in the Struggle for the Vote, 1850–1920*, Rosalyn Terborg-Penn. 1998. Bloomington and Indianapolis, Indiana University Press.

•   *Bengali Harlem and the Lost Histories of South Asian America*, Vivek Bald. 2013. Cambridge, Massachusetts and London, England, Harvard University Press.

•   *Black Women and Politics in New York City*, Julie A Gallagher. 2012. Urbana, Chicago, and Springfield, University of Illinois Press.

•   *Sex Workers, Psychics, and Number Runners: Black Women in New York City's Underground Economy*, Lashawn Harris. 2016. Urbana, Chicago, and Springfield, University of Illinois Press.

•   *City of Eros: New York City, Prostitution, and the Commercialization of Sex, 1790-1920*, Timothy J. Gilfoyle. 1994. New York City, W. W. Norton & Company.

ABOUT THE AUTHOR

Alyssa Cole is a science editor, pop culture nerd, and romance junkie who lives in the Caribbean and occasionally returns to her fast-paced NYC life. When she's not busy writing, traveling, and learning French, she can be found watching anime with her real-life romance hero or tending to her herd of animals.

Find Alyssa at her website, http://alyssacole.com/, on Twitter @ AlyssaColeLit and on Facebook at Facebook.com/AlyssaColeLit.

CPSIA information can be obtained
at www.ICGtesting.com
Printed in the USA
LVOW12s1925310317
529201LV00003B/571/P